STILL LOVERS

He had not betrayed her.

Only failed her, failed her, and made her live ever fearful and unsure — no, never had he played her false, but never had he sustained her — and she could see no end to it: here she stood now, come to beg him to turn back to her, to fill her cup each day to the brim with unsureness and disquiet . . .

He strode in, with the wood-axe in his hand and the dogs tumbling over the threshold before and after him.

The sight of him took away her breath.

He was miserably clad — his blue shirt dirty and ragged. His tight leathern breeches had a rent over the one knee, and the seam behind the other leg was burst.

Yet never, more than now, had he seemed the son of chiefs and nobles . . .

KRISTIN LAVRANSDATTER

by
Sigrid Undset

III

The Cross

nslated by Charles Archer

---

*This low-priced Bantam Book
has been completely reset in a type face
designed for easy reading, and was printed
from new plates. It contains the complete
text of the original hard-cover edition.*
NOT ONE WORD HAS BEEN OMITTED.

RL 7, IL 10-up

KRISTIN LAVRANSDATTER
III: THE CROSS

*A Bantam Book / published by arrangement with
Alfred A. Knopf, Inc.*

PRINTING HISTORY

*Original title: Korset; copyright 1922 by
H. Aschehoug & Company, Oslo
Translated by Charles Archer*

*Knopf edition published February 1927
18 printings through October 1976*

*Bantam edition / January 1979
2nd printing*

*Bantam Books are published by Bantam Books, Inc. Its trade-
mark, consisting of the words "Bantam Books" and the por-
trayal of a bantam, is Registered in U.S. Patent and Trademark
Office and in other countries. Marca Registrada. Bantam
Books, Inc., 666 Fifth Avenue, New York, New York 10019.*

PRINTED IN THE UNITED STATES OF AMERICA

THE CROSS

PART ONE

KINSHIP'S DUES

THE SECOND year Erlend Nikulaussön and Kristin Lavransdatter dwelt on Jörundgaard, the mistress was minded to go herself and lie the summer over at the sæter.

She had thought upon this ever since the winter. At Skjenne it was the use from of old for the wife herself to pass the summer at the out-farm, for once a daughter of that house had been carried off by the mountain folk, and afterwards naught would serve the mother but she must herself lie on the mountain every summer. But in so many things they had their own ways down at Skjenne — and folk in the parish were used to this and thought it was but as it should be.

But elsewhere in the Dale 'twas not the use for the master's womenfolk of the great manors to abide themselves at the sæters. Kristin knew that if she did it, there would be talk and wonderment among the folks.

— In God's name, then, they must even talk. Sure it was that they gossiped about her and hers whether or no.

— Audun Torbergssön had owned no more than his weapons and the clothes he stood up in when he was wed with Ingebjörg Nikulausdatter of Loptsgaard. He had been henchman to the Bishop of Hamar; 'twas the time when the Bishop was in the north here to hallow the new church that Ingebjörg fell into trouble. Nikulaus Sigurdssön took it hardly at first, swore to God and all men that a horse-boy never should be son-in-law of his. But Ingebjörg was brought to bed of twins; and, said folks, laughing, Nikulaus maybe deemed their bringing up too hard a matter to tackle single-handed. However that might be, he gave Audun his daughter in marriage.

This had happed two years after Kristin's wedding. 'Twas not forgotten; folk still bore in mind that Audun was a stranger in the parish — he was a Hallander, of good kin, but his folk had fallen into great poverty. And the man himself was not over well liked in Sil; he was stiff-necked and hard, slow to forget either good or ill; yet was he a notable farmer, and had good knowledge of the laws — so in some ways Audun Torbergssön was a man of standing now in the parish, and a man that folk were little willing to fall in at odds with.

Kristin thought of farmer Audun's broad, brown face set in its curly red hair and beard; of his sharp little blue eyes. He was like more men than one that she had seen — she had seen such faces amongst their serving-folk at Husaby — Erlend's house-carls and ship-folk.

The mistress sighed. It must be easier for such a man to hold his own, even though 'twas his wife's lands he lived on. *He* had never been master of aught before —

Throughout the winter and spring Kristin talked much with Frida Styrkaarsdatter, who had come with them from the Trondheim country and was the chief of her serving-women. Over and over again she would say to the girl that they were wont to have things so and so in the Dale here in summer, the harvest-folk were used to get this, and that was how they did in the fields in autumn — Frida must bear in mind how she, Kristin, had done last year. For it was her will that all things here on the farm should go as they had gone in Ragnfrid Ivarsdatter's time —

But to say outright that she herself would not be there on the farm that summer — this she found hard. She had lived at Jörundgaard two winters and a summer now as mistress, and she knew well that if she went to the sæter and abode there this year, 'twere much as though she ran away.

— She saw well that Erlend's lot was no easy one. From the time he sat upon his foster-mother's knee, he had known naught save that he was born to bid and rule over all and everything around him. And if so be he had let himself be ruled and bidden by others, at least the man himself had never known it.

'Twas impossible he could be within as outwardly he seemed. He must needs be unhappy here. She herself — Her father's manor on the floor of the still, shut-in valley, the flat fields looped in by the river bends shining through the alder woods, the farmsteads on the low ploughed lands at the foot of the fells, and the headlong hill-sides above, with grey scaurs high up against the sky, pale-hued screes below, and pine woods and leaf woods scrambling up and over the slopes from the valley-bottom — no, this no longer seemed to her the fairest and safest home in the world. 'Twas so hemmed in. Surely this must seem to Erlend ugly and cramped and unkindly.

But none could mark aught on him but that he was well content —

At last, the day they let the cattle out on Jörundgaard, she got it said — in the evening, as they sat at supper. As she spoke, Erlend was groping in the fish-platter for a titbit — he sat stark still in wonderment, his fingers still in the dish, gazing at his wife. Then Kristin said quickly — 'twas most because of that throat evil that was ever about among the young children in the Dale; Munan was so weakly; she would take him and Lavrans with her up to the mountains.

Ay, said Erlend. Then 'twould mayhap be best that Ivar and Skule should go with her too.

The twins jumped with joy on their bench. Through the rest of the meal each tried to out-chatter the other. They would go with Erling, they said, who was to lie away to the north among the Graahö fells, with the sheep. Three years ago shepherds from Sil had chased a sheep-stealer and killed him by his own hut in among the Boar-fells — he was an outlaw from the Österdal. As soon as the house-folk had risen from the board, Ivar and Skule bore into the hall all the weapons they owned and set to work on them.

A little later in the evening Kristin went southward, with Simon Andressön's daughters and her sons Gaute and Lavrans. Arngjerd Simonsdatter had been at Jörundgaard the most of this winter. The maid was fifteen years old now; and one day in Yule, at Formo, Simon had said somewhat of how 'twas time that Arngjerd should learn something more than what she could pick up at her home; she knew already as much as the serving-women did. At that Kristin proffered to take the girl home with her and teach her as well as she could, for she knew that Simon held this daughter very dear and thought much on what was to come of her. And the child might well have need to learn other ways than those she saw at Formo. Now that his wife's father and mother were both dead, Simon Andressön was one of the richest men in the country-side. He guided his estates well and heedfully, and was a stirring and skilful farmer on his Formo lands. But within the house things went as best they might — the serving-women ruled and guided all things, and when Simon marked that disorder and waste went beyond all bounds, he would get him one or two serving-wenches more; but he never spoke of such things to his wife, and seemed not to look, nor yet to wish, that she should charge herself more with the house-mistress's work. Almost it was as though he did not deem her full-grown yet — but he was most kind and easy with Ramborg, and poured out gifts upon her and the children in season and out of season.

Kristin grew fond of Arngjerd when she came to know her. Fair the maid was not, but she was of a good wit, and was gentle, good-hearted, quick with her hands, and diligent. As the young girl went about with her in the house, or sat by her side in the weaving-house of an evening, Kristin often thought she could wish now that one of her children had been a daughter. A daughter must be with her mother more —

She was thinking the like this evening, as she walked, leading Lavrans by the hand, and looking on the two, Gaute and Arngjerd, who were on the path before her. Ulvhild Simonsdatter was running hither and thither, trampling to bits the brittle evening ice on the puddles — she was making believe she was a beast of some kind, and had put on her red cloak inside out, so that the white hare-skin was turned outward.

Down in the dale the shadows were thickening into dusk over the bare, brown fields. But the air of the spring evening seemed drenched with light. The first stars shone wet and white in the sky, high up where clear watery green shaded into blue-black night. But over the black edge of the fells on the further side of the dale there lingered yet a band of yellow light, and its sheen lit up the scree that overlay the steep hill-side above them. Highest up of all, where the drifts jutted over the mountain crests, there was the glimmer of snow and the glitter of the ice that hung beneath it, feeding the foaming becks that gushed down everywhere amidst the boulders. Above the valley the air was full of the noise of waters, and from below rose the river's hoarse roar. And there was the song of birds from all the groves and thickets, and from out the forest all around.

Once Ulvhild stopped, took up a stone, and threw it in where the birds were singing. But her big sister caught her by the arm. Then she went quietly for a while, but in a little she broke away and galloped down the slope — till Gaute called her back.

They were come close to where the way led into the fir woods; from among the trees ahead came the clang of a cross-bow. Snow was still lying in the woods; it smelt cold and fresh. A short way on, in a little opening, stood Erlend and Ivar and Skule.

Ivar had shot at a squirrel; the arrow was sticking in a pine branch high up, and he wanted now to get it down. He threw stone after stone; the thick, straight tree rang again when he hit the stem.

"Stay a little; let me try to shoot it down for you," said his father. He shook his cloak back over his shoulders, laid an arrow to his bow, and took aim, carelessly enough, in the deceitful light among the trees. The string twanged; the arrow sang through the air and buried itself in the pine branch close by the boy's shaft. Erlend took another arrow and shot again — one of the two arrows that had stuck in the tree slipped down clattering from branch to branch; the shaft of the other was splintered, but the head still stuck fast in the limb.

Skule ran into the snow to pick up the two arrows. Ivar stood gazing up into the tree-top.

" 'Tis mine, father, the one that sticks fast! 'Tis in up to the socket — 'twas strongly shot, father!" — and he set about telling Gaute why it was he had not hit the squirrel —

Erlend laughed low and flung his cloak about him again:

"Will you turn back now, Kristin? I must be going homewards — we are off after capercailzie at daybreak. Naakkve and I — "

Kristin answered in haste, no, she would go on with the maids to the manor — she had somewhat to talk of with her sister this evening —

"Then Ivar and Skule can go with mother and be with her home — if I may go along with you, father?" said Gaute.

Erlend lifted Ulvhild Simonsdatter in his arms to bid her farewell. And bonny and fresh and rosy as she was, with her brown curls nestled in the white fur hood, he kissed her, ere he set her down, and turned and went homewards with Gaute.

Now that Erlend had naught else to take him up, he was ever about with some of his sons. — Ulvhild took her aunt's hand and walked a little — then she ran on again, bursting in between Ivar and Skule. Ay, she was a fair child — but wild and unruly. Had they had a daughter, no doubt but Erlend would have had her too ever with him for a plaything.

At Formo Simon was in the hall, alone with his little son, when they came in. He sat in the high-seat at the middle of the long board, and watched Andres; the child knelt on the outer bench playing with some old treenails, striving to make them stand upon their heads on the flat board-top. Soon as Ulvhild saw this, forgetting to greet her father, she rushed straight up on to the bench beside her brother, took him by the nape, and knocked his face against the board-top, shrieking out that they were *her* pegs; father had given them to her himself.

Simon got up to part the children, and in rising chanced to knock over a little dish of earthenware that stood by his elbow. It fell to the floor and was broken in pieces.

Arngjerd crept under the board and gathered up the bits. Simon took them from her and looked at them unhappily:

"I misdoubt me your mother will be vexed at this!" 'Twas a little dish of clear white ware, a fair pattern upon it, that Sir Andres Darre had brought home from France; 'twas left to Helga, but she had given it to Ramborg, said Simon; and the women deemed it of great price. At that minute he heard his wife in the outer room, and he hid his hands, with the shards in them, behind his back.

Ramborg came in and greeted her sister and her sister's sons. She took off Ulvhild's cloak, and the little maid ran to her father and clung about him.

"Are we so fine to-day, Ulvhild? — wearing our silver belt on a working day, I verily believe — " but he could not take hold of the child, with his hands full as they were.

Ulvhild cried out she had been to Moster Kristin's at

Jörundgaard to-day, and that was why her mother had dressed her up this morning —

"Ay, your mother keeps you so brave and gay — they might well set you up in the shrine northward in the church, just as you stand," said Simon, smiling. The one work Ramborg busied herself with was sewing clothes for her daughter; Ulvhild went ever bravely decked out.

"Why stand you thus?" Ramborg asked her husband.

Simon showed forth the shards. "I know not what you will say to this — "

Ramborg took them from him: "No need to stand there and look so like a fool — "

Kristin grew ill at ease as she sat there. 'Twas true Simon had looked foolish enough as he stood hiding the shards behind him, and, as it were, playing the child. But there was sure no need for Ramborg to say so.

"I deemed it would vex you, that your bowl had been broken," said the man.

"Ay, you seem at all times so afraid aught may vex me — in small things like this," answered Ramborg — and now the other two saw she was on the brink of tears.

"You know well, Ramborg, 'tis not seeming only," said Simon. "And I trow 'tis not alone in small things either — "

"I know not," answered Ramborg as before. " 'Tis never your wont, Simon, to speak to me of great matters — "

She turned sharply and went back to the outer room. Simon stood a little, looking after her. When he sat him down, the boy, Andres, came and tried to climb upon his father's knee. Simon lifted him up, and sat resting his chin on the top of the child's head, but seemed not to hear the little one's prattle.

After a while Kristin said, haltingly:

"Ramborg is not so young any more, Simon — your eldest child is seven winters old already — "

"What mean you?" asked Simon, more sharply than need was, she thought.

"I mean but that — maybe my sister deems you lay too little on her — could you not try to let her have things in her hands a little more, on the farm here — along with you?"

"*My* wife has all in her hands that she would have,"

answered Simon hotly. "I ask not that she should do more than she herself would, but never have I denied Ramborg the ruling of aught here on Formo. If you deem otherwise, 'tis that you do not know — "

"Nay, nay!" said Kristin. "But one time and another, brother-in-law, it has seemed to me you remember not that Ramborg is more grown-up now than in the days when you were wed. You should bear in mind, Simon — "

"Bear *you* in mind" — he set down the child and sprang up — "that Ramborg and I agreed together — and you and I could not — " Just then the mistress of the house stepped in, bearing a stoup of ale for the strangers; Simon went quickly to his wife and laid his hand upon her shoulder: "Heard you ever the like, Ramborg — here is your sister saying she deems not you are content with things as you have them here — " He laughed.

Ramborg looked up; there was a strange glitter in her great, dark eyes:

"How so? I got what I would have, I as well as you, Kristin — should we two sisters not be well content, I know not — " and she too laughed.

Kristin stood there red and wrathful; she took not the ale-bowl in her hands:

"Nay, 'tis late already — time we were going homeward — " and she looked about her for her sons.

"Nay, nay, Kristin." Simon took the bowl from his wife and drank to the other sister. "Be not angry now. 'Tis not well to weigh so nicely each word that falls 'twixt nearest kin — sit a little and rest your feet; content you again, and forget it, if I answered you in other wise than I ought —

"I am weary," said he, stretching and yawning a little. He asked how far they were got on with the spring work at Jörundgaard — here, now, they had ploughed up all the fields north of the manor road.

Kristin took her leave as soon as she deemed it seemly. Nay, Simon need not come with her, she said, as he took up his hooded cloak and axe — she had the great lads with her. But he would go — and he prayed Ramborg, too, to go with them, at least up through the home-fields. This, at most times, she had no mind to, but to-night she went with them right up to the road.

Without was black night, with clear, twinkling stars.

A little warm springlike breath of new-dunged fields came through the frosty night air. The noise of water was about them everywhere in the darkness.

Simon and Kristin went northward, the three boys running before. She felt that the man walking by her would have said something, but she had no mind to help him to speech, for she was greatly vexed with him still. True it was she was fond of her brother-in-law — but there should be some bounds to what he deemed he might say and then turn it off — with a " 'twas but among kinsfolk." He ought sure to understand — that he had stood by them so steadfastly in their pinch made it the less easy now for her to bear, when he grew hot and unmannerly — 'twas hard for her to take him up. She thought of the first winter, when they were but newly come to the parish: Ramborg had sent for her, for that Simon lay abed with neck-boils, grievously sick. He was much plagued with this ill. But when she was come to Formo and went in to the man, he would not suffer her to touch him or even look at him; he was so unruly that Ramborg prayed her sister miserably to forgive her for having brought her thither. Simon had been no better with her, said she, when she would have tended him the first time he was sick after they were wed. When these throat boils came on him, he hid himself away in the old house they called the Sæmunds hall, and would suffer no one near him but a hideous, filthy, lousy old carl, Gunstein by name, that had served on Dyfrin before Simon was born. — True, Simon came to his sister-in-law afterwards and would have made things good again with her: he liked not, he said, that any should see him lying with such a sickness; it seemed to him such a pitiful ailment for a grown man. Kristin had answered, shortly enough, that she understood him not; 'twas sure neither sin nor shame to have a swollen throat.

He went with her now as far as to the bridge, and all the way they spoke of the weather and the farm work — saying over again things they had said in the hall. Simon bade her good-night — then, of a sudden, he asked:

"Know you, Kristin, what I have done to Gaute, that the boy is so wroth with me?"

"Gaute?" she asked, in wonder.

"Aye, have you not marked it? He shuns me — and if

he must needs meet me, he will scarce open his mouth, when I speak with him — ”

Kristin shook her head; no, she had marked naught of this — “but maybe you have said a word in jest, and he has taken it ill, like the child he is — ”

He knew by her voice she was smiling; he laughed a little: “But I cannot remember aught of the kind — ”

With that he bade good-night again and left her.

At Jörundgaard all was still; dark in the hall, and ashes raked over the fire. Björgulf was lying awake; he said his father and brothers were gone a good while since.

In the great bed Munan lay alone, sleeping — His mother took him into her arms when she had lain down.

— ’Twas hard to speak of it to Erlend, if he himself did not understand — that he ought not to take his great sons and go roaming the woods with them, when there was more than enough work to be done on the farm —

Truly, she had never looked that Erlend should go behind the plough himself. For that matter, he was scarce the man to cope with a spell of real work. And Ulf, like enough, would take it but ill if Erlend meddled with the farming. But her sons could not be suffered to grow to manhood as their father had done — learning but to handle arms, to hunt wild beasts and disport him with his horses — or hang over a draught-board with a priest whose task it was to coax into the knight's son some little lore of Latin and of writing, of singing and playing on strings. ’Twas therefore, in chief, that she had kept the manor short of working folk — her sons should learn, she thought, from childhood on, that they must use them to husbandry. There was small hope now for Erlend's sons in the knightly calling.

But of all the youths Gaute was the only one who had any turn for farming ways. Gaute was a worker — but he was scarce thirteen; naught else was to be looked for but that he would liefer be off with Erlend, when his father bade him come —

But ’twas hard to speak of this to Erlend. For she held fast to this — never from her should her husband hear one word he could take for blame of his deeds or lamentation over the fate he had brought upon himself and his sons. The harder was it for her to bring home to the father that his sons must needs use them to work themselves on their farms. If only Ulf would speak of it, she thought —

When the folk moved with the herds from the lower sæters up to Hövringen, Kristin went with them to the mountain. The twins she would not have with her. They were near eleven years old now, and were the most unruly and self-willed of all her children; 'twas all the harder for her to guide them since there were two of them, and they held together in all things. If it so happed that she could get Ivar alone, then was he good and biddable enough; but Skule was fiery and headstrong — and when the brothers were together, Ivar said and did whatsoever the other would.

2

ONE day in early autumn Kristin went out about the time of nones. The herd had said that, a little down the hillside, if she followed the run of the river, she would find a forest clearing where were many Aaron's-rods growing.

Kristin found the spot: a steep hill-side with the sun beating straight upon it — 'twas even now the best time to pick the flowers. They grew in masses all over the heaps of stones and round about the grey tree-stumps — tall, bright yellow stalks, set thick with little full-blown starlets. — Kristin set Munan to plucking raspberries amid some bushes he could not come away from without her help, and bade the dog stay and guard him. Then she drew her knife and set about cutting the flowers, while ever keeping an eye on the little child — Lavrans kept by her side and helped her busily.

She was ever fearful for her two little ones up here. Otherwise she had no great dread of yonder folk any more. Already from many of the sæters the dairy-folks had gone down home, but she was minded to stay on over the second Maria Mass.* True, the nights were black now, and uncanny when it blew hard — uncanny for them when they must go out late. But for the most part the

---

* 8th September.

weather had been so fair up here — and down in the dale
'twas a year of drought and poor feed. Men had to bide
up here both in the late fall and the winter-time — and her
father had said he had never marked that there were any
Dwellers in their sæter of winters —

Kristin came to a stand under a lone pine on the mid-
hill-side; stood with her hands clasped about the heavy
bunch of flower-stems resting upon her shoulder. From
here one could see northwards, some way up into Dovre.
The corn stood in stooks in many places out on the farm
lands —

The sward was yellow and burnt-up there too. But truly
green 'twas never here in the Dale, it seemed to her now
— not green as in Trondheim —

Ay — her mind went back in longing to the home they
had had there — the manor that lay so high and chieftainly
forth on the broad-bosomed hill-side, fields and meadows
spreading wide around and downward to the leaf woods
in the glen that dipped to the lake in the dale bottom.
The far outlook over low wooded ridges that rolled,
wave behind wave, southwards to the Dovrefjeld. And
the grass-lands, so rank and deep in summer, red with
ruddy flowers under the red of evening skies; and the
aftermath, so green and sappy in the autumn —

Ay, there were times when longing came on her even
for the fiord — The strands at Birgsi, and wharfs with
boats and ships, the boat sheds, the smell of tar and fishing-
gear, and of the sea — all those things she had liked so
little when first she came to the north —

Erlend — he must long, surely, for that smell, and for
the sea and the sea-winds —

She missed now all that once she had deemed did but
weary her out — the great householding, the flocks of
serving-folk, the din when Erlend's men rode into the
courtyard with clashing arms and jingling gear — strangers
coming and going, bearing great tidings from far in the
land and gossip of folks in the country-side and the town
— She felt now how hushed her life had grown, when all
this fell dumb —

The market town with its churches and cloisters and
feasts in the great men's town houses — She longed to pass
along the streets, her own page and serving-maid behind
her; to climb the stairs into the merchants' ware-rooms, to

choose or throw aside; to be set aboard the trading-smacks on the river and to chaffer: English linen head-gear, fine veils, wooden horses, with knights astride of them, who could thrust with their lances when you pulled a string. She thought on the meadows outside the town, by Nida-reid, where she would go with her children and watch the showmen's trained dogs and bears, and buy honey-bread and walnuts —

And at times she would be so fain to deck herself out once more — Silken shifts and thin, fine head-linen. The sleeveless surcoat of light-blue velvet that Erlend had bought for her the winter before mischance fell on them. It had borders of ermine-skin about the deeply cut-out bosom and round the long arm-slits, that reached right down to the hips and showed the belt beneath —

And now and then she longed — oh no, 'twere witless not to be glad of *that*, glad so long as she were spared the bearing of more children. When she fell sick in the autumn, after the big slaughtering — 'twas best things fell out as they did. But she had wept a little over it, the first nights after —

For it seemed to her a long, long time since she had held a little child. Munan was but four winters old — but him she had had to give into strangers' keeping ere yet he was full a year. And when she got him back again, he could both walk and talk, and he knew her not —

Erlend! Oh, Erlend! She knew well that, in her inmost heart, she knew he was not so — careless — as he seemed. He, that had been ever restless — 'twas as though now he was ever still: as a stream of water, striking at last on a steep wall of rock, lets itself be turned aside, and oozes through the peat to make a silent pool with marshland all around. He passed his time on Jörundgaard, doing naught, and taking now one and now another of his sons to keep him company in nothing-doing. Or he went a-hunting with them. The whim might take him to set to work, and tar and patch up one of the boats they kept on the tarns for fishing. Or he would set about breaking one of the young colts. But at that he never made any hand — he was all too hasty —

He kept to himself, and made at least as though he marked not that none sought his company. The sons did as their father did. Liked they were not, these strangers, whom ill-fortune had driven to the Dale, and who went their ways now, proud and strange as ever, seeking not to learn aught of the ways of the parish and of its folk. For Ulf Haldorssön there was sheer ill-will — he scorned the Dalesmen openly, called them thick-witted and old-fashioned; folk that were not bred by the sea-shore *were* not folk —

And she herself — she knew she had not many friends either, here in her own home country. Not now any more —

Kristin straightened herself in her moss-brown wadmal dress, and shaded her eyes with her hand from the golden flood of afternoon sunlight —

Northward she caught a glimpse of the Dale along the river's white-green riband, and then came the throng of mountain-hulks, one behind the other, yellow-grey with scree and marsh, away to where, seen through clefts and scaurs, snow-fields and clouds were one. Straight before her Rostkampen bent forward a knee and hemmed the Dale, thrusting the Laagen aside in a great crook. A far-off thunder rose to her from the river, where it cut deep into the slate rocks below and fell, boiling and foaming, from shelf to shelf. On the moorish hills above Rostkampen's dome rose the rounded backs of the two great Blaahöer, that her father had likened to a woman's breasts —

Erlend must feel it cramped and ugly here — hard to draw breath in —

— A little to the south on this same hill-side, yonder, under the slopes near the sæter, was where she had seen the elf-maiden, when she was a little child —

A gentle, soft, fair, slender child with thick, silky hair about her round, red and white cheeks — Kristin shut her eyes, and turned her sunburnt face full to the flood of light. A young mother with milk-swollen breasts and a heart stirred and fruitful with child-bearing like a new-ploughed field — ay. But for such an one as she was now there was no fear; her they would scarce try to draw into their clutches. Ill would the mountain-king deem a woman so worn and meagre would set off his bridal gold; the elf-wife would scarce be fain to put her child to such dried-up breasts. She felt herself hard and dry as the pine root beneath her foot, that crooked itself over the stones, and clawed itself fast. She struck her heel hard upon it with the thought.

The two little lads had come to her side; they made haste to do as their mother did, kicking the pine root with all their might, and then asking eagerly:

"Why did you so, mother?"

Kristin sat down, laid the Aaron's-rods in her lap, and began to strip off the full-blown blossoms into her basket. "'Twas that my shoe pinched me on the toes," she answered, so long after that the boys minded not that they had asked. But they gave little heed to this — they were so used to have their mother seem not to hear when they spoke to her, or wake up and answer when they had forgot what 'twas they had asked.

Lavrans helped to strip off the blossoms; Munan would have helped too, but he only tore the tassels to shreds. So his mother took the flowers from him without a word, without anger, far away in her own thoughts. Soon the boys began to play and fight with the stripped stalks that she threw aside.

The game went on noisily before their mother's knees. Kristin looked on the two small, round, brown-haired child-heads. Much alike they were still: they had well-nigh the same light-brown hue of hair, but, by all kinds of small scarce-seen marks and signs that came and went in a flash, their mother could see they would grow to be most unlike. Munan would favour his father: he had his sea-blue eyes, and the silky hair that clung, soft and close, in curls and little waves round the narrow head; 'twould darken to sooty black with time. That little face of his, that still was so round below the chin and on the cheeks, so that 'twas a joy to lay a hand on its soft freshness, would narrow and lengthen out, once he grew a little older; he, too, would one day show the high, narrow forehead sunken at the temples, and the straight, out-standing triangle of nose, sharp and narrow on the bridge, with thin, restless nostrils, that Naakkve had already and that the twins had plainly shown they were to have.

Lavrans had had flaxen, silk-fine curls when he was little. Now his hair had the hue of a hazel-nut, but it held golden gleams in the sunlight. 'Twas smooth, and soft enough, but yet much coarser and thicker; deep masses

you could bury your fingers in. Lavrans was like her; he
had grey eyes and a round face, broad of forehead and
with softly rounded chin; 'twas like he would keep the
red and white of his cheeks well on into manhood.

Gaute's skin too had this bright fresh hue; he was so like
her father, with his full oval face, iron-grey eyes, and
light, light yellow hair.

Björgulf alone — she knew not whom he favoured. He
was the tallest of the sons, broad-shouldered, heavy and
strong of limb. Untamed, curly, coal-black hair grew low
over the broad, white brow; his eyes were blue-black, but
strangely lustreless, and they blinked sorely when he
lifted them to the light. She knew not rightly when it had
begun, for it had chanced that this was the child she had
always taken the least heed of. They took him from her
and gave him to a foster-mother soon as he was born;
eleven months afterwards she bore Gaute, and Gaute had
been sickly the four first years he lived. After the twins'
birth she had come to her feet, sick still, with a hurt in
the back, and yet must take up the big boy again, carry
him about and tend him, so that she scarce had time to
look on the new children save when Frida brought Ivar
thirsty and shrieking — and Gaute, too, lay and shrieked
while she sat and gave the little one the breast. She had
not been able — holy mother Mary, thou knowest I *could*
not give more heed to Björgulf than I did — And from the
first he was such an one as would rather go about alone
and fend for himself; strange and silent had he ever been,
seemed ever to mislike it when she would have fondled
him. She had ever deemed him the strongest of her brood;
like a swart, headstrong little bullcalf had Björgulf always
seemed to her —

Little by little it had come home to her that there was
somewhat amiss with his sight. The monks had done something to his eyes when he and Naakkve were at Tautra,
but it seemed that had not helped —

He was still close and silent as ever; she made no way
when now she tried to draw Björgulf to her. His father
fared no better, she saw — Björgulf was the only one of
their sons who did not warm to any heed from Erlend as
a meadow takes the sunshine. Only with Naakkve was
Björgulf otherwise — but when she would have talked
with Naakkve of his brother, he turned the matter off.

She knew not if Erlend fared any better in this — though
greater love than Naakkve's for his father — !

— Oh no, with Erlend's offspring there could be no
mistaking who their father was. — When she was last in
Nidaros, she had seen that child from Lensvik. She met Sir
Thorolf in Christ's Church yard; he came out with a train
of men and women and serving-folk, a maid bearing the
babe in its swaddling clothes. Thorolf Aasulfssön greeted
her with a bow, quiet and courteous, as he went by. His
wife was not there —

She had seen the child's face; in a single glance, but
'twas enough. It was like other children's faces that had
lain at her own breast —

Arne Gjavvaldssön was with her, and he could not refrain him from talking — as his way ever was. Sir Thorolf's kinsmen that were his heirs were but ill pleased
when the child saw the light last winter. But Thorolf had
it christened Aasulf. 'Twixt Erlend Nikulaussön and Lady
Sunniva there had never been more than the friendship
all folk knew of — he made as though he never doubted
this. Loose-tongued and rash as the man was, he had talked
recklessly, without doubt, when bandying jests with her —
and 'twas no more than the lady's duty to warn the king's
wardens when she suspected mischief. But had they been
over-good friends, Sunniva must sure have known that
her own brother was privy to Erlend's plan. When Haftor
Graut made forfeit of his life and his soul's salvation in
the prison, she had gone clean from her wits — no one
could pay heed to what she had laid to her own charge in
that state. Sir Thorolf had laid his hand on his sword-hilt
and looked around the company as he spoke of this, said
Arne —

Arne had named the matter to Erlend too. One time
when she was above in a loft-room, the two men had
stood below under the balcony, knowing not that she
could hear their words. The Lensvik knight was so o'er-
joyed at the coming of the son his wife had borne last
winter — 'twas plain he had no doubt that he himself was
the father.

"Ay, Thorolf himself must sure know best," Erlend
had answered. She knew that tone in his voice — he was
standing now with downcast eyes and the little smile at
one corner of his mouth.

Sir Thorolf hated so those kinsmen of his who should have been his heirs if he died childless. But folk were talking, saying the thing was not as it should be — "Oh, the man must sure know best himself," said Erlend as before —

"Ay, ay, Erlend! That one boy is heir to more than the seven sons you have by your wife — "

"For *my* seven sons shall I care myself, Arne — " But at that she went down; she would not suffer them to talk any more of this thing. Erlend looked a little out of countenance when he saw her. Then he came and took her hand, standing behind her so that her shoulder touched his body. She felt that, as he stood there looking down upon her, he was making over again, wordlessly, the promises he had just made — as it were to give her courage —

— Kristin grew ware now that Munan was gazing up into her face — somewhat fearful. She must have smiled — not a pleasant smile. But when his mother looked down at *him*, he smiled back to her straightway, doubtfully and provingly.

Vehemently she caught him up into her lap. He was little, little, little yet, her youngest — not too big yet to be kissed and fondled by his mother. She winked one eye at him. He did his best to wink back at her, but, try as he would, both eyes *would* shut together — his mother laughed aloud; Munan too went off into peals of laughter, while Kristin hugged and squeezed him in her arms —

Lavrans had been sitting with the dog in his lap. They both turned, listening, towards the woods below.

" 'Tis father!" The dog first and the boy after him went leaping down the steep hill-side.

Kristin sat still awhile. Then she rose and went out on a jutting point. Now they were coming up the path from below: Erlend, Naakkve, Ivar, and Skule. They came along in wild glee, calling their greetings up to her.

Kristin greeted them again. Were they going up to fetch the horses? No, answered Erlend: Ulf, he thought, was sending Sveinbjörn up for them to-night. He and Naakkve were bound further afield after reindeer, and the twins had had a mind to come along with them and see their mother —

She made no answer. She had known how 'twas ere she asked. Naakkve had with him hounds in leash; he and his father were in wadmal jerkins of mingled grey and black, such as make little show against the screes. All four of them had bows.

Kristin asked the tidings from the manor, and Erlend talked as they climbed upward. Ulf was in full swing with the harvest work; he was not ill pleased, but the straw was cutting short; the corn had riped so quickly on the higher fields, the grain was dropping from the ears. And the oats were all but ready to cut — they must keep hard at it, Ulf said —

Kristin nodded as she walked, but said no word.

She went to the byre herself to help in the milking. It was ever pleasant to her, this hour when she sat in the dark close in to the swelling cow-flank, and felt the milk's sweet breath in her nostrils. Swish, swish, came the answer from the inner darkness, where the byre-woman and the herd were milking. 'Twas all so restful, the strong, warm smell in the byre, the sound of a withy-band creaking, of a horn knocking against wood, of a cow moving her feet in the miry earth floor of the stall, or whisking her tail at the flies. — The wagtails that nested in here in the summer were gone now —

The cows were restless to-night. Bluesides put her foot in the milk-pail — Kristin slapped at her and scolded her. The next cow turned restive and ugly, as soon as Kristin sat in to her side. She had sores on her teats. Kristin pulled her wedding-ring from her finger and milked the first jet through it.

She heard Ivar and Skule down by the gate — they were shouting and throwing stones at the strange bull that followed her cattle home each evening. They had offered to help Finn to milk the goats in the pen, but they must have grown tired of that —

When she came by a little later, they were busy tormenting the pretty white bull-calf she had given Lavrans — the little boy stood by whimpering. His mother set down the pails, took the two by the shoulders, and pushed them aside — they must let their brother's calf be, when he bade them to —

Erlend and Naakkve were sitting on the doorstep; they had a fresh cheese between them; they were eating hunch upon hunch, and stuffing Munan, who stood betwixt

Naakkve's knees. Naakkve had laid her strainer over the little one's head, saying that none could see Munan now — for this was no strainer, but a fairy hat. They were laughing, all three, — but no sooner did Naakkve see his mother than he handed her the strainer, stood up, and took the pails from her.

Kristin lingered in the dairy. The upper half of the door to the outer room stood ajar — she saw they had piled the hearth with fuel. Round the fire in the warm flickering glow they sat eating, Erlend, the children, the serving-wench, and the three herds.

When she came in, they had ended their meal. She saw that the two little ones had been put to bed upon the wall-bench; they seemed to be asleep already. Erlend lay huddled up in the bed. She stumbled over his jerkin and boots and, as she went by, picked them up and then went out.

The sky was bright still, with a red streak over the fells in the west; a few dark cloud-wisps swam in the clear heaven. It looked like good weather for to-morrow too, 'twas so still, and so nipping cold, now that night had well fallen — no wind, but an icy breath from the north-west, a steady air-drift from the naked grey-stone mountains. Over the low hills down to the south-east the moon was floating up, nigh the full, big and pale red yet in the thin haze that hung always over the marshes there.

The strange bull was bellowing mournfully somewhere away on the uplands. But for that, all was so still 'twas like an ache — naught but the rush of the river below their milking-place, the little beck tinkling down the grassy green, and a sleepy soughing off in the woods — an unrest among the pines, that stirred, settled for a space, and then stirred again —

She busied herself with some milk-pans and troughs that stood by the sæter wall. Naakkve and the twins came out — whither were they going? their mother asked.

They were going to lie in the barn — there was such a rank smell in the dairy from all the cheese and butter — and from the herds sleeping there.

Naakkve went not at once to the barn. His mother still saw his light-grey form faintly against the green darkness of the hay-field that bordered the woods. A little later the serving-wench came to the door — she started when she saw the mistress standing by the wall.

"Are you not for bed now, Astrid? — 'tis late already — "

The wench mumbled — she was but going behind the byre. Kristin waited till she had seen her in again. Naakkve was in his sixteenth year. 'Twas some time now since his mother had begun to keep an eye upon the serving-women on the manor, when they grew merry with the comely and lively youth.

Kristin went down to the river and knelt upon the stone slab out over the water. Before her the river ran, well-nigh black, in a wide pool; only a few rings showed the current; but a little above, it foamed down, white in the darkness, with a drumming noise and cold puffs of air. The moon had risen so high now that its light was grown strong — here and there it glittered on a dewy leaf. Then a sparkle showed on a ripple of the stream —

Erlend spoke her name just behind her — she had not heard him coming down across the sward. Kristin sank her arm into the icy water and fished up a pair of milk-pans that lay at the bottom with stones on them, scouring in the river; she rose and followed her husband back with both hands full. They did not speak as they passed up the slope.

Once in the hut, Erlend stripped himself wholly and climbed into the bed:

"Will you not come to rest soon, Kristin?"

"I must get me a bite of food first — " She sat her down on her three-legged stool close by the hearth, with some bread and a slice of cheese in her lap, ate slowly, and gazed into the heap of embers that were dying out little by little in the stone-lined hole in the floor.

"Are you sleeping, Erlend?" she whispered, as she rose and shook her skirt.

"No — " Kristin went over and drank a dipperful of sour milk from the tub in the corner. Then she went back to the hearth, lifted a slab of stone and laid it on top, and spread the Aaron's-rod blossoms on it to dry.

But now there was no more she could think on to be done. She undressed in the dark and laid her down in the bed by Erlend. When he put his arms around her, she felt her weariness like a wave of cold sweeping through her whole body; her head grew hollow and heavy, as though all within it had settled down and made a lump

of sheer pain where it joined her neck. But when he
whispered to her, she dutifully put her arms about his
neck.

She awoke in the night and knew not what time it was.
But by the pane above the smoke-hole she could see the
moon must be high.

The bed was narrow and short, so that they needs must
lie close to one another. Erlend slept; he breathed quietly
and evenly; his breast rose and fell gently in his sleep.
At one time she had been wont to nestle close in to his
warm, sound body when she woke of nights and grew
fearful because he breathed so noiselessly — then it had
seemed a sweet joy to feel his breast rise and fall in
slumber against her side.

After a while she crept out of the bed, put on her
clothes in the dark, and stole to the door.

The moon was sailing high over the whole world. Here
and there was a glimmer from water in the mosses, or on
cliffs over whose face it had trickled the day through and
was freezing now to ice. The moon shone over the leaf
woods and the pine woods. On the grass banks hoar-frost
glittered. It was bitter cold — she crossed her arms upon
her breast and stood a little.

Then she went up along the beck. It tinkled and gurgled, with little sounds of ice-needles breaking in sunder —

At the upper end of the fenced field lay a great deep-
bedded boulder. No one went near it unless he must, and
when he went, he crossed himself. They poured cream in
under it when they came in the summer, and when they
left again. True it was she had never known of any that
had seen or heard aught there — but such had been the
custom on the sæter from of old —

She knew not herself what had taken her, to leave the
house in this wise, at dead of night. She came to a stand by
the stone — set her foot in a notch in it. Her belly shrank,
her body grew cold and numb with fear — but cross
herself she *would* not. Then she crept up and sat her down
upon the stone.

From here one saw far and wide around — away over
the ugly grey-stone mountains in the moon-light. The
big hump on Dovre rose mighty and pale against the pale
sky, the snow-field glistened white in the scar on Graahö,

the Boar-fells shone with blue clefts and new-fallen snow.
In the moonlight the mountains were uglier than she had
ever deemed they could be — hardly a single star or two
shone here and there in the endless, icy-cold heavens. She
was chilled through bone and marrow — terror and cold
pressed in upon her from all sides. But she sat on defiant.

She *would* not go down and lay herself in the black
darkness by her husband's warm, slumbering body. For
her there was no sleep that night, she knew —

So sure as she was her father's daughter — her wedded
husband should never hear her blame his deeds. For she
remembered what she had sworn when she besought God
Almighty and all the holy saints in heaven for Erlend's
life —

So it was that she *must* go out into this ghostly night to
take breath, when she felt nigh perishing —

She sat and let the bitter old thoughts come to her like
old acquaintance. And met them with other old and well-
known thoughts — in feigned excuse of Erlend —

True, he had not craved this of her. He had not laid
upon her aught of the burden she had taken upon her
shoulders. He had but begotten seven sons on her. "For
my seven sons *I* shall care, Arne — " God alone might
know what the man meant by those words. Like enough
he had meant nothing — he had but said it —

Erlend had not begged her to set Husaby and his estates
a-going again. He had not begged her fight for dear life to
save him. Like a chieftain he had suffered — that his goods
be wasted, that his life be set on the hazard, that all he
owned be lost. Stripped and bare, he stood amidst mischance loftily unbowed and still; loftily still and unbowed
he abode in her father's manor like some stranger guest —

But all that was hers was her sons' by right. By right
they claimed her sweat and blood and all her strength.
But, if so, the manor and she herself could lay rightful
claim to them in return.

There had been no need for her to take the road to the
sæter like any cottar's wife. But at home, as things were
now, she felt herself crushed and hemmed in on every
side — so that she seemed to fail for breath. Besides, she
had needed to prove to herself that she *could* do a peasant woman's work. True, toil and struggle had been hers

every hour since she rode, a bride, into Erlend Nikulaussön's manor — and saw that here *one* at least must fight to
save the heritage of him she bore below her heart. If the
father could not, then she must be the one. But now she
must needs assure herself — that, if the pinch came, there
was no piece of work she had set her maids and serving-
women to in the old days that she could not do with her
own hands. Up here 'twas a good day when she marked
that she ached not across the loins when she had stood
long a-churning. 'Twas good in the mornings to be along
herself and help let out the cattle — they had grown fat
and fair this summer — the weight on her heart lightened
when she stood in the sunset, crying on the home-coming
cows. She loved to see the food growing under her own
hands — 'twas as though she were reaching down to make
firm the very groundwork on which her sons' fortunes
were to be built up again.

Jörundgaard was a good estate, but 'twas not so good as
she had deemed. And Ulf was a stranger here in the dale
— he fell into mistakes and he lost patience. As folk reckoned in this country-side, they ever did well with their
hay on Jörundgaard — they had water-meadows along
the river and out on the holms — but 'twas not *the best*
hay, nor such as Ulf was used to in the Trondheim country. He was unused to have to garner in so much moss
and leaf fodder, so much heather and twigs, as was needful
here —

Her father had known every inch of his land, had had
all a farmer's lore: of the whims of seasons; of the way the
divers fields took wet or dry years, windy summers or
burning summers; of the strains of cattle that, generation
after generation, he himself had coupled, fed and reared
and sold from — all the knowledge that was needed for
just this place. She knew not her manor so by heart. But
she would yet — and her sons should —

But Erlend had never asked the like of her. He had not
wed her to plunge her into toil and trouble; he had but
wed her that she might sleep in his arms. And thus, ever,
when her time was come, a child lay by her side, craved
its place upon her arm, at her breast, in her cares —

Kristin moaned through her clenched teeth. She sat
shivering with cold and wrath.

"*Pactum serva* — that is, in the Norse tongue, keep thy troth!"

'Twas in that time when Arne Gjavvaldssön and brother Leif of Holm had come to Husaby and fetched away her goods and her children's to Nidaros. That, too, had Erlend left her to deal with — he had taken lodging out at the Holm cloister. She sat in the town mansion — the monks owned it now — and Arne Gjavvaldssön was with her, helping her with rede and deed; Simon had sent letters praying for his help.

Arne could have been no more eager had it been for himself he was to save the goods and gear. The very evening he brought it to the town, he must needs have both her and Lady Gunna of Raasvold, who had come in with the two little ones, out to the stables. Seven picked horses — folk were minded to deal fairly towards Erlend Nikulaussön, and gave assent when Arne averred the five eldest sons each owned a riding-horse, and the lady of the house one for herself and one for her serving-man. As to the Castilian, Erlend's Spanish stallion, he could bring witness that him Erlend had made over in gift to his son Nikulaus — even though it might have been more jest than earnest. Not that Arne was much taken with the long-legged beast — but he knew Erlend loved the horse well —

'Twas an ill thing, said Arne, that he had to let the armour of state go, with the great helm and the gold-mounted sword — true, all this gear was fit for naught but the tournament; still 'twas worth a great sum. But he had got Erlend's body-shirt of black silk with the red lion broidered on it. And he had claimed the English battle-harness for Nikulaus. And that was so choicely wrought that Arne deemed there was not the like to be found in Norway's land — for them that had eyes to see. But 'twas much worn — ay, indeed, Erlend had worn his weapons more than most sons of nobles in these times — Arne fondled each piece — helm, gorget, vambraces, greaves, gauntlets of the finest steel plates, corslet and hauberk of chain-mail, so light and easy-fitting and yet withal so strong. And then the sword — it had but a plain steel hilt, and the leather on the handle was chafed — but the like of such a blade one saw not every year —

Kristin sat and held the sword across her lap. She knew Erlend would take it to him like a much-loved bride — he had never used any other of all the swords he owned. It had been left to him when he was but a lad by Sigmund Torolfssön, who had been his bedfellow when first he joined the body-guard. Once only had he spoken of this friend to her: "Had God not been in such hot haste to take Sigmund from this world, 'tis like that much had gone otherwise with me. After his death I was ill at ease at the Court, and so with much begging I got me King Haakon's leave to go north with Gissur Galle that time. — Yet but for that I trow I had never won you, my sweeting — for belike I had been a wedded man long ere you were grown maid — "

From Munan Baardssön she had heard that Erlend had nursed his friend day and night, as a mother tends her babe, taking no sleep but a short doze now and then on the sick man's bed-side — that last winter, when Sigmund Torolfssön lay spitting out his lungs piecemeal, and his heart's blood. And when Sigmund had been brought to earth in Halvard's Church, Erlend had gone to his grave late and early, and lain flat on the gravestone sorrowing. But to her he had never spoken of him but that one time. In Halvard's Church, too, Erlend and she had had their trysts sometimes, that sinful winter in Oslo. But he had never named with a word that the dearest friend of his youth lay there. — 'Twas thus he had mourned over his mother, she knew; and when Orm died he had been wild and ungoverned in his despair; yet them too he never named. She knew he had been in to the town and seen Margret — but he never spoke of his daughter.

— Right up under the hilt she saw some writing graven into the blade. 'Twas runes mostly, and she could not read them, nor Arne either; but the monk took the sword and looked on it a while. "*Pactum serva*," said he at last. "That means, in the Norse tongue, keep thy troth."

Arne and brother Leif spoke, too, of how a great part of her lands here, north of Dovre, Erlend's morning-gift to her, had been pledged and thrown away. Could not some device be found to save somewhat of this? But Kristin would not — 'twas honour one must save first of all; she would not have any question raised whether her husband's dealings were lawful. And besides, she was well-nigh plagued to death by Arne's talk, well meant as it was. That night, when he and the monk had bidden good-night and gone to their lodging, she threw herself upon her knees before Lady Gunna and hid her face in her lap.

In a little the old woman lifted up the young one's head. Kristin looked up at the other — Lady Gunna's face was heavy, yellow, and fleshy, with three thick folds, as though moulded in wax, right across her brow, lightly freckled, with sharp, kind blue eyes and an indrawn, toothless mouth shaded by long, grey lip-hairs. Kristin had seen this face look down on her in so many an hour of torment — Lady Gunna had been with her each time she bore a child, save when Lavrans came, for then Kristin had been at home by her father's death-bed.

"Ay, ay, my daughter," said the lady, pressing a hand on her forehead. "I have stayed you more times than one now, when you needs must to your knees — ay. But in this trial, my Kristin, you must lay you down before God's mother Mary herself and pray her to help you through — "

— Ah, and she had done it too, Kristin thought. She said her prayers and somewhat of the psalter every sabbath eve; she kept the fasts Archbishop Eiliv had laid upon her when he gave her remission of her sins; she gave alms, and tended herself each wayfarer who begged night's lodging, looked he fair or foul. But she felt no longer now that the light shone within her when she did these things. That there *was* light without she knew, but it seemed as though mists shut in her soul. It must be what Gunnulf spoke of — the drought of the spirit. No soul should lose courage by reason of that, said Sira Eiliv; be steadfast in prayer and good deeds, as a farmer ploughs and dungs and sows — God will send the quickening rain in His own good time. — But then Sira Eiliv had never been a farmer —

Gunnulf she had not seen that time. He was making a term north in Helgeland, preaching and gathering gifts for his cloister. Ay! there was the one of the knight's sons of Husaby — and the other —

But Margret Erlendsdatter had come to her sometimes at the town mansion. Two servants followed the merchant's wife; she was in goodly clothing and shone with rich trinkets — her father-in-law was a goldsmith, so they had them handy in the house. She seemed happy and content — albeit she had no children. She had got her dowry from her father in good time. God only knew whether she ever gave a thought to the poor cripple, Haakon, out at Gimsar — he could but just drag himself round the court-yard on two crutches, Kristin had heard. —

But even then she had not thought on Erlend with bit-terness, it seemed to her. She must have felt that what waited Erlend, now he was a free man again, was the worst of all for him. 'Twas therefore he hid himself away out with Abbot Olav. Take order for the flitting, show himself now in the town — it might well be too much for even Erlend Nikulaussön to face —

And there was the day they sailed out over Trondheim's fjord — on the Laurentius galleass, the selfsame bark by which Erlend had shipped her bridal gear to the north when they first got leave to wed each other —

A still day, well on in autumn — a pale, leaden glimmer upon the fjord, the world about them cold, white-barred, unquiet — the first snow drifted into ridges across the frozen lands, the cold-blue hills streaked white with snow. The highest clouds, too, where the skies were blue, seemed spread out thin as flour by a wind high up in the dome of heaven. The ship drifted along slowly, sullenly, close under the land — the town ness. Kristin stood looking at the white surf against the cliff — wondering if she should be seasick when they got further out into the fjord.

Erlend stood by the rail, further forward near the bow, his two eldest sons with him. The wind blew their hair and cloaks about.

Now they were looking up Kors fjord, toward Gaularos and the landing at Birgsi. A gleam of sunshine lit up the brown and white hill-side above the strand in there —

Erlend said somewhat to the lads. At that Björgulf turned sharply round, left the bulwark, and came aft. With the spear he always bore and used as a staff he groped his way among the empty rowing-benches; he came past his mother — his curly black head thrust low down upon his breast, his eyes blinking, well-nigh shut, his lips pressed close together. He went in under the poop —

The mother looked forward at the other two, Erlend and his eldest son. Then she saw Nikulaus kneel down upon one knee, as a page does homage to his lord, take his father's hand, and kiss it.

Erlend tore away his hand — Kristin had a glimpse of his face, deathly white, quivering, as he turned from the boy and went behind the sail away from view —

They put into a small haven down the Möre coast that night. More sea was running now — the galleass tugged at her land moorings, pitching and rolling. Kristin was down in the room below, where she was to sleep with Erlend and the two little children. She felt qualmish with sickness, could not keep her footing on the boards, which seemed to rise and sink beneath her feet; the lantern swung over her head, the tiny candle flickered — and she stood struggling with Munan, trying to get him to make water down between the planks. When he awoke, drugged with sleep, he would be sick or worse in their bed; and he raged and shrieked and would not suffer that the strange woman, his mother, should lay hands on him to help him and hold him over the side. Then Erlend came down.

She could not see his face, as he asked, very low:

"Saw you Naakkve? — He was so like you in the eyes, Kristin." Erlend drew in his breath, short and hard. " 'Twas so your eyes looked that morning by the wall of the nuns' garden — when you had heard the worst of me — and you plighted me your troth — "

It was then that she had felt the first drop of bitter gall well up in her heart. God shield the lad — may he never see the day when he must fix his faith on a hand that lets all slip through its fingers like cold water and dry sand —

A little while before, she had thought she heard the sound of hoofs from somewhere far south in the hill wastes. Now it came again, from nearer by: 'twas not the noise of stray horses, 'twas some rider; he rode sharply over the rock slabs below the hillock yonder.

Fear came over her, icy cold; who rides abroad so late? Dead men ride north under a waning moon — heard she not horsemen following the first, far behind — ? Yet she sat on; she knew not herself whether 'twas that she was palsied, or that her heart to-night was so hardened —

He was bound hither, the rider — now he was crossing the stream below the home-pasture. She saw the glint of a spear-head above the willow bushes. Then she found strength to come down from the stone, and would have run back to the hut — but now the rider sprang from his horse, bound it to the wicket-post, and threw his cloak over it for a covering. He came up the green; 'twas a big, broad man — and now she knew him — it was Simon.

When he saw her coming towards him in the moonlight, he seemed as affrighted as she had been before:

"Jesus, Kristin, is't you yourself or — how comes it you are out at dead of night — ? Did you look for me to come?" he asked quickly, as in great dread; "have you had warning of my coming?"

Kristin shook her head:

"I could not sleep. — Brother-in-law, what ails you — ?"

"Andres is so sick, Kristin — we are afeared for his life. And so we thought — we know you are the most skilful of women in such things — bear in mind he is your own sister's son. Will you do a good deed and go home with me to him? — You know well I would not come to you thus, but that I know full surely the boy's life is the stake," he said beseechingly.

Inside the hut he said the same to Erlend, who sat up in the bed, still half asleep, in silent wonderment. Then Erlend tried to comfort his brother-in-law, speaking as one with knowledge: such young children so easily went off into a high fever and wandered in their talk, even if they had only taken some little chill; mayhap there was not so much peril as there seemed. "You may well know, Erlend, I had never come to fetch Kristin out at such hours of the night as this, had I not seen all too plain that the child is lying fighting with death — "

Kristin had blown up the embers and laid wood on the hearth; Simon sat staring into the fire; he drank eagerly of the milk she proffered him, but would have no food. He had a mind to set off down the hill as soon as the others came, " — if you are willing, Kristin?" One of his henchmen was bringing with him a widow that served at Formo, a notable woman, who could take the charge here for a time — Aasbjörg was a most handy woman, he said again.

When Simon had lifted Kristin to the saddle, he said:

"Fain am I that we should take the short cut southwards — if you have naught against it?"

Kristin had never been on that side of the fell, but she

knew there was a path there going sheer down into the
dale over the hill-side above Formo. She answered, ay —
but then his man must ride the other way, round by
Jörundgaard, to fetch her casket and the bags of roots
and herbs. He must waken Gaute; the boy knew best
about them.

By the edge of a wide moss they were able to ride side
by side, and Kristin made Simon tell her again of the
boy's sickness. The children at Formo had had the throat
sickness about Olav's Mass, but had got over that lightly.
This new sickness had taken hold on Andres quite of a
sudden, when he seemed in the highest health — in the
middle of the day three days ago. Simon had taken him
out with him; he was to have a ride on the corn-sled down
to the field — but he began to complain that he was cold,
and, when Simon looked, the child was in a shivering fit,
his teeth chattering in his head. Later came the hot fit and
the cough; and he spat up an evil-looking brown slime,
and had a sore pain in the breast — but, to be sure, he
could not tell them much of where he felt worst, the
poor little being —

Kristin spoke to Simon as cheerly as she could, and now
she had to ride for a stretch behind him. Once he turned
and asked if she were cold; he would have her to put on
his mantle over her cloak —

Then he talked again of his son. 'Twas true, he had
marked it — the boy was not strong. But Andres had
grown much more hearty this summer and autumn — his
foster-mother deemed so too. Ay, the last days before he
fell sick he had been a little strange and startlish —
"frighted," he said when the dogs sprang up on him in
play. And the day he took the fever Simon had come
home at sunrise with some wild-ducks. Other days the
boy would ever beg his father for the birds he brought
home, to play with them awhile; but now Andres had
shrieked out loud when his father had made as if to toss
the leash of birds at him. He had indeed stolen across
afterward and handled the ducks, but he got some blood
upon him, and at that he grew quite wild with terror.
And now to-night, as he lay moaning sore, getting no sleep
nor rest — he had cried out somewhat of a hawk that was
after him —

" — Mind you that day the tidings came to me at Oslo, and you said: ' 'Twill still be the Darre stock that will hold Formo when you are gone — '?"

"Talk not so, Simon — as though you deemed you would die sonless. God and his gentle mother can surely help — 'Tis unlike you, brother-in-law, to be so faint of heart."

"Halfrid, my first wife, said the same to me when she had borne our son as you said at Oslo. Knew you, Kristin, that I had a son by her?"

"Ay — But Andres is all but three years old — 'Tis the first two years that are hardest to bring children through alive — " But even to herself it seemed that her words availed little here. And they rode, and they rode; the horses nodded as they mounted a rise, and tossed their heads so that the bits jingled; not a sound in the frosty night, save of their own riding, and at times the ripple of water as they crossed a beck; and the moon shone high and low; and scree and greystone crag glimmered grimly pale as death, where they rode on under the hill-sides.

At length they had come where they could look down upon the parish. Moonlight filled all the dale; the river and the marshes and the lake farther south shone like silver — fields and meadows were wan.

"Ay, to-night 'tis freezing in the lowlands too," said Simon.

He got down from his horse and led hers as they went down over the edge. The path was so steep in many places, Kristin felt she scarce dared look ahead. Simon steadied her with his back against her knee, and she held on with one hand behind the saddle. Now and then a stone rolled from under the horses' hoofs, trundled downward, stopped a little, then rolled again, loosening others and carrying them along —

At last they were down. They rode over the barley-fields north of the manor between the rime-covered corn-stooks. The aspens crackled and pattered eerily above their heads in the bright, still night.

"Said you sooth," asked Simon, wiping his face with his sleeve, "that you had had no warning — ?"

Kristin answered that it was true. Then said he:

"I have heard tell that sometimes a forewarning goes

forth when any one yearns sorely for another — Ramborg and I said to each other more than once that had you been at home you might have known a way — "

"None of you have been in my thoughts all these days," said Kristin. "You must believe me, Simon." But she could not see that this comforted him.

In the courtyard a couple of house-carls sprang out at once and took the horses. "Ay, 'tis even as when you went, Simon; 'tis no worse," said one of them quickly; he had looked up at his master's face. Simon nodded; he went in front of Kristin towards the women's house.

Kristin saw clear enough that here was great peril of life. The little boy lay alone in the great, fine bed, moaning and gasping and tossing his head without cease to and fro on the pillows. He was burning hot, and dark red in the face; he lay with half-open, glistening eyes, fighting for breath. Simon stood, holding Ramborg's hand, and all the women of the manor, who were gathered in the room, pressed round Kristin while she handled the boy.

But she spoke as calmly as she could, and heartened the parents as best she was able. Sure enough 'twas the lung fever. But this night was now near an end without the evil having changed for the worse — and 'twas the way of this sickness to take a turn the third or seventh or ninth night, before cock-crow. She prayed Ramborg to send all the serving-women to bed save two, so that she might at all times have women, rested and fresh, to help her. And when the man came from Jörundgaard with her leech-wife's gear, she brewed a sweating-drink for the boy and opened a vein in his foot to draw the humours somewhat away from his breast.

Ramborg's face blanched at the sight of her child's blood. Simon put an arm around her, but she pushed the man aside and sat down on a chair by the bed-foot; there she sat gazing at Kristin with big, black eyes, while her sister busied herself with the child.

On in the day, the boy seeming a little better, Kristin talked Ramborg over to lie down on the bench. She heaped cushions and coverings about the young wife; sat by her head, stroking her forehead gently. Ramborg took Kristin's hand:

"Surely now, you wish us naught else but good?" said she in a moaning breath.

"Could I wish you aught but well, sister — we two, sister, left here in the country of our home, alone of all our kindred — ?"

Ramborg broke into sobs — a few half-choked sobs through lips pressed hard together. Kristin had but once seen her sister weep — the time they stood by their father's death-bed. Now a few small, hasty tears sprang to her eyes and trickled down her cheeks. She lifted Kristin's hand and looked upon it. It was long and slender, but red-brown now and rough —

"Even yet 'tis fairer than mine," she said. Ramborg's hands were small and white, but the fingers were short and the nails square.

"Yes," said she, almost angrily, as Kristin shook her head, smiling. "And you are even yet fairer than I have ever been. And our father and our mother held you dearer than me — all our days. You wrought them sorrow and shame; I was duteous and obedient and set my heart on the man they most fain would have me wed — yet withal 'twas you they loved much more — "

"Nay, sister. Be sure they held you every whit as dear. Be glad, Ramborg, to think you never gave them aught but joy — you know not how heavy the other thought is to bear. But you were younger the time when I was young; and therefore, maybe, they spoke more with me."

"Aye, I trow that all were younger that time when you were young," said Ramborg, sighing as before.

She slept soon after. Kristin sat and gazed at her. She had known her sister so little; Ramborg was yet a child when she herself was wed. And now it seemed to her that the other in some ways had never ceased to be a child. She had looked like a child as she sat by her sick boy — a pale, frighted child, striving to bear up against terror and unhappiness.

It befell at times that beasts stopped short in their growth if they bore young too early. Ramborg had not been full sixteen years when she bore her daughter, and since then it seemed as though she had never rightly taken up her growth again; she had stayed frail and small, without bloom or fruitfulness. She had had this one son since, and he was strangely ailing — comely of face, fine-

featured and fair of hue, but piteously small and puny—
he had been backward in walking, and he still spoke haltingly, so that only those about him daily understood
aught of his prattle. He was so fearful and peevish with
strangers, too, that he had scarce ever let his mother's
sister touch him till now. Would God and Holy Olav
but grant her grace to save this poor little being—oh! she
would be thankful all her days. Such a child as this mother
of his was, sure it was that she could never endure the loss
of him. And she felt that for Simon Darre too 'twould be
bitter hard to bear the blow well, if this only son were
taken from him—

That she had grown to love her brother-in-law heartily
she marked well, now that she understood how sorely he
suffered in this sorrow and dread. She could well understand now her father's great love for Simon Andressön.
And yet she wondered if he had not done Ramborg
wrong in making such haste to bring about this match. For
when she looked upon this little sister beside her, it came
home to her that, after all said, Simon must be both too
old and too sober and heavy to be husband to this young
child.

3

THE DAYS went by and Andres lay sick; there was no great
change either for the worse or for the better. The worst
was he scarce got any sleep; the boy lay there with half-
open eyes and seemed not to know any; cough and breath-
lessness wrung his wasted little frame, and the flickering
fever rose and fell. One evening Kristin had given him a
soothing drink—after it he sank into rest; but in a while
she saw the child had gone a bluish-white, and his skin felt
cold and clammy.

In all haste she got a draught of hot milk poured down
his throat, and laid hot stones to the soles of his feet; but
thereafter she no longer dared give him a sleeping potion.
—She saw that he was too young to support it.

Sira Solmund came and brought him the Holy Elements
from the church; Simon and Ramborg vowed perpetual

prayer, fasts and alms, if God would hear them and grant their son his life.

Erlend came thither one day; he would not light from his horse and go within, but Kristin and Simon came out into the courtyard and spoke with him. He looked on them most sorrowfully. 'Twas strange that this look of his ever stirred in Kristin a vague dull anger. Certain 'twas that it gave him pain when he saw any sick or sorrowing, but he seemed most of all mazed and shamefaced — he ever looked so helpless when he was sorry for folk.

After that Naakkve or the twins came each day to Formo to ask for Andres.

The seventh night brought no turn in the sickness, but as the day drew on the boy seemed a little better — not so hot. Simon and Kristin were sitting alone by him towards midday.

The father pulled out a little gilded amulet he wore on a cord about his neck under his clothes. He bent down over the boy, dangled the amulet before his eyes, thrust it into the child's hand, and pressed the little fingers together around it — but Andres seemed not to heed.

This amulet Simon had had given him when a child, and he had borne it ever since — his father had brought it with him from France. It had been blessed in a cloister named St. Michael's Mount, and there was on it the likeness of St. Michael with great wings; this Andres liked right well to look upon, Simon told her, very low. But the little fellow deemed it was a cock; *he* called the chief of all the angels "the cock" — At last he had got the boy taught to say "the angel." But one day they were standing in the courtyard Andres saw the cock pecking at one of his hens; "Angel angry now, father," said he.

Kristin looked up at the man beseechingly — it cut her to the heart to hear him, albeit Simon spoke so evenly and calmly. And she was so worn out by all these nights of watching; she felt she must break down if she began now to weep —

Simon thrust the charm into the bosom of his shirt again:

"Oh, ay. I shall give a three-year-old ox to the church on St. Michael's even, each autumn so long as I live, if

he will but tarry a little ere he come to fetch this soul.
Methinks too he would weigh in the balance no more than
a plucked chicken — Andres — so little — " but when he
tried to laugh, his voice broke a little.

"Simon, Simon!" the woman begged him.

"Ay, 'twill be as 'tis willed to be, Kristin. And 'tis God
Himself that wills it; he must sure know best — " The
father spoke no more, but stood looking down upon his
son.

On the eighth night Simon and one of the serving-
women watched, while Kristin slumbered a little over on
the further bench. When she awoke, the girl was sleeping.
Simon sat, as he had sat most nights, on the bench at the
bed head; he sat with his head bowed down over the bed
and the child.

"Doth he sleep?" whispered Kristin, going forward to
him.

Simon raised his head. He brushed his hand over his
face; she saw that his cheeks were wet, but he answered
low and calmly:

"I deem not, Kristin, that Andres will sleep any more
till he lies beneath the turf in holy ground — "

Kristin stood — 'twas as though she grew stark and
stiff. Slowly she blanched beneath her sunburnt skin,
grew white to the very lips.

Then she went to the corner and took her outdoor
cloak.

"You must order it so — " she spoke as though her
throat and mouth were dry — "that you are here alone
when I come back. Stay you with him — and, when you
see me enter, speak no word, and speak no word of this
after, neither to me nor to any. Not even to your
priest — "

Simon rose up — came slowly over to her. He too had
grown pale.

"Nay — Kristin!" His voice could scarce be heard. "I
— I dare not — have you go that road — "

She wrapped her cloak about her, took a cloth of linen
from the chest in the corner, folded it together, and hid
it in her bosom.

"I dare. You wot well not one must come nigh us after,

before I call — no one must come nigh us after, nor speak
to us, ere he wakes and himself has spoken — "

"What, trow you, would your father think of this?" he
whispered, faintly as before. "Kristin — do it not — "

"I have done before now what my father deemed was
wrong — then 'twas but to forward my own lusts —
Andres is *his* flesh and blood too — *my* own flesh, Simon
— my only sister's son — "

Simon breathed hard, trembling; he stood looking down.

"But if you would not that I should make trial of this
last shift of all — " He stood as before with bowed head,
and made no answer. Thereon she said again — and knew
not that a strange, nigh scornful half-smile had come about
her white lips:

"Would you that I should not go?"

He turned his head aside, and she went by him, stepped
through the door noiselessly, and closed it softly behind
her.

Without was thick darkness, with little puffs of south
wind, so that all the stars flickered and blinked unsteadily.
She had come no farther than into the road between the
fences, and yet it seemed as though she had passed out
into the everlasting itself. An endless road behind her and
before her. As though she would never come away from
what she had stepped into when she set foot out into
this night —

The darkness itself seemed a power that she pressed
forward against. She was walking in deep mud — the way
had been ploughed up by the dung-carts and was thawing
in the south wind. At each step she must tear herself loose
from the night and the raw cold that clung about her
feet, sucked its way up, and clogged the hem of her skirts.
Ever and anon a falling leaf brushed by her — as though
a living thing in the dark touched her, softly, sure of its
power: go back, go back! —

When she came out upon the highway, walking grew
easier: it was grass-grown; her feet stuck in the mud no
longer. She felt her face stiff as stone, her body strung and
taut — each step bore her mercilessly towards the wood
she must go through. An inner palsy seemed to mount
up in her — 'twas impossible she could dare go through

that murky passage — yet she had no thought of turning.
Terror had struck her body numb, yet she kept striding
forward as though in sleep, stepping surely over stones
and roots and puddles, all unaware — heedful not to
stumble, not to drop her even gait and give her terror
the mastery.

Now the firs sighed nearer and nearer in the night; she
passed in among them, still calm, as if sleep-walking. She
was ware of every sound, and scarce dared move an eye-
lid for the darkness. The thunder of the river, the heavy
sighing in the trees, the tinkle over stones of a beck that
she drew near to, passed, and left behind. Once, up on the
scree, a stone rolled, as if some living thing stirred up
there — sweat burst out over her whole body, but she
dared neither slacken nor hasten her gait —

Kristin's eyes were now so used to the dark that, when
she came out of the wood, she could see a little — there
was a faint gleam upon the river, upon the waters of the
marshes. The farm-lands showed now against the blackness; the clusters of houses looked like cores of blacker
gloom upon them. The sky, too, was surely lightening
high above her as she went — she felt it, but dared not
look up at the black hill-sides that towered up to heaven.
But she knew it must soon be time for the moon to rise —

She tried to remind herself — in four hours' time 'twill
be day: folk will be setting about the day's work on all
the farms — the air will be grey with dawn; 'twill grow
light above the hills. The way will not be long then — in
the light 'tis not far from Formo to the church. And
long ere that she herself would be home and within-doors.
But something told her that she must needs be another
then than she was when she went forth —

She knew — had it been for one of her own children's
lives, she had never dared to try this last shift of all. Turn
God's hand aside, when He had stretched it forth to take
a living soul! As she sat over her own sick little ones,
when she was young and her heart bled with tenderness,
she had tried to say, when ready to sink with dread and
anguish: Lord, Thou lovest them better than I — Thy
will be done —

Yet now went she here this night defying her own
terror — This child which was not hers — this child she
would save, whatsover she might save it for —

— For you too, Simon Darre, when the dearest thing you owned on earth was the stake, took at my hands more than a man may take with honour unabated —

"Would you that I should not go — ?" And he had not been man enough to answer. In her heart of hearts she knew — were the child to die, that too Simon would somehow make shift to bear. But she had swooped down upon that single hour when she found him at the breaking-point — had seized the chance that moment gave her and gone her way. This secret now she would share with him — that he knew she too had seen *him* in an hour when he stood not firmly on his feet —

For he had come to know her too nearly. At the hands of the man she had thrown off she had taken help each time there was need, to save the man of her choice. The lover she had cast aside was the man she had turned to, each time she stood in need of a shield for her love. And she had never besought Simon in vain — time after time had he stepped forth to screen her with his kindness and his strength.

— So she walked this road through the night that she might lighten a little the load of debt whose crushing weight still that hour she had never felt to the full.

Simon had forced her to understand at the last that he was the strongest — stronger than she herself and stronger than the man she had chosen to give herself to. She must indeed have felt it from the very hour when they three had met face to face in that shameful den in Oslo — though she *would* not see it then — that this lumpish, round-cheeked, talking youth was stronger than —

So went she here, and dared not call upon a good and holy name, and took upon herself this sin, that she might win — she knew not what — was it revenge? — revenge for that she had been forced to see he was worthier than they two — ?

But now you too know it, Simon — when 'tis for the life of him one loves more than one's own being — a poor human soul will grasp at aught, at aught —

The moon had risen over the edge of the hills as she went up the slope towards the church. Again 'twas as though she must ride over a fresh wave of terror — the moonlight lay like a thin cob-web layer over the tar-sprent mass; the church itself stood under the thin veil, awful

and threateningly black. For the first time she saw the
great cross on the green outside and dared not go thither
to bow down before the holy tree. She crept across where
she knew the churchyard wall of turf and stone was
lowest and easiest to climb.

A gravestone here and there glistened like water in the
long dewy grass. Kristin went straight across the churchyard, down to the poor folks' graves away by the south
wall.

She went to the place where lay a poor new-comer to
the parish. The man had frozen to death on the mountains
one winter; his two motherless daughters had been passed
from house to house as bedesfolk, till Lavrans Björgulfsön had proffered to keep them for Christ's sake, and to
give them nurture. They grew up and turned out well,
and her father had himself sought out honest, hard-working men for them, and had given them away in wedlock,
each with cow and calf and sheep; while Ragnfrid gave
them beds and bedding and iron pots — now they were
thriving housewives, well-to-do in their own way of life.
One had been Ramborg's serving-maid, and Ramborg had
borne children to baptism for her —

So now must you spare me a turf from your covering,
Bjarne, for Ramborg's son. She knelt down and drew out
her dagger.

The sweat burst out in ice-cold beads upon her brow
and upper lip as she dug her fingers in under the dew-wet
turf. Something held it from below — 'twas but roots —
she cut them with the dagger.

In guerdon the drow must have gold, or silver heired
for three generations. She drew off the little gold ring
with rubies that had been her grandmother's betrothal
ring — the child is of my father's house. She thrust the
ring down into the earth as deep as she could, wrapped
the turf in the linen cloth, and covered the spot whence
she had taken it with moss and leaves.

As she rose to her feet, her legs beneath her trembled —
she had to stand a little ere she could turn. If she looked
under her elbow now, she would see *them* —

And there was a dreadful dragging within her, as though
they would force her to it — all the dead who had known
her in days gone by. Is't you, Kristin Lavransdatter —

come you hither thus?— Arne Gyrdssön in the grave without the western porch. Ay, Arne, well may you wonder
— I was not such an one when you and I were friends —

Then she climbed over the wall again and went her way
downward.

The moon shone now over the whole country-side.
There lay Jörundgaard out on the river flat — dew glittered in the grass on all the roofs. She looked down yonder, well-nigh unmoved — 'Twas as though she herself
were dead to that home and all therein — the door barred
for ever against her who went by that night on the
highroad —

Nigh all her road back was shadowed by the hills. The
wind blew stronger now — gust after gust pressed straight
against her — Withered leaves blew against her and would
have turned her thither whence she last came —

Nor seemed it to her that she walked alone. Of a sudden there would come a sound as of stealthy footsteps behind her. Is it you, Arne —? Look behind you, Kristin;
look under your elbow, it whispered —

And yet 'twas as though she was rightly afraid no
longer. Only cold and numb, sick with longing to give
up and sink down to the ground. Surely after this night
she could never know fear again in this world —

Simon sat in his wonted place at the head of the bed,
bent over the child, when she opened the door and stepped
in. For one short moment he looked up — Kristin wondered whether *she* had grown in this time to look as worn
and marred and old. Then Simon bowed his face wholly
down and hid it on his arm.

He reeled a little as he rose. He turned his head away
from her as he went by towards the door, with stooping
neck and shoulders.

Kristin lit two candles and set them on the board. The
boy opened his eyes a little, looked up unseeingly, frowned
a little, and tried to turn his head from the light. When
Kristin laid the little body out straight, as one lays out a
corpse, he tried not to change his posture — he seemed
too weak to move.

Then she covered his face and breast with the linen
cloth and laid the strip of turf across it.

With that the horror rushed upon her anew, like a breaking sea.

She must sit by the bed. The window was right over the short bench. She dared not sit there with her back to it — better to look them in the eyes, if any stood without looking in. She drew the high-backed chair up to the bed, and sat facing the pane — the night pressed in upon it, pitchy black; one of the candle flames was mirrored in the glass. Kristin stared hard at it, clenching her hands round the chair arms, so that the joints stood out white and her arms behind them trembled. Her legs had no feeling in them, so cold and wet were they — she sat with her teeth chattering from fear and cold, the icy sweat pouring down her face and back. She sat moveless — threw but now and then a lightning glance upon the linen cloth that rose and fell ever so little with the child's breathing.

At length the window-pane began to grey. Cocks crew shrilly. And then she heard men in the yard — they were going to the stables —

Limply she fell back against the back of the chair, shaking as in spasms, and tried to lie so as to still the twitching and jerking of her limbs.

Then beneath the linen cloth something moved strongly — Andres pulled it from his face, whimpering peevishly — he seemed to have his senses in a fashion, for he grunted crossly at her when she started up and bent over him —

She snatched up the cloth and the turf, ran to the fire-place, stuffed in twigs and wood and flung the demon-ware into the fresh, hissing new-lit fire. But then was she fain to stand a little, leaned against the wall — tears trickling down over her face.

She dipped milk from the little pot which stood by the hearth and took it to the child — Andres was asleep again already. It seemed now to be a healthy sleep —

She drank the milk herself. 'Twas so delicious that she was fain to swallow two or three dipperfuls of the warm drink.

She dared not speak yet — the boy had said no word that could be understood. But she fell upon her knees by the bed-foot and said over to herself, noiselessly:

Convertere, Domine, aliquantulum; et deprecare super

*servos tuos. Ne ultra memineris iniquitatis nostræ: ecce
respice; populus tuus omnes nos —* *

— Ay, ay, ay, 'twas a fearful thing she had done —

But he was their only son. She, she had seven! Ought she
not to venture *all* to save her sister's only son — ?

All that in this night she had been thinking — 'twas but
a delusion of the night. Sure it was she had done it for
naught else but that she could not bear to see the child
die in her hands —

Simon — he that had never failed her. He, that had been
faithful and kind to every mother's child she knew of —
and best of all to her and hers. And this son that he loved
more than the apples of his eyes — ought she not to make
trial of all to save the boy's life — Even if 'twere a sin —

Ay, 'twas sinful; but God, visit it on me. This little fair,
innocent child of Simon and Ramborg — God would not
let His wrath fall on Andres —

She crossed the room and bent over the bed — breathed
down upon one of the little wax-white hands. Kiss it she
dared not — he must not be waked —

Bright and sinless. — It was in those nights of horror,
when they sat together alone at Haugen, that Lady Aashild
had told her of this — told her of her faring to the graveyard in Konungahelle: "That, Kristin, be sure, is the heaviest task I ever took on my shoulders." — But Björn Gunnarssön was no innocent child when he lay at death's
door, for that Aashild Gauttesdatter's sister's sons had
come over-nigh his heart with their swords. He had been
the death of one of them ere he had fallen, and the other
was never whole man again after the day he changed
sword-strokes with Sir Björn —

Kristin stood by the window and looked out on the
court-yard. Folk went hither and thither among the
houses at their daily tasks. Some little heifer calves wandered about in the yard — so comely as they were —

All manner of thoughts spring up in the dark — like to

---

* Psalm xc. 13. Return, O Lord, how long? and let it repent
thee concerning thy servants.

Isaiah lxiv. 9. [Be not wroth very sore, O Lord,] neither
remember iniquity for ever: behold, see, we beseech thee, we
are all thy people.

those filmy plants that grow in the sea and wave and rock
themselves, strangely, weirdly fair—awesome and entic-
ing, they draw us with a strange dark lure while yet they
grow within their own living, wavering dusk. But plucked
up by the children and pulled into a boat, they are naught
but a brown, slimy clot. In the night many and strange
are the thoughts that spring up to lure and affright.
Surely 'twas brother Edvin that had said once, the
damned in hell would not themselves be parted from their
torment — hate and sorrow were their delight — therefore it was that Christus could not save them. This had
seemed to her wild talk then — A cold shudder ran
through her — now did she begin to understand what the
monk had meant —

She bent over the bed again — drinking in the air that
breathed from the little child. Simon and Ramborg should
not lose him. Even if 'twere true that she had done this
out of her need to set herself right in Simon's eyes — to
show him that she too was willing to do more than take
gifts at his hands; a need had been in her to dare all that
she might requite him —

Then again she knelt down and said over again and
again as much as she knew of the psalter —

That morning Simon went out and sowed winter rye
on the new-broken field, south in the wood. He had it in
mind that he must make as though it seemed to him fitting
that the work on the farm should go its wonted way. The
serving-women had fallen into great wonderment when
he had come in to them in the night and said that Kristin
would be alone with the boy till she sent for them. He
told Ramborg too, when she awoke — Kristin had prayed
that none should go near the women's house to-day.

"Not you either?" she asked quickly, and Simon said
no. 'Twas then that he had gone out and fetched the seed-
box.

But after the midday meal-time he stayed up at the
manor — he had no heart to go far from the houses. And
he liked not the look in Ramborg's eyes. It came, a while
after the midday rest: he was standing by the corn-barn,
and he saw his wife rush across the yard. He sprang after
— Ramborg flung herself at the door of the women's house

and beat upon it with her clenched fists, shrieking wildly
to Kristin to open.

Simon put his arms about her, trying to soothe her —
thereon she bent, quick as lightning, and bit him on the
hand; she seemed like some wild beast in her rage:

"He is *my* child! What have you done with my son?"

"You know well your sister is going naught but good
to Andres" — when he took hold of her again, she shrieked
and struggled against him.

"Come now," said the man, in a voice of feigned harsh-
ness: "Ramborg — are you not ashamed, before our house-
folk — "

But she went on screaming:

"He is mine, mine, I tell you — You were not with us
when I bore him, Simon," she cried; "then we were not so
dear to you — "

"You know well yourself what I had in hand in those
days," answered the men wearily. He dragged her away
towards the hall by main strength.

Thereafter he dared not leave her. In a while Ramborg
grew quiet, and, when the evening was come, she gave
in to him and let the women undress her.

Simon sat on by her side. His daughters were sleeping
in their own bed; the serving-women he had sent out.
Once, when he rose and went across the room, Ramborg
asked from the bed — she was wide-awake by her voice
— whither he was going.

"I had a mind to lie down a little by you," he answered
after a moment. He took off his outer coat and shoes, and
crept in between the skins and the woollen coverlid. Then
he put an arm under his wife's neck: "I know well, my
Ramborg, that this has been a long day and a heavy for
you — "

"Your heart beats so hard, Simon," she said soon after.

"Ay, you may believe I am in dread for the boy, I too.
But we must wait in patience till Kristin sends us
word — "

He started up in the bed — lay propped on his elbow —
looked up wildly into Kristin's white face — it was close
above his own, and shone wet with tears in a glimmer of
light; her hand was on his breast. For one moment he
thought — this time 'twas not a dream only — Simon

threw himself back against the bed-head; with a stifled moan he hid his face on his arm. He felt sick, the heart in him hammered so wildly and so hard —

"Simon, wake up!" Kristin shook him again. "Andres is calling on his father; hear you not? — 'twas the first word he spoke — " Her face shone with smiles, while the tears ran down it without cease.

Simon sat up, and passed his hand once and again across his face. Surely he had not said aught as she woke him, while yet amazed with sleep — He looked up at Kristin — she was standing by the bed with a lantern in her hand.

Softly, not to wake Ramborg, he crept out with her. The qualmish sickness still weighed upon his breast. He felt as though something would break within him — why was he ever haunted by this hateful dream? He who, awake, strove and ever strove to drive all such thoughts from him. And then, when he lay sleeping, will-less and helpless, ever to dream this dream of the devil's own sending — even now, while she sat watching over his son that lay sick to death, to dream like some monstrous wretch —

'Twas raining, and Kristin could not say rightly what time of night it might be. The boy had been half awake in the day, but he had not spoken. 'Twas not till on in the night that it had seemed to her he slept well and soundly — and she had dared to lie down a little and rest — with Andres in her arms, that she might feel if he moved. Then she had fallen asleep —

The boy looked a tiny, tiny thing, lying alone in the bed; woefully pale he was, but his eyes were clear and his face lit up with smiles when he saw his father. Simon went down on his knees by the bedside, but when he would have taken the little one to his breast, Kristin caught him by the arm:

"Nay, nay, Simon, he is all a-sweat, and 'tis cold here — " She pulled the bed-clothes closer about Andres. "Rather lay yourself in by his side — then will I send hither a women to watch. I go now to the hall to lie down by Ramborg — "

Simon crept in under the covering. There was a warm hollow where she had lain, a faint, sweet scene of her hair on the pillow. Simon moaned very softly once — then he drew his little son in to him and pressed his face against

the soft, damp child-head. He was so small now, he was
well-nigh nothing to hold in one's arms, was Andres, but
he lay there happily enough, saying a little word ever
and again.

Then he took to fumbling and groping in the opening
of his father's shirt, put his little clammy hand in on the
man's breast, and pulled out the amulet:

"The cock," he said, well pleased; "here he is—"

The day Kristin stood ready to set forth for home,
Simon came to her in the women's house and handed her
a little wooden box:

"Methought maybe you would like to have this—"

Kristin knew by the wood-carving that 'twas her
father's work. Within there lay, wrapped in a bit of glove
leather, a small, small golden clasp, set with five emeralds.
She knew it at once—Lavrans had used to wear it in his
wristband at especial times, when he would go richly
clad.

She thanked Simon, but then she blushed blood-red. It
had come upon her of a sudden that she had surely never
seen her father wear this trinket after she had come home
from the cloister in Oslo.

"When gave father this to you—?" She repented her
of the question as soon as asked.

"I got it for a parting gift, once when I was riding from
the manor—"

"This seems to me to be all too great a gift," she said
low, with eyes cast down.

Simon laughed a little as he answered:

"You will have need of many such, Kristin—when the
time comes for you to send forth all your sons with
bridal gifts—"

Kristin looked at him and said:

"You know well, Simon—I deem that the things that
have come to you from him—you know that I hold you
as dear as though you were his own son—"

"Do you so—?" He touched her cheek lightly with
the back of his hand, stroking it downwards, and smiled, a
strange little smile, while he spoke as to a child:

"Ay, ay, Kristin, I have marked it—"

4

SOMEWHAT later in the autumn, Simon Andressön had an errand that took him to his brother's house at Dyfrin. While he was there, a wooer made suit to him for his daughter Arngjerd.

The matter was not concluded, and Simon was somewhat restless and troubled in mind as he rode northward. Maybe he should have struck the bargain, for then the child would have been well settled and he himself quit of all fear for her future lot. Maybe Gyrd and Helga were right — 'twas witless in him not to seize the chance, when he got such an offer for this daughter of his — Eiken was a greater manor than Formo, and Aasmund owned outright more than the third part; he had never thought of wooing for his son a maid of Arngjerd's condition, low-born and kinless on the mother's side, had it not been that Simon held three hides of the manor's land in pledge. They had had to borrow moneys both from the nuns of Oslo and from Dyfrin, when Grunde Aasmundssön had to pay forfeit for manslaughter the second time. Grunde was wild and ungoverned when in drink — yet was he in all other ways an upright and well-natured fellow, said Gyrd, and 'twas sure he would let himself be guided by a clear-witted and kindly woman such as was Arngjerd —

But the thing was, that Grunde was not many years younger than Simon himself. And Arngjerd was young. And naught would serve the folk at Eiken but to have the wedding this coming spring —

A sore remembrance clung to Simon — he thought not on it when he could forbear. But now, since the matter of Arngjerd's wedding had been stirred, 'twas ever thrusting up its head. An unglad man had he been that first morning when he woke at Ramborg's side. He had been, for sure, no more flustered and wanton when he went to bed than a bridegroom should be — albeit to see Kristin amid the brideswomen had made him strange and wild of mood — and Erlend, his new brother-in-law, among the men who brought him up to the loft. And yet when he awoke the next morning and lay looking at the bride that still slept beside him, he had known a sore and bitter shame deep down in his heart — 'twas as though he had mishandled some young child —

— Though all the time he knew he might have spared himself that sorrow.

She had laughed when she opened her great eyes.

"Now you are *mine*, Simon" — she pressed her hands on his breast. "My father is your father, and my sister your sister" — and he had grown clammy with fear, for he thought: what if she had felt the heart in his bosom start at her words?

Else was he well content with his marriage — to that he held firmly. His wife was rich, come of high kindred, young and fresh, fair and kindly. She had borne him a daughter and a son — and on that a man sets much price, when he has known what 'tis to have wealth and be without children to hold his estate together when their parents are gone. Two children — and their welfare was assured — and he was rich enough besides to make a good match for Arngjerd —

One other son he would fain have had — ay, 'twould be no grief to him if one, ay or two more children came to Formo. But he saw Ramborg was best pleased to scape those troubles. So 'twas somewhat to the good, that too. For he could not deny it: it made much for comfort in the house when Ramborg was in humour. He could have wished her, indeed, a more even temper. He knew not always how he stood with his wife. And 'twould not have been amiss had things been something better ordered within-doors at his home. But no man can hope that all his measures shall brim over, as the byword has it — Simon said thus to himself again and again, as he rode homewards —

Now was Ramborg to go to Kruke the week before Clement's Mass * — it ever livened her up to get from home awhile —

Yet God knew how things were to go there — this time. 'Twas her eighth child that Sigrid went with now. And he had been frighted when he looked in on his sister but now, on the way down — she looked not as though she had the strength for much more —

---

* 23rd November.

He had bestowed four thick wax tapers to set before the old picture of Mary Virgin at Eyabu — 'twas of a rare wonder-working virtue, folk said — and vowed goodly gifts, if Sigrid came through this with life and health. For how 'twould fare with Geirmund and all the children if their mother died and left them — nay, that was hard to say —

And they lived in good accord, Sigrid and Geirmund. Never had she heard an ungentle word from the man, she said; never had he left aught undone he deemed would pleasure her. When he saw that Sigrid was pining for the child she had had in her youth by Gjavvald Arnessön, he had had Simon fetch the boy, so that his mother might have him by her for a while. But sorrow and hope deceived were all that Sigrid had reaped from the meeting with that spoiled young spark. Thereafter Sigrid Andresdatter had clung to her husband and the children she had had by him, as a poor sick sinner to priest and sacrament.

In a fashion she seemed now well content. And this Simon could understand — few men were so good to be with as Geirmund. So tunable was his speech that, talked he but of the hoof-bound horse they had passed off on him, 'twas well-nigh like listening to harp-playing.

Ugly and strange of face Geirmund Hersteinssön had ever been, but at least he had been strong and comely in build of body and limbs; the best of bowmen, a rare hunter, and ahead of most others in all sports. But for these three years past he had been a cripple — ever since he came crawling down the valley from a hunt, on his hands and one knee, dragging the other leg crushed behind him. Now could he not cross the floor without a staff, nor come up on a horse, nor crawl, without help, round his steep hill-side fields. Mischance was ever at his heels; the man was full of strange ways, and little fitted to care for his farm or his own fortunes; 'twas easy for any that had the heart to fool him in his dealings. But he was deft of hand, a skilful workman in wood and iron, and shrewd and kind in speech. And when this man took a harp upon his knee, he could make folk laugh or weep at will with his singing and playing. Ay, 'twas most like hearkening to the knight that Geirmund sang of, who played the leaves from off the lindens and the horns from off the living beasts.

Then would they take up the burden and sing with their
father, the eldest children — and 'twas fairer to hear than
all the bells a-ringing in Bishop's Hamar. The youngest
child but one, Inga, could but just walk when she held
to the bench; speak she could not yet, but she hummed
and sang the livelong day, and her tiny voice was fine and
clear as a little silver bell —

They dwelt huddled together in a little, black old
hearth-room house, husband and wife, children and serving-folk. The loft Geirmund had talked of building all
these years 'twas not like he would ever get put up —
hardly had he made shift to get a new barn built in place
of the one burnt two years agone. But none of their many
children could the parents bring themselves to part with.
Simon had made offer, each time he was at Kruke, to take
some of them and give them nurture — Geirmund and
Sigrid thanked him, but said no —

None the less, maybe 'twas she of all his brothers and
sisters who had come off best, thought Simon at times.
True, Gyrd said Astrid was well content with her new
husband — they lived far south in Ryfylke, and Simon
had not seen them since they were wed. But Torgrim's
sons wrangled much with their step-father, Gyrd had
said —

And Gudmund was marvellous glad and well-content —
But if this were happiness for a man, Simon deemed
'twere no sin to thank God their father had not lived to
see it — Hard upon Andres Darre's death, as soon as ever
'twas seemly, Gudmund had drunk the bride-ale with the
widow his father would not hear of his mating with. The
Dyfrin knight deemed that, if none too good fortune had
come to Gyrd and Simon through the rich and comely
maid of noble birth and unstained fame he had sought
out for his two eldest sons, naught but sheer wretched-
ness could come of it for Gudmund if his father let him
have his witless will. Tordis Bergsdatter was much older
than Gudmund. She was indifferent well-to-do and had
no children by her first husband. But since then she had
had a daughter by one of the priests of Maria Church in
Oslo, and folk said, moreover, that she had been over kind
to other men besides — to Gudmund Darre among them,
when first she came to know him. Ugly as a troll she was,
and, for a woman, foul-mouthed and rough of speech,

deemed Simon — but she was quick and witty, of good understanding and well humoured — he himself would have liked Tordis well enough, he knew — if only she had not married into their kin. But Gudmund throve so, 'twas uncanny to look on him; he was near as fat and heavy now as Simon himself — and 'twas not Gudmund's nature so to be; in youth he had been slender and comely. He had grown so lazy and lumpish that Simon's hands itched to thrash the fellow, each time he saw him. A moonstruck calf had Gudmund been all his days, truth to tell — and that his children took their wits from their mother and their looks from him was, after all, a piece of luck in ill luck — But Gudmund throve —

So there was no need for him to vex himself as he did for that brother's sake. And in a way 'twas needless too that he should grieve so for Gyrd — Yet each time he went home to his father's manor and saw how things stood there, it jarred upon him so that 'twas with a right sore heart he rode away —

They prospered greatly — was not that brother-in-law of his brother, Ulf Sakseson, in the King's full grace and favour now? — and he drew Gyrd Andressön along with him into the ring of men who had most power and profit in the land. But Simon misliked the fellow — and he felt that Gyrd liked him not either. Unwillingly and ungladly Gyrd of Dyfrin went the way his wife and her brother would have him go — to win a little peace at home.

Helga Saksesdatter was a troll — But most like 'twas still more those two sons of his that made Gyrd look so grief-worn nowadays. Sakse, the elder, was a good sixteen winters old by now — And well-nigh every single night his body-servant had to drag the whelp to bed, dead drunk. He had drunk wits and health away already — like enough he would drink himself to death ere he won to a grown man's age. And 'twould scarce be a great loss — Sakse had got himself a bad name in the country-side, young as he was, for an overweening churl. That was the mother's darling; Gyrd loved the younger, Jon, the most: and t'was true he had much more of the turn of mind that might have made him an honour to his kin, if only he had not been — ay, he was somewhat misshapen, high-shouldered, and wry-backed. And then he had some in-

side stomach evil — could brook no other meat than milk
gruel and bannocks —

In his loving-kindness for his own kin Simon Andressön
had ever found a kind of secret refuge when his own life
seemed to him — ay, out of gear, or whatever one might
call it. If aught went awry with him, it touched him much
less nearly if he could call to mind his brothers' and sisters' fortune and prosperity. Had things but been at
Dyfrin as they were in his father's time — when peace,
content, and well-being ruled at the manor — 'twould
have done much, Simon thought, to ease his hidden unrest. 'Twas as though his own life-roots were twined in
with those of his kindred, somewhere deep down in the
darksome earth. Every blow that struck one of them,
every ill that sucked the marrow of any, was felt by all —
    With Gyrd and him assuredly it had been so — at least
in old days. He knew not so surely if Gyrd felt so now —
    This eldest brother — and Sigrid — had been most dear
to him of all. He minded — when a growing lad: he would
sit and gaze at his youngest sister till he joyed in her so
that he *must* do something to show it. So he would begin
nagging at her, tease and fret her, pluck at her plaits, and
pinch her arms, for it was as though he could show his
love in no other wise and not be ashamed. All this bickering between them had to be, else had he been too shamefaced to give her all his hidden store of good things, or to
join the little maid in her games, when he built mills in the
beck, made houses for her, or cut willow whistles for the
girls in springtime —
    Like a burnt-in brand mark was his memory of the day
when first he knew the whole truth of her mischance. The
winter through he had watched Sigrid grieving well-nigh to
death over her dead groom — but more he saw not. Then
came a Sunday towards the spring — he stood on the balcony at Mandvik, vexed that the women were so late of
coming — out in the yard stood horses decked and saddled
for church, and the men had waited long. At length he
grew wroth and went in to the women's house. Sigrid
still lay abed — wondering, he asked if she were sick. His
wife was sitting on the bed-edge — a tremor passed over
her gentle, faded face as she looked up: "Sick is she truly,

the poor child — but yet more afraid I trow — of you —
and of all her kindred — how you will take this — "

His sister shrieked aloud, and threw herself headlong
over Halfrid's lap, clinging to her, twining her thin, bare
arms about her brother's wife — Her scream cut Simon
so to the quick, it seemed his heart grew grey and blood-
less. Her grief, her shame, so pierced him through that no
feeling was left in him — and then came fear, and he grew
wet with sweat — Their father, what would he do with
Sigrid now —

His dread was such that, as he struggled towards his
home in Raumarike over roads deep in slush, the man with
him, knowing naught of the matter, began at last to jest
at his lighting down so often. For long now he had been
a full-grown wedded man, yet fear so gripped him as he
thought on the meeting with his father, that his bowels
turned to water —

And his father had spoken scarce a word — But he had
sunk together — as though lightning-struck. It befell yet,
sometimes, that Simon, when dropping into sleep, would
see it all again, and all at once start broad awake. His
father, sitting swaying, swaying, his head bowed down
upon his breast; Gyrd standing by, his hand upon the
high-seat's arm, something paler than his wont, with downcast eyes —

"God be thanked that she was not here when this came
out — At least 'tis well she is with you and Halfrid — "
Gyrd had said, when they two were left alone.

'Twas the one time Simon had heard Gyrd say such a
word as might betoken that he set not his wife above all
other women —

Yet seen it he had — how Gyrd seemed to wither and
dwine from the day he was wed with Helga Saksesdatter.

That time they were betrothed — Gyrd's words were
ever few — but each time he had seen his bride, Gyrd
went about so shining fair that Simon was most strangely
moved at sight of him. He had seen Helga long since,
Gyrd let Simon understand, but never had speech with
her, and never could he have deemed her kinsfolk would
give to him a maid so rich and beautiful —

Gyrd Darre's wondrous comeliness in his youth Simon
had felt to be, as 'twere, an honour to himself. He was
fair with a winsomeness all his own — 'twas as though all

must see that in this fine and still young man there dwelt goodness, high-mindedness, a brave and noble heart. Then he was wed with Helga Saksesdatter — and then there seemed an end to him —

Silent he had always been — but the two brothers were ever together, and Simon was well able to talk for both. Simon was glib-tongued, passed for a youth of parts, and was hail-fellow-well-met with all — for drink and frolic, for hunting and racing, for all manner of youthful sport, Simon had friends in crowds, all alike dear and near to him. His eldest brother went with him — said little, but smiled his sweet and sober smile, and what few words he dropped seemed all the more weighty —

Dumb as a locked chest was Gyrd Andressön now —

The summer that Simon came home and told his father Kristin Lavransdatter and he of one accord were minded that the bargain concerning them should be undone — Simon knew then that Gyrd had guessed the most that lay behind: that Simon loved his bride; that some weighty cause had brought him to give up his right — and that the cause was such that Simon was heart-scalded within with grief and wrath. Very quietly, Gyrd had counselled his father to let the matter fall. But to Simon he breathed no word that hinted of his knowledge. And Simon felt, could he ever have loved his brother more than he had done all his days, 'twould have been now, for his silence —

Simon *would* be glad and blithe of mood as he rode northwards towards his home. Upon the way he made himself errands to his friends' homes along the Dale, to bear them his greetings and to drink himself merry — and his friends saddled their horses and bore him company to the next manor where their own cronies dwelt. 'Twas good and easy riding in this clear and frosty weather —

The last stretch he rode in the dusk. His ale-born mettle was gone out of him. His men were lusty and loud-voiced — but the master seemed to have run dry of laughter and jest — he must sure be weary.

And now he was home. Andres toddled after, wherever his father stood or went. Ulvhild hung about the saddle-bags — had he brought home any gifts for her? Arngjerd bore forth ale and food; his wife sat down beside him while he ate, chatted and asked of the tidings. When the

children had gone to bed, Simon took Ramborg on his
knee, while he gave her messages and told her of kin and
friends.

'Twas a shameful thing and an unmanly, so he deemed,
if he could not be content, so well off as he was in all
ways —

The day after, Simon was sitting in the Sæmund's Hall
when Arngjerd came in to him bearing meat. He thought
'twere well to speak with her of her suitor while they
were alone, and so he told his daughter of his talk with
the Eiken men-folk.

Oh, no, she is none too fair, thought the father — he
looked up at the young girl as she stood before him. Squat
and broad-built she was, with short, coarse-grained, pale
face; her grey-yellow hair was bushy; down her back it
hung in two big plaits, but straggled above her forehead
and hung in tufts about her eyes, and she had a trick of
brushing it back every moment.

"It must be as you will, father," she said quietly, when
he was done speaking.

"Ay, you are a good child, I know; but what think you
yourself of this?"

"Nay, I think nothing. You must judge for me, dear
father."

" 'Tis thus, Arngjerd — 'twould please me well for you
to go free for some years yet — from child-bearing and
household cares and pains — all such things as fall to
women's lot when first they wed. But I have thought that
maybe you think long till you have a house of your own
and can be your own mistress — ?"

"I am in no haste," said the girl, smiling a little.

"You know that, were you to wed at Eiken, you would
have your rick kinsfolk near by — bare is back without
brother behind it" — he saw a little gleam in Arngjerd's
eyes, and her sly smile. "I mean Gyrd, your uncle," he
said quickly, somewhat put out.

"Ay, I deemed well you meant not my kinswoman,
Helga — " and they both laughed.

Simon's heart grew warm — in thankfulness to God and
Mary Virgin, and to Halfrid, who had brought him to
own this daughter of his. When it chanced that they

laughed together thus, he and Arngjerd, he needed not any other proof that she was his own.

He rose and dusted off some flour she had got on her sleeve: "And your wooer — what think you of the man?" he asked.

"Oh! I like him, the little I have seen of him — and 'tis well not to hearken to all that's said — But you must judge for me in this, father — "

"Then shall it be as I have said. Aasmund and Grunde can wait a while — we shall see if they are still of the same mind when you are somewhat older — For the rest, you know well, my daughter, you have freedom to choose yourself whom you shall wed, so far as you have wit to judge of your own good. And of wit you have no lack, Arngjerd — "

He put his arms around her. She blushed when her father kissed her — and Simon bethought him it must be many a long day since last he had done this. He was not, for the most part, a man who feared to fondle his wife in the light of day, or romp with his children. But 'twas ever as in play — and Arngjerd — It came home to Simon of a sudden that here on Formo this young daughter was the only being he spoke with in earnest now and then —

He went over and pulled the stopping from out of the slit in the south wall. Through the little hole he gazed out over the Dale. There was a southerly draught in the air, and below, where the hills met and hemmed in the sight, big grey clouds were rolling up. When a beam of sunlight broke through, all colours shone out, rich and clear. The mild weather had licked away the pale grey rime — the plough-lands were brown, the fir woods blue-black — and farthest up, along the treeless hill-brows, clothed with moss and lichen, the light streamed yellow-gold.

Simon felt as though there were a marvellous virtue to be drawn from the autumn wind out there and the fitful brightness over the country-side. Should there come rain in plenty at All Hallows' Mass, the streams might well have water for the mills, at least till on near Yule: and 'twould be worth while sending men to the hills to gather

moss. Such a dry autumn had it been — the Laagen ran
shrunk and little 'twixt frets of yellow gravel and whitened
stones.

Here, northward of the parish, 'twas only Jörundgaard
and the priest's farm that had mill-houses on the river. He
was loth to pray for leave to grind at Jörundgaard —
were't but that the whole parish doubtless went thither
with their corn. For Sira Eirik took toll for grinding. And
folk deemed, besides, he got to know too well what corn
they had — he was so greedy for his tithes. But Lavrans
had ever let folk grind at his mill without price, and Kristin would have things go on as in his time —

The slightest thought of her, and there came a sick,
strained trembling round his heart —

'Twas the day before Simon's and Jude's Mass;* he had
ever been wont to go to shrift that day. 'Twas to com-
mune with himself, to fast and pray, that he was sitting
here in the Sæmund's-hall to-day, whilst the house-carls
threshed in the barn —

It took no long time to bring to mind his sins — he had
sworn, told cock-and-bull tales to folk that asked of things
that concerned them not; there was the reindeer he had
shot long after he had seen by the sun that the sabbath
was begun; and he had hunted a Sunday morning while
folk down in the parish were at mass —

What had newly befallen whilst the boy lay sick he
might not and he dared not name. But 'twas the first time
in his life that, unwillingly, he kept secret a sin from his
parish priest. He had thought much on it, and it weighed
much on his heart. A deadly sin it must sure be — whether
he had trafficked with sorcery, or as much as lured another on to do the like —

Neither could he find in his heart to repent it — when
he thought that but for this his son had surely lain now in
the earth. But he was all the time cast down and fearful —
spying to see whether the child was changed at all since
that night. He deemed not he could see aught —

He knew it happened with many kind of fowl and
wild beasts — if hand of man had lain upon their eggs, or
their young, the parents would have naught more to do

---

* 28th October.

with them, but turned from their offspring. A man, who
had from God the light of reason, could not do the like —
with him now things were rather so that, when he took
his son to his arms, he felt scarce able to let the child out
of his hands again, so fearful had he grown for Andres.
But none the less he could understand how 'twas the
heathenish, unthinking brutes took such a misliking for
their own brood once they had been *touched*. He, too, felt
as though his child had been in some way soiled —

Yet he repented not — wished not that the thing had
not been done. But he would that it had been another than
Kristin. — 'Twas hard enough for him, at all rates, to have
these folk living in the parish —

— Arngjerd came in — to ask after a key. Ramborg
thought not she had had it back again since her husband
had the use of it.

The housekeeping on this manor of his was growing
worse and worse — Simon remembered he had given the
key back to his wife; 'twas before he set off southward,
too — "Ay, then I shall find it, surely," said Arngjerd.

She had such a good smile — and wise eyes — and she
was none so ill-favoured either, thought her father. Her
hair was goodly, and when she let it flow loose on holy-
days and feast days, 'twas thick and bright.

Erlend's bastard daughter had been fair enough — and
naught but mischance had come of that —

But Erlend had had that daughter by a fair and well-
born woman. 'Twas like Erlend had never cared to cast
his eyes on such an one as Arngjerd's mother. He had
flung on his haughty way through the world — and, where
he went, proud and comely ladies and maidens had stood
arow, proffering him love and adventure —

His own one sin in that sort — his boyish pranks while
in the King's household he counted not — a little more
nicety about that sin had not been amiss, if indeed he must
needs wrong his good and noble wife — 'Twas not as if he
had even looked much at the woman, Jorunn — he could
not so much as bring to mind how 'twas he first came to
make too free with the wench. He had been abroad at
merry-makings that winter with friends and acquaintance,
and when he came home to his wife's manor, there sat the
wench to see to it that he came to bed without setting the
place afire.

No more glorious than so had *that* adventure been.

— All the less had he deserved that the child should promise so fairly and bring him so much gladness — But he ought not to harbour such thoughts now — he should be thinking on his confession —

As Simon took his way home from Romundgaard in the dusk, fine rain was falling. He went slantwise across the fields. In the last wan rays of daylight the stubble gleamed pale and wet. Over by the wall of the old bath-house something small and white lay shining on the slope. Simon went thither and looked. 'Twas the shards of the French bowl that was broken that day in the spring — the children had laid the table with them on a board set upon two stones. Simon reached out with his axe and tumbled the whole down the bank —

He was vexed with himself the next moment. But he cared not to have that evening called to his mind.

To make some little amends for keeping back a sin, he had spoken to Sira Eirik of those dreams. Ay, and because too he felt a need to ease his heart of *that* at least. He stood ready to go — when it came upon him of a sudden — he must speak of this thing. And this old, half-blind priest had been his ghostly father these twelve years and more —

So he went back and knelt again at Sira Eirik's knees.

The priest sat unmoving till Simon had said his say. Then he spoke — his mighty voice came aged and veiled now from out the everlasting twilight — Sin it was not. Each member of the Church militant must be proven in battle with the enemy; therefore did God suffer the devil to beset a man with manifold temptations. So long as a man threw not away his weapons — so long as he forsook not the standard of his Lord, nor, open-eyed and in privity with the foe, yielded to the visions that unclean spirit would beguile him with — so long such sinful promptings were not sin —

"Nay!" Simon was shamed by the sound of his own voice.

Yielded he *never* had. He was tortured, tortured, tortured by them. When he awoke, having dreamed these sinful dreams, he felt as though he himself had been abused the while he slept.

* * *

Two stranger horses stood tied to the fence when he came into the courtyard. They were Erlend Nikulaussön's Soten and Kristin's riding-horse. He shouted to the horse-boy — why had they not been stabled? The strangers had said there was no need, the fellow answered sulkily.

He was a lad who had but now taken service with Simon, since he had come home — he had served at Dyfrin before. There all things must go now as 'twere in knightly fashion; Helga had had her way in that. But if this lout of a Sigurd deemed, because he, Simon, chose rather to talk cheerly and jestingly with his folk, and would sometimes suffer a pert answer from a serving-man, that, here at Formo, anyone might answer the master back, the devil was in it — Simon was starting to rate the fellow soundly — but he caught himself up; had he not even now come from shrift? Jon Daalk would have to take this new-comer in hand, and teach him that good country breeding was no more to be set at naught than the courtly ways of Dyfrin —

So he did but ask, mildly enough, if Sigurd had but just come out of the mountain this year, and bade him put the horses in. But he was vexed —

The first thing that met his eyes, as he stepped into the hall, was Erlend's laughing face — the light from the taper on the board fell straight upon him, where he sat on the bench, and warded off Ulvhild, who was kneeling beside him, seeking to scratch him, or somewhat of the kind — she was clawing with her hands at the man's face, laughing till she hiccoughed —

Erlend sprang up and would have put the child aside, but she clung to his coat-sleeve and hung on his arm, as he came across the floor straight and light-footed, to greet his brother-in-law. She kept on teasing about something: Erlend and Simon could scarce come to speech.

Her father bade her, some what harshly, to go with the serving-women out to the kitchen — they were just done setting the board. When the little maid answered him back, he grasped her by the arm and dragged her away from Erlend.

"There then — !" Erlend took a lump of resin from his mouth and stuffed it into the child's. "Take it then, Ulvhild, blossom-cheek! — that daughter of yours, brother-in-law," said he, laughing, as he looked after the child, "will scarce be so biddable as Arngjerd!"

Simon had not been able to refrain him from telling his wife how well Arngjerd took this matter of her wedding. But it had not been his intent that she should speak of it to the Jörundgaard folk. 'Twas unlike Ramborg too — he knew that she loved Erlend but little. He liked it not — liked not that Ramborg had talked of this matter, liked not that she was so unstable, nor that Ulvhild, young child as she was, seemed so fond on Erlend — like most of the tribe of women —

He went and welcomed Kristin; she sat in the corner by the fire-place, with Andres in her lap. The boy had grown right loving with his mother's sister, since she had nursed him in the autumn when he lay gathering strength after his sickness.

Simon saw they must have some errand to him, since Erlend had come thus. 'Twas not often he darkened the doors of Formo. Simon could not but own that Erlend bore himself well in a case that was none too easy — things having come to be as they were betwixt the brothers-in-law. Erlend held himself aloof from the other as much as he well could, but they met as often as was needful, that no talk of unfriendliness betwixt the kinsmen should get about in the country-side, and when they met, 'twas as the best of friends; Erlend was quiet, and held back somewhat when they were together, yet was his bearing free and unabashed.

When the food had been cleared from off the board and ale set forth, Erlend spoke:

"Methinks you will wonder at my errand, Simon — we are here to bid you and Ramborg to a bride-ale feast with us — "

"Nay, sure, you jest? I knew not that you had folk of age to marry on your manor?"

"That is as a man takes it, brother-in-law. 'Tis Ulf Haldorssön — "

Simon smote his thighs:

"Nay, now shall I hear next that my plough-oxen are to calve at Yule!"

"Never call Ulf a plough-ox," said Erlend, laughing.

"It seems the mischief is that the man has been all too forward — "

Simon whistled. Erlend laughed again, and said:

"Ay, you may believe I scarce could trust my own ears when they came in on us to-day, the Herbrandssöns from Medalheim, and made claim that Ulf should wed their sister."

"Herbrand Rambra's — ? But they are but young lads — their sister cannot be so old that Ulf — ?"

"She has twenty winters to her score. And Ulf is nearer the fifties. Ay." Erlend had grown grave. "You understand, Simon — they must account this no great match for Jardtrud; but 'tis the better choice of two bad ones, for her to wed him. Though, 'tis true, Ulf is a knight's son and a well-to-do man — he has no need to seek his bread in another man's house. But he came with us, for that he would rather dwell with us, his kinsfolk, than live upon his own farm in Skaun — after what had come and gone — "

Erlend fell silent a little while. His face grew soft and winning. Then he spoke again:

"Now, we are minded, Kristin and I, to hold this wedding in every wise as though he were our brother. 'Tis our intent that Ulf and I shall ride south to Medalheim a-wooing, this coming week. For appearance' sake, you understand. And now I had thought to crave a boon of you, brother-in-law — I know, Simon, that I owe you much already. But Ulf is but ill liked here in this countryside. And you stand so high with folk that few men are your fellows — while I myself — " he shrugged his shoulders and laughed a little. "Will you do us this friendship, Simon: to ride with us and be spokesman for Ulf? — he and I have been comrades since ever we were boys," said Erlend, beseechingly.

"That will I, brother!" Simon had gone red in the face — at Erlend's open-hearted speech he felt himself grow strangely abashed and pitiful. "All I can do to do honour to Ulf Haldorssön, that will I gladly do."

Kristin was still sitting over in the corner with Andres — the boy had set his heart on having his aunt undress him. Now she came forward into the light — the child sat half-naked on her arm, clasping her round the neck.

"This is kindly done of you, Simon!" said she, low, holding out her hand. "For this we thank you, all of us — "

Simon held her hand a moment, loosely:

"Nay, Kristin — I ever liked him, Ulf — be sure, I do this gladly — " He reached up to take his son, but Andres feigned coyness, and kicked at his father with his little naked feet, laughing and clinging to the woman.

Simon listened to the two while he sat talking with Erlend of Ulf's money affairs. The boy was in a fit of laughter all the time — she knew so many little chants and nursery jingles; and she laughed along with him, cooingly soft and gentle, deep down in her throat. Once, when he glanced their way, she had twisted her fingers into a kind of winding stairs, and Andres' fingers were folk that walked up them. At last she got him to his cradle, and set herself down by Ramborg. The sisters chatted together, whispering —

'Twas true enough, he thought, when he had lain down that evening — he had liked Ulf Haldorssön always. And since that winter in Oslo, when, together, they had striven to help Kristin, he had felt, in a fashion, knit to the man in a bond of fellowship. Naught else ever crossed his mind than that Ulf was his equal — a great man's son; and that he had no lawful footing amid his father's kin, being gotten in whoredom, made Simon yet more heedful in his dealings with Ulf — somewhat deep down in his own heart there dwelt ever a prayer for Arngjerd's welfare. Else was this none too seemly a matter for a man to be mixed with — an ageing man and a young girl like this. — Ay, well, if Jardtrud Herbrandsdatter had tripped when she was at the Thing last summer, it touched not him — he was no kin to these folks, and Ulf was a near kinsman to his brother-in-law.

Unasked, Ramborg had proffered to help Kristin and to wait at the wedding-feast. He deemed this kindly done of her. When aught of weight was toward, Ramborg ever showed what manner of folk she came of. Yes, truly! Ramborg was kind —

5

THE DAY after Katrine's Mass * Erlend Nikulaussön held his kinsman's wedding with great state and pride. Many good folk were come together — Simon Darre had cared for that; he and his wife had many friends in the parishes all about. Both the priests from Olav's Church were there, and Sira Eirik blessed the house and bed — this was counted an honour, for Sira Eirik said mass now on high holy-days only, and rendered ghostly service to some few folk who had been his penitents these many years. Simon Darre read out the deed concerning Ulf's extra-gift and morning-gift to the bride; Erlend spoke right lovingly to his kinsman over the board; Ramborg Lavransdatter, along with her sister, played hostess at the feasting and helped to undress the bride in the loft.

Yet was it no rightly merry bridal. The bride was of an old and honoured yeoman stock here in the Dale; her kin and neighbours could in no wise deem she had made a fitting match, since she must put up with a stranger to the country-side, and one who served in another man's house, albeit a kinsman's. Neither Ulf's birth — son of a rich man and a knight by his serving-wench — nor his kinship with Erlend Nikulaussön, did the Herbrandssöns seem to count for any great honour —

Nor seemed it that the bride herself was over well pleased with what she had made of things. Kristin seemed much disheartened when she spoke to Simon of it — he had an errand to Jörundgaard a few weeks after the wedding. Jardtrud was plaguing her man to move to his estate in Skaun — she had said in Kristin's hearing, weeping bitterly, she deemed it the worst that could befall, that her child should be pointed at for a serving-man's son. To that Ulf had answered naught. The newly-married folk dwelt in the house that had been called the steward's house ever since Jon Einarssön abode there, before Lavrans bought the whole of Laugarbru and moved him thither. But this name was not to Jardtrud's liking. And she was wroth because she must keep her cows in Kristin's byre — she

---

* 25th November.

feared, belike, that folk might think she was Kristin's handmaid. The mistress deemed this was but reason — she must have a byre built for the steward's house, if so be Ulf did not flit to Skaun with his wife. And maybe that would be the best — he was not so young but that he must find it hard to change his way of life; maybe 'twould come easier to him in a new place —

In this Simon thought she might well be right. And Ulf was ill liked in the country-side. He hid not his scorn of the Dale and all its ways. Good, hard-working husbandman as he was, there were many things on this side of the land that he had no skill of — he reared more cattle in the autumn than he could feed through the winter — and when the beasts fell dead, or when, on towards spring, he had, after all, to kill off part of the half-starved brutes, he grew angered, and would blame it on his being unused to the cottar ways of this country-side, where, as early as Paul's Mass,* folk must begin stripping bark to feed to their beasts.

Another thing was this: in the Trondheim country the custom 'twixt landlord and tenant had come to be that the landlord took for rent such goods as most he needed, hay, hides, meal, butter, or wool, even though at lease time they had agreed for some especial ware, or a money rent. And, furthermore, 'twas the landlord or his bailiffs that fixed the worth of rent-goods, as betwixt ware and ware, much as seemed good to them. But when Ulf came on Kristin's leaseholders with claims like these, folk called it high-handed and grossly unlawful — as, truly, it was — and the tenants made complaint to the mistress. She set Ulf right, soon as she heard of the matter, but Simon knew well that folks blamed not only Ulf, but also Kristin Lavransdatter. He had striven to make it clear, wherever this matter came up, that the mistress had not known aught of Ulf's demands, and that in the country the man came from these were warranted by use and wont. But Simon feared this had availed but little — though none gainsaid him to his face.

So he scarce knew whether to wish that Ulf would stay with her or go. How things would speed with her without

---

* 15th January.

this stout and faithful helper he could not think. Erlend was most unfit to take the guidance of the farm, and their sons were all too young. But Ulf had set the parish against her more than enough already — and now, on top of all, he had done wrong to a young maid of well-respected and well-to-do kindred here in the Dale. And yet, God knew, Kristin must toil hard enough even as things were —

Otherwise, too, the Jörundgaard folks were ill placed here. Erlend himself, 'twas sure, was no better liked than Ulf. If Erlend's head man and kinsman set folks on edge with his overweening ways, the master's easy-going, somewhat lazy bearing was yet more galling. For sure, it never crossed Erlend Nikulaussön's mind that he set folks against him — he seemed not to think but that, rich or poor, he was what he ever had been, and never dreamed that for *that* any man could call him haughty. He had plotted to raise rebellion against his King — he, Magnus' kinsman and vassal, and sworn to his service; and these same plans he had brought to naught by his own witless folly — and yet it seemed no thought ever came to him that in the eyes of any, by reason of these things, he might be brand-marked with the name of nithing. Simon could not mark, indeed, that Erlend thought much at all —

He was not easy to make out: when one sat talking with him, he was far from lacking wit, so Simon thought; but 'twas as though it never came to his mind to take to himself the wise and worthy things he often said. 'Twas no wise possible to bear in mind that this man would soon be old — might have had well-grown children's children this long time past. When one marked him nearly, 'twas plain to be seen that his face was furrowed and his hair sprinkled with grey — and yet he and Nikulaus together were more like two brothers than father and son. He was straight and slender, as when first Simon saw him, his voice as young and full of tone. He went about among folk free and self-assured as ever, with that somewhat of lazy grace in his bearing — With strangers he had ever kept himself somewhat quiet and retired — had let others seek him, rather than sought himself for company, whether in fortune or mischance. But that none now sought his company Erlend seemed not to mark. And the whole band of esquires and great yeomen up and down the Dale, close allied by marriage and by fellowship as they were, waxed wroth over

this haughty Trondheim chieftain, cast into their midst by
mischance, who yet reckoned himself all too high in birth
and in *kurtèisi* to seek their company.

But in truth what most of all had made bad blood for
Erlend Nikulaussön, was that he had dragged down the
men of Sundbu with him into ill-fortune. Guttorm and
Borgar Trondssön were under ban of outlawry in Norway, and their shares of the great Gjesling estates, as
also their half part of the udal goods, were forfeit to the
Crown. Ivar of Sundbu had had to buy grace of King
Magnus. When now the King gave the forfeit estates —
not without a price, folk said — to Sir Sigurd Erlendssön
Eldjarn, Ivar, and Haavard, the youngest of the Trondssöns, who had not been privy to his brothers' treason,
sold their shares of the Vaage estates to Sir Sigurd, who
was cousin to them and to the Lavransdatters: his mother,
Gudrun Ivarsdatter, was sister to Trond Gjesling and to
Ragnfrid of Jörundgaard. Ivar Gjesling moved to Ringheim at Toten, an estate he had with his wife; 'twas like
his children would find a home there, where were their
mother's kin and udal lands. Haavard still owned much
land, but it lay for the most in Valdres, and now, by marriage, great estates in the Borgesyssel had come to him. But
to the men of Vaage and the northern Dalemen it seemed
a most grievous mischance that the offspring of the old
barons had been parted from Sundbu, where their fathers
had lived and ruled the country-side time out of memory.

— For a short time Sundbu had been in the hands of
King Haakon Haakonssön's faithful baron, Erlend Eldjarn of Godaland in Agder — the Gjeslings had never been
warm friends of King Sverre and his line, and they had
joined with the Duke Skule when he raised revolt against
King Haakon. But Ivar the young had gotten Sundbu
back by barter of lands with Erlend Eldjarn, and had
wed his eldest daughter Gudrun to him. Ivar's son, Trond,
had done his kin no honour in any wise, but his four sons
were comely men, well liked and bold, and folk took it
much to heart that they had lost their father's seat.

And ere yet Ivar had left the Dale, a mischance befell
which woke yet more grief and wrath amongst the people
over the Gjeslings' evil fate. Guttorm was unwed, but,
when Borgar fled, his young wife was left behind at
Sundbu. Dagny Bjarnesdatter had ever been somewhat

weak of wits, and had ever plainly shown that she loved
her husband beyond all measure — Borgar Trondssön was
a comely youth, though something loose-lived. The winter
after he had fled the land, Dagny fell into a lead in the
ice on Vaage lake. Mishap, 'twas called, but folk knew
well that grief and longing had robbed Dagny of the
little wit she ever had, and men pitied with all their hearts
the simple, sweet, fair young woman who had met such
an ill death. Thereafter folks' wrath rose higher yet —
against Erlend Nikulaussön, who had brought all this ill-
fortune upon the best folk in the parish. And now, too,
'twas in all mouths how he had behaved him in the days
when he was to wed Lavrans Lagmandssön's daughter —
ay, and she too was a Gjesling, on the mother's side —

The new master of Sundbu was ill liked, though, for that
matter, none had aught to say against Sigurd himself. But
he was a stranger from Egde, and his father, Erlend Eldjarn, had made foes of every soul in the country-side who
had dealings with him. Kristin and Ramborg had never
met this cousin of theirs. Simon had known Sir Sigurd in
Raumarike — he was near of kin to the Haftorssöns, and
they were near kinsmen of Gyrd Darre's wife. But, so
tangled as these things were now, Simon made shift to
meet Sir Sigurd as little as might be. He had no heart now
to go to Sundbu; the Trondssöns had been his dear friends;
Ramborg and Ivar's and Borgar's wives had been wont,
each year, to change visits. Sir Sigurd Erlendssön, too,
was much older than Simon Andressön — a man nigh
upon the sixties.

Therefore did it seem to Simon Darre, so tangled had
all things grown through Erlend and Kristin's coming to
dwell at Jörundgaard, that, even though their steward's
marriage could not be deemed in itself any greater matter,
yet 'twas enough to make the coil still worse. 'Twas not
his wont at other times to trouble his young wife with the
matter, if he were hard-set or crossed. But now he could
not forbear to speak somewhat with Ramborg of these
things. And 'twas both a wonder and a joy to him to see
how understandingly she spoke of the matter, and with
what a good will she sought to do all she could to help.
She was with her sister at Jörundgaard much more often
than had been her wont, and she quite cast off her sullen

bearing toward Erlend; on Yule-day, when they met upon the church-green after mass, Ramborg kissed, not Kristin only, but her brother-in-law too. And ever before she had scoffed sourly at these outlandish tricks of his—at his using to kiss his mother-in-law in greeting and the like.

It flashed through Simon, when he saw Ramborg lay her hands about Erlend's neck—then he might do the like by his wife's sister. But yet—he felt he could not. Besides, he had never taken up this fashion of kissing women of his kin—his mother and his sisters had so laughed at him, if he offered to try it with them at his home-comings when he was a page in the body-guard.

At the Yule-tide feast Ramborg set Ulf Haldorssön's young wife in a high and honourable seat, and showed both to him and to her all the honour befitting a bride and bridegroom. And she betook her to Jörundgaard and was with Jardtrud when she bore her child.

This came to pass a month after Yule—two months before the time—and the boy was still-born. Jardtrud now fretted bitterly—could she have thought that 'twould go thus, she would never have wedded Ulf. But 'twas done now and could not be helped.

What Ulf Haldorssön thought of the whole matter, none could tell—he said naught.

The week before mid-Lent, Erlend Nikulaussön and Simon Andressön rode together southward to Kvam. Some years before he died, Lavrans, along with two other farmers, had bought a small farm in that parish; the udalmen were now minded to buy it again, but 'twas not wholly clear how the law stood in the matter in that country-side, nor how far the kinsmen of the sellers had claimed their rights in lawful wise. After Lavrans' death, when his estate was parted among his heirs, this farm, and certain other small holdings, the title whereto might give cause for suits at law, were left undivided, and the sisters shared between them the revenues therefrom. Therefore it was that both of Lavrans' sons-in-law came now to the meeting in their wives' behalf.

Folks were come together in good number, and, since the tenant's wife and children lay sick in the house, the men were fain to hold their tryst in an old shed that stood in the farm-place. It was tumbledown and leaky, and so folk kept on their fur cloaks. Each man had his weapons lying close by him, and his sword in his belt — no one had a mind to stay here longer than was needful. But a bite of meat they must have ere they parted; so toward nones, when the business had been brought to an end, each man took his wallets, and sat and ate, with the sacks by him on the bench, or before him on the ground — board there was none in the shed.

In behalf of the parish priest of Kvam, his son, Holmgeir Moisessön, had come to tryst. He was a loose-tongued and trustless young man, that few folk liked. But his father was much beloved, and his mother had been of a good kindred; and, besides, Holmgeir was a big, strong fellow, and fiery and swift to fly up at folk; wherefore no one cared to fall out with the priest's son — many, too, deemed him sharp and witty of speech.

Simon knew him but little, and had no liking for his looks — he had a long and narrow, palely freckled face, with short upper-lip, so that the great yellow front teeth peeped out like a rat's. But Sira Moises had been a good friend of Lavrans, and the son, until his father had owned him at law, had for a while been nurtured at Jörundgaard, half as servant and half as foster-son. Therefore had Simon ever been wont to meet Holmgeir Moisessön in friendly wise.

He had rolled a wood-block forward to the hearth, and sat sticking bits of his victuals — roasted thrush and shreds of bacon — on his dagger and heating them at the fire. He had been sick, and had had to get fourteen days' indulgence, he told the others, who sat munching bread and hard-frozen fish, while the savoury smell of Holmgeir's food rose to their nostrils.

Simon was out of sorts — not outright ill-humoured, but somewhat dull and flat. 'Twas no easy matter to make head or tail of the case, and the letters left by his father-in-law were in no wise clear; yet, when he rode from home, he had deemed, none the less, that he had come to a right understanding of them — having compared them with other letters. But when here, at the tryst, he came to hear the testimony of the witnesses and saw the letters that were put in by others, he felt that his view of the matter could not be upheld. Yet for that matter none of the other men were better able to set things straight — even the Warden's sheriff, who was there too, was quite at

sea. Some had begun to say that belike the case must go
before the Thing — when, of a sudden, Erlend spoke
up and prayed that he might see the letters.

Hitherto he had sat and listened, much as though he
had no part in the matter. Now 'twas as if he waked up.
He read carefully through all the papers, some of them
more than once. And thereupon he made plain the whole
case, shortly and clearly — the lawbooks read so and so,
and thus were they most commonly understood; the unclear and clumsy wording of the letters must mean either
this or that; were the matter to go before a Thing, judgment would fall either thus or thus. Thereafter he put
forward a settlement which might well content the udalmen, and yet was not over unfavourable to the present
owners.

He stood while he spoke, his left hand resting lightly on
his sword-hilt, and holding the bundle of letters carelessly in his right. He bore him as though 'twere he that
held the reins in the meeting — but Simon saw that he
thought not of this himself. 'Twas thus he had been wont
to stand and speak when he held the Warden's Thing in
his county — when he turned to one of the others and
asked whether 'twere not so, whether they understood
what he put forward, he spoke as though he questioned
witnesses — not uncourteously, but none the less as though
'twere his part to ask and the others' to answer him. When
he was done speaking, he handed the letters to the sheriff,
as though the man had been his servant, and sat him down
again; and, while the others spoke together, and Simon
too had his say to the company, Erlend listened indeed,
yet in such wise as though he himself had had no con-
cern in the case. He gave short, clear, enlightening answers when any spoke to him — all the while busy scraping with his finger-nails some grease spots that had come
upon the bosom of his coat, settling his belt, drawing his
gloves through his hands, and seeming to wait, something
impatiently, the ending of the debate.

The others fell in with the settlement Erlend had laid
before them, and 'twas one that gave Simon no great cause
for miscontent; he could scarce have won aught more in
a suit at law.

But he was out of heart. He deemed himself 'twas childish beyond measure that he should be vexed that his

brother-in-law had understood the case, and he himself
had not. It was but reason that Erlend should have more
skill in making plain the words of the law and clearing
up the drift of unclear letters, since it had been the man's
office to make inquiry and guide folk aright in disputed
causes. But it had come upon Simon quite unlooked-for:
the evening before, at Jörundgaard, when he spoke with
him and Kristin of this meeting, Erlend had said no word
of what he thought — 'twas like he had listened with but
half an ear. Ay, 'twas clear that Erlend must be better
read in the law than plain farmers — but 'twas as though
the law touched not himself, as he sat there guiding the
others with careless friendliness — there came to Simon
a dim feeling that in one way or another Erlend had
never set aught by the law, as a rule to his own life —

And 'twas so strange, besides, that he could stand up
thus, quite unabashed. He must know that this turned the
minds of all to think who and what he had been, and
what his state now was. Simon felt that the others sat
and thought upon it — some grew wroth, doubtless, at
this man who never list to heed what folk deemed of him.
But no one said aught. And when the blue-frozen clerk,
that was with the Warden's sheriff, sat him down and took
the writing-board upon his knees, he kept all the time
asking of Erlend, and Erlend spelt out for him what to
write, playing the while with some straws he had picked
from off the floor, twining them round his long, brown
fingers and plaiting them to a ring. When the clerk was
done, he reached forth the parchment to Erlend; and he
cast the straw ring on the fire, took the deed, and read it
half aloud:

"To all men to whose ears or sight this deed may come,
send Simon Andressön of Formo, Erlend Nikulaussön of
Jörundgaard, Vidar Steinssön of Klaufastad, Ingemund and
Toralde Björnssöns, Björn Ingemundssön of Lundar, Alf
Einarssön, Holmgeir Moisessön, God's greetings and their
own — Have you the wax ready?" he asked the clerk, who
stood blowing upon his frozen fingers. "Be it known unto
you that in the year from our Lord's birth one thousand
three hundred and eight-and-thirty, on the Friday before
mid-Lent Sunday, we, the aforesaid, met at Granheim in
the church parish of Kvam — . . .

" — We can take the chest, Alf, that stands in the outhouse, and use it for a board." He turned to the sheriff, giving back the deed to the writer.

Simon remembered how Erlend had been whilst he lived and moved among his fellows in the north. Self-assured and bold enough, nothing lacking in that regard — reckless and wanton of tongue — yet ever with somewhat flattering in his ways that was his own; he was in no wise careless what they thought of him, those whom he counted as his fellows and kinsmen. Nay, for he had set much store by the winning of a good report among them.

With a strangely vehement bitterness, Simon felt himself of a sudden one with these farmers of the Dale — whom Erlend held in so low esteem that he cared not to wonder what they thought of him. 'Twas for Erlend's sake he had become one of them — 'twas for his sake that he had bidden farewell to the company of rich men and nobles. 'Twas well enough to be the wealthy farmer at Formo — ay, but he could not forget that he had turned his back upon his fellows, his kinsmen and the friends of his youth, because he had gone round amongst them on such a beggar's errand that he could not bear to meet them again — could scarce bear to think on it. For this brother-in-law of his he had as good as defied his King and stepped out of the ranks of guardsmen. To Erlend he had laid himself bare in such wise that the thought of it was more bitter to him than death. And Erlend bore himself to him as though he had understood naught and remembered naught. It recked not this fellow overmuch that he had maimed another man's life —

Just then Erlend spoke to him:

"We must see and be on our way, Simon, if we are to win home to-night — I go now to see to the horses — " Simon looked up, with a strange, sick distaste, at the other's tall, comely form. Under the hood of his cloak Erlend wore a small, black silk cap, lying close around his head and tied beneath his chin — the narrow, dark face, with the great light-blue eyes deep in the shadow of the brows, looked, within it, yet more young and fine. — "And buckle up my wallet the while," said he from the door, as he went out.

The other men had gone on talking of the case. 'Twas strange enough, none the less, said some, that Lavrans should have ordered this matter with so little forethought; the man was wont else to know what he did — he was more skilled than any in the Dale in all that concerned the buying and selling of land.

"Likely 'tis my father who is to blame for this," said Holmgeir Prestesön. "He said himself this morning — had he listened to Lavrans that time, all had been straight and clear. But you know how 'twas with Lavrans — with priests he was ever biddable and meek as a lamb — "

For all that, Lavrans of Jörundgaard was wont to know what was for his own good, said someone.

"Ay, maybe he thought he did so when he hearkened to the priests' counsel," said Holmgeir, laughing; "'tis the part of wisdom, sometimes, even in worldly things — so long as one squints not at the same morsel the Church has set its eyes on — "

Marvellous pious had Lavrans been, for sure, deemed Vidar — he had never spared either goods or cattle when 'twas for the Church or the poor.

"No," said Holmgeir, musingly. "Ay, had I been so rich a man, I too might have been minded to spend somewhat for my soul's peace. But I had not been fain to strew out my goods with both hands, as he did, and go about besides with red eyes and white cheeks each time I had been to the priest and shrived me of my sins — and Lavrans went to shrift each month, he did — "

"Tears of repentance are the Holy Ghost's fair gifts of grace, Holmgeir," said old Ingemund Björnssön; "blessed is he who can weep for his sins in this earthly home; much the easier doth he enter in unto the next — "

"Ay, then must Lavrans be in heaven long ere now," said the other. "So as he fasted and mortified his flesh — Good Friday he locked him in the storehouse loft and lashed him with a scourge, I have heard tell — "

"Hold your tongue," said Simon Andressön, trembling with fury; he was blood-red in the face. Whether 'twere true, what Holmgeir said, he knew not. But when he was setting in order his father-in-law's private chests, at the bottom of the book-chest he had found a long, narrow, little wooden box, and in it lay such a scourge as in the cloisters they call a "discipline"; the plaited leather thongs were darkly flecked: it might be with blood. Simon had burned it — with a kind of sorrowful awe: he felt he had come upon something in the other's life which Lavrans had not meant that living soul should know of.

" — Howsoever it be, he talked not of it, I trow, to his serving-lads," said Simon, when he could trust himself to speak.

"Nay, like enough 'tis but a tale that folk made up," answered Holmgeir, mildly. "I trow well he had no such sins to atone for that he should need — " the man smirked a little — "had I lived as virtuous and Christian a life as Lavrans Björgulfssön — and had been wedded to that unglad woman, Ragnfrid Ivarsdatter — I had rather wept for the sins I had *not* wrought — "

Simon sprang up and struck Holmgeir hard on the mouth, so that the fellow tumbled backward towards the hearth-place. The dagger fell from his grasp — next moment he clutched it up and rushed upon the other. Simon warded off with the arm his cloak was over, gripped Holmgeir by the wrist, and tried to wrest the dagger from him — while the priest's son struck him blow after blow in the face. Now Simon got a grip round both the other's arms, but on that the youth fixed his teeth in the man's hand.

"Would you bite, dog — ?" Simon let go, sprang back a few steps, and tore his sword from its sheath. He thrust at Holmgeir — the young man's body bent backwards, a couple of inches of steel in his breast. Then at once Holmgeir's body sank from off the sword-point and fell heavily, half over the hearth-fire.

Simon threw down his sword and stooped to lift Holmgeir from out the fire — then he saw, just above his head, Vidar's axe lifted for a blow. He ducked down and to the side, caught up his sword again, and was but just in time to strike aside Alf Einarssön the sheriff's blade — whirled round on guard once more against Vidar's axe — when with the corner of his eye he caught a glimpse, behind him, of the Björnssöns and Björn of Lunde thrusting at him with their spears from the far side of the hearth. On this, he drove Alf before him against the further wall, but marked that now Vidar came at him from behind (Vidar had dragged Holmgeir out of the fire; they were cousins, those two) and the carles of Lunde were closing on him round the hearth. He was hemmed in and uncovered on all sides — and amidst it all, with more than enough to do to guard his life, he felt a vague, unhappy wonder that all men's hands should be against him —

— The next instant Erlend's sword flashed between the Lunde men and him. Toralde reeled aside and away, crumpled up against the wall. Quick as lightning Erlend shifted his sword to his left hand and struck Alf's weapon from his grasp, so that it flew clanging across the floor, while at the same time, with his right, he clutched Björn's spearshaft and bent it down —

—"Get you out," he said to Simon, under his breath, as he guarded his brother-in-law against Vidar. Simon ground his teeth, and rushed inwards to meet Björn and Ingemund. Erlend was at his side, shouting, through the trampling and the clash of arms: "Come out, hear you not — blockhead? Get you towards the door — we must run for it!"

When he saw Erlend meant they should both get out, he drew backwards, fighting, towards the door. They ran through the outer room, and stood fast in the courtyard — Simon a step or two farther from the house, Erlend right in front of the doorway, with his sword half lifted, facing the men who now came crowding after.

For a moment Simon was near blinded — the winter day without was so dazzling bright and clear — under the blue sky the white dome of the fell-top shone golden in the last sunshine; the woods stood smothered with snow and rime. All over the fields was a sparkling and glittering as of gems —

He heard Erlend say:

" 'Twill not better this mischance that more men be slain. Let us come back to our wits, good men, and have no more bloodshed. 'Tis ill enough as it is for my brother-in-law to have been a man's bane — "

Simon went forward to Erlend's side.

"Sackless have you slain my cousin, Simon Andressön," said Vidar of Klaufastad — he stood foremost in the doorway.

"Wholly sackless he fell not, I trow. But you know well, Vidar, I shall not shun the reckoning — shall make good the mischief I have wrought you. You all know where you can find me at home — "

*

Erlend spoke some words more with the farmers: "Alf — how fared it with him — ?" He went in with the men.

Simon was left behind, struck strangely speechless. Erlend came out in a little while: "Let us ride now," said he, and went down towards the stable.

"Is he dead?" asked Simon.

"Ay. And Alf and Toralde and Vidar all have wounds — but naught grievous, I trow. He has singed off his back hair, Holmgeir." Erlend had spoken most soberly — now, suddenly, he burst into a laugh: "*Now* is there a rare stink of roast thrush in there, trust me! What the devil — how was't possible you could fall so by the ears in so short a space?" he asked, in great amaze.

A half-grown boy stood holding their horses — neither of the brothers-in-law had brought his henchmen with him on this journey.

Both still bore their swords in their hands. Erlend took up a wisp of hay and dried the blood from his. Simon did the like — when he had got off the most of it, he thrust the sword back into its sheath. Erlend scoured his with careful pains, and, at the end, furbished it with the skirt of his cloak. Then he made some little playful passes in the air before him — smiling the while, fleetingly, as at a memory — threw the sword high into the air, caught it again by the hilt, and stuck it into the scabbard.

"Your wounds — we must go into the house, and I will bind them — " Simon said 'twas nothing:

"You are bleeding, too, Erlend!"

"For me there's no fear. My flesh heals up so well. Fat folk ever heal slower, I have marked. And now, in this cold — we have far to ride — "

Erlend got grease and cloths from the tenant on the farm, and dressed the other's wounds with care — they were two flesh-wounds close together in the left breast; they bled much at first, but grievous they were not. Erlend had gotten a scratch from Björn's spear-point on the outer thigh — it must be irksome to ride with, Simon said, but his brother-in-law laughed: it had scarce pierced his leathern hose. He plastered a little grease upon it and bound it well about, against the frost.

It was biting cold. Before they were come down from the hillock where the farm stood, rime began to gather

on the horses, and the fur edging on the men's hoods
grew white.

"Hoo, hoo!" Erlend shivered. "Would we were home!
We must turn in at the farm down here that you may
give yourself out the slayer —"

"Is it needful?" asked Simon. "I spoke, you wot, with
Vidar and the —"

"'Twere best that you did it," said Erlend. "That you
told the tidings here yourself. Let them not have aught
they can say against you —"

The sun was behind the ridges now, the evening a pale
grey-blue, but still light. They rode along a beck, under
birch trees yet more shaggy with rime than the woods
around: there was a tang of raw frost fog in the air down
here, fit to choke the breath in a man's throat. Erlend
grumbled impatiently at the long cold they had had, and
at the cold ride that lay before them.

"You have not got your face frost-bit, think you,
brother-in-law — ?" He peered uneasily in under Simon's
hood. Simon chafed his face — frost-bitten 'twas not, but
he was somewhat pale as he rode. It set him ill, for his big,
fat face was weather-bitten and red-besprinkled, and the
paleness spread over it in grey patches and made his hue
seem as 'twere unclean.

"Saw you ever a man pitchfork dung with his sword?"
said Erlend — he burst out laughing at the thought of it,
leaned forward in his saddle and aped the motions " — like
yonder Alf — a rare fellow for a sheriff, that! You should
have seen Ulf at swordplay, Simon — Jesus Maria!"

Play — ay, now, indeed, he had seen Erlend Nikulaussön at that play. Again and again he saw himself and those
men, in the mellay there by the hearth, like peasants hew-
ing wood or pitching hay — Erlend's slender, flashing
figure amidst them, his lightning glances, his sure wrist,
while he sported with them, swift-thinking, skilled of
fence —

'Twas twenty years and more since the time he himself
had been accounted one of the first in skill of arms amongst
the youth of the body-guard — when they practised them
on the play-green. And from that time on he had had but
little use of an esquire's swordcraft.

And here he rode now, sick at heart for that he had
slain a man — saw ever Holmgeir's corpse pitch from off

his sword down into the fire; had his short, hoarse death-cry in his ears, and saw, again and again, glimpses of the short, furious fight that followed. Heart-sore was he, downcast and mazed — they had turned on him in a single instant to slay him, all those men he had sat with, feeling he belonged to their fellowship — and *Erlend* had come to his rescue —

A coward he had never deemed himself to be. He had hunted down six bears in the years he had dwelt at Formo — and twice he had risked his life as recklessly as well could be. With a slender fir-stem between him and a mad, wounded she-bear, without other weapon than his spear-head and a scant handbreadth of shaft — the peril of the game had not ruffled his sureness of thought and deed and sense. Now, down there in the hut — he knew not whether 'twas fearful he had been — but he had been mazed, his wits had failed him —

And when he sat at home, after that bear-hunt, with his clothes huddled on him as they best would hang, with his arm in a sling, burning with fever, his shoulder stiff and torn, he had felt naught but an overweening joy — things might have gone worse — how, he thought not on over-much. But now he must think and think, endlessly, how all would have ended had Erlend not come so timely to his help. He had been — not afraid, surely, but strangely dashed. It was the look on the other men's faces — and Holmgeir's dying carcass —

Manslayer he had never been before —

— That Swedish trooper he had cut down — 'Twas the year King Haakon carried war into Sweden to avenge the dukes' murder. He had been sent out to scout — three men sent with him, and he to be the leader — full blithe he was and proud. Simon remembered that his sword had stuck fast in the trooper's steel head-piece, so that he must twist and wrench it loose; there was a notch in the edge when he looked on it in the morning. He had never thought on that deed with aught but content — there were eight of the Swedes, too — he had got at least a taste of war; that fell not to the lot of all men who marched with the guard that year — When daylight came, he saw that blood and brains had spurted out over his coat of mail — he had striven to seem lowly and not puffed up while he washed it off —

But 'twas no help to think on that poor devil of a trooper now. No, yonder time was not like this. He could not rid him of a gnawing sorrow for Holmgeir Moisessön.

And this too, that now he owed his life to Erlend. He knew not yet how much that might bring with it. But he felt as though all things must be changed now that he and Erlend were quits —

— On that score they were quits now, ay —

The brothers-in-law had ridden with scarce a word. Once Erlend said:

"Ay, 'twas foolish of you, too, Simon that you bethought you not to make for the door at the first — "

"How so?" asked Simon, something shortly. "Because you were without — ?"

"Nay — " there was a little laugh in Erlend's voice. "Ay, that too — though I thought not on that. But out of that narrow door, see you, they could not have come at you more than one at a time — And besides, 'tis wonder often to see how quick folks come to their wits again once they get out beneath open sky. Much do I marvel now that no more than one man was slain."

Once and again he asked after Simon's wounds. The other said he felt them not much — though the truth was they burned sorely enough.

They came to Formo late at night, and Erlend turned in there with his brother-in-law. He had counselled him to write to the Warden, betimes in the morning, of what had befallen, so as to have order taken for a grace-deed * as soon as might be. Erlend might as well make up the letter for Simon that night — doubtless the wounds in his breast would hinder his writing: "And to-morrow you must lie quiet in your bed, I trow, for like enough you will have some touch of wound-fever — "

Ramborg and Arngjerd were sitting up waiting. Because of the cold, they had crept up on the bench against the warm fire-place wall, and had drawn up their feet beneath them — a draught-board lay between them — they looked like two children.

Simon had scarce got a few words said of what had be-

---

* See Note 1.

fallen ere his young wife flew to him and flung her arms about his neck. She drew his face down to hers, pressed her cheek to his — and she wrung Erlend's hands so that he said, laughing, he had never deemed Ramborg had such strength of fingers —

Naught would serve but that her husband must sleep in there that night, and she herself sit up by him. She begged this, almost in tears — but on this Erlend proffered to stay there and lie by Simon, if she would send a man north to Jörundgaard with a message — 'twas late after all for him to ride home: "and 'twere pity Kristin should sit up so late in this cold — she, too, waits for me always herself; good wives are you Lavransdatters — "

While the men ate and drank, Ramborg sat nestled close to her husband. Simon patted her arm and hand now and again — he was much moved, but a little put out as well, at her showing so much love and fearfulness. Being that 'twas now Lent, Simon was sleeping alone in the Sæmunds hall, and when the men went over there, Ramborg went with them and set a great kettle with honey-ale by the stone hearth-brim to warm.

The Sæmunds hall was a little, ancient hearth-room house, warm and wind-tight — the timber was so massy that there were but four logs in the wall. 'Twas cold there now, but Simon threw a mighty armful of pine roots upon the fire and hunted his dog up on to the bed — it could lie there and warm it up for them. They drew the block-chair and the settle right up to the hearth and made themselves snug, for they were chilled through and through from their journey, and their meal in the great hall had but half thawed them.

Erlend wrote the letter for Simon. Then they set about loosing their clothes — as Simon's wounds began to bleed again if he moved his arms much, his brother-in-law helped him to get his doublet over his head and his boots from off his feet. Erlend himself halted on his wounded leg a little — 'twas stiff and tender from the ride, he said, but naught to matter. And they settled them down by the fire again, half undressed — 'twas so good and warm here now, and a plenty of beer in the kettle yet.

"You take this over-hardly, brother-in-law, I see well," said Erlend once. They had been sitting dozing, gazing into the fire. "He was none so great a loss, this Holm-geir — "

" 'Twill not seem so to Sira Moises," said Simon, low. "He is an old man and a good priest — "

Erlend nodded gravely.

" 'Tis a grievous thing to have made an enemy of such a man. And you know well I often have errands in that parish — "

"Oh! — but, when all is said, the like may hap so easily — to any one of us. Like enough they will doom you to pay ten or twelve marks in gold for weregild. Ay, and you know too Bishop Halvard is a stern lord, when he is to shrive a man of a deed of blood — and the boy's father is one of his priests. But you will come off not much the worse from both reckonings — "

Simon said naught. Erlend went on again:

"I shall have to make amends for wounding, I trow" — he smiled to himself — "and I hold no more of Norway's ground for my own than that farm in Dovre — "

"How great a farm *is* Haugen?" asked Simon.

"I mind not rightly — it stands written in the deed. But the folks who farm the land pay only some hay for rent. None will dwell on it — the houses are nigh in ruins, they tell me — you know folk say Aashild and Sir Björn walk there in death — "

" — But at the least I wot well that for this day's work I shall have much thanks of my wife. Kristin loves you, Simon, as though you were her own brother."

Simon's smile could scarce be marked, where he sat in shadow. He had thrust the block-chair back a little and screened his eyes with his hand from the heat of the blaze. But Erlend joyed in the fire like a cat — he sat close in to the hearth, leaning into a corner of the settle, with one arm over the back, and his wounded leg stretched out over the other arm-rest.

"Ay, she spoke so fairly of it here, one day in autumn," said Simon in a while; 'twas well-nigh as though his voice had a mocking sound. "She showed here last autumn, when our son was sick, that she is a faithful sister"; he spoke gravely now — but then again came the little tone of mocking. "Now, Erlend, have we kept faith one with another, even as we swore that time we laid our hands together in Lavran's and vowed to stand by each other like brothers — "

"Ay," said Erlend, simply. "I am glad of this day's work; I too, brother Simon." For a time they both sat silent. Then Erlend, as though provingly, stretched out a hand towards the other. Simon took it; they crushed each other's fingers hard, let go, and shrank back shamefacedly, each into his seat.

At length Erlend broke the silence. He had sat long with his chin in his hand, staring into the hearth-fire, where now only one little flame and another flickered, flared up, flapped a little, and played along the charred sticks that snapped and fell to pieces with small brittle sighs. Soon naught would be left of the blaze but black charcoal and embers.

Erlend said very low:

"So high-heartedly have you borne you towards me, Simon Darre, that I deem few men could be your like. I — I have not forgotten — "

"Be still! — you know not, Erlend — God in heaven alone knows," he whispered, in fear and distress; " — all that harbours in a man's mind — "

"It is so," said Erlend, as low and earnestly. "We need, all of us, I trow — that He judge us with His Mercy —

" — But man must judge man by his *deeds*. And I — I — God reward you, brother-in-law!"

After that they sat in dead silence — dared not to move lest they be put to shame.

Till, of a sudden, Erlend let his hand fall upon his knee — a fiery blue ray flashed from the stone of the ring he bore on his right forefinger. Simon knew he had had it of Kristin when he came out from his prison-cell.

"But you must mind, Simon," said he softly, "there goes an old word: Many a man wins what is meant for another, but another's lot none may win."

Simon lifted his head with a sudden start. Slowly he grew blood-red in the face — the veins in his temples stood out like dark, twisted cords.

Erlend glanced at the other — and withdrew his eyes swiftly. Then he too reddened — a strangely fine and girlish flush speading under his dark skin. He sat still, shy and abashed, with mouth a little open, like a child.

Simon rose vehemently and went over to the bed:

"You had liefer lie outermost, I trow"; he tried to speak evenly and calmly, but his voice shook.

"Nay — be it as you will," said Erlend, haltingly. He rose up to his feet as in a maze. "The fire?" he asked. "Shall I rake it under — ?" he began to shovel ashes over.

"Enough now — come and lie down," said Simon, as before. His heart beat so, he could scarce speak.

In the dark, Erlend crept, silent as a shadow, in among the skins at the outer edge, and lay down, still as a beast of the forest. To Simon it seemed that to have that other by him in his bed must stifle him.

6

EVERY year, in Easter-week, Simon Andressön held an ale-feast for the folk from all the parish. They came to Formo the third day after the mass and tarried there till Thursday.

Kristin had never had much delight in these feastings. When mirth and merry-making were afoot, both Simon and Ramborg seemed to deem the more bustle and uproar there was at the feast the better was it. Simon ever prayed the guests to bring their own children, and their serving-folk with their children, as many as might be away from home. The first day things went quietly and peacefully; the great folk and the elders led the talk, while the youth listened and ate and drank, and the small children were for the most in another house. But on the second the host went about from early morning and egged on the young and unstaid folk and children to drink and make merry, and 'twas not long then, for the most part, till the mirth grew so wild and wanton that wives and young maids shrank into the corners and stood there in groups, tittering, ready to run out; while many of the most worshipful house-wives gathered in Ramborg's ladies' house, whither already the mothers had carried off the smaller children out of the hurly-burly in the great hall.

But this year Easter had brought wondrous fair spring weather. On the Wednesday, from early morn 'twas so warm and sunny that, the morning meal scarce over, all the company swarmed out into the courtyard. Instead of racketing and raising riot, the young folks were soon busy playing ball, shooting at a mark, or hauling on the rope; then began the game of stag, and dancing on the log; after that they got Geirmund of Kruke to pluck his harp and sing — and thereon all, both young and old, were soon footing it in the dance. The snow still lay low on the fields, but the alder woods were brown with blossoms, and the sun shone warm and fair on every bare hill-side; when folks came out after the supper, there was such singing of birds everywhere — and they built a bonfire on the field beyond the smithy and sang and danced till far into the night. Next morning the guests lay long abed; and thus they broke up and took their leaves later than was their use. The folk from Jörundgaard were wont to be the last to leave — and now Simon prevailed on Erlend and Kristin to tarry over the next day — the Kruke folk were to stay the week out at Formo.

Simon had gone up to the highway with the last flock of guests. The evening sun shone so fair over his lands, lying spread out on the hill-slopes; he was warm and of good cheer with the drink and all the junketing, and as he went down between the fences, home to the quiet and easy fellowship that follows when, after a great banquet, a little ring of near kinsfolk are left together, he felt himself gladder and more light of heart than he had been for long.

Down on the fields by the smithy they had set the bonfire a-going again — Erlend's sons, Sigrid's eldest children, Jon Daalk's sons, and his own daughters. Simon hung over the fence awhile, watching them. Ulvhild's holy-day frock flared scarlet in the sun — she ran about dragging branches to the fire — and there she lay her length on the ground! Her father shouted to them, laughing, but they did not hear —

In the courtyard sat two wenches minding the smallest children — they sat close by the bower wall sunning themselves; over their heads the evening light burned like melted gold upon the small glass pane. Simon took little Inga Geirmundsdatter, heaved her high into the air, and set her upon his arm: "Can you sing to-day for your uncle, Inga winsome may — ?"; and at that her brother and Andres set upon him, and would be thrown high on loft, they too —

Whistling, he climbed the stairway to the upper hall.

The sun shone in so bravely — they had set the door wide. The folk within sat in goodly quiet. Up at the end of the board Erlend and Geirmund bent them over the harp, putting new strings to it; they had the meadhorn beside them on the board. Sigrid lay upon the bed, giving her youngest son the breast; Kristin and Ramborg sat by her; a silver mug stood on the foot-board between the sisters.

Simon filled his own gilded beaker with wine, went to the bed, and drank to Sigrid:

"All folks here have the wherewithal to slake their thirsts, I see, save you, my sister!"

Laughing, she raised herself on her elbow and took the beaker. The little child, disquieted at his meal, burst into a wrathful howl.

Simon sat down on the bench, still whistling softly and hearkening to the others with half an ear. Sigrid and Kristin gossiped of their children; Ramborg sat silent, toying with a little windmill of Andres's. The men by the board fingered the harp-strings to try them — Erlend sang a stave very softly; Geirmund picked out the air on the harp and sang the verse after him — they had such tuneful voices, both of them —

A little after, Simon went out on the balcony, stood leaning against the carven pillar, and gazed around. From the byre came the everlasting hungry bellowing. If this weather would but hold a while, maybe the spring dearth would not last so long this year.

'Twas Kristin who came. He needed not to turn — he knew her light tread. She stepped out and stood by his side in the evening sunlight.

So fair and fine, that she had never seemed to him so fair. And all at once he felt as though, in some wise, he were lifted up, as though he floated in this sunlight — he drew a long breath: suddenly it came upon him — 'twas good, 'twas good to live. A rich and golden happiness flooded all his being —

She was his own sweet love — and all the heavy, bitter thoughts he had thought were but as half-forgotten follies. Poor, poor love of mine — could I but do you aught of good. Could you but be glad once more — gladly would I lay down my life, if that might help you —

O ay! for well he saw her lovesome face was worn and aged. Fine, small wrinkles had gathered beneath her eyes, her skin had lost its pure shining — had grown coarser far and sunburned, and she was pale beneath the brown. But to him for sure she would be ever alike fair; for her great grey eyes and her fine, still mouth, and her little round chin — her restful, tempered bearing, too, were the fairest things he knew on earth.

And 'twas good too — once more to see her clad as beseemed a high-born lady — The thin little silken kerchief but half hid the masses of her yellow-brown hair — the plaits were caught up, so that they peeped forth above her ears — there were streaks of grey in her hair now, but 'twas no matter. And she bore a stately, blue outer robe of velvet, edged with ermine — it was cut so deeply at the bosom, and the arm-slits were so long, that over breast and shoulders it showed no more than the breast-straps of a horse's gear — 'twas brave to look on. Underneath, there clung a somewhat, yellow as sand, an under-robe that lay smooth to the body, stood high around her throat and ran down to the wrists. 'Twas buttoned with many small gilded buttons, and they touched him to the heart — God forgive him, all these little gilt buttons gladdened him like the sight of a troop of angels.

He stood, feeling his own heart's strong, quiet beat. Something had slipped from him — ay, like fetters. Evil, hateful dreams — they were but shadows of the night, and now he saw his love for her by light of day, in full sunshine.

"You look at me so strangely, Simon — why smile you so? — "

The man laughed, low and joyously, but did not answer. Out before them lay the Dale, filled with the evening sun's golden glow; flocks of birds twittered and chirruped shrilly in the borders of the woods — then from somewhere deep in the forest a thrush's full, clear song ran out. And here she stood, warmed by the sun, shining in her festal pride — escaped from out the dark, cold house and the coarse, heavy garmets reeking of sweat and toil — Kristin mine, 'twas good to see her thus again —

He took her hand, that lay before him on the railing — lifted it up toward his face: "This ring you bear upon your finger is a fair one!" He turned the finger-ring a little, and laid her hand down again. The hand was chafed and reddened now, and he knew not how he could ever do enough to make it amends — so fair had it been, her long, slender hand —

" 'Tis Arngjerd and Gaute," said Kristin. "Those two are quarrelling again — "

From below the loft-balcony came the voices, high and angry. Now the maid broke in with a cry of rage:

" — Ay, mind me of that, you! — meseems 'tis more honour to be called bastard daughter to my father than to be true-born son of yours!"

Kristin turned sharp about and ran down the stairway. Simon, following after, heard the sound of two or three buffets on a cheek. He saw her standing under the balcony holding her son by the shoulder.

The two children stood looking down, red-faced, silent and sullen.

"I see well you know how to behave you to your hosts — you do us honour, forsooth, your father and me — "

Gaute gazed down on the ground. Low and wrathfully he answered his mother:

"She said somewhat — I will not say it again — "

Simon took his daughter by the chin, forced her to look up at him. Arngjerd grew redder and redder, and dropped her eyelids under her father's look.

"Ay" — she broke away from him — "I minded Gaute that his father was judged nithing and traitor to his King — but first he had called you, father — you, said he, you were the traitor, and you had Erlend to thank that you sat here rich and scatheless, on your own manor — "

"I had deemed you were a grown maid now — would you let you be egged on by a child's chatter, to forget both manners and the dues of kin?" — he pushed the girl from him in wrath, turned to Gaute, and asked, most soberly:

"How mean you, friend Gaute, that I have betrayed your father? I have felt before this that you were wroth with me — now must you say what the cause may be?"

"That know you well!"

Simon shook his head. And then the boy cried out, flaming with fury:

"The letter they broke my father on the rack for, to make him tell who hung their seals below it — I saw it. 'Twas I who went off with it and burnt it — "

"Be still!" Erlend burst in amongst them. His face was white to the very lips, his eyes burned.

"Nay, Erlend — 'twere best, now, we came at the truth of this. Was my name in that letter then?"

"Be still!" In furious rage his father seized Gaute by the breast and shoulder. "I trusted you — you, my son! If I killed you, 'twere but your due — "

Kristin sprang forward; Simon too. The boy broke loose and clung to his mother. Quite beside himself with passion, he shouted at furious speed, while he hid himself behind the woman's arm:

"I looked on the seals before I burned it — father! I deemed the day might come when I could serve you thereby — "

"God's curse upon you — !" There broke from Erlend's frame a short, dry sob.

Simon, too, had grown pale, and then flushed dark red, with shame for the other. He dared not look towards where Erlend stood — the sight of the man's humiliation seemed to choke him.

Kristin stood as though spellbound — still with her arms about her son to guard him. But, within her brain, thought fitted into thought with lightning speed:

Erlend had had Simon's privey seal in his ward a short time that spring — the brothers-in-law were selling Lavrans's warehouse on Veöy to the Holm cloister-brothers. Erlend had said himself that it might well be this was unlawful, but 'twas like none would question it. He had shown her the seal and said that Simon might well have got him one more fairly graven — all three brothers had had their seals graven with their father's arms, only the legends were diverse. But Gyrd's was graven much finer, said Erlend —

— Gyrd Darre — Erlend had brought her greetings from him, both the last times he came from the south country — She remembered she had marvelled that Erlend should visit Gyrd at Dyfrin — they had seen each other but the once, at Ramborg's wedding — Ulf Sakseson was Gyrd Darre's brother-in-law; Ulf had been in the plot —

"You saw wrong, Gaute," said Simon, low and firmly.

"Simon!" Blindly Kristin grasped her husband's hand. "Remember — there are other men besides you who bear that device on their seal — "

"Be still! Would you too — " Erlend tore himself from his wife with a tortured cry and rushed across the court-yard towards the stable. Simon sprang after him:

"Erlend — was it my brother — ?"

"And send for the lads — come you after me," cried Er-lend back to his wife.

Simon caught him up again in the stable door, seized him by the arm:

"Erlend — was it Gyrd — ?"

Erlend answered not — tried to wrench himself free. His face was set and drawn and white as death.

"Erlend — answer me — was my brother with you in the plot?"

"Maybe you would measure swords with me too — " Erlend snarled out the words, and Simon, as they wrestled, felt the other's whole body tremble.

"That you know I will not." Simon loosed his hold and staggered backwards against the door-jamb. "Erlend — for the love of God, that died for us — say if it was so!"

Erlend led Soten out, forcing Simon aside from the doorway. A too forward house-carl brought saddle and bridle; Simon took them and sent the man away; Erlend took them from Simon.

"Erlend — sure you can tell it *now!* — to *me!*" He knew not himself why he should beg thus, as though he were begging for his life. "Erlend — answer me — by Christ's wound-marks, I conjure you — tell me, man!"

"You can go on thinking what you thought," said Er-lend, in a low biting voice.

"Erlend — I thought — naught — "

"I *know* what you thought." Erlend swung himself into the saddle. Simon caught the horse by the head-stall; it reared and flung about wildly.

"Let go — or I ride you down," said Erlend.

"Then will I ask Gyrd — No later than to-morrow will I ride south — by God, Erlend, you *shall* tell me — "

"Ay, you will get an answer from *him*, I doubt not," said Erlend scornfully — he spurred the stallion, and Simon must needs leap aside. The other galloped from the manor —

Half-way up the courtyard, Simon met Kristin; she had her cloak on. Gaute walked by her side, carrying the wallet with their clothes. Ramborg was with her sister.

The boy glanced up an instant, fearful and at a loss. Then he looked away. But Kristin fixed her great eyes full upon him — they were dark with sorrow and anger:

"Could you believe this thing of Erlend — that he could betray you so?"

"I believed naught," said Simon hotly. "I believed 'twas foolish babble of that young scamp there — "

"Nay, Simon — I will not have you go with me," said Kristin, low.

He saw that she was unspeakably hurt and sorrowful.

In the evening, when he was left alone with his wife in the great hall — they were putting off their clothes, and their daughters were asleep already in the other bed — all at once Ramborg asked:

"Knew you naught of this, Simon?"

"No — ? Knew *you* aught?" he asked, anxiously.

Ramborg came across and stood just within the light of the taper on the board. She was half undressed — in shift and laced bodice; her hair hung loose in tresses about her face.

"Knew? — I had my thoughts. Helga was so strange" — her face twisted into a kind of smile, and she seemed as she were cold. "She spoke of how now there would be other times in Norway. The great nobles" — Ramborg smiled a wry, fluttering smile — "were to come to their rights here as in other lands. Knights — and barons — they would be called once more —

" — Afterward, when I saw you take up their cause so hotly — you were from home almost all the year — you could not find time to come north to me at Ringheim, when I was to bear your child in a strange man's house — afterwards, I thought maybe you knew — that there was question of others than Erlend — "

"Ho! Knights and barons!" Simon laughed, short and angrily.

"Was't for Kristin's sake alone you did it?"

He saw her face was pale as it were bit with frost; 'twas impossible to pretend he did not understand her meaning. Desperately and defiantly he burst out:

"Ay!"

Then he bethought him — why, she was mad — and he

himself was mad. Erlend was mad — all the world had lost their wits that day. But now there must be an end to it.

"I did it for your sister's sake, ay," said he, soberly, "and for the children's sake, who had no man nearer of blood or of kin than I to take their part. And for Erlend's sake, since we were to be true brothers one to the other. — And now begin not you to bear you witlessly — for of that have I seen more than enough in this house to-day — " He flamed up, and flung the shoe he had taken off against the wall.

Ramborg went and took it up — looked at the log where it had struck:

" 'Tis shame that Torbjörg could not think of it herself — to wash the soot off in here for the banquet — I forgot to tell her of it." She wiped the shoe — 'twas of Simon's best pair, with long toes and red heels — then took up the other and laid the pair in his clothes-chest. But he marked that her hands shook sorely while she was about it.

On that, he went and took her to his arms. She twined her slender limbs vehemently about her husband, while she shook with strangled weeping, and whispered, on his bosom, that she was so weary —

The seventh day thereafter Simon and his henchman were riding north from Dyfrin through Kvam. They struggled forward against a storm of great, clinging snow-flakes. Towards midday they came to the little farm by the highway where there was a tavern.

The woman came out and begged Simon to step into their house — only small folk were sent to the rest-house. She shook his wet outer garments and hung them to dry on the cross-beam by the hearth, while she talked away: Such a filthy weather — 'twas pity of the horses — and he must have had to ride the whole way round — belike there was no riding over Mjös now?

"Oh, yes, if a man be tired enough of his life — "

The woman, and the children standing beside her, laughed with a good will. The bigger ones made themselves errands into the room with firewood and beer; the little ones bunched them together away by the door. Often they got pennies from Master Simon of Formo when he stopped there, and if he had with him something good for his children from Hamar market, they were like

enough to get a taste. But to-day it seemed he list not to
look at them.

He sat on the bench, bent forward, with his hands hanging out over his knees, staring into the hearth-fire, and
answering a word now and again to the woman's flood
of talk. Then she let fall that Erlend Nikulaussön was at
Granheim to-day — 'twas to-day that the Udalmen were
to pay the first of the redemption-money to the whilom
owners. Should she send one of the children to his
brother-in-law and tell him, so that they might ride home
together?

No, said Simon. She might give him a little food, and
after that he would lie down and sleep a while.

—Erlend he would meet soon enough. What he meant
to say he would say in Gaute's hearing. But he had liefer
not speak of the thing more than once.

His man, Sigurd, had settled down in the kitchen-house
while the woman was cooking the food. Ay, a toilsome
journey — and, besides, the master had been like an angry
bull nigh the whole way. Simon Andressön was wont to
hearken gladly enough to all the news of his home parish
that his men could pick up, when they had been at Dyfrin.
He had most often one or more Raumerike men eating his
bread: folk came and sought service with him when he
was at Dyfrin, for he was known for a kindly man and an
open-handed, merry-hearted and not wont to be too high
and mighty with his men. But "hold your tongue" was
well-nigh the softest answer he, Sigurd, had had of his
master that journey.

Moreover, it seemed he had quite fallen out with his
brothers — he had not even slept overnight at Dyfrin;
they had taken lodging on a lease-hold farm near by in the
parish. Sir Gyrd — ay, for, she must know, the King had
made his master's brother a knight at Yule-tide — Sir
Gyrd had come out into the yard and prayed Simon, right
fairly, to stay — Simon had scarce answered his brother.
And they had roared and bellowed and shouted, the gentry
in the high-loft hall — yonder Sir Ulf Saksesön and Gudmund Andressön had been at the manor — enough fairly
to fright folk. God only knew what they had fallen so
by the ears about —

Simon came past the kitchen-house door, stood a moment, and glared in. Sigurd said, quickly, he was getting

an awl and a buckle to put the saddle-gear to rights that
was broke that morning.

"Have they such-like things in the kitchen on this
farm — ?" Simon flung back at him, and went his way.
Sigurd shook his head, and nodded to the woman, when
he was out of sight.

Simon thrust the platter from him and sat on at the
board. He was so weary he could scarce bring himself to
rise. But after a while he went and threw himself upon the
bed in his boots and spurs — but bethought him then
'twere pity, too, of the bed: it was clean and good for
such a humble house. He sat up and pulled off his foot-
gear. Stiff and weary as he was, he sure should be able to
sleep now — and he was wet through and shivering with
cold, though his face burned after the long ride against
the storm.

He crept in under the bed-spread, turned and tossed
about the pillows — they smelt so strangely of fish. Then
he lay still, half raised upon his elbow.

His thoughts began to go round again in a ring. He had
thought and thought these days, as a beast tramps round
in a tether-rope.

— Even if Erling Vidkunssön had known it might cost
Gyrd and Gudmund Darre life and goods if Erlend
Nikulaussön let himself be driven to speak — ay, that made
it none the worse that he had gone all lengths to win the
Bjarkö knight's help. Rather the contrary — surely a man
owed it to his brothers to stand by them, to the death if
need be. Yet would he be fain to know if indeed Erling
had known it. Simon weighed the chances for and against.
Quite without knowledge that a rising was a-brewing he
sure could not have been. But *what* Erling knew — ?
Gyrd and Ulf, at least, seemed not to know if the man had
knowledge that they were in it. But Simon minded that
Erling had named the Haftorssöns, had counselled him to
seek help there, for 'twas rather their friends who had
need to be afraid — The Haftorssöns were cousins of Ulf
Saksesön and Helga. The nose is near to the eyes — !

But even if Erling Vidkunssön had believed that Simon
was thinking of his own brothers too, what he had done
was none the worse, surely, for *that*. And Erling might
well have seen, too, that he knew naught of his brothers'

peril. Besides, had he not said himself — he minded, he had said it to Stig — he believed not that they could wring speech from Erlend.

Nevertheless, they might well have need to fear Erlend's tongue. Having held his peace in despite of bonds and torture, he was the very man to betray himself after by a slip of the tongue. 'Twould be like him — And yet — that, he felt, was the one thing he could be sure Erlend would not do. He was dumb as a stone each time the talk turned that way, for very fear he might be drawn on to say too much. Simon saw that such was Erlend's fevered, well-nigh childish dread of breaking his troth — childish, for, that himself had betrayed the whole emprise to his para-mour, Erlend, it seemed clear, deemed not such a stain on his honour as he need regard. Such a thing, he seemed to hold, might happen to the best. So long as he held his tongue himself, he counted his shield untarnished and his troth unbroken — and Simon had seen well that Erlend was tender of his honour, so far as he understood what good fame and honour were. Had he not gone clean beside himself with despair and wrath at but the thought that any of his fellow-plotters should be betrayed — (now, so long after, and in such wise that 'twas not possible it could matter aught to the men he had shielded with his life — and his honour and his wealth) — by the words of his child spoken to him who was nearest of kin to these same men — ?

— He would order it so that, if things went awry, he would pay the price for them all — this Erlend had sworn upon the crucifix before all who joined with him in this emprise. But that grown men in their right minds could put their trust in such an oath! — for 'twas clear the issue rested not with Erlend. Now that he knew all about the plot Simon deemed 'twas the most witless folly he had heard on. Erlend had been willing to be torn limb from limb that he might keep the letter of his oath. And all the while the secret lay in a ten-year-old boy's hands — Erlend had himself seen to that. Nor seemed it to be his fault, either, that Sunniva Olavsdatter knew no more than she did know — Could anyone make such a fellow out? —

So, if he had for a moment thought — ay, what Erlend and his wife deemed he had thought — God knows, that thought lay close enough to hand when Gaute came out with this tale of having seen his seal below the treasonous

letter. And they two might have remembered he knew
one thing and another of Erlend Nikulaussön that gave
him less ground than most men to believe at all times the
best of that gallant. But 'twas like they had forgotten long
ago how once he had come upon them and seen into the
depths of their shamelessness —

So 'twas with little reason he lay there, ashamed as a
beaten dog for that he had done Erlend wrong in his
thoughts. God knew, 'twas not that he gladly deemed ill of
his brother-in-law — naught but unhappiness had he felt
at the thought. But he knew himself 'twas a witless, foolish
misthought — he would have seen straightway, even without Kristin's words, that so it could not be. Well-nigh as
soon as the thought came to him — that Erlend might have
misused his seal — he had felt: nay, Erlend could never
have done the like. Never in his life had Erlend done a dishonourable deed that had aught of forethought in it — or
aught of sense —

Simon flung himself about in the bed and groaned. They
had driven him half-crazy himself with all this foolishness.
It hurt him so to think that Gaute had gone for years
believing this of him — yet 'twas against reason to take
it so hardly. Even though he were fond of the boy, fond
of all Kristin's sons — they were scarce more than children
after all; did he need to care so much what they deemed
of him?

And why should such boiling wrath come on him when
he thought on the men who had laid their hands on Erlend's sword-hilt and sworn to follow their chieftain? If
so be they were such sheep as to let themselves be dazzled
by Erlend's glib tongue and his hardihood, and to deem
that man had the stuff of a chieftain in him — then 'twas
no more than was to be looked for that they should behave them like frighted sheep once the whole plan went
awry. He still felt giddy when he thought on what he had
heard at Dyfrin but now — *so* many men had been willing
to sell the peace of the land and their own welfare into
Erlend's hands — and Haftor Olafssön, and Borgar
Trondssön —! And not *one* had had the manfulness to
step forth and crave of the King that Erlend be granted an
honourable atonement and safety for his udal lands. They
were so many that, had they but stood together, it had
been no hard matter to force their will through. It seemed

that amongst the gentry of Norway there was less of man's wit and of manhood than he had deemed —

Angry, too, he was that he himself had been altogether left out of these counsels. Not that they could have got *him* to join with them in such a senseless complot. But because both Erlend and Gyrd had gone behind his back and kept him in the dark — Was he not every whit as much a noble as any of the rest, and did he not count more than a little in the country-side where folk knew him — ?

In a fashion he owned that Gyrd was right. So as Erlend had made wreck of his leadership, the men could not crave, with reason, that his fellows in the plot should come forth and own themselves leagued with him. Simon knew that, had he found Gyrd alone, he had not come to part from his brothers in this wise. But there lay yonder Sir Ulf, with his long legs stretched out before him, discoursing on Erlend's lack of wit — now, after the fray! And then Gudmund chimed in. Neither Gyrd nor he himself had ever before suffered their youngest brother to gainsay them in aught. But since he had wedded with the priest's leman — his own leman thereafter — the boy had grown so puffed up and self-glorious — as Simon sat there he soon grew wild at the very sight of him — he prated so pertly, and his round, red face looked so like a child's back-side, that Simon's hands itched to smack it — In the end he had scarce known himself what he said to the three men.

— So now, 'twas come to a breach betwixt him and his brothers. He felt as though he must bleed to death when he thought on it — as though bonds of flesh and blood had been torn asunder. It had made him poor. Bare is brotherless back —

But whether 'twere so or so, in the midst of their angry broil he had understood, of a sudden — he himself knew not how — that Gyrd's numbed, half-hearted bearing came not alone from his sore need of a little peace at home. He had seen in a flash that Gyrd loved Helga still; 'twas this that made his brother seem so fettered and strengthless. And strangely, he understood not how, this roused him to fury against — ay, against the whole of life.

— Simon hid his face in his hands. Ay, this it was to have been good, dutiful sons. It had come easy to both Gyrd and himself to feel love for the brides their father came and said he had chosen for them. The old man had

spoken to them one evening right goodly words of counsel — so that at length they sat there, quite shamefaced,
the two of them — of marriage, and friendship and faith
'twixt honourable, clean-living wedded folk; ay, and last
of all their father had even talked of prayer and intercession and masses. 'Twas pity their father had not vouchsafed them counsel how to forget as well — when friendship is shattered, and honour dead, and faithfulness a sin
and a secret, shameful torture, and the bond has left naught
behind it save a bleeding sore that never can be healed —

After Erlend was set free, a kind of peace had fallen
upon himself — if but because a man cannot go on suffering such pain as he had suffered that time in Oslo. Either
somewhat happens — or it grows better of itself.

Glad he had not been when she moved in to Jörundgaard
with her husband and all their children, and he had to
meet them, and keep up friendship with them and the dues
of kin. But he comforted himself — so much worse had it
been when he had to dwell with her so as a man cannot
bear to live with a woman he loves, if she be not his wife
nor his blood kin. And what had befallen betwixt Erlend
and himself that night they made festival for his brother-
in-law's deliverance from prison — he made light of that:
Erlend, like enough, had not understood more than half,
and 'twas like he thought little on the matter. Erlend had
such a rare gift for forgetting. And he himself had his
manor, and his wife, who was dear to him, and his children.

He had found peace, after a fashion. 'Twas not his fault
that he loved his wife's sister. She had been his betrothed
maid once — 'twas not he who had broken his troth to her.
When first he set his heart on Kristin Lavransdatter, 'twas
but his duty, for then he deemed she was to be his wife.
That 'twas her sister he got — that was Ramborg's doing
— and her father's. Lavrans, wise man though he was, had
never bethought him to ask whether Simon had forgotten.
Howbeit he knew, not even Lavrans would he have suffered to ask *that*.

He was no good hand at forgetting. 'Twas not his doing
that it was so. And he had never said *one* word that should
have been left unsaid. He could not help it if the devil
tempted him with dreams and promptings that did wrong
to the bond of blood — of his own free will he had never
given himself up to sinful thoughts of love. And in *deeds*

he had been as a trusty brother to her and hers. That he knew himself.

At length he had come to be not ill content with his lot. So long as he knew 'twas he who had served those two yonder — Kristin and the man she had cast him off for — They had ever been forced to take succor at his hands.

Now 'twas so no longer. Kristin had staked her life and her soul's heal to save his son's life. 'Twas as though all the old wounds had burst open since he had let this be.

And since then it had come to pass that he owed Erlend his life.

— And then, in return, he had wronged him — not with his will, in his thoughts only — but yet — !

" — *et dimitte nobis debita nostra, sicut et nos dimittimus debitoribus nostris.*" 'Twas strange that the Lord had not taught us also to pray: "*sicut et nos dimittimus creditoribus nostris.*" He knew not whether it were good Latin — he had never been strong in that tongue. But he knew he could ever bring himself to forgive his debtors fairly enough. To him it seemed much harder to forgive one who had laid a load of debt upon *his* shoulders —

And now that they could call themselves quits — he and those two — he felt every ancient grudge that he had trampled underfoot these many years sprout up and quicken —

No longer could he thrust Erlend aside in his thoughts — for a witless babbler, who could neither see, nor learn, nor think, nor bear aught in mind. The other weighed now upon his spirit, just because none could know *what* Erlend saw and thought and remembered — there was no counting on him.

"Many a man wins what is meant for another, but another's lot none may win."

'Twas a true word.

He had loved his young bride. Had he got her, for sure he had been a well-contented man; most like they had come to live well together. And she would have been still as she was when first they met: gentle and pure, shrewd, so that a man might take counsel of her even in greater matters; something wilful in small things, but yielding in the main, used as she was, when in her father's hands, to let herself be led and helped and guarded. — But then this man got a hold on her — one not fit to guide himself, who never had guarded aught. He had ravaged her sweet maidenliness, broken her proud calm, torn asunder her woman's soul, and forced her to stretch to the uttermost all her powers. *She* had had to stand up for her lover, as a little bird guards its nest, with throbbing body and shrilling cries, when any draws near to its home. Her sweet, slender body had seemed to him made to be lifted aloft in a man's arms and shielded lovingly — he had seen it strained with wild resolve, and while her heart beat within her with fear and courage and lust of battle, and she fought for husband and children, as even a dove will grow fierce and fearless when she has young.

Had it been he who was her husband — had she lived fifteen winters through in the shelter of his honest goodwill — full well he knew for him too she would have stood up, if aught of mischance had come his way. With wisdom and firm will would she have stood by his side. But never would he have come to see the stony face she turned on him that night in Oslo, as she sat and told him she had been to that house and looked around within it. Never would he have heard her cry out his name in a voice of such wild despair and woe. And 'twas not the pure and honourable love of his youth that had answered in his heart. The wild craving that rose and cried out in answer to her wildness — never had he learned that aught such could harbour in his soul, had it gone with him and her as their fathers planned —

Her face as she went past him out into the night to find help for his child — she had never dared to tread that road, had she not been Erlend's wife, and long used to go on undaunted, even though her heart might shake with dread. The smile on her tear-stained face when she woke him and said the boy was calling for his father — so piercing sweet can none smile who knows not what it is to lose a fight and what to win it —

'Twas Erlend's wife he loved — as now he loved her. But then must his love be sin, and so belike there was no help for it — he must needs be unhappy — For he was so unhappy that at times he felt naught but a great wonder — that 'twas he who had come to this pass, and who could see no way out of his unhappiness.

— When, treading underfoot his own honour and all gentle breeding, he had reminded Erling Vidkunssön of things no man of honour would have whispered that he

knew aught of — he had done it, not for brothers or kinsmen, but *only* for her. Only for her sake had he brought
himself to beg of the other man as the lazars beg at church
doors in the great towns, showing their loathly sores —

He had thought — some time she shall know of it. Not
all, not how deeply he had abased himself. But when they
both were come to be old folk, he had thought he would
say to Kristin thus: I helped you as best I might, for I
minded how dear I loved you that time you were my
promised bride.

One thing there was he dared not to turn his thoughts
upon. Had Erlend said aught to Kristin? — Ay, he had
thought, some time she should hear it from his own mouth:
— I have never forgot that I loved you when we were
young. But if so it were that she knew, and that 'twas from
her husband she had learned it — nay, then he deemed he
could bear no more —

To her alone he had meant to say it — some time, long
hence. When he thought on that hour when he himself
had bewrayed it — of Erlend's stumbling upon the thing
he had deemed hidden in his most secret heart! And Ramborg knew it — though how she had seen it he could not
understand —

His own wife — and *her* husband — they knew it —

Simon cried out, a wild and choking cry, as he flung
himself suddenly on his other side in the bed —

— God help him! 'Twas his turn now to lie, stripped
naked, outraged, bleeding from torture wounds and quivering with shame —

The woman set the door ajar; from the bed Simon's hot,
dry, glittering eyes met hers: "Did you not get to sleep?
— Erlend Nakulaussön rode by even now, with other
two — belike 'twas two of his sons that rode with him."
Simon muttered some kind of answer, angry and unmean-
ing.

He would let them get well ahead. But else 'twould
soon be time he too was thinking of the homeward road —

— As soon as he was come into the hall and had taken
off his outer gear, Andres would seize his fur cap and put
it on his own head. Whilst the boy sat astride the bench
and rode to his uncle at Dyfrin, the big cap would slip

down, now upon the little nose and now back over his
bonny bright locks — But it helped him not much to try
to think on such things — God knew when the boy was
like to go a-visiting to his uncle at Dyfrin now —

And, instead, came the memory of that other son of his
— Halfrid's child. Erling — 'twas not so oft that he
thought on him. A little ashy-blue child body — the days
that Erling lived he had scarce seen him — he had to sit by
the dying mother. Had the child lived, or had it lived
longer than its mother — then had Mandvik been his own.
And then like enough he had sought a new mate there, in
the south country. Only now and again would he have
come to his estate here, north in the Dale. And so, maybe,
he would have — not *forgotten* Kristin — she had led him
too wondrous a dance for that ever to be — The devil — a
man might, sure, have leave to remember, as an adventure,
that he had been fain to fetch his bride, a high-born maid,
bred up in chaste and Christian ways, home from a bordel
and another man's bed. But then, maybe, he had not gone
on so remembering her that it racked him and took all
relish from whatsoever else of good life held for him —

Erling — he would have been fourteen winters old by
now. When in due time Andres drew so near to man's
estate, he himself would be old and laid aside —

Oh, ay, Halfrid — you were not over happy with me.
Maybe 'tis not so undeserved that things have gone with
me as they have—

And then, for sure, Erlend Nikulaussön had had to pay
for his folly with his life; and Kristin had been sitting now
at Jörundgaard, a widow —

And he himself going about, maybe, rueing that he was
a wedded man! There was naught so witless but that he
could believe it of himself now —

The gale had died down, but big, wet flakes of spring
snow still fell, as Simon rode from the tavern yard. And,
now, towards evening, the birds were beginning to pipe
and trill in the woody thickets, in despite of the falling
snow.

As a cut in the skin bursts open again at a hasty movement, a chance memory gave him pain — Not many days
ago, at his Easter feast, they — a whole troop of them —
had stood without, basking in the mid-day sun. High

above them, in a birch-tree, sat a robin, piping out into the warm, blue air. Geirmund came round the house corner, limping, dragging himself along on his staff, with one hand on his eldest son's shoulder. He looked up, stopped, and mimicked the bird. The boy, too, pursed his mouth and whistled. They could copy well-nigh every bird note. Kristin stood a little way off, amidst of some other women. Her smile was so fair as she listened —

Towards sunset the clouds thinned out in the west — rolled in golden drifts along the white fell-sides, filled glens and little dales with thick grey mist. The river had a dull gleam, as of brass — it rushed and eddied, wide and dark, round the stones in its course, and on each stone lay a little white cushion of new-fallen snow.

The wearied horses made but slow going over the heavy roads. It was milk-white night, with a full moon peering out through driving haze and clouds, when Simon rode down the steep banks of the Ula. When he was come over the bridge and out upon the flat fir tree heath, where the road ran in winter, the horses made better speed — they knew they were nearing their stalls. Simon patted Diger-bein's wet, steaming neck. He was glad, at all rates, that this journey was near an end. Ramborg, belike, was asleep long ere now.

Where the road makes a sharp turn to leave the woods, there stood a little house. He was right upon it, when he grew ware that some men on horseback had drawn rein before the door. He heard Erlend's voice cry:

"Then 'tis sure you will come the first day after holy-day — I may tell my wife so — ?"

Simon shouted a greeting. 'Twould seem too out of the way not to stay and ride on in their company; but he bade Sigurd go on ahead. Then he rode up to the others: they were Naakkve and Gaute. Erlend came forth from the house door at the same moment.

He greeted them again — the three gave back his greeting somewhat uneasily. He could see their faces but dimly in the glimmering light — it seemed to Simon they looked at him doubtfully — seemed at once curious and resentful. So he said straight out:

"I come from Dyfrin, brother-in-law."

"Ay, I heard tell you were gone south." Erlend stood

with his hand on the saddle-bow, looking down. "You have ridden hard, 'twould seem," he added, as if to break an irksome silence.

"Nay, stay a little," said Simon to the youths, as they made to ride on. "You, too, must hearken to this. 'Twas my brother's seal you saw on the letter, Gaute. And I wot it must seem to you they kept their troth but ill with your father, he and the other knights who set their seals to that letter to Prince Haakon your father was to bear to Denmark — "

The boys looked down in silence. Erlend spoke:

"One thing, I trow, you thought not on, Simon, when you rode to tryst with your brother. Dearly bought I safety for Gyrd and those others — with all I owned, save the name of a trusty man that held to his word. Now Gyrd Darre deems, for sure, not even that name is left to me — "

Simon bowed his head, abashed. Of that he had not thought.

"Why said you not this to me, Erlend, when I told you I would ride to Dyfrin — ?"

"You must sure have seen yourself I was so mad with rage, when I rode from your manor, there was neither thought nor counsel in me — "

"I was scarce in my full wits either, Erlend — "

"No, but meseems you might have had time to bethink you on yonder long road. Nor could I well have prayed you give up your intent to question your brother, without bewraying things I had sworn a dear oath to keep hidden — "

Simon said naught for a little — at first it seemed to him the other was in the right of it. But then it struck him — nay, now was Erlend wrong-headed as could be. Should he have sat still and suffered Kristin and the boys to think such evil of him? He asked this something hotly.

"I have never breathed a word of this, kinsman, either to mother or to my brothers," said Gaute, turning his comely, bright face to Simon.

"Ay, but none the less they learnt of it in the end," answered he, stubbornly. "I trow, after all that befell yonder day at my house, great need there was that we should clear the matter. And I see not how it could come upon your

father so unawares — much more than a child you are
not yet, my Gaute, and right young were you when you
were made a sharer in these — secret counsels."

"My own son I sure might well deem I could trust,"
cried Erlend hotly. "And choice I had none, when I
must save the letter. 'Twas either give it to Gaute or let
the Warden find it —"

It seemed to Simon bootless to speak more of the matter.
But he could not refrain him from saying:

"Little did I like it when I learned what the boy had
gone about believing of me these four years. I have ever
set much by you, Gaute."

The boy urged his horse forward a few paces; he held
out his hand, and Simon saw his face grew darker, as
though he flushed:

"You must forgive me, Simon!"

Simon gripped the boy's hand. At times Gaute's face
could be so like his mother's father that it moved Simon
strangely. He was something bow-legged and low of
stature when afoot, but he was a rarely good rider, and on
horseback he was as fair a sprig of young manhood as
could gladden a father's eyes.

Now they rode northwards, all four, the boys ahead.
When they were out of ear-shot, Simon said:

"Understand you, Erlend — I trow you cannot rightly
blame me for seeking out my brother and praying him to
tell me truth about this matter. But I wot you had cause
for anger against me, you and Kristin. For as soon as these"
— he groped for words — "these strange tidings came
out — what Gaute said of my seal — I cannot deny I
thought — I understand your believing that I thought what
I should have had wit to know was unthinkable. So I say
not but you have reason to be wroth — " he said again.

The horses plashed through the snow-slush. 'Twas a little while till Erlend answered, and then his voice sounded
most meek and mild:

"I know not, after all, what else you could have thought.
'Twas sure the easiest thing to think — "

"Ah no, I should have known well 'twas impossible,"
Simon broke in, sorely. A little after he asked:

"Did you deem that I knew of this — of my brother?
That 'twas for their sake I tried to help you?"

"Nay," said Erlend, wonderingly. "I knew for sure

that you could not know it. That *I* had said naught, I knew. And that your brother had not let slip aught, that I deemed I could be full sure of." He laughed a little. Then he grew grave. "I know well," said he, softly, "you did it for our father-in-law's sake — and because you are good —"

Simon rode on for a time, and said no word.

"You were bitter wroth, I can conceive?" he asked in a little.

"Oh! — When I got time to bethink me — I see not that there was any other meaning you could put on it —"

"And Kristin?" asked Simon, still lower.

"Ay, she —!" Erlend laughed as before. "You know well she brooks not that any point a finger at me — save her own self. She deems, I trow, she can see to that well enough herself. 'Tis the same with our children. God have mercy on me if I but speak a word of blame to them! But, trust me, I set her right —"

"You did that — ?"

"Ay — when time and season serve I surely shall make her understand. You know well Kristin is such an one that, when she has bethought her, she will remember you have shown us such trusty friendship that —"

Simon felt his heart quiver with a tingling wrath. He felt 'twas more than he could bear — the other seemed to think that now they might cast this matter quite from their thoughts. His face, in the pale moonlight, showed utterly at peace. Simon's voice shook with the hurry of his spirits as he spoke again:

"Forgive me, Erlend, I understand not how I could believe —"

"You hear," the other broke in, a little impatiently, "that I understand. Methinks it had been hard for you to believe otherwise —"

"Would to God those two witless young ones had never spoken," said Simon, vehemently.

"Ay — Gaute has never had such a beating in his life before — And to think it all came of bickering over their far-off forbears — Reidar Birkebein and King Skule and Bishop Nikolas." Erlend shook his head. "But come, brother-in-law, think no more on it — 'twere best we forget all this soon as we can —"

"I *cannot!*"

"Nay, Simon!" This came by way of protest, gentle and wondering. " 'Tis not worth taking so hardly — !"

"I *cannot*, hear you! I am not so good a man as you!"

Erlend looked at him in a maze:

"Now know I not what you mean."

"I am not so good a man as you! I cannot forgive so easily them that I have wronged."

"I know not what you mean," said the other, as before.

"I mean — " Simon's face was drawn and marred with pain and passion; he spoke low, as though he crushed down a longing to cry aloud. "I mean — I have heard you speak fair words of Sigurd, the Lagmand at Steigen, the old man whose wife you stole from him. I have seen and known that you loved Lavrans with all a son's love. And never have I marked that you bore me grudge for that you — lured from me my promised maid — I am not so high-minded as you deem, Erlend — I am not so high-minded as you — I — *I* bear a grudge to the man whom *I* have wronged — "

His cheeks palely flecked with passion, he stared into the other's eyes. Erlend had listened to him with mouth half open.

"This had I never dreamed on till this hour! Do you *hate* me, Simon?" he whispered, astounded.

"Seems it not to you that I have cause — ?"

Without knowing it, both men had stayed their horses. They sat gazing into each other's faces: Simon's little eyes glittered like steel. In the hazy-white light of the night he saw that Erlend's thin features worked, as though something stirred within him — an awakening — He looked up from under half-closed eyelids, biting his quivering under-lip.

"I cannot bear to meet you any more!"

"Man! — 'Tis twenty years agone," Erlend burst out, in amaze.

"Ay. Deem you not that — she — is worth remembering for twenty years?"

Erlend drew himself upright in his saddle — met Simon's gaze, full and steadfastly. The moonlight kindled a blue-green spark within his great light eyes.

"Yes. God — God bless her!"

So he sat for a moment. Then he set spurs to his horse

and dashed forward along the miry track, splashing the water high behind him. Simon held Digerbein back — he was well-nigh thrown, so suddenly did he rein in the horse. He tarried there, on the edge of the woods, struggling with the impatient beast, for so long as he could hear the hoof-strokes in the slush.

Remorse had rushed over him in the moment he had said it. Remorse, and shame — as though he had struck the most defenceless of creatures — a child — or a fine and gentle, reasonless beast — in senseless wrath. His hate seemed like a shivered lance — he himself seemed shivered by the clash with this man's witless simplicity — so little understanding had this bird of ill omen, Erlend Nikulaussön, 'twas as though he must be held both helpless and innocent —

He cursed and swore under his breath as he rode on. Innocent — the fellow was long past two score years — 'twas high time he learnt to suffer being spoken to, man to man. If Simon had wounded himself — ay, devil take him if 'twas not a cheap price to pay if he had but got a blow home on Erlend for once.

Now was he riding home to her — "God bless her," he mocked wryly. And then there would be an end to all this struggling for brotherly love — 'twixt those two there, and him and his. He need nevermore meet with Kristin Lavransdatter —

— The thought took away his breath — Yet, devil take it! why not — ? "If thine eye offend thee, pluck it out," said the priests. 'Twas for this mostly, he told himself, that he had done this thing — to escape this make-believe of brother and sister's love with Kristin — he could bear it no more —

One only wish he had now — that Ramborg might not wake when he came home.

But when he rode down between the fences, he saw a dark form in a cloak standing under the aspen trees. Her head-linen showed white.

She had been waiting there, she said, ever since Sigurd came home. The serving-women were abed, and Ramborg herself ladled out the porridge from the pot which stood against the fire to keep warm, set bacon and bread on the board, and fetched fresh-drawn ale.

"Will you not to bed now, Ramborg?" asked the man, while he ate.

Ramborg answered not. She went over to her loom and began to thread the little many-coloured balls in and out of the warp. She had set up a tapestry before Yule, but she was not come far with it yet.

"Erlend rode northwards, a while ago," she said; as she stood with her back to him. "I deemed, from what Sigurd said, you were coming with him?"

"No — it fell not out so — "

"Erlend longed more for home and bed than you?" She laughed a little. As she got no answer, she said again: "He, I trow, ever longs to come home to Kristin, when he has had an errand from home — "

Simon kept silence for a good while ere he answered: "Erlend and I parted not as friends." Ramborg turned sharp round — he told her, then, what he had heard at Dyfrin, and of the first part of his talk with Erlend and his sons.

"Methinks 'tis scarce reason to fall at odds over this — when you have been able to keep friends till now."

"Maybe — yet so it fell out. But 'twere too long to tell the whole tale to-night."

Ramborg turned to her loom, and busied herself with the work again.

"Simon," she asked, all at once, "mind you a saga Sira Eirik read to us once upon a time — out of the Bible — of a young maid named Abishag the Shunammite?"

"No."

"What time King David grew old, and his strength and manhood began to fail," began the wife, but Simon broke in:

"My Ramborg, the night is too far spent; 'tis no time to begin telling sagas now. — And I mind, too, now, how 'twas with her you named — "

Ramborg beat the weft up with the reed; she held her peace for a little. Then she spoke again:

"Mind you that saga, then, that my father could tell — of Tristan the comely, and Isolde the fair, and Isolde the dark?"

"Ay, that one I mind." Simon pushed the dish from him, rubbed the back of his hand across his mouth, and stood up. He came over to the fire-place; with one foot up on the edge, elbow on knee and chin in hand, he stood looking into the fire that was burning itself out in the stone-built cavern. From the corner by the loom came Ramborg's voice, quavering and ready to break:

"I thought always, when I heard those sagas, that such men as King David and Sir Tristan — it seemed foolish — and cruel — that they loved not the young brides who brought them their maidenhood and their heart's love in all gentleness and seemly purity, more than suchlike women as the Lady Bath-sheba or yonder Isolde the fair, who had made waste of themselves in other men's arms. Methought had I been a man, I had not been so prideless — or so heartless" — she stopped, overcome. "Meseemed 'twas the hardest of fates — the lot they had; Abishag and that poor Isolde of Bretland — " She turned, vehemently, came across the room, and stood before her husband.

"What ails you, Ramborg?" Simon spoke low and with an ill grace. "I know not what you mean by this — "

"Yes, you know," said she, vehemently. "You yourself are like yonder Tristan — "

"That can I scarce trow," he tried to laugh, "that I am like — Tristan the fair — And the two women you named — if I mind me aright, they lived and died spotless maids, untouched of their husbands — " He looked over at his wife: her little, three-cornered face was white, and she bit her lips.

Simon put his foot to the ground, stood upright, and laid both hands upon her shoulders:

"My Ramborg, have we not had two children, you and I?" he said softly.

She answered not.

"I have striven to show you I was thankful to you for that gift. I deemed myself — I have tried to be a good husband to you — "

She still said naught, and, letting fall his hands, he went and sat him down upon the bench. Ramborg followed, stood before him, looking down upon her husband: the broad thighs, in wet, muddied breeches, the unwieldy body, the heavy, red-brown face. She pursed up her lips in distaste:

"Ill-favoured, too, have you grown with the years, Simon."

"Ay, I have never deemed myself aught of a comely man," he said, soberly.

"And am I not young and fair—" She set her on his lap; the tears started from her eyes, as she clasped his head in both her hands: "Simon—look on me—wherefore can you not repay me for this?—never have I wished that any should have me save you—methought, even from the time I was a little maid, my husband should be such an one as you were—Mind you how you led us both by the hand, Ulvhild and me—? you were to go with father to the west paddock to look upon his foals—you bore her over the beck, and father would have taken me up, but I screamed out that you must bear me too. Mind you?"

Simon nodded. He remembered well he had been much taken up with Ulvhild, the lovely crippled child had seemed to him so pitiful. Of the youngest he had had no memory, save that one there was younger than Ulvhild.

"You had the goodliest hair—" She ran her fingers through the thick-waved, light-brown forelock that hung somewhat down over her husband's brow. "Not one grey hair have you yet in your head—Erlend's hair will soon be as much white as black.—And I liked so well that there came those deep dimples in your cheeks when you smiled —and that you were so merry of speech—"

"Ay, like enough I was something better-favoured then than I am now—"

"No," she whispered vehemently—"not when you look kindly on me—Mind you the first time I slept in your arms?

"—I lay abed, crying with the toothache—father and mother had gone asleep; 'twas dark in the loft-room, but you came over to the bench where we lay, Ulvhild and I, and asked why I wept. You bade me to be quiet and not wake the others, and then you took me up into your arms, and then you lit the taper and cut a splint and pricked around the bad tooth till blood came. Then you said a blessing over the splint, and then I was soon well again, and I got leave to sleep in your bed and you held me in your arm—"

Simon laid his hand upon her head and pressed it in to his shoulder. Now she spoke of it, he remembered: 'twas that time he was at Jörundgaard and had told Lavrans that the bond 'twixt him and Kristin had best be loosed again.

He had slept little that night — and now he remembered that he had got up once and done somewhat to help little Ramborg, who lay whimpering with the toothache —

"Have I so borne me to you at any time, my Ramborg — that you deem you have a right to say I love you not — ?"

"Simon — seems it not to you that I deserve you should love me more than Kristin? Wicked and false she was to you — I have followed you about like a little lap-dog all these years — "

Simon lifted her gently down from his lap, stood up, and took her hands in his:

"Speak no more of your sister now, Ramborg — in that wise. I wonder if you understand yourself what you say. Think you not that I fear God — can you believe of me that I could be so dreadless of shame and the worst of sins, or that I should not remember my children and all my kin and friends? I am your husband, Ramborg — forget it not, and speak not so to me — "

"I know you have not broken God's law, or cast away faith and honour — "

"Never have I spoken one word to your sister or touched her with my hand in other wise than I can answer for on the judgment-day — God and Saint Simon, the apostle, are my witness — "

Ramborg nodded silently.

"Think you your sister would have met me as she has done all these years, if she thought as you do, that I loved her with sinful lust? Nay, then you know not Kristin."

"Oh, she has never so much as thought whether any other man save Erlend bears love to her. It scarce comes to her mind that we others are flesh and blood — "

"Ay, belike you speak truly there, Ramborg," said Simon calmly. "But then sure you can understand for yourself how witless 'tis for you to plague me with jealousy."

Ramborg drew away her hands.

"I meant it not so either, Simon. But never have you cared for me as you cared for her. She is for ever in your thought even yet — of me you think but seldom, when you see me not."

" 'Tis not my doing, Ramborg, that a man's heart is so made that what is writ thereon when 'tis young and fresh

stands more deeply graven than all the runes cut afterward — "

"Have you never heard the word that says: a man's heart
is the first thing that quickens in his mother's womb, and
the last thing in him to die?" said Ramborg, softly.

"Nay — Is there a word that says the like — ? Ay, and
it may well be true, too." He stroked her white cheek
lightly. "But if we are to sleep this night, we must to bed
now," he said, wearily.

Ramborg slept after a while, and Simon stole his arm
from under her neck, moved him gently towards the outer
bed-edge and drew the fur coverlid right up under his
chin. His shirt, at the shoulder, was wet through with her
tears. He was bitterly heartsore for his wife — and he
understood too, with a new desperation, that he could no
longer make shift to live with her by taking her as though
she were a blind, unlessoned child. Now must he make up
his mind that Ramborg was a grown woman.

The window-pane was grey already with dawn — the
May night was nigh its end. He was deathly weary —
and to-morrow was mass-day. Go to church to-morrow
he would not — though sure enough he had great need of
it. He had promised Lavrans once, never would he miss
a mass without full good cause — but, he thought bitterly,
it had not helped him overmuch that he had kept his word
all these years. To-morrow he would not ride to mass —

THE CROSS

PART TWO

DEBTORS

I*

KRISTIN learned but in part what had befallen 'twixt Erlend and Simon. Her husband told her and Björgulf what Simon had said of his journey to Dyfrin, and that, afterwards, they had changed high words, and in the end had parted unfriends. "More I cannot tell you of this matter."

Erlend was a little pale, his face set and resolved. She had seen it thus some few times before, in the years she had been wedded to him. And she knew 'twas a sign that these were matters he would say no more on.

She had never liked it when Erlend had met her questions with this look. God knew she craved not to be held for more than a simple woman; she had liefer had to answer for naught but her children and her housekeeping. But she had been driven to put her hand to so much that seemed to her fitter for a man to deal with — and Erlend, 'twas clear, had deemed it fitting that he should let such things rest upon her shoulders. And thus it beseemed him ill to carry things so high and answer so curtly, when she sought to know the rights of doings of his own which touched the welfare of them all.

She took this unfriendship 'twixt Erlend and Simon Darre hardly. Ramborg was her only sister. And when she thought on it, that now Simon would come among them no more, she understood fully, for the first time, how fond she had come to be of this man and how much of thanks she owed him — in the troublous lot that was hers she had had a sure stay in his trusty friendship.

And she knew now that, all over the country-side, the folk would have a new titbit of gossip — that yonder Jörundgaard people had broken with Simon of Formo too. Simon and Ramborg were liked and held in esteem by every soul. And for the most part she herself, her

---

* For explanation of the title of Part II, see Note 2.

husband, and her sons were looked on with distrust and misliking — that she had known for long. Now would they be left quite unfriended —

Kristin felt as though she must sink into the ground with sorrow and shame the first Sunday when she came on to the church-green and saw Simon standing there, a little way off, in a cluster of yeomen. He bowed his head in greeting to her and hers, but 'twas the first time he came not forward to shake hands and chat with them.

But Ramborg went up to her sister and took her hand:

" 'Tis ill, sister, that our husbands have fallen out — but I see not that you and I need fall out for that — " She raised herself upon her toes and kissed Kristin, so that the folk in the churchyard could see it. But Kristin knew not how it was — she seemed to feel within her that, none the less, Ramborg was not greatly grieved. Never had she brought herself to like Erlend — God knew whether she had not set her husband against him, knowingly or unknowingly —

Yet thereafter Ramborg ever came and greeted her sister when they met at the church. Ulvhild called out aloud to know wherefore her aunt came not south to them any more; then she ran across to Erlend, and clung about him and his eldest sons. Arngjerd, standing quietly by her stepmother's side, took Kristin by the hand and looked troubled. Simon and Erlend and his sons held aloof from each other most diligently.

Kristin missed her sister's children sorely too. She had grown fond of the two young maids. And one day, when Ramborg had brought her son to mass, and Kristin, after worship, was kissing Andres, she fell a-weeping. This weak, sickly boy had grown so dear to her — and she could not but feel, now that she had no truly little children any more, 'twas in a way a comfort to her to care for this little sister's-son at Formo and spoil him, when his parents brought him with them to Jörundgaard.

From Gaute she heard somewhat more of the matter, for he told her the words that had fallen between Erlend and Simon that night they met by Skindfeld-Gudrun's cottage. The more she pondered these things, the more it seemed to her that Erlend was the most at fault. She had been wroth with Simon — so much he should sure have known of Erlend as to know that he could not have thus basely played his brother false — how strange so ever the things he might do through thoughtlessness or hot temper — and when he saw what he had brought to pass, he bore himself often most like a shy stallion that has broken loose, and goes wild with fright at what he drags behind him.

But that Erlend never could understand that, sometimes, other men must needs cross him, to guard their own welfare against the mischief he had such a rare gift for making! And that then he cared not what he said, or how he bore himself! She remembered those days when she herself yet was young and tender — time after time she had felt as though he were trampling on her heart with his reckless doings. His own brother he had cut him off from — even before Gunnulf went into the cloister, he had drawn away from them, and she had known that Erlend was to blame — so often he had given offence to his pious and worthy brother, though never had Gunnulf done Erlend aught but good, that she wist of. And now he had thrust Simon from him, and when she would have known what 'twas that had brought unfriendship between him and their only friend, he but put on a lofty mien and answered that he might not tell her —

To Naakkve he had said more, she saw well.

The mother waxed sore and uneasy in mind when she marked that Erlend and their eldest son grew silent, or turned their talk to some other matter, so soon as she came near them — and this befell not seldom.

Both Gaute and Lavrans and Munan held closer to their mother than Nikulaus ever had done, and she had always talked more with them than with him. Nevertheless it ever seemed to her that, of all the children, her first-born stood, in a way, closest to her heart. And since she was come to dwell on Jörundgaard again, the memories of the time when she bore this son under her heart, and of his birth, had grown strangely living and near. For she was made aware in many ways that, here in Sil, folks had not forgotten the sin of her youth. 'Twas almost as though they accounted her to have smirched the honour of the whole country-side of her birth when she, the daughter of the man all here looked up to as their head, had gone astray. They had not forgiven that, nor yet that she and Erlend

had added insult to his shame and sorrow when they
fooled him into giving away an erring maid with the most
stately bridal that had been held in man's memory here
in the northern Dale.

Kristin could not tell if Erlend knew that now folk
were raking these old tales up again. But if know it he
did, 'twas like he cared naught for the matter. He accounted her countrymen of the Dale naught but wadmal-
farmers and village hinds, one and all — and he taught her
sons to think the like. It seared her soul to know that these
men and women, who had thought much of her and
wished her so well in those days when they called her
Lavrans Björgulfsön's winsome daughter, and the Rose of
the Dale, now held Erlend Nikulaussön and his wife in
scorn and judged them hardly. She besought not these
folk, she wept not for that she was become a stranger
amongst them. But it hurt her sorely. And it seemed to her
that even the headlong hill-sides about the Dale, that had
sheltered and guarded her childhood, now looked down
upon her and her home in other guise — with darkling
menace and hard, stony-grey will to cow her spirit.

Once she had wept bitterly — Erlend had known of it,
and he had not long had patience with her then. When he
learned that she had gone lonely through those many
months with his child a heavy weight beneath her sad,
fearful heart, he had not taken her into his arms and comforted her with gentleness and loving words. Angered and
shame-struck had he been when he saw that now 'twould
come to light how unworthily he had dealt with Lavrans
— but he had not thought how much worse it needs must
be for her, the day when she should stand shamed before
her proud and loving father.

Nor had Erlend greeted his son with overmuch joy
when, at last, she had borne this child forth to life and the
light. In that hour, when she was delivered from her endless agony of soul and terror and torment, and saw the
ugly, shapeless burthen of her sin take life under the
priest's powerful prayers, and change to the loveliest child,
whole and without blemish — in that moment it had
seemed as though her heart melted with humble gladness,
and that even the hot, defiant blood of her body turned to
white, sweet, innocent milk. Ay, with God's help he may
grow human in time, said Erlend, as she lay there in bed

and would have had him rejoice with her over this costly treasure, that she could scarce suffer from out her arms long enough to let the women tend the child. Yet his children by Eline Ormsdatter he loved; that she had both seen and known. But when she bore Naakkve to his father and would have laid him in the man's arms, Erlend had pulled a wry face and asked what should he do with this brat who leaked both top and bottom. For long had Erlend looked askance at his eldest true-born son — could not forget that Naakkve had come into the world at an untoward time — though yet the boy was so fair and winsome and likely a child that any father might well rejoice who saw such a son growing up to fill his place.

And Naakkve had loved his father so that 'twas marvel to see it — even from the time when he was a tiny babe. He had beamed like the sun over the whole of his little comely face if his father took him between his knees for a moment and said but two words to him, or if the man let him hold his hand crossing the courtyard. Staunchly had Naakkve striven to win his father's favour in those days when Erlend liked all his other children better than this one. Björgulf had been his father's favourite while the boys were small. Then would Erlend sometimes take his little sons with him up to the knights' armoury, when he had an errand thither — all the armour and weapons not in daily use at Husaby were kept there. While the father talked and jested with Björgulf, Naakkve would sit still as a mouse on a chest — panting for very joy that he had leave to be there.

But as time went on, and, by reason of his bad sight, Björgulf could not, so well as his brothers, go abroad with Erlend, and as the boy himself grew more withdrawn and silent when with his father, all this was changed. 'Twas now well-nigh as though Erlend were a little shy of this son. Kristin wondered at times whether Björgulf blamed his father in his heart because he had wasted all their substance and had dragged down his sons' fortunes with him in his downfall — and whether Erlend knew or guessed this. Howsoever it might be, it seemed as though Björgulf alone, of all Erlend's sons, looked not up to him with blind love and with unbounded pride in calling him father.

One day the two smallest boys had marked that their

father was reading the psalter in the morning and keeping fast on bread and water. They asked why he did thus — for 'twas no fast-day. Erlend answered 'twas for his sins. Kristin knew that these days of fasting were a part of the penance laid upon Erlend for his adultery with Sunniva Olavsdatter, and that the eldest sons at least knew of this. Naakkve and Gaute seemed to think naught of it, but it chanced that she looked just then at Björgulf: the boy sat there blinking near-sightedly down into his meat-bowl and smiling to himself — so had Kristin seen Gunnulf smile one time and another when Erlend got on the high horse. The mother liked not the sight —

Now 'twas Naakkve whom Erlend would ever have by him. And the lad lived as though all the roots of his being were knit to his father. Naakkve served his father as a young page his lord and chieftain: he would have none but himself care for his father's horse, and keep his riding-gear and arms in good order; he buckled the spurs on Erlend's feet, and bore hat and cloak to him when he would go forth. He filled his father's beaker and carved for him at board, where he sat on the bench to the right of Erlend's seat. Erlend laughed a little at the lad's *kurteisi*, but he liked it well, and more and more he made Naakkve all his own.

Kristin saw that now he had quite forgot how she had striven and prayed to win from him a little fatherly love for this child. And Naakkve had forgot the time when he was young and little, and 'twas to her he came to seek comfort for all ills, and counsel in all his troubles. To his mother he had ever been a loving son, and this he was still in a fashion, but she felt that the older the boy grew the farther he drifted from her and all her concerns. Of all she had upon her hands Naakkve took no thought at all. He was never loth to do her will when she set him to any task, but he was strangely wooden-handed and clumsy at all that might be called farm work — he did it lifelessly and listlessly, and never could bring aught to an end. He was not unlike his dead half-brother, Orm Erlendssön, in many ways, his mother thought — was like him, too, in looks. But Naakkve was strong and sound, lusty in the dance and in all sports, a good marksman with the bow, and passably skilled, too, in the use of other weapons, a

good rider and a ski-runner of the best. Kristin spoke of
this one day with Ulf Haldorssön, Naakkve's foster-father.
Ulf said:

"None has lost more through Erlend's folly than this
lad. Better stuff than Naakkve for a knight and a great
noble grows not in Norway in these days."

But his mother saw that Naakkve never thought of all he
had been bereft of by his father's fault.

At this time there was again great unrest in Norway, and
rumours flew northward over the parishes of the Dale,
some likely enough and some wholly unbelievable. The
great lords south and west in the realm and throughout
the Uplands were so miscontent with King Magnus' rule —
'twas said they had openly threatened to take to arms, to
rouse the commons, and bring Sir Magnus Eiriksson to
govern after their will and counsel, or else take for king
his mother's sister's son, the young Jon Haftorssön of
Sudrheim — his mother, the Lady Agnes, was daughter to
King Haakon Haalegg, of blessed memory. Of Jon himself but little was heard, but 'twas said his brother, Sigurd,
was the head and font of the whole emprise, and Bjarne,
Erling Vidkunssön's young son, was of their counsels —
folk told how Sigurd had sworn, if Jon became king, he
should take one of Bjarne's sisters to his queen, for the
maidens at Giske, too, were of the race of the old Norse
kings. Sir Ivar Ogmundssön, who before had been King
Magnus' stoutest stay, 'twas said had now gone over to the
party of these young nobles, and many others of the land's
richest and best-born men as well — of Erling Vidkunssön himself and the Bishop of Björgvin, folk said that
they were pushing behind.

Kristin hearkened but little to these rumours; bitterly
she thought: they were but small folk now, the matters
of the realm touched them not. Yet, in the autumn gone
by, she had spoken somewhat of them with Simon Andressön, and she knew, too, that he had talked of them with
Erlend. But she had seen that Simon was not fain to talk
of these things — in part, maybe, because he liked not
that his brothers should mix themselves in such perilous
doings; and Gyrd at least, she knew, was led by the nose
by his wife's kinsfolk. But he was fearful too that talk of
suchlike things might discomfort Erlend, since he was

born to sit among the men who met in counsel for Norway's realm, and now mischance had barred him out from the fellowship of his peers.

But Kristin knew that Erlend spoke of these things with his sons. And one day she heard Naakkve say:

"But should these lords make good their right against King Magnus, they could not be so base, father, for sure, as not to take up your cause and force the King to mend the wrong he did you."

Erlend laughed; but his son went on:

"You first showed these lords the way, and brought to men's minds that 'twas not the wont of Norway's chiefs of old to sit still and brook oppression by their kings. It cost you your udal lands and fiefs — the men who had leagued them with you came off without a scratch — you alone paid for them all — "

"Ay, then have they the better reason to forget me, I trow," said Erlend laughing. "And Husaby hath the archbishopric got in pledge. I trow the lords of the council will scarce pester King Magnus, poor moneyless wretch, to redeem it — "

"The King is your kinsman, and so is Sigurd Haftorssön and most of these men," answered Naakkve vehemently. "How, without shame, can they forsake that man of all Norway's nobles who bore his shield with honour to the northern Marches, and purged Finland and the Gandvik coast of the King's foes and God's — caitiffs would they be — "

Erlend whistled.

"Son — one thing can I tell you. I know not how the Haftorssöns' emprise will fare, but I wager my neck they will not dare show Sir Magnus a naked Norse sword. Talk and bargaining I trow there will be, but not a bolt shot. And these gentry will never put on harness in my cause, for they know me, and know well that I am not so qualmish at sight of cold steel as be some others —

" — Kinsmen, say you — ay, they are your third cousins, both Magnus and the Haftorssöns. I remember them from the time I served in King Haakon's court — 'twas well for your kinswoman, the Lady Agnes, that she was daughter of the King — else had she, belike, been fain to go upon the wharves and gut fish, if some such lady as your mother had not hired her to help in the byre out of pious charity.

More times than one have I dried these Haftorssöns about
the snout, when they were to be brought before their
mother's father, and they came running into the hall as
snotty-nosed as they crept off their mother's lap — and if
I caught them a buffet, in cousinly kindness, to teach them
somewhat of manners, they shrieked like stuck pigs. I hear
it said these oafs of Sudrheim have been made men of at
last. But to look for a kinsman's help from that side — as
well shear the sow for wool — "

Afterwards Kristin said to Erlend:

"Naakkve is so young, dear my husband — deem you not
'tis unwise to talk so freely with him on such matters?"

"And you are so mild of speech, dear my wife," said
Erlend, smiling, "that I see well you would take me to
task — When I was of Naakkve's age, I fared north to
Vargöy the first time. Had Lady Ingebjörg been loyal and
true to me," he burst out hotly, "then had I sent her
Naakkve and Gaute to serve her — yonder in Denmark
'tis like there had been advancement for two mettlesome
blades with warm blood in their veins — "

"I thought not," said Kristin, bitterly, "the time I bore
you these children, that our sons should seek their bread
in a foreign land."

"You know I thought not so either," said Erlend. "But
man proposeth, and God disposeth — "

So Kristin said to herself, 'twas not alone that it hurt
her heart to mark that Erlend, and her sons, now they
were growing up, bore them as though their affairs were
beyond a woman's kenning. She was afraid, too, of Erlend's reckless tongue — never did he call to mind that his
sons were little more than children.

This, too, there was, that, young as the sons were —
Nikulaus was now seventeen winters old, Björgulf would
be sixteen, and Gaute fifteen at harvest-time — these three
already had a way with women that made their mother
uneasy.

True it was, naught had befallen that she could point to.
They did not run after women-folk; they were never gross
of tongue or foul-mouthed, and liked it little when the serv-
ing-carls offered to crack ribald jests or bring lewd tales to
the manor. But Erlend, too, in such matters had ever borne
him right seemly and modestly — she had seen him

abashed at talk that made both her father and Simon laugh heartily. But at such times she had felt, dimly, that the others laughed as peasants laugh at tales of the devil's dull-wittedness — while learned men, who know better his wicked wiles, care little for such jesting.

And Erlend, too, might have claimed to be guiltless of the sin of running after women — only folk who knew not the man could think him loose, in the way of luring women to him and leading them astray of set purpose. She never denied to herself that Erlend had had his will with her without use of love-philtres, without force or guile. And as for the two wedded women he had sinned with, she was sure that 'twas not Erlend had been the tempter. But, when light women met him half-way with bold and luring laughter, she had seen that he grew curious as a young kid — a drift of secret, heedless lightness would seem to breathe from the whole man.

And, with dread, she deemed she saw the Erlendssöns were like to their father in this — they ever forgot to think, before doing aught, of the judgment of other folk — though afterward they took to heart keenly what was said. And, when women met them with smiles and on-coming, they grew not abashed or shy and sullen, like most lads of their age — they smiled back, chatted, and bore them as easily as freely as had they been to the King's court and learned a courtier's ways. Kristin grew fearful lest they should be drawn into trouble through sheer simplicity — to their mother, rich housewives and their daughters, as well as poor serving-women, seemed all too forthcoming in their bearing towards these fair youths. — But they would grow hot with wrath, like other young men, if afterward any rallied them about a woman. Frida Styrkaarsdatter in especial did this often — she was a fool in grain, old as she was, not many years younger than the mistress herself; and she had had two bastard children — for the last she had even been hard put to it to find a father. But Kristin had held a shielding hand over the poor creature; because she had fostered Björgulf and Skule with care and love, the mistress was long-suffering with the woman — though it vexed her that the old creature should ever prate to the boys of young maids.

Kristin thought now, 'twere best if she could get her sons wedded at a young age. But she knew 'twould not be easy — the men whose daughters might be equal matches for Naakkve and Björgulf in birth and blood would deem that her sons were not rich enough. And the King's enmity, and the judgment their father had brought down upon himself, would stand in the way if the lads should try to better their lot in the service of great lords. With bitterness she thought of the times when Erlend and Erling Vidkunssön had talked of a match 'twixt Nikulaus and one of the High Steward's daughters.

She knew, indeed, of one growing maid and another amongst the dales that would be a fitting match — rich and of good kindred, though their forbears, for the space of some lives back, had held themselves without the service of the court, and stayed at home in their own country. But she could not brook the thought that she and Erlend might get no for an answer if they made suit to these great landowners. Here Simon Darre might have been the best of spokesmen — and now had Erlend bereft them of this helper.

To the service of the Church she deemed none of her sons had a bent — unless 'twere Gaute or Lavrans. But Lavrans was still so young. And of all her sons Gaute was the only one whose help on the farm was of some avail to her.

Storm and snow had wrought havoc with the fences this year, and the snow-fall in the days about spring Holy Cross Mass* had hindered the work, so that the folk were hard driven to get through in time. Therefore, one day, Kristin sent off Naakkve and Björgulf to mend the fencing round a field that lay up nigh to the highway.

In the afternoon their mother went up to see how it fared with the lads at this unwonted work. Björgulf was working on the farm-road fence — she stopped a while and spoke with him. Then she went on northward. Soon she caught signs of Naakkve leaning over the fence talking with a woman on horseback who had stopped at the road's edge close by the paling. He fondled the horse, then he caught the girl by the ankle, and presently he moved his hand a little upward, as though heedlessly.

The young maid saw the lady first; she reddened and said

---

* 3rd May.

somwhat to Naakkve. He drew away his hand quickly, and looked something dashed. The girl would have ridden on, but Kristin called out a greeting; afterwards she spoke a little with the maid, and asked after her kinswoman — the girl was sister's daughter to the mistress of Ulvsvoldene, and lately come a-visiting there. Kristin made as though she had seen naught, and talked a little with Naakkve of the fencing after the maid was gone.

Not long after, it chanced that Kristin was at Ulvsvoldene for the space of two weeks; the woman there was in the straw, and, after the child was born, lay gravely sick; Kristin was there as her neighbour, and one who was deemed the most skilled leech-woman in the parish. In this time Naakkve came often over with messages and errands to his mother, and this girl, Eyvor Haakonsdatter, found means always to meet him and talk with him. Kristin liked this little — she had no liking for the maid, nor could she see that Eyvor was fair, as she heard most men deemed. She was glad, the day she learned that Eyvor was gone home again to Raumsdal.

Yet she deemed not that Naakkve had cared aught for Eyvor; the more so when she heard Frida prating of the daughter of the house at Loptsgaard, Aasta Audunsdatter, and teasing Naakkve about her.

Kristin was in the brew-house one day, boiling a juniper brew, and she heard Frida's tongue busy again with this. Naakkve was with Gaute and his father without in the back courtyard; they were at work on a boat they meant to have for the fishing on the lake up in the fells — Erlend was a not unskillful boat-builder. Naakkve waxed wroth, but now Gaute joined in the teasing — Aasta would be a fitting match, he said —

"Ask for her yourself, if you deem so," said his brother, hotly.

"Nay, I will have none of her," answered Gaute, "for I have heard that red hair and fir woods thrive on barren ground — but I wot well you have a leaning to red hair — "

"Ay, but that word holds not for women neither, my son," said Erlend, laughing. "Red-haired wives are wont to be white and soft of flesh — "

Frida laughed noisily, but Kristin grew angry; this seemed to her unseemly talk before such young boys. She remembered, too, that Sunniva Olavsdatter had had red hair, though her friends had called it golden. Then Gaute said:

"Be glad that I said not: I durst not, for fear of sin. On Whitsunday watch-night you sat with Aasta in the tithe-barn all the time we danced on the church-green — so sure you must like her —"

Naakkve would have flown at his brother — but just then Kristin came out. When Gaute was gone, the mother asked her other son:

"What was this that Gaute said of you and Aasta Audunsdatter?"

"Methinks, mother, that naught was said you did not hear," answered the boy — he reddened and frowned angrily.

Kristin said vexedly:

"'Tis an ill thing that you young folks cannot keep a watch-night but you must dance and frolic about between the services. 'Twas not our use when I was a maid —"

"You have said yourself, mother, that when you were young, my grandfather would often sing for them, when folk danced upon the church-green —"

"Ay, but they were not such songs, and 'twas not such wild dancing," said his mother, "and we young folks kept us in seemly wise each by our parents — we went not off in pairs to sit in barns —"

Naakkve seemed ready to make a wrathful answer, when Kristin chanced to look over at Erlend. He was smiling stealthily, while he looked with one eye along the plank he was trimming with his axe. Angry and grieved, she went back into the brew-house again.

— But she thought not a little on what she had heard. Aasta Audunsdatter was none so bad a match — there was wealth at Loptsgaard and three daughters only, but no son, and Ingebjörg, Aasta's mother, came of most worthy kindred.

That they at Jörundgaard should some day call Audun Torbergssön kinsman by marriage she had never thought. But he had had a stroke in the winter, and folk deemed not that he would live long — And the girl was well mannered and winsome in her ways, and notable in the house, by what Kristin had heard. If Naakkve truly liked the maid, 'twere not wise to set oneself against this match.

They must wait two years yet with the wedding — so young as both Aasta and Naakkve were — but she would gladly make Aasta welcome then as her son's wife.

But one fair day, in the middle of the summer, Sira Solmund's sister came in to Kristin to borrow somewhat. The women were standing outside before the storehouses saying farewell, when the priest's sister said: Nay, but Eyvor Haakonsdatter! Her father had driven her from his house, for she was with child — so now had she come back for shelter to Ulvsvoldene.

Naakkve had been an errand up in the storehouse loft — he stopped short on the lowest step. When his mother caught sight of his face, such a sickness came on her, she felt as her legs would scarce bear her up. The boy was red to the roots of his hair as he went past towards the dwelling-house.

But she saw soon from the other's gossip that things must have been so with Eyvor long ere she first came to the parish that spring. My poor, harmless boy, thought Kristin with a lightened sigh — he is shamed now because he had thought well of the girl.

A few nights later Kristin lay in her bed alone, for Erlend was gone from home a-fishing. She knew not but that both Naakkve and Gaute were with him. But she was waked by Naakkve's touching her and whispering that he must speak with her. He crept up and sat him down on the bed by the footboard:

"Mother — I have been over and spoken with that poor woman, Eyvor, this night — I knew that they lied about her — I was so sure, I had gladly taken a red-hot iron in my hand to prove she lied, yonder magpie from Romundgaard — "

His mother lay still and waited. Naakkve strove to speak steadily, but all the time his voice kept shifting up and down with the hurry of his spirits:

"She was on her way to matins the day after Yule — she went alone, and the road from their farm lies, a long stretch, through forest. There she met two men — 'twas yet dark, she knows not who they were; maybe outlawed robbers from the fells — At last she could keep them off no longer, poor weak young thing. To none durst she make her moan — when her mother and father saw her mischance, they dragged her by her hair and drove her from home with blows and curses. She wept so, mother, when she told me all this, 'twould have melted the very stones in the hill-sides." Naakkve stopped speaking suddenly and drew a long breath.

Kristin spoke of how it seemed to her a sore mischance that these villains had escaped. She hoped that God's justice would overtake them, and bring them to their due reward on the gallows-tree.

Thereupon Naakkve began to talk of Eyvor's father, how rich he was, and kin to one worthy family and another. The child Eyvor would send away to be fostered in another parish. Gudmund Darre's wife had had a bastard by a priest — and there sat Sigrid Andresdatter at Kruke, a good and honoured woman — A man must be both hard of heart and unjust to deem Eyvor an outcast, for that, sorely against her will, it had been her lot to suffer shameful mischance — she might well be fit, none the less, to be wife to a man that held honour dear —

Kristin pitied the girl and cursed the ravishers — and, in her heart, thanked and praised fortune that not for three years yet would Naakkve be of age. Gently she prayed him to bethink him that now must he walk most heedfully, not seek Eyvor in her bower late of an evening, as he had done this night, nor show himself at Ulvsvoldene save when he had an errand to the folk of the house, else he might, all unwittingly, bring it about that folk should spread abroad yet uglier gossip of the luckless young child. Ay, 'twas well enough to say that they who doubted Eyvor's word, and believed not she had come to harm blamelessly would find his arm no nerveless one — nevertheless, 'twould be an evil thing for the poor girl if there were more talk —

Three weeks later, Eyvor's father came and fetched his daughter home to her betrothal and wedding. 'Twas a good farmer's son of her own parish that was the man; at first the parents on both sides had been against the match, because they were at odds about some farm lands. In the last winter the men had made friends again, and the two young folk were to have been betrothed, but then, suddenly, Eyvor would not — she had set her fancy on another man. But, afterwards, she saw it might well be something late to throw away her first lover. None the less

she went to be with her mother's sister in Sil, deeming, belike, that here she would find help to hide her trouble, for
now she was set upon having this new man. But when
Hillebjörg at Ulvsvoldene saw how it was with the girl,
she sent her back to her parents. That her father had flown
in a fury and had beaten his daughter once and again, and
that she had fled hither once more, was true enough. But
now had he come to an accord with the first suitor — and
now Eyvor must put up with him, little as she might like it.

Kristin saw that Naakkve took this hardly. For many
days he went about scarce speaking a word, and his mother
had such pity of him she scarce dared look his way — for if
he met his mother's eye, he turned so red and looked so
abashed that it cut Kristin to the heart.

When the serving-folk at Jörundgaard would have gossiped of these doings, the mistress bade them, sharply, to
hold their tongues — she would not have that dirty matter
or that wretched woman named in her house. Frida marvelled greatly: had she not many and many a time heard
Kristin Lavransdatter judge mildly and help with bounteous hands a maid who had fallen into such mischance —
Frida herself had twice found safe shelter in her mistress's
pity. But in the little she said of Eyvor Haakonsdatter she
spoke as ill of her as any woman can of another.

Erlend laughed when she told him how sadly Naakkve
had been fooled — 'twas one evening when she sat out on
the green spinning, and her husband came and stretched
himself on the grass at her side.

"No great harm has been done, I trow," said the father;
"rather seems it to me that the boy has learned a man's lesson at a cheap rate: put not your trust in women — "

"Say you so?" asked his wife; her voice shook with
smothered anger.

"Ay — " Erlend smiled. "See, of you I believed, the
time I met you first, you were so gentle a maid, you could
scarce find in your heart to bite a slice of cheese — Yielding as a silk ribbon and mild as any dove — but therein
you fooled me finely, Kristin — "

"How think you 'twould have gone with us all," said
she, "had I been so soft and gentle?"

"Nay — " Erlend took her hands, so that she was fain to
stop her work; he smiled up at her, shining with gladness.

Then he laid his head in her lap. "Nay, I knew not, my
sweet one, *how* good was the luck God gave me when he
led you into my path — Kristin!"

But, because she must ever and at all times keep herself
in check, to hide her despair at Erlend's eternal heedlessness, it would chance at times that her temper took the
upper hand when she must correct her sons: she grew
heavy of hand and hot of speech. 'Twas oftenest Ivar and
Skule that bore the brunt.

They were at the worst age now, in their thirteenth
year, and so wild and self-willed that Kristin, at her wits'
ends, thought many a time, was there any mother in Norway who had the rearing of two such ruffians. Comely
they were, like all her children, with black, silky-soft
ringletted hair, blue eyes beneath black brows, and narrow,
fine-cut faces. They were tall for their age beyond the
common, but narrow-shouldered still, with long, lean
limbs — their joints stood out like the knots of a corn-
stalk. They were so like that none outside their home knew
them one from the other, and throughout the parish folk
named them the Jörundgaard dirksmen — and 'twas not
meant as a title of honour. Simon had first given them this
nickname in jest, for that Erlend had made them each
the gift of a dirk, and these small swords they never laid
from them, save when they were in church. Kristin liked it
little that they had got the dirks, and yet less that they ever
went about with axes, spears, or bows; she feared that these
hot-headed boys might bring some mischief on themselves
with such-like things. But Erlend said, curtly, they were
so old now 'twas time they used them to bear arms.

She lived in one unending terror for these her twin sons.
When she knew not whither they were gone, the mother
wrung her hands in secret, and besought Mary Virgin and
St. Olav to lead them home again, alive and unscathed.
They climbed the fell-sides through rifts and up the face
of headlong cliffs where none before had gone; they
robbed eagles' nests, and came home with ugly, yellow-
eyed, hissing fledgelings within the bosoms of their coats;
they scrambled among the slate rocks along the Laagen,
northward in the gorge, where the river dashes from fall
to fall; once Ivar had been dragged by his stirrup and half
killed — he was trying to ride a half-broken young stal-

lion that the boys had got a saddle on, God only knows how. Errandless, for naught but prying's sake, they had ventured into the Finn's hut in the Toldstad woods — from their father they had learned some words of the Lapps' tongue, and when they greeted the old Finn witch-wife with these, she had feasted them on meat and drink, and they had stuffed them full to bursting, and that on a fast-day. And Kristin had ever held so strictly to it that when the grown folk fasted, the children must content them with little food and such-like things as they had no mind to — for to this had she been used by her parents when she was little. This time, for once in a way, Erlend, too, was stern with his sons, took and burnt the sweetmeats the Finn wife had given them to take with them, whilst he strictly forbade them ever again to go even to the edge of the forest where the Finns were. But, none the less, it tickled him to hear of the boys' adventure; and after, he would often tell Ivar and Skule tales of his doings and travels in the north, and of what he had seen there of these folks' ways, and he talked to the boys in this ugly heathenish speech of theirs.

For the rest, Erlend scarce ever chid his children, and turned it aside in jest when Kristin bewailed the twins' ways. At home on the manor they did endless mischief, though they could be useful too, when they must — unhandy, like Naakkve, they were not. But time and again, when their mother had set them some work and came to see how it fared, the tools would be lying there, and the boys standing watching their father, while he showed them how seamen made knots and suchlike —

Lavrans Björgulfsön had often been wont, when he made a cross with tar over the byre door, or on suchlike places, to paint a little with the brush round about — paint a ring outside or draw a stroke over each cross-arm. One day the twins bethought themselves to make a target of one of these old cross-marks. Kristin was beside herself with despair and wrath at such Jewish doings, but Erlend took the children's part — they were so young, one could not look that they should think on the holiness of the cross each time they saw it tarred over a byre-door or on a cow's back. Let the boys go up to the cross on the church-green, kneel before it and kiss it, and say five paternosters and fifteen aves — no need to drag Sira Solmund to the manor for this. But this time Björgulf and Naakkve stood by their mother; the priest was fetched, and he sprinkled holy water on the wall and corrected the two young sinners most sternly.

— They gave Kristin's bulls and he-goats the heads of snakes to eat, to send them horn-mad. They teased Munan because he clung still to his mother's skirts, and Gaute too — he was the one they were oftenest at odds with — for the most part the Erlendssöns held together in the goodliest brotherhood. But now and again, when they got past bearing, Gaute would give them a drubbing. To chide them in words was like talking to a wall — and, if their mother grew hot with them, they would stand, their bodies stiff, their fists clenched, scowling at her with glittering eyes from under wrinkled brows, red as fire with fury. Kristin thought on what Gunnulf had told of Erlend — he had cast his knife at his father, and lifted his hand against him more times than one while he was yet a child. So she thrashed the twins, and thrashed hard, for she thought with terror: what would come of these children of hers if they were not tamed betimes.

Simon Darre was the only one who could do aught with these two madcaps — they loved their uncle, and ever grew meek and towardly when he talked to them good humouredly and quietly. But, now that they saw him no more, their mother could not see that they missed him. Sadly Kristin thought: the heart of a child is fickle.

And secretly, in her heart, the mother knew that, in spite of all, 'twas of these two sons she was well-nigh proudest. Could she but break this ill-omened defiance and wildness, it seemed to her none of the brothers promised a fairer manhood than these two. They had good health and were strong and sound of body, were fearless, truthful, generous, kindly to all poor folk, and more times than one had they shown a readiness and swiftness in counsel that far outwent, she thought, what one could look for from such young lads.

One evening in the hay harvest Kristin had been kept late in the kitchen-house, when Munan came rushing in, shouting that the old goat-shed was afire. There were no men at home or near by — some were at the smithy hammering their scythes sharp; some had gone north to the bridge, where the young folk were wont to gather on

summer evenings. The mistress caught up a pair of buck-
ets and ran, calling to her serving-women to follow after.

The goat-shed was a little old house with a roof going
right down to the ground, and stood in the narrow way
between the court-yard and the farm-yard, against the
middle of the main stable wall and with other houses built
close to it on either side. Kristin ran into the hearth-room
penthouse and caught up a broad-axe and a fire-hook, but
when she came round the corner of the stable, she saw no
fire, but only a thick cloud of smoke pouring forth from
a hole in the goat-shed roof. Ivar sat up on the roof-ridge
hacking down at the roof, Skule and Lavrans were within
the house tearing down burning flakes from the roofing,
and trampling and stamping out the fire. Now came running Erlend, Ulf, and the men who had been at the smithy
— Munan had run on thither and given warning — and
now the fire was soon put out. But the worst mischance
might well have befallen — the evening was still and sultry,
but with a puff of wind from south ever and anon, and
had the fire once been let blaze up in the goat-shed, most
like all the houses round about the north end of the yard,
the stables, the store-houses, and the dwelling-houses themselves, had been swept away.

Ivar and Skule had been up on the stable roof — they
had trapped a hawk and had gone up to hang it from the
gable cross — when they smelt burning, and saw smoke
coming from the roof below them. Straightway they
leaped down on the roof, and, with the small axes they had
in their hands, began to hack away the smouldering turf,
while they sent off Lavrans and Munan, who were playing
near by, the one for hooks and the other to their mother.
By good fortune the laths and rafters of the roof were too
rotten to burn freely; but 'twas clear this time the twins
had saved their mother's manor, by setting to work
straightway to tear down the burning roof and wasting no
time in running first for grown folks' help.

'Twas not easy to understand how the fire had arisen, if
'twere not in this wise, that Gaute, an hour before, had
passed by that way with embers for the smithy, and he
owned that the fire-pan had not been covered — so, belike,
a spark had flown on to the tinder-dry turf roof.

But of that less was said than of the twins' and Lavrans's
readiness — at the fire-watch that Ulf set, and wherein

the whole household kept him company late into the night, while Kristin had strong ale and mead borne out to them. All three boys had burns on hands and feet — their foot-gear was so scorched it broke in bits. Young Lavrans was but nine years old, so 'twas hard for him to bear the pain with patience for long, but at the first he was the proudest of all, going about with bound-up hands and hearing all the manor-folk praise him.

That night, when they had gone to rest, Erlend pressed his wife in to him.

"Kristin mine, Kristin mine — be not so careful and troubled about your children — see you not, dear one, what metal our sons are made of? You bear you ever towards these two mettlesome lads as though you looked that their path must lie 'twixt gallows and block. Methinks now you should joy in your reward for all you have borne of pangs and pains and toils, in those years you went ever with a child beneath your belt and a child at your breast and a child upon your arm — naught would you speak of then but the little bratlings, and now, when they have grown to wit and manhood, you go about amongst them as though you were both deaf and dumb, scarce paying heed enough to answer if they speak to you. God help me, 'twould seem as though you loved them less, now you have not the cares of their childhood to plague you, and our fair, well-grown sons are joy and a blessing to you — "

Kristin did not trust herself to answer a word.

But she lay there and could not fall asleep. And towards morning she climbed over the sleeping man quietly, went on bare feet over to the peep-hole, and opened it.

The sky was cloudy grey and the air cool — far to the south, where the hills drew together and closed the Dale, a rain-shower was sweeping over the uplands. The mistress stood a while looking out — 'twas ever hot and close here in the new storehouse loft, where they slept in summer. On the breath of dampness that was in the air, the scent of hay was borne in to her, so strong and sweet. A bird here and there, out in the summer night, twittered a little in its sleep.

Kristin found her fire-steel and lit a stump of candle. She crept over to where Ivar and Skule slept on their bench bed — let the light shine upon them and felt their cheeks with the back of her hand — sure enough they had a little fever. Softly she said an Ave Maria, and made the sign of the cross over the two. Gallows and block — that Erlend could make a jest of such things — he who himself had been so near —

Lavrans moaned and murmured in his sleep. The mother stood a little, bent over the two youngest, who had their couch on a small bench cot behind the foot-board of their parents' bed. Lavrans was hot and flushed, and tossed about, but did not wake when she touched him.

Gaute lay with his milk-white arms behind his neck, in among his long flaxen-yellow hair — the bed-clothes he had thrown clean off him. Such hot blood had he, that he would ever sleep naked; and he was shining white of skin — the sun-burnt hue on face, neck, and hands stood out sharply. His mother drew the covering up above his waist.

— 'Twas hard for her to be vexed at Gaute — he was so like her father. She had said but little to him of the mischance he so nearly had brought upon them all. So clearheaded and thoughtful was this boy, she deemed full surely he would take it to heart of his own accord and not forget it.

Naakkve and Björgulf had the second of the two beds in the loft. For a long time the mother stood and let the light shine upon the two sleeping youths. Black down already shadowed their childishly soft red mouths. Naakkve's foot stuck out from under the coverlid — narrow, high of instep, deep-arched in the sole — and not over clean. And yet it seemed to the mother 'twas not long since this man's foot was so little 'twas quite hidden in her closed hand, and she had pressed it in under her breast and lifted it to her mouth, gently biting each single little round toe-bud, for they were as pink and sweet as the flower-bells on a bilberry bush.

— It might well be that she was not thankful enough for the portion and the lot God had granted her. The memory of the time before Naakkve was born, and of the visions of horror she had writhed under — might shoot at times hot as fire through her mind: *she* had been delivered, as when one awakes from dream horrors and the crushing weight of nightmare to the blessed light of day. — But other women had wakened to find the day's misery worse than the worst they had dreamed. Even now, when she saw a cripple or a misshapen creature, Kristin would grow heartsick with the memory of her own fear for her unborn child. Then would she humble herself with burning ardour before God and Holy Olav; she would throw herself into good works; she would strive to wring tears of true repentance from her eyes the while she prayed. Yet ever did she feel within her heart this unyielding discontent, and the warm glow faded, and the tears of penitence sank back into her soul as water oozes away in sand. Then she comforted herself: 'twas that she had not that gift of holiness she had one time hoped was her heritage from her father. She was hard and sinful, but like enough she was no worse than most folk, and like most folk she must lay her account with suffering, in her second home, the fervent fires that were needful to melt and cleanse her heart.

Yet, between-whiles, she longed to be another. When she looked upon the seven fair sons who sat at her board; when, on mass-day mornings, she walked up towards the church, while the bells rang out and called so sweetly to gladness and God's peace, and saw the flock of tall, well-clad young lads, her sons, go up the slope before her. She knew of no other woman who had borne so many children and never had to know what 'twas to lose one — and all were fair and healthful, without blemish in body or mind — Björgulf alone was something near-sighted. She longed to be able to forget her cares altogether, to grow gentle and thankful, to love God and fear him, as her father had done — she remembered her father had said that he who with contrite heart minds him of his sins, and bows him before the Lord's cross, never needs to bend his neck beneath this world's mischance or wrong.

Kristin blew out the light, snuffed the wick, and put the stump in its place up under the topmost wall-log. She went to the peep-hole again — already 'twas light as day without, but grey and dead — upon the lower house-roofs that she looked over, the scant, sun-burnt grass shook gently in a breath of wind; a little whispering sound ran through the leaves of the birch trees that showed over against her above the hall-house roof.

She looked at her hands, clasping the peep-hole frame. They were rough and toil-worn, her arms right up to the elbows were brown, and the muscles swollen, hard as wood. While she was still young, the children had sucked blood and milk from her till all trace of a maiden's smooth, fresh roundness had been worn from her body. Now each day's toil took away something of what was left of the comeliness that had marked her out as daughter and wife and mother of men of noble blood — the narrow white hands; the soft fair-skinned arms; the clean and tender hue of face that she had shielded from the sun so heedfully with a kerchief, and tended with cunningly brewed washes. Long ere now she had grown careless whether the sun beat straight upon her sweat-stained face and burnt it brown as any poor peasant wife's.

Her hair was all that was left to her of her maiden beauty. 'Twas thick and brown as ever, seldom though she found time to wash and tend it. The heavy, tangled plait that hung down her back had not been undone these three days.

Kristin flung it forward over her shoulder, unplaited the hair, and shook it out — it still wrapped her about like a cloak and reached below her knee. She took a comb from out her case, and, shivering a little now and again, as she sat there in her bare shift beneath the little window that stood open to the morning chill, she combed out the tangled masses heedfully.

When she had smoothed her hair and plaited it again in a firm and heavy rope, 'twas as though she felt a little better. Then she lifted Munan, sound asleep, carefully in her arms, laid him down next the wall in the great bed, and herself slipped between him and the sleeping man. She took her youngest in to her arms, laid his head to rest against her shoulder, and then she fell asleep —

She overslept next morning; when she awoke, Erlend and the lads were up. "I trow verily you suck your mother still, when no one sees," said Erlend, when he saw that Munan lay by his mother. Angered at this, the boy ran out and crept over the headpiece of one of the beams which bore the balcony — he would fain show his manhood. "Jump!" shouted Naakkve from the court-yard below; he caught his little brother in his arms, turned him upside down and flung him to Björgulf — his two grown brothers tumbled him about till he laughed and screamed.

But next day, when Munan stood weeping because a

bow-string had caught his fingers in its rebound, the twins took and wrapped him up in a coverlid, bore him thus up to his mother's bed, and stuffed into his mouth a lump of bread so huge the boy was well-nigh choked.

2

ERLEND's house-priest at Husaby had taught the three eldest sons their books. They were not over-diligent scholars, but they were apt to learn, all three, and their mother, who herself had been brought up so learnedly, watched over them, so that they learned not so very little.

And the year Björgulf and Nikulaus were at Tautra cloister with Sira Eiliv, they had sucked — so said the priest — at the breasts of Lady Knowledge with fiery zeal. The teacher there was an aged monk who, busy as a bee, had gathered learning his whole life long from all the books he could come by, Latin or Norse. Sira Eiliv was himself a lover of wisdom, but, in the years at Husaby, he had had little chance to follow his bent towards book-lore. For him the fellowship with Lector Aslak was like sæter-pasture to starved cattle. And the two young boys, who, among the monks, clung to their home-priest, followed, open-mouthed, the two men's learned talk. And brother Aslak and Sira Eiliv found delight in feeding the two young minds with the most delicious honey from the cloister's bookshelves, whereto brother Aslak himself had added many copies and excerpts from the choicest books. Soon the boys became so skilled that the monk had rarely need to speak to them in the Norse tongue, and, when their parents came to fetch them, they both could answer the priest in Latin, glibly and without many slips.

This learning the brothers had kept up since. There were many books at Jörundgaard — Lavrans had owned five; of these, 'twas true, two had gone to Ramborg at the parting of the estate, but she had never had a mind to learn to read, and Simon was not so skilled in letters that he cared to read for pleasure's sake, though he could both make out a letter and print one himself well enough. Therefore he had prayed Kristin to keep the books until his children grew bigger. Three books, which had belonged to his par-

ents, Erlend gave to Kristin some little time after they were
wed, and yet another book she had got in gift from Gunnulf Nikulaussön; he himself had had the matter of it
brought together and written down for his brother's wife
out of books on Holy Olav and his miracles, some other
sagas of the saints, and the writing the Franciscans in Oslo
had sent to the Pope concerning brother Edvin Rikards-
sön, praying that he might be canonized. And, last of all,
Naakkve had got a prayer-book of Sira Eiliv when they
parted. So Naakkve read much to his brother — he read
easily and well, with somewhat of a singing voice, just as
brother Aslak had taught him; but he liked best the Latin
books — his own prayer-book and one that had been Lavrans Björgulfsön's. Yet most of all he prized a great book,
of a passing fair script, that had come down an heirloom
in his kin from their renowned forefather, Bishop Nikulaus
Arnessön himself.

Kristin would fain have got some learning for her
younger sons, too, as was but fitting for men of their birth.
But 'twas not easy to see how this could be: Sira Eirik
was all too old, and Sira Solmund could but read from
the books he used at mass; and many things in what he read
he understood not well himself. Lavrans would now and
again of an evening find pleasure in sitting by Naakkve
and letting his brother teach him the letters on the wax
tablet — but the other three had no mind at all to win such
knowledge. One day Kristin took a Norse book and bade
Gaute see if he remembered aught of what he had learned
in his childhood of Sira Eiliv; but Gaute could not con-
trive to spell out three words, and when he came upon the
first sign standing for several letters, he shut the book up,
laughing, and said he liked not to play that game.

Now, 'twas for this reason that Sira Solmund, one evening in the late summer, came and prayed Nikulaus to
come home with him. An outland knight, who was come
from the Olav's Mass at Nidaros, had borrowed a house
at Romundgaard, but neither he nor his esquires and servants had the Norse tongue; the guide who had brought
them hither understood but a word or two of their prate;
Sira Eirik lay sick — could not Naakkve come and speak
with the knight in Latin?

Naakkve seemed nowise ill pleased to be sent for thus
to interpret, but he made as though 'twas nothing, and

went with the priest. He came home very late in the night, in high feather and not a little drunken — 'twas wine he had been given; the stranger knight had store of it with him, and had set it flowing, for the priest and the deacon and Naakkve too, something too freely. He was named somewhat like Sir Allan or Allart of Bekelar; he was from Flanders, and was on pilgrimage to the holy places round about the north countries. He was friendly beyond measure, the talking had gone smoothly. — And then Naakkve brought forth his message. The knight was bound hence to Oslo, and thereafter to places of pilgrimage in Denmark and Germany, and he was bent on having Nikulaus ride with him and be his interpreter, at least while yet he was here in Norway. And besides, he had dropped a hint that if the young man would follow him out into the world, Sir Allart was the man to make his fortune — it seemed as though, in the land he came from, golden spurs and neck-chains, heavy money-purses and goodly weapons did but lie waiting for such a man as young Nikulaus Erlendssön to come and pick them up. Naakkve had answered that he was yet under age, and must have his father's leave — but Sir Allart had pressed a gift upon him none the less; 'twould in no wise bind him, he had said plainly — a half-length, plum-coloured silken jerkin with silver bells on the sleeve-flaps.

Erlend listened to him, all but silent, with a strangely high-wrought look. When Naakkve was done speaking, he sent Gaute for the casket with his writing-gear, and straightway set about inditing a letter in Latin — Björgulf had to help him, for Naakkve was in no case to be of much use, and his father sent him to bed. In the letter 'twas written that Erlend bade the knight to his home next day after prime, that they might talk of Sir Allart's proffer to take the well-born young man Nikulaus Erlendssön into his service as his esquire. He begged the knight to forgive that he sent back the proffered gift, with the prayer that Sir Allart would have it in his keeping until Nikulaus, with his father's allowance, had taken oath in the service of the stranger, in accordance with the use prevailing among the knighthood of all lands.

Erlend dropped a little wax at the bottom of the letter and pressed his small seal — that on his ring — lightly down on it. Then, forthwith, he sent a serving-man to Romundgaard with the letter and the silken jerkin.

"Husband — surely you cannot think to send your young son out into foreign lands with an unknown man and an outlander," said Kristin, trembling.

"We must see — " Erlend smiled so strangely. " — But I deem not that 'tis like to be," said he, when he saw her disquietude; he smiled something more broadly, and stroked her cheek.

At Erlend's bidding, Kristin had strewn the floor of the upper hall with juniper and flowers, spread the best cushions on the benches, and set the board with a linen cloth, and good meat in trenchers of fine wood, and drink in the rare, silver-mounted drinking-horns that the manor had in heritage from Lavrans. Erlend had shaven himself with care, curled his hair, and clad himself in a black, richly broidered, long coat of foreign cloth. He went to the gate of the manor to meet the guest, and when they came across the court-yard together, Kristin could not but deem her husband looked far more like one of those knights of Valland of whom the sagas tell, than did the fat, fair stranger in gay and motley garments of sarsenet and velvet. She stood upon the balcony of the upper hall, bravely decked and adorned with a silken coif; the Fleming kissed her hand when she bade him *"Bien venu,"* and more words passed not between her and him in the hours he was with them. She did not understand aught of the men's parleyings; neither did Sira Solmund, who was with his guest. But the priest said to the mistress that hereby he had surely made Nikulaus' fortune. She answered neither yea nor nay.

Erlend had a little French, and spoke glibly such German as hireling soldiers use, and the talk changed betwixt him and the stranger knight went smoothly and in courtly wise. But Kristin marked that the Fleming seemed not over well pleased as it went on, although this he strove to hide. His sons Erlend had bidden wait over in the new storehouse loft, till he sent them word to come up hither — but no message was sent for them.

Erlend and the mistress went with the knight and the priest to the gate. When the guests were lost to sight among the fields Erlend turned to Kristin and said, with a smile that she misliked:

"With yonder fellow would I not send Naakkve from home as far as to Breiden even — "

Ulf Haldorssön came up to them. He and Erlend spoke somewhat that Kristin could not hear, but Ulf swore fiercely and spat. Erlend laughed and patted the man's shoulder:

"Ay, had I been such a stay-at-home as the good farmers here — but I have seen so much, I promise you 'tis not I will sell my fair young falcons from out my hands and into the devil's — Sira Solmund had not understood aught, the holy calf's-head — "

Kristin stood with hanging arms; the colour came and went in her face. Horror and shame took hold on her, so that she felt sick; her legs seemed to fail her. Sure enough, she had known that such things were — as of somewhat immeasurably far off — but that this unnamable thing dared thrust itself forward right to her very threshold — 'Twas as the last billow that must needs overset her storm-tossed, over-laden boat. Holy Mary, must she go in dread of *such* things too for her sons — ?

Erlend said, with the same ill-favoured smile:

"I thought my own thoughts, yester-eve already — Sir Allart seemed to me something too *kurteis*, by what Naakkve told. I wot well 'tis no knightly use anywhere in the world to greet a lad one would take in service with a kiss on the mouth, nor to give him costly gifts ere ever he has made proof of his worth — "

Trembling from head to foot, Kristin said:

"Why bade you me strew my floor with roses and spread my board with linen cloths for such a — ?" She spoke the worst of words.

Erlend knit his brows. He had picked up a stone — keeping an eye on Munan's red cat, which was stealing flat on its belly, through the long grass under the house wall, towards the chickens by the stable door. Whiz — he flung the stone; the cat was round the corner in a flash, and the bevy of hens flounced hither and thither. He turned to his wife:

" —Methought I might as well *see* the man; had he been a trustworthy fellow, then — and to see him I must needs show him courtesy — *I* am not Sir Allart's confessor. And you heard, belike, he is bound for Oslo." Erlend laughed again. "Now, like enough, some of my true friends and dear whilom kinsmen may hear tell that we sit not here at Jörundgaard either, lousing our rags and eating herring and oat-meal bannock — "

Björgulf had the headache and lay abed when Kristin came up into the loft at supper-time; and Naakkve said somewhat of not going over to the hall to supper.

"Methinks you are dull this evening, son," said his mother to him.

"Nay, how can you think so, mother?" — Naakkve smiled scornfully. "That I seem to be a bigger fool than other men, and 'tis easier to throw dust in my eyes, is naught to mope for, sure — "

"Take comfort," said his father, when they sat at the board, and Naakkve was still more silent than his wont. "You will come out into the world yet to try your fortune — "

"It depends, father," answered Naakkve, low, as if he meant Erlend alone to hear, "on whether Björgulf can bear me company." Then he laughed quietly. "But say to Ivar and Skule what you have said to me — 'tis their one longing, I trow, to grow up and be of an age to fare forth — "

Kristin stood up, and drew on a hooded cloak. She thought to go north to the old beggar-man in Ingebjörg's cottage, she told them. The twins proffered to go along and carry the sack for her, but she would liefer go alone.

The evenings were somewhat dark already, and north of the church the road ran through woods and under the shadow of Hammer-hill. Here, cold gusts ever blew from out the gorge, and the river's roar seemed to bring with it a breath of damp. Swarms of great white moths hovered and flickered under the trees — sometimes they swept right against the woman; it seemed as, in the dusk, the palely shining linen about her head and breast lured them. She beat at them with her hands as she hastened upward, slipping on the smooth pine-needle carpet and stumbling on the writhen roots that wound across the path she followed.

— There was a dream that had haunted Kristin for many a year. The first time she had dreamed it was the night before Gaute was born, but even now it would chance that she waked all a-sweat, with her heart hammering as if 'twould beat itself in sunder in her breast, and knew that she had dreamed the selfsame dream.

She saw a flowery lawn — a steep hill-side, deep in pine forest that hemmed in the greensward on three sides, thick and murky; at the foot of the slope a little tarn mirrored the dark woods and the green, spangled clearing. The sun was behind the trees — from the very top of the hill-side the last golden light of evening sifted in long rays through the firs, and in the depths of the tarn shining sunset clouds swam amidst the water-lily leaves.

In the midst of the slope, standing deep in the scree of campions and buttercups and foamy clouds of the green-white angelica, she saw her child. Naakkve it must have been, the first time she dreamed it — she had but the two then, and Björgulf yet lay in his cradle. Afterwards she never knew surely which of her children it might be — the little round sunburnt face under the round-cropped yellow-brown hair seemed to her now like one, now like another, but ever the child was two to three years old, and clad in just such a little dark-yellow coat as she was used to sew for her little boys' everyday wear — of homespun wool, dyed with litmus and edged with red binding.

She herself, it seemed to her at times, was on the farther side of the tarn. Or she was not at the place at all, but yet she saw all that befell —

She saw her little son move hither and thither, and turn his face as he plucked the flowers. And a dull fear pressed heavy on her heart, a foreboding of an evil thing to come; yet first there came ever with this dream a mighty aching sweetness, as she gazed at the fair child there in the meadow.

Then she grows ware that from out the dark up in the forest fringe there parts itself a shaggy, living bulk. It moves without a sound; two tiny wicked eyes glare out. Right out on to the upper meadow comes the bear, stands and sways its head and shoulders, sniffing downwards. Then it springs. Kristin had never seen a living bear, but she knows they spring not thus; this is no right bear. This moves like a cat — now it turns grey — like a grey, shaggy giant-cat it leaps, with long lithe bounds, down the grassy slope.

The mother watches with the anguish of death upon

her — and she cannot come where the little one is to save him; she cannot warn him with a sound. Then the child grows ware that *something* is there; it turns half round and looks over its shoulder. With a dreadful, little low cry of fear it tries to run down the slope, lifting its legs, as little children do, high in the long grass, and the mother hears clearly the little sounds of the sappy stalks breaking as the child pushes its way through the tangled growth of flowers. Then it stumbles on something in the grass, falls head-long, and next moment the monster is on top of it, with arched back and head thrust deep between its fore-paws. Then she wakes —

— And each time she lay awake for hours before it availed aught to try to calm herself — by thinking 'twas but a dream! Her smallest child, that lay betwixt her and the wall, she would draw close in to her — would think of how, had it been real, she might have done this or that — frightened the monster with shrieks or with a staff — and at her belt there hung ever the long keen knife —

No sooner had she talked herself into quietness in this wise, than 'twould break over her anew, the unbearable agony, as, in her dream, she stood strengthless, and saw her little one's poor, vain efforts to flee from the deadly swift and strong and cruel beast. She felt as though the blood boiled and surged within her, as though her body swelled and her heart must burst, since it could not contain such a wave of blood —

The cottage called Ingebjörg's cot lay up on Hammer-hill, a little below the highway, which here pressed up the height. It had stood empty many a year, and the ground was leased to a man who had got leave to clear a place and build close by. An old beggar-man, left behind from a gang of mumpers, had now got leave to creep in there. When she had heard of it, Kristin had sent up meat and clothes and healing simples, but she herself had till now had no time to go thither.

'Twould soon be all over with the poor man, she saw. She gave her sack to the beggar-woman who had stayed behind with him, did the little she now could to ease him, and, when she learned that they had sent for the priest, she washed his face, hands, and feet, that they might be clean, and ready for his last anointing.

'Twas thick with smoke in the little hovel, and there

was a horribly sickly, foul stench. When two of the
settler's women-folk came in, Kristin prayed them send
to Jörundgaard for all they might need, then said farewell
and went. A strange, sick fear of meeting the priest with
the Lord's body had come upon her, and she turned aside
into the first by-path she came to.

That 'twas naught but a cattle-path she soon saw; she
found herself plunged in trackless wilderness. Fallen trees
with their high, tangled masses of roots were fearsome to
look on; she must creep over them, when she could not
find a way round. Flakes of moss slipped from under her
feet when she had to scramble down amongst great stones.
Cobwebs clung to her face, and branches struck her and
took hold on her clothes. When she must pass over a
trickling beck, or come to a low swampy opening in the
forest, 'twas nigh impossible to find a place where she
could slip through the thick, wet scrub of leafy bushes.
And the loathly white moths were everywhere, thick
under the trees in the dark, swarming up in great clouds
from off the heather tufts where she trod.

But at length she came out on the low hills down
towards the Laagen. Here the fir wood was scant and
sparse, for here the trees must send their roots twisting
far over the barren rock, and the forest floor was little
else but dry, grey-white reinder-moss that crackled beneath her feet—amid it stray tufts of heather stood out
black. The smell of the pine-needles was hotter and dryer
and sharper than higher up—hereabout the forest ever
showed scorched and yellow needles from right early in
the spring. The white moths still kept after her—

The thunder of the river drew her downward. She
went right out on the edge and looked down. Deep down
below the water shimmered white, where it boiled, thun-
dering, over the slaty rocks from pool to pool.

The changeless roar of the falls went quivering through
her overwrought body and soul. It minded and minded
her of somewhat—of a time endlessly long since—even
then she had known that she could not bear the lot she
had chosen for herself. She had laid open her shielded,
tender girlhood's life to ravaging, fleshly love—in dread,
in dread, in dread had she lived ever since, a bondswoman
from the first hour of motherhood. To the world she had

given herself up in her youth, and the more she struggled and fluttered in the world's snare, the more straitly she found herself bound and prisoned by the world. Her sons she strove to guard, with vainly flapping wings tied down by worldly cares. Her dread, her unspeakable weakness, she had striven to hide from all men, had gone forward with a straight back and a calm face, held her peace, and fought to safeguard her children's welfare in every wise she could —

But ever with that hidden, breathless fear — if they fare ill, 'twere more than I can bear. And the deeps of her heart made moan at the memory of her father and mother. Even as they had walked, laden with fear and care for their children, day after day forward unto death, they had had strength to bear their burden; and 'twas not that they loved their children less, but that they loved them with a better love —

And was she now to see her strife end thus? — Had she but reared a brood of restless eyases, who lay in her nest impatiently waiting the hour when their wings would bear them out over the farthest blue fells — ? And their father clapped his hands together and laughed — fly, fly, my young birds —

Bloody fibres from her heart's roots would they drag with them when they took flight, and they would know naught of it. And she would be left behind to sit alone; and all the heart-strings which once had bound her to this old home of hers she herself had torn asunder long ago — Surely 'twould be such a life as is neither life nor death.

She turned, and half ran, with stumbling steps, up over the pale, sere carpet of reindeer-moss, her cloak gathered tightly about her, for 'twas so uncanny when it caught in the bushes. At last she came out upon the small hay-fields a little north of the gild-shelter and the church. As she went slantwise across the field she was ware of some-one standing in the road. He called: "Is it you, Kristin?" — she knew 'twas her husband.

"You were long away," said Erlend. " 'Tis deep night already, Kristin. I began to grow afraid."

"Were you afraid for me?" Her voice came from her harder and haughtier than she would have had it.

"Not so much afraid either. But it came to my mind that I had best come and meet you."

They scarce spoke a word as they went southward. All was still when they came into the courtyard. Some of the horses they had at home shambled along under the house walls, grazing, but all the folk were abed.

Erlend went straight to the storehouse loft, but Kristin turned her steps to the kitchen-house. "I must look for somewhat," she answered to her husband's question.

He stood hanging over the balcony waiting for his wife — and then he saw her come out from the kitchen-house with a lighted pine-root torch in her hand, and go over to the hearth-room house. The man waited a while — then he ran down and went in after her.

She had lit a candle and set it on the board. Erlend felt a strange chill of fear go through him as he saw her standing there by the lone taper in the empty house — there was naught in the room but the fixed furnishings, and in the candlelight the worn wood glistened, stripped and bare. The hearth was cold and clean swept, save for the pine-root brand, which lay there where it had been thrown, yet glowing. They were not wont to use this room, Erlend and Kristin; it might well be half a year since fire had been kindled there. The air was strangely close; the many blended, living odours left by man's abidings, his comings and goings, were lacking, and smoke-vent and door had not been opened in all that time — so the place smelt of wool and hides; some rolled-up skins and sacks, which Kristin had taken out from the wares in the store, were piled up in the empty bed that had been Lavrans' and Ragnfrid's.

Strewn on the top of the board lay many small skeins — sewing thread and yarn for mending with, both linen and wool, which Kristin had set apart when she was dyeing. She stood fingering them and setting them in order.

Erlend sat him down in the high-seat at the board end. The room seemed strangely wide and empty about the slender man, as it gaped there, stripped of cushions and hangings. The two warriors of St. Olav with cross-marked helms and shields, that Lavrans had carven for high-seat posts, scowled, grim and moody, out from under Erlend's narrow brown hands. No man could carve out leafage and beasts fairlier than Lavrans, but with men's semblances he had never been over happy.

For long the two kept so still that not a sound was to be heard, save the dull thuds on the sward without, where the horses wandered in the summer night.

"Are you not for bed soon, Kristin?" he asked, at length.

"Are not you?"

"I thought to wait for you," said the man.

"I have no mind to go up yet — I cannot sleep —"

"What is't then that lies so heavy on your mind, Kristin, that you deem you will not sleep?" he asked after a little.

Kristin drew her upright. She stood with a skein of heather-green wool in her hands; she pulled at it and twisted it between her fingers. "What was it you spoke with Naakkve to-day —" She swallowed once or twice, she was so dry in the throat. "Some plan — 'twould not do for him he seemed to think — but you talked of how Ivar and Skule —"

"Oh — that!" Erlend smiled a little. "I but said to the lad — *I* have a kinsman by marriage, too, now that I bethink me. — Though Gerlak, I trow, will scarce be so ready to kiss my hands and take from me cloak and sword as before he was. But he has ships on the sea — and rich kinsmen, both at Bremen and at Lynn. And sure the man must understand that it behoves him to help his wife's brothers — *I* spared not my goods and gear when I was a rich man and gave my daughter to Gerlak Tiedekenssön to wife."

Kristin said naught. At last Erlend said, somewhat hotly:

"Jesus, Kristin, stand not so, staring as you were made of stone —"

"Little thought I, the time we first came together, that our children should need to wander the world around, begging their bread in strangers' houses —"

"Nay, devil fetch me if I meant that they should beg! But should they have, all seven of them, to wring their bread from your farms here, 'twill be but peasant's fare, my Kristin — and I trow my sons are little fit for that. Bully-boys they seem like to be, Ivar and Skule — and out in the world is there both wheaten bread and cake for the man who will carve out his meat with his sword."

"Hirelings and vassals would you have your sons to be — ?"

"Hire I took myself, in the days when I was young and followed Count Jacob. God be gracious to him, say I — I learned somewhat then that a man gets not the knowledge of at home in this land of ours — here, either he sits pea-cocking in his high-seat with silver belt about his belly, swilling himself full with ale, or he walks behind his plough smelling to the rumps of his jades. 'Twas a hearty life I lived in the Count's service — I say it, even though I had got that block fast to my leg while yet I was of Naakkve's age. — At least I had some joy of my youth — "

"Be still!" Kristin's eyes seemed to grow black. "Would you not deem it the deadliest harm if your sons were ensnared in such sin and mischance — ?"

"Ay, God defend them from the like of that — but 'twere not needful either that they should copy all their father's follies. A man *can*, sure, take service with a noble, Kristin, without such hangers-on to clog him — "

"'He who draws the sword shall perish by the sword,' so stands it written, Erlend!"

"Ay, I have heard it, my dear one. Yet did the most of both your forefathers and mine make a good and Christian end in their beds, with the last anointing and all ghostly comfort. You need but call to mind your own father — he had shown in his youth that he was a man that could wield the sword — "

"'Twas in war, Erlend, at the bidding of the King they had gone to help to guard our homes and hearths, that my father and the others took up arms. Yet father himself said 'twas not God's will with us that we should bear arms — christened, Christian men — one against the other — "

"Nay, that know I. But the world is what it is, since ever Adam and Eve ate of the tree — and that was fore my time; 'tis not my blame that we are born with sin within us — "

"Shameful is your talk — !"

Erlend broke in, vehemently:

"Kristin — you know it well — never was I slow to repent and make amends for my sins as well as might be. No godly man am I, 'tis true. I saw too much when I was child and youth — My father was such a dear friend of the great lords of the chapter — they came and went in his house like grey swine; Lord Eiliv, when he was priest, and Sir Sigvat Lande and all their following; and little

else came with them but wrangling and jars — hard-hearted
and unmerciful they showed them to their own archbishop
— no more holy and peace-loving than so were they, they
who each day held in their hands the holiest of holy things
and lifted God Himself aloft in the bread and wine — "

" 'Tis not for us to judge the priests — father ever said
'twas our duty to bow down before their priesthood and
obey them, but that their natural man lies under the
judgment of Almighty God alone — "

"A — ay." Erlend lingered a little on the word. "So I
know he said, and you have said it too, ere now. I wot
well you are more godly in such-like things than I can
ever be — yet, Kristin, 'tis hard for me to see how it
should be a right reading of God's word to go on, as your
way is, ever storing up wrath and never forgetting. A
long memory he too had, Lavrans — oh, no! I say naught
of your father but that he was pious and nobly good, and
that are you too, I wot — but often when you speak so
soft and sweet, as your mouth were filled with honey, I
fear me you are thinking most upon old wrongs, and God
may judge whether your heart is full as pious as your
mouth — "

Of a sudden she dropped down, lay over the board with
her face hidden on her arms, and wept aloud. Erlend
sprang up — she lay weeping, with hoarse, racking sobs
that shook her frame. Erlend laid his arm on her shoulders.

"Kristin, what is it — ? What is't?" he said again, sitting
down on the bench by her and trying to lift her head.
"Kristin — nay, weep not so — methinks you have lost
your wits — "

"I am frighted!" She sat up, clenched her hands in her
lap. "I am so frighted; Mary, gentle lady mine, help us
all — I am so frighted — what will become of all my
sons — ?"

"Ay, Kristin mine — but you must use you to the
thought — you *cannot* hide them longer beneath your
skirts — soon will they be grown men, all our sons. And
you are like the bitch still — " He sat with one leg over
the other, his hands folded over his knee, looking down
somewhat wearily at his wife — "you snap blindly both
at friend and foe, when 'tis aught that touches your
children."

She got up sharply, and stood a moment dumb, wring-

ing her hands. Then she began to walk swiftly up and
down the room. She said naught, and Erlend sat silent,
looking at her.

"Skule —" She stopped before the man. "A luckless
name you gave your son. But you would have it — you
willed that the duke should live again in the child —"

" 'Tis a good name enough, Kristin. Luckless — there is
ill luck of many kinds. Well I remembered, when I named
my son after my father's mother's father, that fortune
betrayed him, but, none the less, king he was, with better
right than the comb-maker's seed * —"

"You were proud enough, you and Munan Baardssön,
that you were of King Haakon Haalegg's near kindred —"

"Ay, for you know that my father's aunt, Margaret
Skulesdatter, brought kingly blood into Sverre's stock —"

For a long time man and wife stood and gazed into each
other's eyes.

"Ay, I know what you are thinking on, my fair lady
wife." Erlend went and sat him down again in the high-
seat. With his hands resting on the two warrior-heads he
leaned forward a little; he smiled a cold and galling smile.
"But you see, Kristin mine — me it has not broken, that I
am become now a poor and friendless man. 'Tis well you
should know it — I am not afraid that with me my father's
line has fallen for all time from might and honour. I too
was betrayed by fortune — but had my plan but sped,
then had I and my sons now sat in the seats on the King's
right hand, that we, his near kinsmen, are born to. For me
the game is up now, mayhap — but I can see it on my
sons, Kristin — they will win back the place that befits
their birth. You need not to grieve so for them, and strive
not so to bind them fast here in this nook-shotten dale
of yours — let them prove them freely, and you will see
maybe, ere you die, they will have won firm footing again
on their father's rightful heritage —"

"Oh, you can talk!" Hot, bitter tears of wrath were
pricking in the woman's eyes, but she forced them back
and laughed, with mouth twisted awry:

---

* See Note 3.

"Methinks you are yet more childish than the lads, Erlend! You can sit and talk thus — and no longer ago than to-day Naakkve had well-nigh come to such fortune as a Christian man's mouth dare not name — had not God preserved us — "

"Ay, but this time 'twas I that had the luck to be God's instrument" — Erlend shrugged his shoulders. But then he said most earnestly:

"Such things — you need not to fear, my Kristin — is't this that has clean scared the wits from you, poor soul?" He looked down, and said almost shamefacedly: "You must mind, Kristin — your father of happy memory prayed for our children, as he prayed for all of us, early and late. And I deem, most sure and firmly, it avails for deliverance from much — from the worst things of all — so good a man's intercession — " She saw the man cross his breast with his thumb as though by stealth.

But, so beside herself was she, it but embittered her the more:

"So — you comfort you with the thought, Erlend, as you sit there in my father's high-seat, that your sons shall be saved by his prayers, even as they are fed by his lands — "

Erlend grew pale:

"Mean you, Kristin — that I am unworthy to sit in Lavrans Björgulfsön's high-seat — "

His wife's lips moved, but could bring forth no sound. Erlend rose and stood moveless:

"Mean you this — for then say I, as sure as God is above us both — I will sit there never more.

"Answer," said he again, as she stood speechless. A long tremor shook the woman's body.

"He was — a better master — he who — sat there before you" — she could scarce get the words out so as to be heard.

"Heed your tongue now, Kristin!" Swiftly Erlend strode a step or two nearer. She stood upright with a start:

"Ay, strike me — I have borne that too ere now; I can bear it again."

"Strike you — I thought not on it." He stood with his hand resting on the board; again they gazed at one another, and again his face had that strange far-off calm which she had seen on it at some rare times. Now it drove her to distraction. She knew 'twas she was in the right — Erlend's talk was witless, reckless; but that face of his made her feel as though all the wrong was hers.

She looked at him, and, sick with dread herself at what she said, she spoke:

"I fear me 'twill not be in *my* sons that your line will flourish again in the Trondheim country —"

Erlend flushed blood-red:

"You could not forbear to mind me of Sunniva Olavsdatter, I see —"

" 'Twas not I who named her, but you."

Erlend reddened yet more deeply.

"Have you never thought, Kristin — that *you* were not wholly without blame in that — mischance —

"Mind you that night in Nidaros — I came and stood before your bed. Most humble was I, and sorrowful for that I had offended against you, my wife — I came to beg of you — to forgive me my wrong. Your answer was to bid me go and lay me where I had lain the night before —"

"Could I know that you had lain by your kinsman's wife — ?"

Erlend stood a little. He grew pale, and again red. Then he turned and went from the room without a word.

The wife did not stir — long she stood moveless, her clenched hands pressed up beneath her chin, staring into the light.

Then she raised her head with a jerk — drew a long breath. Some time he must endure to hear it —

Then she grew ware of the sound of a horse's hoofs in the courtyard — heard by its gait that 'twas a horse being led by a house-carl. She stole to the door and out into the penthouse, stood behind the doorpost, and peered out.

Already the night was growing grey with dawn. Out in the courtyard stood Erlend and Ulf Haldorssön. Erlend held his horse, and she saw that it was saddled and the man clad for riding. The two spoke together for a while, but she could not catch one word. Then Erlend swung himself into the saddle and began to ride at a foot-pace northward to the manor-gate; he looked not back, but seemed to talk with Ulf, who walked by the horse's side.

When they were gone from sight up towards the road, she crept out, hastened as noiselessly as she could up to the gate, stood there and listened — she heard now that Erlend had started Soten at a trot up on the highway.

A little while after, Ulf came back. He stopped short when he caught sight of the woman there at the gate. For a while they stood looking at each other in the grey twilight. Ulf's feet in his shoes were bare, and he had but a linen shirt beneath his cloak.

"What is this?" asked the mistress wildly.

"You must sure know — I know not."

"Whither rode he?" said she again.

"To Haugen." Ulf stood a little. "Erlend came in and waked me — he said he would ride thither to-night — and he seemed in haste; there were some things he prayed me to see and have brought up after him."

Kristin was silent for a space.

"He was angry, then?"

"He was quiet." In a little Ulf said, low: "I am afeared, Kristin — I marvel if you have not said what you had best have left unsaid."

"For once, surely, Erlend might endure to be talked to as he were a grown man," said the wife, vehemently.

They went slowly downward. Ulf turned towards his own house, and at that she came after him.

"Ulf, kinsman," she prayed him, fearfully, "in old days 'twas you who told me, late and soon, that, for my sons' sakes I must harden my heart and speak to Erlend."

"Ay — I have grown wiser with the years, Kristin, and that have you not," he answered as before.

"You give me fair comfort, in sooth," said she, bitterly.

He laid a hand heavily upon the woman's shoulder, but at first he said naught. They stood there — 'twas so still that they both heard the endless roar of the river, that other times came not to their ears. Out on the farms around the cocks were crowing, and, from the stable, Kristin's farm-cock sent forth a ringing answer.

"Ay — I have had to learn and deal heedfully with comfort, Kristin — heavily has that ware been drawn on these many years — we must go sparingly with it now, for we know not how long yet it will need to last — "

She shook herself free from his hand; with teeth set

hard into her lower lip, she turned her face aside — then she fled downward, back to the hearth-room house.

The morning was biting cold; she wrapped her cloak close about her, and pulled the hood down over her head. Crouched together, with her dew-wet shoes drawn up beneath her skirt and her arms crossed upon her knees, she sat on the edge of the cold hearth, brooding. Now and again her face quivered, but she did not weep.

She must have slept — she started up with aching back, stiff-limbed and frozen to the marrow. The door stood ajar — she saw that out in the courtyard the sun was shining.

Kristin went out into the penthouse — the sun was high already, from down in the home pasture she heard the bell on the horse that had gone lame. She looked across at the new storehouse. And then she was ware that little Munan was standing up on the balcony peeping out through the railing arches.

Her sons — it flashed through her. What had they thought, when they awoke and saw their parents' bed unslept in?

She ran across the courtyard and up to the child — Munan had naught on but his shirt. As soon as his mother came to him, he thrust his hand in hers, as if he were afraid.

Within the loft none of the lads was yet full clad — none had waked them, she saw. All looked up quickly at their mother, and then down again. She took Munan's hose and would have helped him to draw them on.

"Whither is father gone?" asked Lavrans, wonderingly.

"Your father rode north to Haugen at early dawn," she answered. She marked that the big ones hearkened, and she said: "You know he has long said he must go up some time and see how it fares with his farm."

The two little ones looked up into their mother's face with wide-open, wondering eyes, but the five older brothers hid their gaze from her as they went out of the loft.

3

THE DAYS went by. At first Kristin felt no fear: she cared
not to ponder what Erlend might mean by these doings —
running off from home in sudden wrath at dead of night
— or how long he was minded to sit up north there on his
hill farm and punish her with his absence. She was bitterly
wroth with her husband, angered all the more because she
denied not to herself that she too was in the wrong, and
had spoken words that she wished from her heart could
be unsaid.

Sure enough, she had been in the wrong many a time,
and had often, in wrath, said hateful and unseemly things
to her husband. But what hurt her most bitterly was that
Erlend could never offer to forget and to forgive, except
she first humbled her and begged it of him meekly. 'Twas
not so often either, thought she, that she had done amiss
— could he not understand, 'twas oftenest when she was
wearied and worn with cares and fears that she had
striven to bear in silence? — 'twas then she most readily
lost the mastery of herself. She deemed that Erlend might
have remembered that, beside all the disquietude for their
sons' future that she had borne these many, many days,
twice this summer she had gone through a time of deadly
fear for Naakkve. Her eyes had been opened now to see
that, after the young mother's pains and travail are over,
there come for the ageing mother fears and woe of a new
kind. — His careless talk of having no fear for the fortunes of their sons had goaded her till she was like a wild
mother-bear — or like a bitch with whelps; she cared not
if Erlend likened her to a bitch in all that touched her
children. For them would she be watchful and unsleeping
as a mother-bitch, so long as life abode in her.

And if, for such a cause, he could forget that she had
stood by him in every time of need, with all her powers;
that, in despite of her anger, she had been both just and
forgiving, when he struck her, and when he was false to
her with the hateful, wanton Lensvik woman; then he
must even forget. Even now, when she thought on it, she
could not feel so much wrath and bitterness against Erlend
for this, the worst of his offences against her — when she
turned on him with reproaches for *that*, 'twas because she

knew that he repented it himself, that in this he saw and felt he had done evil. But never had she been so wroth with Erlend — neither was she now — that the memory of his blow and of his faithlessness, with all it brought with it, did not trouble her, most of all, for the man's own sake — she felt ever that in these outbursts of his ungoverned spirit he had sinned against himself and his soul's welfare far more than against her.

What went on rankling in her spirit were all the little wounds he had dealt her with his unkind heedlessness, his childish lack of patience — even with his wild and thoughtless way of loving, when at times he showed that, despite of all, he loved her. 'Twas all the years when she was young and soft of soul, and had felt that both health and courage must fall short — cumbered as she was with all those helpless little children — if the father, the husband, would not show that he had strength and loving-kindness wherewith to guard her and the little sons upon her knees. It had been such a torment to feel herself weak of body, simple and unlessoned in mind, and not dare trust securely in her husband's strength and wisdom — 'twas as though she had got heart-wounds then that would never heal again. Even the sweet delight that 'twas to lift up her suckling, set its lovesome mouth to her breast, and feel the little warm, soft body upon her arm, had been made bitter by fear and fret — so small, so defenceless you are, and all too oft your father forgets that his first thought should be to make you secure.

And now, when her little children's bones were set and their heads had hardened, but they yet lacked somewhat of a grown man's wit — now he lured them from her. They melted away from her, the whole flock, husband and sons, in that strange, boyish light-mindedness that she thought she had seen glimpses of in all the men she had met, and where a sad, careful woman can never follow.

So, for her own part, 'twas but sorrow and anger she felt when she thought on Erlend. But she grew fearful when she wondered what her sons were thinking.

Ulf had been up to Dovre with two pack-horses, to bear to Erlend the things he had asked should be sent after him — clothes, weapons in plenty; all his four bows, sacks full of arrow-heads and cross-bow bolts, and three of the dogs. Munan and Lavrans wept bitterly when Ulf took the little smooth-haired bitch with silky soft, hanging earlaps — she was a fine, outlandish beast that Erlend had had of the Abbot at Holm. That their father owned such a rare dog seemed, more than aught else, to raise him above all other men in the eyes of the two little ones. And then their father had promised them that, when the bitch had pups again, they should each choose him one from out the litter.

When Ulf Haldorssön came back, Kristin asked if Erlend had said when he thought to turn him home again. "No," said Ulf. "It looks as though he had a mind to bide on there."

Of his own accord Ulf said but little more of his journey to Haugen. And Kristin was loath to ask.

In autumn, when they flitted in from the new store-house, the eldest sons said they would like, this winter, to sleep above stairs in the upper hall-room. Kristin gave them leave, and thus she was left to sleep with the two youngest in the great hall below. The first evening she said that Lavrans too might lie in the bed with her now.

The boy lay blissfully rolling about and boring himself down into the bedding. The children were used to have their couch made up on the bench, on leathern sacks filled with straw, and to have fur skins to wrap them in. But in the bed there were blue bolster mattresses to lie upon, and fine coverlids beside the furs — and the parents had fine white linen covers on their pillows.

" 'Twill be but till father comes home that I may lie here," asked Lavrans; "then, belike, we must go back to the bench again, mother?"

"Then you may sleep in Naakkve's and Björgulf's bed," answered his mother; "if the lads change not their minds and move down again, once the weather grows cold." Upstairs, too, there was a small masoned fire-place, but it gave out more smoke than heat, and the wind and weather were felt much more in the upper story.

As the autumn drew to an end, a vague fear came creeping over Kristin; it waxed from day to day, and the strain made life heavy to bear. No one seemed to hear word or whisper of Erlend.

In the long, black autumn nights she lay awake, heard

the two little boys' even breathing, listened to the march
of the storm about the house corners, and thought on
Erlend. Had it only not been on that farm that he was —

She had liked it ill when the cousins had fallen to talking of Haugen — Munan Baardssön was with them at their
lodging one of the last evenings ere they were to set forth
from Oslo. At that time Munan was sole owner of this
little farm — it had come to him from his mother. He and
Erlend had been making merry, and both were not a little
drunken, and while she sat chafing that they must needs
bring up that unchancy place in their talk, things fell out
so that Munan gave Erlend the farm — so should he be not
wholly landless in Norway's land. The thing was settled
amid jest and laughter — even those rumours that folk
could not dwell there because 'twas haunted they made
sport of. The terror that had taken hold on Munan
Baardssön when his mother and her husband came to their
miserable end up there, seemed by this time in some
measure to have worn off the knight.

And, sure enough, he made over Haugen to Erlend by
lawful deed. Kristin could not hide how hateful 'twas to
her that her husband should own that uncanny place. But
Erlend had turned it off with a jest:

" 'Tis little like that either you or I will ever set foot
in the houses up there — if they yet stand and are not
quite in ruin. And I trow Moster Aashild and Sir Björn
will not bring us home the rents themselves. So it sure
can matter naught to us if 'tis true, as folk say, that they
walk there — "

As the year waned, and Kristin's thoughts ran ever on
how it might fare with Erlend north on Haugen, she grew
so tongue-tied that she scarce spoke a word to her children, or to the serving-folk, unless she must answer their
questions — and they grew loath to speak to the mistress
save when they needs must, for she made them short and
impatient answers when they broke in upon and troubled
her uneasy, overwrought brooding. She herself was so
little ware of this that, when at last she marked that the
two youngest children had stopped asking after their
father or speaking of him to her, she sighed and thought:
children forget apace — for she knew not how often she

had frighted them from her with impatient answers, and bidden them be still and not plague her.

With the older sons she spoke scarce at all.

As long as the dry frost lasted she still could answer stranger-folk, who came to the manor and asked for the master, that he lay out in the fells trying his luck in hunting. Then there came a heavy snow-fall, both in the parish and in the hills, the first week in Advent.

Early in the morning of St. Lucia's Eve,* while 'twas yet pitch-dark without, and the stars showed clear, Kristin came from the byre. Then she saw, by the light of a pine-torch stuck into a heap of snow, that three of her sons stood without the house-door with ski in their hands, binding them on their feet — and a little way off stood Gaute's gelding with wicker snow-shoes on its feet and a pack-saddle on its back. She guessed whither they were bound; and she dared say naught more than to ask, when she saw that one of the lads was Björgulf — the two others were Naakkve and Gaute:

"Would you go out to-day on ski, Björgulf? — 'tis like 'twill be bright weather, son!"

"As you see, mother."

"Maybe you will be home ere midday, then?" she asked, somewhat at a loss. Björgulf was ill at ski-running; the glare from the snow soon hurt his eyes, and he kept him mostly within-doors in winter-time. But Naakkve answered that they might be gone some days.

Kristin was left at home, uneasy and fearful. The twins were surly and sour — she saw that they had been fain to go too, but that their grown-up brothers would not let them.

Early on the fifth day, at breakfast time, the three came back. They had set out at cockcrow for Björgulf's sake, said Naakkve — that they might be home ere the sun got up. Those two went straightway up to the upper hall — Björgulf seemed like to drop with weariness — but Gaute bore the sacks and the pack-saddle into the room. He had with him two goodly little whelps for Lavrans and

---

* 13th December.

Munan — at the sight the little boys forgot all questions and all cares. Gaute seemed to be troubled, but strove to hide it:

" — And this," said he, drawing it out of a sack, "this father bade me give to you."

'Twas fourteen ermine skins, passing fair. His mother took them, with somewhat of an ill grace — she could not find a word to say in answer. There was all too much that she would fain have asked; she was afraid she might lose the mastery of herself if she gave her heart the smallest vent — and Gaute was so young. She brought out naught but:

"They are white already, I see — ay, we are far on in the winter half-year now — "

When Naakkve came down, and he and Gaute set them down to the porridge dish, Kristin said hastily to Frida that she herself would bear his food up to Björgulf in the loft. It had come to her all at once that with the silent boy, who she guessed was far riper in mind than his brothers, she could mayhap talk of this matter.

He had lain down on the bed, and held a linen cloth over his eyes. His mother hung a kettle of water on the pot-hook in the fire-place, and, while Björgulf lay propped on his elbow and ate, she brewed a wash of dried eyebright and celandine.

Kristin took from him the empty porridge bowl, bathed his red and swollen eyes with the wash and laid damped linen cloths upon them; and then, at length, she took courage to ask:

"Said he naught, your father, of when he thought to come home to us?"

"No."

"You are ever chary of your words, Björgulf," said his mother in a little while.

"It seems to run in the breed, my mother." — He said, a little after: "We met Simon and his men near by, north of the gorge — with loaded sleighs, driving northwards."

"Did you speak with them?" asked the woman.

"No — " He laughed as before. "It seems to run like a sickness through our kindred — friendship thrives not among us."

"Mean you to blame me for that?" his mother flashed out. "One moment you complain that we hold our peace

too much — and then you say we cannot keep friendship — "

Björgulf only laughed again. Then he raised him on his
elbow, as though he were hearkening to his mother's
breathing:

"In God's name, mother, do not fall a-weeping now —
I am down-hearted and weary — so unused am I to go on
ski — and take no account of what I say: I know full well
that you are no contentious woman."

Kristin went forth from the loft soon after. For now
she dared not, for aught in the world, ask this son what
the young ones thought of these matters.

So she lay, night after night, when the lads had gone
up to the loft — waking and listening: did they talk together when they were alone up there? she wondered.
There was a thumping of boots thrown on the floor, a
clatter of knife-belts falling down — she heard their voices,
but could make out no words — their tongues all went at
once; their voices rose — it seemed to be half quarrel, half
jesting. One of the twins cried out aloud — then someone
was dragged over the floor, so that dust showered from
the planks above her down into the room — the balcony
door flew open with a crash — something fell heavily on
the balcony floor, and then Ivar and Skule's voices threat-
ening and clamouring out there, while they beat on the
door — then she caught Gaute's voice, high and laughing.
He stood within the door, she could hear — 'twas clear
he and the twins had fallen out again, and the end had
been that Gaute had thrown them out. Lastly she heard
Naakkve's grown man's voice — he was making peace;
the two came in. Yet a while the noise of talk and laughter came down to her, then the sounds of their getting
into bed. Silence fell at last. In a little she heard an even
drone, with stillness ever and anon — a drone like far-off
thunder, away in the hills.

The mother smiled in the dark. Gaute snored when he
was wearied out. So, too, had her father done. 'Twas
strange, this matter of likeness — the sons who took after
Erlend in outward looks were like him too in that they
slept as noiselessly as birds. And while she lay thinking
on all the little marks of kinship one can find so strangely,
lifetime after lifetime, in the offspring of a stock, she

could not forbear to smile to herself as she lay there. The torturing strain in the mother's mind slackened for a time, and drowsiness came and tangled all the threads of her thought, while she sank away, first into blissful ease and then into forgetfulness.

— They were young, she comforted herself — 'Twas like they took it not so hardly —

But one day, when the new year was begun, Sira Solmund, the chaplain, came to Kristin at Jörundgaard. It was the first time he had come thither unbidden, and Kristin gave him fair welcome, though her mind foreboded evil straightway. As she had thought, so it proved — he deemed 'twas his duty to find out if she and her husband had wilfully and in ungodly wise severed their fellowship, and, if so it were, which of the pair bore the blame for this breach of God's law.

Kristin felt herself that she grew shifty-eyed and over glib of tongue, and that she used too many words, as she set forth to the priest how Erlend deemed he must look after his estate north in Dovre; it had lain quite uncared for these many years; the houses, for sure, were well-nigh fallen to ruin — with the many children they had, 'twas needful they see to their welfare — and much more to the like purpose. She glossed the matter in so many words that even Sira Solmund, no sharp-sighted man, must needs mark that she felt herself unsure — and now she talked and talked of how eager a hunter Erlend was, as the priest well knew. She brought out and showed him the ermine skins she had had from her husband — in her confusion she had given them to the priest almost ere she herself knew of it, ere she could bethink her —

She fretted when Sira Solmund was gone — Erlend might have known that, when he stayed from home in this wise, a priest such as they had now would surely take in his head to come and pry out whether aught were amiss —

Sira Solmund was a paltry little man to look on; 'twas not easy to guess his age, but folk deemed he was near about forty winters by now. He was not over bright-witted, and of a certainty he had no learning to spare; but he was an honest, pious, well-living priest. An oldish sister of his, a childless widow and a parlous tale-bearer, cared for his small household.

He would fain have shown himself a zealous servant of the Church, but 'twas mostly on small matters and small folk that he fastened — he was fearful of spirit and shy of grappling with the big landowners or taking up ticklish questions; but if once he had done so, he was apt to grow passing stubborn and hot-headed.

For all this, he was well enough liked by his parishioners. For one thing, folk held him in esteem for his quiet, seemly way of life; for another, he was not near so greedy of money or so stiff in matters that touched the Church's rights or folks' duties as had been Sira Eirik. Like enough this came in the main from his lacking altogether the old priest's boldness.

But Sira Eirik was loved and honoured by every man and every child in the parishes round about. Folk had often taken it amiss in the old days, when the priest had striven, with unseemly greed, to enrich and make secure the children he had had unlawfully by his serving-wench; and when he first came to dwell in the parish the people of Sil could ill brook his masterful sternness toward all who transgressed the least of the Church's laws. A warrior had he been before he took the priestly vows, and he had followed the sea-rover earl, Sir Alf of Tornberg, in his youth; 'twas easy to mark it in his ways.

But even then the parish folk had been proud of their priest, for he was far above most priests of the country parishes in learning, wisdom, strength of body, and chieftainly bearing, and he had the noblest singing-voice. And with the years, and under the heavy trials that God seemed to have laid upon this His servant by reason of his youthful untowardliness, Sira Eirik Kaaressön had so grown is wisdom, piety, and righteousness that his name was now known and honoured over the whole bishopric. When he journeyed to the synod at Hamar town, he was honoured as a father by all the other priests, and 'twas said that Bishop Halvard would gladly have preferred him to a church which carried with it noble rank and a seat in the cathedral chapter. But 'twas said Sira Eirik had begged he might be left where he was — he had pleaded his age, and that his sight had been dim these many years past.

In Sil there stood by the highway, a little south of
Formo, the fair cross of potstone which Sira Eirik had
set up at his own cost, where a stone-slip from the moun-
tain-side had taken from him both his young, hopeful
sons forty years agone. Even now the older folk of the
parish passed it not by without stopping to say Paternosters and Aves for Alf's and Kaare's souls.

His daughter the priest had wedded from his manor
with a fair dowry of goods and cattle; he gave her to a
comely and well-born farmer's son from Viken; none
thought other than that Jon Fis was a good young fellow.
Six years after, she came home to her father, starved,
broken, ragged and lousy, with a child by each hand and
one beneath her belt. The folk who had lived in Sil in
those days knew well, though they never spoke of it:
the children's father had been hanged for a thief in Oslo.
The Jonssöns turned out but ill — and now they were
dead, all three.

Even while his issue were yet alive, it had been Sira
Eirik's zealous care to deck and do honour to his church
with gifts. Now 'twould be it, belike, that would get the
greater part of his wealth and his costly books. The new
church of Saint Olav and St. Thomas in Sil was much
greater and statelier than the old one that burned down,
and Sira Eirik had bestowed upon it many noble and
costly adornments. He went each day to church for
prayer and meditation, but for the folks he now said
mass on the high holy-days only.

'Twas Sira Solmund, too, who now carried on most of
the duties of the priestly office. But when folk had a
heavy grief to bear, or were vexed at soul by great
troubles or the stings of conscience, they rather sought
the old parish priest, and all deemed that, from a com-
muning with Sira Eirik, they ever brought comfort home
with them.

And so, one evening on towards spring, Kristin Lavransdatter went to Romundgaard and knocked upon the door
of Sira Eirik's house. But she knew not herself rightly how
she should set forth what she had to say; so, when she
had made her offering, she sat talking of this and that.
At length the old man said, something impatiently:

"Have you come in but to greet me, Kristin, and see
how I fare? 'Tis kindly done of you, if so — but methinks

you have somewhat else upon your heart, and if so it be, speak of it now, and waste not time with empty talk — "

Kristin laid her hands together in her lap and looked down:

"It mislikes me much, Sira Eirik, that my husband bides on up yonder at Haugen."

"I trow the way is not so long," said the priest, "but that you can get you up thither easily enough, to speak with him and beg him to return home soon. So much there cannot be for him to see to, up on that little one-man's croft, that he need tarry there longer."

"I am afraid, when I think of him dwelling there alone these winter nights," said the wife, shuddering.

"Erlend Nikulaussön is sure old enough and bold enough to look to himself."

"Sira Eirik — you know all that befell up there once upon a time," whispered Kristin, so low as scarce to be heard.

The priest turned his dim old eyes towards her — once they had been coal-black, bright, and keen. He said naught.

"You have heard, belike, what folk say," she said as low as before. "That — the dead — walk there."

"Mean you you dare not seek him out for that — or are you feared that the drows will break your husband's neck? If so be they have not done it yet, Kristin, 'tis like they will let him be hereafter also" — the priest laughed harshly. " 'Tis folly, naught but heathenish, superstitious prate, the most of the tales folks spread about of drows and of dead men that walk. There are stern doorkeepers, I fear me, where Sir Björn and Lady Aashild are."

"Sira Eirik," she whispered, trembling, "deem you then there is no salvation for those two poor souls — ?"

"God forbid that I should be so overbold, to judge of the bounds of His mercy. But scarce can I deem those two can have been able to quit their score so soon — not yet have all the tablets been shown forth on which they two carved their witness — her children that she forsook; you two that were prentices in the wise lady's school. If I deemed it could help, so that somewhat of the ill she did might be righted, then — but since Erlend tarries on there, 'tis like God deems not it would avail aught if his mother's sister should show her and warn him. For this

we know, by God's mercy and Our Lady's pity and the
prayers of the Church, it may befall that a poor soul have
leave to come back to this earthly home out of the fires of
purgatory, if his sin be such that it can be made good by
the help of living men and his time of torture shortened
thereby — as 'twas with the unhappy soul who had shifted
the boundary between Hov and Jarpstad, and the farmer
in Musdal with the false letters concerning the mill-race.
But no soul can come out from purgatory fire except it
have such a lawful errand — 'tis trumpery else, the most
of what folk prate of drows and ghosts; or 'tis the devil's
juggleries, that melt away like smoke when you ward you
with the sign of the cross and the Lord's name — "

"But the blesséd who are with God, Sira Eirik?" she
asked again, low.

"The holy ones with Him you wot well He can send
on His errands with good gifts and messages from
Paradise."

"I told you once that I had seen Brother Edvin Rikards-
sön," she said as before.

"Ay, either 'twas a dream — and it might have been
sent by God or by your guardian angel — or else the
monk is a holy saint."

Kristin whispered, trembling:

"My father — Sira Eirik, I have prayed so much that it
might be granted me to see his face but once. I long to
see him so unspeakably, Sira Eirik — and maybe I might
understand by his mien what he would that I should do.
Could I but once have counsel of my father, then — "
She had to bite her lips and, with the fall of her coif,
brush away the tears that would out.

The priest shook his head.

"Pray you for his soul, Kristin — though I well believe
that Lavrans, and your mother with him, are now long
since comforted, in the house of them whose comfort
they sought in all their sorrows while they lived here on
earth. And true and sure it is that Lavrans holds you fast
in his love in that place too — but your prayers and
masses for his soul's peace bind you and us all to him —
Ay, the way of it, 'tis one of the secret things which are
hard to understand — but doubt not that this way is better
than that he should be disquieted in his peace that he
might come hither and show himself to you — "

Kristin was forced to sit awhile, ere she grew so far mistress of herself that she dared speak. But then she told the priest all that had befallen betwixt her and Erlend that night in the hearth-room house, saying over every word that was spoken, as near as she remembered it.

The priest sat long silent when she had done speaking. Then she smote her hands together vehemently:

"Sira Eirik! Deem you that most of the wrong was with me? Deem you that *so* much of the wrong was with me that 'tis no sin of Erlend to have fled from me and all our sons in this wise? Think you 'tis just for him to crave that I should seek him out, kneel before him, and eat my words that I spoke amiss? — I know without that he will not come home to us!"

"Think you you need to call Lavrans back from his other home to ask his counsel in this matter?" The priest rose, and laid his hand upon the woman's shoulder: "The first time I saw you, Kristin, you were a tender little maid — Lavrans took you between his knees, laid your little hands cross-wise on your breast, and bade you say Paternoster to me — clearly and sweetly could you say it, though you understood not one word — afterward you learned the meaning of every prayer in our tongue — maybe you have forgotten it now — ?

"Have you forgotten that your father taught you and did honour to you and loved you — he did honour to this man you are now so afeared to humble yourself before — or have you forgotten how fair he made the feast in honour of you two? And how you rode from his manor like two thieves — stealing away with you Lavrans Björgulfsön's worship and honour?"

Sobbing, Kristin hid her face in her hands.

"Can you remember yet, Kristin — did he crave of you two that you fall down on your knees before him, ere he deemed he could raise you up again into his fatherly love? Think you 'twere all too hard a morsel for your pride if you must bow yourself now before a man whom you have wronged, maybe, less than you sinned against your father — ?"

"Jesus!" Kristin wept most piteously. "Jesus — have mercy — "

"You remember yet His name, I hear," said the priest, "the name of Him your father strove to follow as a

disciple and to serve as a faithful knight." He touched
the little crucifix which hung above them. "Sinless, God's
Son died upon the cross to atone for our transgressions
against Himself —

"Go home now, Kristin, and think over this that I
have said to you," said Sira Eirik, when her weeping was
a little allayed.

But in these same days southerly storms set in; gales,
sleet, and rain in torrents — at times it so raged that folk
found it hard to cross over their own courtyards without
risk of being blown clean over the house-tops, as one
might almost think. None could travel by the parish
roads. The spring floods came down so sudden and
furious that folk fled from the farms most in danger.
Kristin shifted most of her goods up into the new storehouse loft, and she got leave to put the cattle in Sira
Eirik's spring byre — the Jörundgaard spring byre lay
on the further side of the river. 'Twas cruelly toilsome
work in the rough weather — all through the paddocks
the snow lay soft as melting butter — and the beasts were
poor and weak; it had been a hard winter. Two of the
best young steers broke a leg as they walked — they
snapped like brittle stalks.

The day they shifted the cattle, Simon Darre, with four
of his house-carls, appeared of a sudden, half-way. They
set themselves to help. Amidst the wind and rain and all
the press and bustle, with cows that had to be held up and
sheep and lambs that must be borne, there was no making
oneself heard, nor leisure for the kinsfolk to talk. But
when they were come in to Jörundgaard in the evening,
and Kristin had got Simon and his men seated in the hall
— all who had been at work that day stood much in need
of a draught of warm ale — Simon was able to have some
speech with her. He begged her to come to Formo with
the women and children, and he and two of his men
would stay here with Ulf and the lads. Kristin thanked
him, but said she would stay on her manor; Lavrans and
Munan were at Ulvsvoldene already, and Jardtrud had
sought refuge at Sira Solmund's — she had come to be
such good friends with the priest's sister. Simon said:

"Folks deem it strange, Kristin, that you two sisters

never meet together. Ramborg will be ill content if I turn me home without you."

"I know well that it looks strange," said the woman, "but 'twould seem yet stranger, methinks, were I to go a-visiting my sister now, when the master of this house is from home — and folk know that you and he are unfriends."

On this, Simon said no more, and soon after he and his men took their leave.

Rogation week came in with a fearful storm, and by Tuesday news went round among the farms in the north of the parish that now had the flood swept away the bridge up in the gorge, which folk must cross when they were bound for the Hövring sæters. They began to fear for the great bridge south by the church. 'Twas built most strongly, of the stoutest timbers, and arched high in the middle, propped below with great tree-trunks set deep in the river-bed; but now the water swept over the bridge-ends, where they joined the banks, and the bridge-arch was packed and choked with all manner of driftage whirled down the stream from the north. The Laagen had flooded the low fields on both banks now, and at one place on the Jörundgaard lands, where was a hollow in the meadows, the water ran inwards, like a bay, almost up to the houses — and the roof of the smithy and the tops of the trees showed above it like small islands. The out-barn on the holm was gone down-stream already.

From the farms on the east side of the river but few men had come to church. They were fearful that the bridge might go in church-time, and cut them off from their homes. But up on the other bank, on the hill-side under the Laugarbru barn, where there was a little shelter from the storm, might be espied, between the snow flurries, a black clump of people. The word went round that Sira Eirik had said he would bear the cross over the bridge and set it on the eastern bank, even if none dared follow him.

A snow squall swept straight in the men's faces as the procession stepped out from the church. The snow drove through the air in slanting streaks — of the country-side but glimpses could be seen — now and again a cantlet of the blackening lake where the meadows had been; cloud-scud sweeping across the screes and the tongues of forest on the hill-sides; glimpses high up of fell-tops against the high-piled clouds. The air was loaded with a mingled roar — the river's drone, rising and falling; the rushing noise of the woods; the howling of the wind —and ever and again there was a dull booming echo of the raging of the storm among the mountains, and the thunder of slides of new snow.

The tapers were blown out as soon as they were borne from out of the church cloister-way. This day grown young men had donned the choir-boys' white surplices — the wind tore at them; they walked, a whole cluster of them, holding the banner, with hands grasping the cloth that the wind might not tear it in shreds, while the procession, with bodies bent forward, clove its way against the wind across the hill-side. But over the raging of the storm rose, now and then, a few notes of Sira Eirik's ringing voice, as he fought his way forward, singing:

Venite: revertamur ad Dominum; quia ipse cepit et sanabit nos: percutiet, et curabit nos, et vivemus in conspectu ejus. Sciemus sequemurque, ut cognoscamus Dominum. Alleluia.*

Kristin stopped, she and all the other women, when the procession came to the place where the water had overflowed the road, but the white-clad young men, the deacons, and the priests, were up on the bridge already, and well-nigh all the men followed after — the water reached to their knees.

The bridge trembled and shook, and now the women were ware that from upstream a whole house was coming driving down upon the bridge. Round and round it was spun by the stream as it bore downwards; it was rent half in twain and the logs were spread asunder, but yet it hung together. The wife from Ulvsvoldene clung close to Kristin Lavransdatter and wailed aloud — her husband's two half-grown brothers were amongst the choir-lads. Kristin cried silently upon the Virgin Mary, and strained

---

* Come, and let us return unto the Lord: for he hath torn, and he will heal us; he hath smitten, and he will bind us up. . . . And we shall live in his sight. Then shall we know, if we follow on to know the Lord. . . . Hosea vi. 1–3.

her eyes towards the crowd on the middle of the bridge, where she could make out Naakkve's white-clad form among the men holding the flag. Through all the hubbub the women deemed they still could hear tones of Sira Eirik's chant.

He halted on the crown of the bridge, and lifted the cross high as the house struck. The bridge tottered and groaned — to the folk on both banks it seemed as though it settled somewhat towards the south. Then the procession went on, was lost from sight behind the bridge's arching back — came into sight upon the other shore. The wrecked house had tangled itself in the mass of other driftage clinging to the lower timbers of the roadway.

Then, sudden as a heavenly sign, silvery light dropped through the wind-driven cloud masses — a faint gleam, as of molten lead, was spread over the swollen river, far and wide. Mists and clouds burst asunder — the sun broke through, and when the procession came back across the bridge again, its beams sparkled on the cross; on the priest's wet, white alb the crossed stripes of the stole shone a wondrous purple-blue. Golden and glittering wet the Dale lay, as in the bottom of a cave of blue darkness, for, smitten down by the sun's rays, the storm-clouds clung high up round the brows of the fells and made the uplands black — between the heights the mists were fleeing, and the great mountain-dome above Formo rose up from the blackness, blinding white with new-fallen snow.

She had seen Naakkve go by. The dripping wet vestments clung about the boys, while they sang with might and main, out into the sunshine:

Salvator mundi, salva nos omnes. Kyrie, eleison; Christe, eleison; Christe, audi nos — *

The priests, the cross, had gone by; the crowd of farmers followed, heavy in their soaking clothes; but they looked about them with wondering, shining faces at the parting storm, as they joined in the pealing supplication — *Kyrie eleison!*

Then she saw — she believed not her eyes, 'twas she now who must cling to her neighbour-woman for support.

---

* Saviour of the world, save us all. Lord, have mercy; Christ, have mercy; Christ, hear us.

'Twas surely Erlend who walked there in the procession; he was clad in a dripping-wet, reindeer-skin coat with the hood over his head — but it was he; with half-open mouth, he cried *Kyrie eleison* like the rest — now he looked straight at her as he went by — she could not read the look on his face aright; there was somewhat — like the shadow of a smile upon it —

Together with the other women she followed the procession up over the church-green, chanting loud with the others in unison with the young lads who sang the litany. She was ware of naught but the wild hammering of her own heart.

During the Mass she had a glimpse of him one only time. She dared not stand in her wonted place — hid herself in the gloom in the northern aisle.

Soon as the service was at an end she hasted out. She fled from her serving-women who had been in the church. Outside, the whole valley was steaming in the sun. Kristin ran home, heedless of the bottomless mire of the way.

She spread her board, and set the brimming mead-horn before the master's high-seat, before she gave herself time to change her wet clothes for her holy-day wear — the dark-blue broidered dress, the silver belt, the buckled shoes, and the coif with the blue borders. Then she fell on her knees in the closet. She could not think, she could find no words of her own, as she so fain would — over again and over again, she said Ave Maria — Blessed Lady mine, dear Lord, Son of the Virgin — Thou knowest what I would say —

Time dragged slowly by. From her maids she heard that the men had gone to the bridge again — they were plying axes and hooks to loosen the mass of wreckage that had stuck fast — striving to save the bridge. The priests had gone thither too, when they had laid aside their vestments.

It was long past midday when the men came in. Her sons, Ulf Haldorssön and the three house-carls, an old man and two small parish boys who were kept on the manor.

Naakkve had already set him down in his place, the right of the master's high-seat. Suddenly he rose, left his place, and made for the door.

Kristin called him by name, half aloud.

On that he came back, and sat him down again. The colour came and went in the young face; he kept his eyes cast down, and ever and anon would set his teeth in his under-lip. His mother saw he was hard put to it to keep the mastery over himself — yet he won through the trial.

And at last the meal was at an end. The sons on the inner bench rose, came round the end of the board where was the empty high-seat, settled their belts a little, as of wont, after they had stuck their knives back into the sheaths, and went out.

When they were all gone, Kristin followed. The sun shone warm, and runnels were pouring from every roof. There was not a soul in the courtyard save Ulf — he stood on the stone slab outside his own house door.

A strangely helpless look came to his face as the mistress came towards him. He said no word — she asked, low:

"Spoke you with him?"

"Not many words. Naakkve and he talked together, I saw — "

A little after, he spoke again:

"He was somewhat fearful — for all of you — when there came down such a flood. So the thought took him to come home-about and see how things were going. Naakkve told him how you had managed —

"I know not where he had heard it — that you had given away the skins he sent you by Gaute in the autumn. He was angered at that. And so, too, when he found you had slipped straight home after Mass — he had thought you would have stayed and spoken with him — "

Kristin said naught; she turned and went in.

This summer there were endless broils and bickerings betwixt Ulf Haldorssön and his wife. Ulf's half-brother's son, Haldor Jonssön, had come to his kinsman in the spring and brought his wife with him; he had wedded the year before. Now 'twas meant that Haldor should take on lease the farm Ulf owned in Skaun, and flit thither on term-day; but Jardtrud was wroth, for she deemed Ulf had given his brother's son over-good terms, and she saw that the men had in mind that, in one way or another, things should be so ordered that the heritage of the farm be assured to Haldor.

Haldor had been Kristin's page-boy at Husaby, and she had much liking for the young man; his wife, too, a quiet, winsome young woman, she liked well. A little after midsummer the two young folk had a son born to them, and Kristin lent her the weaving-house, where the mistresses of the manor had themselves been wont to lie when they bore children — but Jardtrud took it ill that Kristin waited on the lying-in woman as the chief of the midwives — though Jardtrud herself was young and most unskilled, and could neither help a woman in child-birth nor care for a new-born babe.

Kristin was godmother to the boy, and Ulf gave the christening feast; but Jardtrud deemed that he spent too much on it, and that the gifts he laid in the cradle and on the mother's bed were by far too great. To stop her mouth a little, Ulf gave his wife, before all men's faces, divers costly things from among his chattels: a gilt cross and chain, a fur-lined cloak with a great silver clasp, a finger-ring of gold, and a brooch. But she saw that he would not give her a single rood of the land he owned, beyond what was her extra-gift when he wedded her — all his land was to go to his half-brothers and sisters, if he himself had no children. And now Jardtrud bemoaned herself that her child had been still-born, and that it looked not as though she should have more children — she was soon a laughing-stock among all the neighbours, for talking of this to everyone.

By reason of these bickerings Ulf had to pray Kristin to let Haldor and Audhild dwell in the hearth-room house when the young wife had held her churching. Kristin agreed gladly. She held aloof from Haldor, for it brought back to her so much that was sore to think on when she talked with him that had attended her in those old days. But much talk fell between her and the wife, for Audhild was bent on helping Kristin in every wise she could. And in the end of summer the child fell sorely sick; and on that Kristin took it in hand and tended it for the young, unlessoned mother.

When, in autumn, the two young folk set forth north-wards, she missed them, but most of all the little baby boy. Foolish as she herself knew it was, yet she had not been able, these last years, to rid her of a kind of sorrow because, all at once, she seemed to have grown barren — though she was no old woman, not yet forty years.

It had helped her to keep her mind from grievous thoughts that she had the young, childish wife and the little babe to help and tend. And, heavy as she deemed it to see that Ulf Haldorssön had not had better fortune in his marriage, yet had the happenings in the steward's house helped to take her thoughts away from other things.

For, after the fashion Erlend had borne him on Rogation day, she dared scarce think how it all would end. That he had come down to the parish and to the church, before all folks' eyes, and then had made off north again without greeting his wife with so much as one word, seemed to her so cruel that she deemed now at last she no longer cared what he might do —

With Simon Andressön she had not changed a word since that day of the spring flood when he came to help her. At the church she greeted him, and most often spoke a few words with her sister. What they thought of her affairs, and of Erlend's betaking him up to Dovre, she knew not.

But the Sunday before St. Bartholomew Mass * Sir Gyrd of Dyfrin came with the Formo folks to church. Simon looked wondrous glad as he went in to Mass by his brother's side. And, after the service, Ramborg came over to Kristin, and whispered eagerly that she was with child again and looked to be brought to bed at Maria Mass, in the spring:

"Kristin, sister, can you not come home and drink with us this day?"

Kristin shook her head sorrowfully, patted the young wife's pale cheek, and prayed that God might turn this to joy and blessing for the parents. But go to Formo she could not, she said.

After the breach with his brother-in-law, Simon had forced himself to believe that 'twas best so. He was so

---

* 24th August.

placed that he needed not to ask what folk judged of his doings in all things; he had helped Erlend and Kristin in their greatest need, and as for the stay he could be to them here in the parish, 'twas not so much worth that, to yield it them, he should make such a tangled web of his own life.

But when he heard that Erlend was gone from the parish, 'twas no longer possible for Simon to uphold the heavy, stubborn calm he had striven to feel. In vain he told himself that none, sure, knew rightly what was at the bottom of Erlend's long tarrying from home — folks prated so much and knew so little. And howsoever it might be, he could not mix himself in the matter. Yet was his mind never at rest. At times he pondered whether he should not seek out Erlend at Haugen, and eat the words he had said when they parted — thereafter he might see whether he could not find some way to set things right between his brother-in-law and his wife's sister. But he came no further than to think on it.

He believed not, indeed, anyone could mark on him that he was so uneasy in mind. He lived as he was wont, worked his farm and cared for his estates, was merry and drank manfully with his boon companions, lay out in the fells a-hunting when he had time, spoiled his children when he was at home, and never did an unkind word fall 'twixt him and his wife. To the folk on the manor it must rather seem as if the love between him and Ramborg were greater than ever before, since his wife was much more quiet and even in her bearing, and no longer fell into those fits of whimsy and childish anger over trifling matters. But in secret Simon felt himself shy and unsure in his dealings with her — no longer could he bring himself to take her as though she too were still half a child, to be teased and spoiled. He knew not now how he should behave him towards her.

And so he knew not, either, how he should take it, when one evening she said to him that now was she with child again.

"You are not over-glad of it, belike," he said at length, stroking her hand.

"But *you* are glad, I trow?" Ramborg nestled close to him, half laughing, half crying, and he laughed somewhat shamefacedly as he took her in his arms.

"This time I will be good and quiet, Simon, and not moan and wail as before. But you must *stay* with me — hear you? — if all your brothers-in-law and your brothers were in bonds and being led arow to the gallows, you must not forsake me!"

Simon laughed sadly:

"Whither should I go, my Ramborg — ? 'Tis not like that Geirmund, poor cripple, will broil himself in any great matter — and you know well he is the only man now, of my blood or kin, that I am not at odds with — "

"Oh! — " Ramborg laughed, too, through her tears. "Those quarrels will last no longer than till they need a helping hand and you deem you can give it. I know you well now, my husband — "

'Twas fourteen days later that, all unlooked for, Gyrd Andressön came to the manor. The Dyfrin knight had but one henchman attending him.

Few words passed between the brothers at their meeting. Sir Gyrd said somewhat of how he had not seen his sister and brother-in-law at Kruke these many years, and how the thought had come to him that he might journey up hither and give them greeting; and, once he was in the Dale, Sigrid thought surely he ought to visit at Formo too, "and I thought, brother, 'twas like you were not *so* wroth with me but that you would give me and my man food and shelter till to-morrow."

"You may believe that," said Simon — he stood looking down, flushed dark red in the face. "It was — kindly done of you, Gyrd, to come to me."

The brothers strolled out together after they had eaten. The corn was beginning to yellow here on the sunny slopes down towards the river. 'Twas most goodly weather — the Laagen shone gently enough now, in little white gleams down among the alder woods. Great white clouds sailed over the summer sky — sunshine filled the great bowl of the Dale, and the fell right over against them lay all soft blue and green in the haze of the heat and the drifting shadows of the clouds.

From within the paddock behind them came the thudding of horses' hoofs on the dry ground — the herd came trotting through the alder bush. Simon leaned over the fence: "Coltie — coltie — He begins to grow old now,

Bronsvein?" said he, as Gyrd's horse put his head over the paling and nosed at his master's shoulder.

"Eighteen winters" — Gyrd fondled the horse. "Methought, kinsman — this matter — 'twere all too ill a thing if it should part the friendship betwixt you and me," he said — and looked not at his brother.

"It has grieved me every day," answered Simon, low. "And I thank you for your coming, Gyrd."

They went farther along the fence: Gyrd first, Simon tramping after. At last they sat them down on the edge of a little stony stretch of burned-up yellow sward. There was a sweet, strong scent from the small hay-cocks that lay here and there amid the stone heaps, where the sickles had scraped together a little short, flowery hay. Gyrd told of the parley between King Magnus and the Haftorssöns and their following. After a while Simon asked:

"Deem you 'tis not to be thought of that any of those kinsmen of Erlend Nikulaussön should try to win him a full pardon and bring him back to the King's favour?"

"*I* cannot do much," said Gyrd Darre. "And they have no love for him, Simon, they that might perchance have the power. Ay, I have little mind to speak of that *now* — Methought he seemed a bold, winning fellow; but he showed up ill in that emprise of his; so deem the others. But I would liefer not talk of this now — I know well this brother-in-law of yours is so dear to you — "

Simon sat gazing out at the silvery gleams in the tree-tops on the slope below, and at the glittering sheen of the river. Wonderingly he thought — ay, in a way 'twas true too, what Gyrd said.

"Howbeit, in these days we are unfriends, Erlend and I," said he. " 'Tis a good while since we spoke together."

" — Meseems you have grown passing quarrelsome with the years, Simon," said Gyrd, laughing a little.

"Have you never thought," he asked a little after, "to leave these dales? We kinsmen might be of more help one to the other if we dwelt more near together."

"Can you think of such a thing — ? Formo is my udal heritage — "

"Aasmund of Eiken owns his part of that manor by right of udal. And I know he is not unwilling to change udal against udal — 'tis still in his thoughts that he might get your Arngjerd for Grunde according to the terms he proffered — "

Simon shook his head.

"Our father's mother's kin have had their seat on Formo manor ever since this land was heathen. And 'tis here I have ever meant that Andres shall dwell after me. I trow you have lost your wits, brother — should I part me from Formo?"

"Nay, 'tis but reason, what you say." Gyrd grew somewhat red. "I thought but that — maybe — in Raumarike you have most of your kinsfolk — and the friends of your youth — that perchance you might think that there you would thrive more happily."

"I thrive *here*," Simon, too, was grown red. "Here is the place where I can set the boy in a safe seat." He looked at Gyrd, and his brother's fine-cut, lined face took on somewhat of a bashful look. Gyrd's hair was well-night white now, but he was as slender and lithe of body as ever. He moved a little uneasily — some stones slipped from the heap he leaned on and rolled down the slope into the corn.

"Would you rake the whole scree down on my fields?" asked Simon, laughing, with a feigned gruffness. Gyrd sprang up, light and nimble, and held out a hand to his brother, who had a heavier weight to move.

Simon kept his brother's hand in his for a moment after he had got to his feet. Then he laid his own hand upon his brother's shoulder. On that Gyrd did the like; with their hands lying lightly on each other's shoulders the brothers went slowly up over the hill-side towards the manor.

They sat together over in the Sæmund's hall in the evening — Simon was to sleep with his brother. They had said their evening prayers, but they felt they must empty the ale-bowl before they went to rest.

"*Benedictus tu in muliebris — muliebris —* mind you?" laughed Simon all at once.

"Ay, it cost me a basted back many a time or ever Sira Magnus got my grandmother's false doctrine out of my head." — Gyrd smiled at the memory. "Hard-handed as the devil he was, too. Mind you, brother, once as he sat scratching his legs and had lifted the skirt of his habit

— you whispered to me that, had you been so crook-legged as Magnus Ketilssön, you, too, had been a priest and gone ever in a long gown — ?"

Simon smiled — it seemed to him he *saw* all at once his brother's boyish face, bursting with choked laughter for all its piteous rueful eyes: they were yet young boys then, and Sira Magnus *was* sorely hard of hand when he set to correcting them —

Over-bright Gyrd had not been when they were children. Ay, and 'twas not because he was an over and above wise man that he loved Gyrd now. But he grew warm with thankfulness and tenderness towards his brother as he sat here — for every day of their brother-hood, well-nigh forty years now — for Gyrd, even as he was, the most guileless, the most true-hearted of men.

And so this, that he had won back his brother Gyrd, seemed to Simon much as though he had at the least got a fast foothold with one foot. And for long now his life had been so woefully warped and tangled.

He felt a warm glow each time he thought on Gyrd, who had come to him to make good again the breach he himself had made, when he rode from his brother's manor in anger and with unseemly words. His heart overflowed with thankfulness — he had others to thank besides Gyrd.

A man like Lavrans, now — how *he* would have taken such a happening he knew well enough. He could follow his father-in-law as far as he was worthy to follow — with almsgiving and the like. Such things as a broken and contrite heart and adoration of the Lord's wounds were beyond him, unless he stared his eyes out at the crucifix — and that was not what Lavrans had meant. Tears of repentance he could not weep — he deemed not he had wept more than maybe two or three times since he had left childhood behind, and not then when he had the most need to have done so — those times when he had fallen into great transgression — with Arngjerd's mother, while he was a wedded man, and then that man-slaying a year back. And yet he had repented sorely — it seemed to him he repented his sins heartily at all times, confessed them fully, and made amends according to the priest's behest. He said his prayers ever with diligence, took heed to give the right tithes and abundant alms — most of all to the honour of St. Simon the Apostle, St. Olav, St. Michael and Mary Virgin. Otherwise he rested content with what Sira Eirik said, that in the cross alone was salvation, and how else a man should meet and fight the enemy was in God's hand, not his.

But now he felt himself drawn to show, with somewhat more fervency, his deep thankfulness to all the holy ones. He had been born on the birthday of Mary Virgin, so his mother had said — it came to his mind that he would fain pay the Lord's mother his homage by a prayer he was not wont to say daily. He had had written down a goodly prayer, the time he was at the King's court, and now he sought out the little scroll.

He feared, indeed, now he thought of it, 'twas more to please King Haakon than for the sake of God and Mary, that he had got him, while he was with the body-guard, some such little rolls with prayers, and learnt them. All the young men did it, for 'twas the King's wont to question his pages on what they knew of such profitable lore, when he lay abed of nights and could not sleep.

Oh, ay — 'twas long ago now. The King's bedchamber in the stone hall of the royal castle at Oslo. On the little board by the bed stood a single taper burning — its gleam fell upon the fine-cut, wan, and aged face that lay propped upon the red silk pillows. When the priest had ended his reading aloud and was gone, the King himself often took the book, and lay reading with the heavy tome leaned against his drawn-up knees. On two footstools, away by the great stone-walled chimney, sat the pages — he himself kept watch nigh always along with Gunstein Ingasön. 'Twas pleasant in the chamber — the fire burned clear and hot and gave out no smoke, the room seemed so warm and snug with its cross-vaulted ceiling and walls ever hung with tapestry. But they grew sleepy sitting so — first hearing the priest read and afterwards waiting for the King to fall asleep; 'twas scarce ever much before midnight. When he slept, they had leave to take turns at watching, and to rest between-whiles on the bench 'twixt the chimney and the door of the Council Hall. So they sat, longing for him to fall asleep, and swallowing down their yawns.

It might happen that the King would fall into talk

with them — not often — but when he did he was marvellous kindly and winning. Or he would read aloud from a book a wise saw, or some few staves of verse that he thought might profit the young men or be wholesome for them to hear.

One night he was waked himself by King Haakon calling him — 'twas pitch dark; the taper was burned out. Miserably shamed, he made shift to blow the embers alive again, and lit a new candle. The King lay smiling slyly:

"Doth this Gunstein ever snore so fearfully?"

"Ay, my lord!"

"You share his bed in the hostel too, I trow? Methinks 'twere but reason you should crave to be given for a while a bedfellow that makes less hubbub in his sleeping."

"I thank my good lord — but it matters naught to me, Lord King."

"But you must needs wake, Simon, when this thunderpeal breaks loose right by your ear — is't not so?"

"Ay, your Grace, but I have but to give him a jog and turn him over somewhat."

The King laughed.

"I marvel if you young men understand that such a stomach to sleep is a great gift from God. When you are come to my years, friend Simon, mayhap then you will remember these my words — "

'Twas endlessly far away — and yet clear; but it seemed not as if it could be the man sitting here that had been the young page —

One day when Advent was beginning, and Kristin was well-nigh alone at the manor — her sons were carting home firewood and moss — she wondered to see Simon Darre come riding into the courtyard. His errand was to bid her and her sons to a feast at Formo at Yule.

"Sure you must know, Simon, that we cannot do as you would," she said soberly. "Friends we can be, as much as ever, in our hearts, you and Ramborg and I — but you know well that it rests not always with us to do as we would."

"You cannot mean that you will go so far in this as not to come to your only sister's help when she is to lie in the straw?"

Kristin prayed that all might go well, and end in joy
for them both, "but I cannot say for sure if I can come."

"All folk will deem it passing strange," said Simon
vehemently. "You have the name of being the best of
midwives — and she is your sister — and you two are
mistresses of the two greatest manors in this northern
country-side."

"Not a few children have been born into the world on
the great manors here these last years, and I not even
prayed to come. No longer is it so, Simon, that 'tis not
reckoned that all is done fittingly in the lying-in room if
the mistress of Jörundgaard be not there." She saw that
he grew much disheartened at her words, and she went
on: "Greet Ramborg, and say I will go to her and help
her when the time comes — but to your Yule-tide feast
I cannot come, Simon."

But on the eighth day of Yule she met Simon coming
to Mass without Ramborg. No, all was well with her, he
said; but 'twas well for her to rest and gather strength,
for to-morrow he was faring south to Dyfrin with her
and the children — the roads were so good for sleigh
travel; and since Gyrd had begged them to come, and
Ramborg had such a mind to it, why —

4

THE DAY after Paul's Mass * Simon Darre rode north over
Mjös, with two henchmen in his company. It was set in
hard frost, but he deemed he could not stay from home
longer; the sledges with the women-folk must come later,
as soon as the cold was somewhat bated.

At Hamar he met a friend, Vigleik Paalssön of Faga-
berg, and they rode on together. When they were come
to Little Hamar they rested a while at a farm where was
an ale-tap. While they were sitting at their drink, some
drunken fur-hawkers in the room fell foul of each other
and came to blows; at last Simon got up, thrust in between,
and parted them, but so doing he got a knife-cut in the
right forearm. 'Twas little more than a scratch, and he

---

* 15th January.

took no heed of it, but the woman of the house made him suffer her to bind a cloth about it.

He rode home with Vigleik, and slept the night at his house. The men shared a bed, and on towards morning Simon was wakened by the other crying out aloud in his sleep. Vigleik called out his name more times than one; so Simon waked him up and asked what was amiss with him.

Vigleik could not remember his dream rightly. "But an ugly dream it was, and you were in it. One thing I mind — Simon Reidarssön stood here in the room and bade you go with him — I saw him so plain I could have told the freckles on his face."

"That dream I would you could sell me," said Simon, half in jest and half in earnest. Simon Reidarssön was his father's brother's son, and they had been good friends in their youth; the cousin had died when he was thirteen or thereabout.

In the morning, when the men were sitting down to break their fast, Vigleik saw that Simon had left the right sleeve of his jerkin unbuttoned at the wrist. The flesh was red and swollen all down the back of the hand. He spoke of it, but Simon laughed. And when, a little later, his friend begged him to stay there some days — to wait for his wife there — Vigleik could not forget his dream — Simon Andressön answered something peevishly: "Sure, you dreamed not aught so ill about me, Vigleik, as that I kept my bed for a louse-bite — ?"

About sunset Simon and his men rode down to Losna lake. It had been the fairest day; now the high blue and white fells were grown golden and pink in the evening light, but the rime-laden thickets along the river stood all shaggy grey in the shadow. The men had rarely good horses, and they had a brisk ride before them over the long lake — small bits of ice flew out tinkling and clinking from under the horses' hoofs. A biting wind blew hard against them; Simon was bitter cold — but soon after strange, qualmish surges of heat ran through him, despite the cold — then ice waves that seemed to pierce right to the marrow of his spine. At times he felt his tongue swell and grow strangely thick far back in his throat. Ere yet they had got over the lake, he had to stop and pray one

of his men to help him fasten up his cloak, for a sling for
his right arm.

The men had heard Vigleik Paalssön talk of his dream;
now they would have had their master show them the
wound. But Simon said 'twas naught — it smarted a little:
" — Belike I must content me to be left-handed some few
days."

But as the evening wore on — the moon had risen and
they were riding high up on the ridges north of the lake
— Simon felt himself that his arm might likely be troublesome after all. It ached right up in the arm-pit; the jolt-
ing on the horse's back tormented him sorely — the blood
throbbed and throbbed in the ailing limb. And his head
throbbed and ached from the nape upwards. He grew hot
and cold by turns.

The winter road went high up the hill-side here, in
parts through forest, in parts over white farm-lands.
Simon saw it all — the full moon sailed silver bright in
the pale blue heavens; it had driven all the stars far from
its path; only one or two great ones dared to show their
face away far off in the sky. The white fields glittered and
sparkled; the shadows fell short and sharp upon the
snow — within the woods the light lay vaguely in splashes
and stripes between the snow-laden firs. Simon saw all
this —

— But at the same time he saw most plain, in sunshine
of early spring, a field of tufted, ashy-brown grass. Some
stunted firs had pushed up here and there in the outskirts;
they shone like green velvet in the sun. He knew it
again; 'twas the home-paddock at Dyfrin. The stems of
the alder trees in the woods beyond the field stood glossy
grey as in spring, and their tops brown with blossom —
behind lay the long low Raumarike ridges, shining blue,
still flecked with snow. They were on their way down
to the alder thicket, Simon Reidarssön and he; they had
fishing-tackle and pike-spears — they were bound for the
lake lying there dark grey with rotten ice, to fish in the
open water at the lake end. — His dead cousin walked by
his side: he saw his playmate's curly hair bushing out
from underneath his cap, reddish of hue in the spring
sunlight; he could count each freckle in the boy's face.
The other Simon stuck out his under-lip a little and

blew — ph, ph, when he deemed his namesake's talk foolish. They hopped across the water-hills, sprang from tuft to tuft over the oozing snow-water in the grass-land. There was a mossy growth at the bottom — it frothed and mantled a lovely green, down below the water.

Though his senses had not left him — though he saw all the time the bridle-path uphill and downhill, through forest, over white farmlands in glittering moonshine — saw the sleeping, clustered houses under snow-buried roofs cast shadows across the fields, saw the mist-belt over the river in the bottom of the dale — and knew that 'twas Jon who rode just behind him and spurred up alongside when they came out on open clearings — yet he found himself more than once calling the man Simon. He knew 'twas wrong, but he could not help doing it, though he saw that his men grew afraid.

"We must see and come as far as the monks' at Roaldstad to-night, men," he said, once when his head grew clearer.

The serving-men pleaded with him — they should rather see and get within doors as soon as might be; they named the nearest priest's house. But the master would have his way.

" 'Twill be hard for the horses, Simon —" The two henchmen glanced at each other.

But Simon laughed a little. They must abide it for once in a way. He thought on the weary miles. The pain drove through his whole body with each jolt in the saddle. But home he must and would. For now he knew that he was fey —

And though in the winter night he froze to the marrow and burned by turns, yet all the time he felt the mild spring sun in the grazing-paddock at home, and the dead boy and he went on and on towards the alder brake.

For brief moments the vision melted away, and his head grew clear — only that it ached fearfully. He prayed one of the men to cut open his sleeve over the aching arm. He went white, and the sweat trickled down over his face, as Jon Daalk warily ripped open his jerkin and shirt from wristband to shoulder, while he himself stayed the swollen limb with his left hand. That eased it for a while.

Thereafter the men fell a-talking — at Roaldstad they

must see and have word sent south to Dyfrin. But Simon
would hear naught of it. He would not disquiet his wife
with such a message, when, belike, 'twas not needful — a
sledge journey in such bitter cold was not good. Mayhap
when he was come home to Formo; they would see. He
tried to smile at Sigurd to hearten the lad — he looked
awestruck and forlorn.

"But you must send for Kristin at Jörundgaard, as soon
as we come home — she is so good a leech-woman." He
felt his tongue thick and hard as wood as he said it.

Kiss me, Kristin, my promised maid! First she would
think 'twas wandering talk. No, Kristin. Then would she
marvel.

Erlend had seen it. Ramborg had seen it. But Kristin —
she sat there full of her cares and her wrath — so vexed
and so bitter as she was with yonder man Erlend — for
others than him she had no thought even now. You never
set so much by me, Kristin, my beloved, as to think if
'twere a heavy lot, to be brother to her who once was
promised me to wife —

— In sooth he himself had not known it, that time he
parted from her outside the cloister gate in Oslo — that
he would go on ever thinking of her thus; that in the
end 'twould seem to him naught he had got in life since
then could make up fully for what then he had lost. For
the maid that was sealed to me in my youth.

She should hear it before he died. One kiss should she
give him

— I am he who loved you, and who loves you still —

These words had he heard once, and he had never been
able to forget them. They were from Mary Virgin's
miracle book; 'twas a tale of a nun who fled away from
her convent with a knight. Mary Virgin — in the end she
saved these two, and forgave them in despite of their
sin. If 'twere sin for him to say it to his wife's sister ere
he died, then God's mother must win his forgiveness for
this too — 'Twas not so oft that he had troubled her by
craving aught —

— I believed it not myself, that time — that never again
should I be rightly glad or merry —

"Nay, Simon, 'twere all too heavy for Sokka, should
she bear us both — so far as she has had to fare this
night," he said to him who had got up behind him on his

horse, and held him up. "Ay — I see 'tis you, Sigurd, but
I deemed you were another — "

Towards morning they had come as far as the pilgrims'
hostel, and the two monks, who were charged with the
care of the place, took the sick man in hand. But when,
under their tending, he had grown somewhat better and
his fever wanderings were abated, naught would serve
Simon but they must lend him a sledge to drive on
farther north.

The going was good, and they changed horses by the
way, journeyed all the night, and came to Formo next
morning at daybreak. Simon had lain and dozed under
the many coverings that had been spread over him. They
weighed upon him so — sometimes he felt as he were
lying crushed beneath huge rock slabs — and his head
ached so. Between-whiles he seemed as 'twere to lose
himself. Then the pains began to rage again within him
— 'twas as though his body boiled and boiled up, grew
monstrously huge, and was like to burst in bits. His arm
throbbed and throbbed —

He tried to get from the sledge and walk in on his
feet — with his good arm over Jon's shoulder; Sigurd
came behind to hold him up. Simon was ware that the
men's faces were grey and drawn with weariness — for
two whole nights on end had they sat in their saddles.
He would have said somewhat to them of this, but his
tongue obeyed him not. He stumbled over the threshold
and fell forward into the room — with a roar of pain, as
his shapeless, swollen arm struck against something. The
sweat streamed from him, as he strove to choke down
the groans that were wrung from him while he was
unclothed and helped to bed.

Not long after, he saw that Kristin Lavransdatter stood
over by the fire-place, pounding somewhat in a wooden
bowl with a pestle. The sound tramped so through his
head! She poured somewhat from a little pot into a
beaker, and dropped drops into it from a glass flask that
she took from her case — emptied the pounded stuff from
the bowl into the pot and set it on the fire. How still and
deft in all her ways — !

Now she came over to the bed with the beaker in her hand. She walked so lightly. She was straight and fair as the maid had been, this slender housewife with the thin, grave face under the linen coif. It hurt him, for the back of his neck was swollen too, when she passed one arm under his head and lifted him somewhat. She propped his head against her breast while she held the beaker to his mouth with her left hand.

Simon smiled a little, and when, warily, she let his head sink back upon the pillows, he caught her hand in his whole one. 'Twas not soft or white any more, the fine, long, narrow woman's hand.

"These fingers of yours are ill at sewing silk now, I trow," said Simon. "But good and light are they — and blessedly cold is your hand, Kristin!" He laid it on his brow. Kristin stood thus till she felt the palm of her hand grow warm; then she took it away and pressed her other hand gently upon his burning brow — close under the roots of the hair.

"You have an ugly arm, Simon," she said. "But with God's help I trust all will go well."

"I fear me, Kristin, me you cannot heal, skilful leech as you are," said Simon. But he looked almost cheerly. The drink was beginning to work; he felt the pains much less. But his eyes felt so strange — as though he could not guide them — it seemed to him he must be lying there with his eyes squinting one to either side.

"'Twill go with me as 'tis doomed to go, I trow," he said as before.

Kristin went back to her pots — smeared a paste upon linen cloths, came back and swathed the hot bandages around his arm from the finger-tips right round behind his back and over his breast, where the swelling spread from his arm-pit in red stripes. It hurt sorely at first, but soon it brought a little ease. She wrapped woollen over all and laid soft down cushions under the arm. Simon asked what 'twas she had put upon the bandages.

"Oh, 'tis divers simples — salsify and swallow-wort for the most," said Kristin. "Had it but been summer, I could have gathered it fresh from my herb-garden. But I had a plenty — thanks to God — this winter I have had no need of it till now."

"What was it you told once of swallow-wort — you had heard it of the abbess when you were in the cloister — of the name — ?"

"Mean you that in all tongues it has a name that means swallow-blossom — all the way from the sea of Greece hither to the northern lands?"

"Ay — for in all lands it springs into bloom when the swallows wake from their winter sleep." Simon shut his lips a little closer. By then he would have lain long in the earth —

"I would have my resting-place at the church here," said he, "if it so befall that I die now, Kristin. Now am I so rich a man that Andres, belike, will sit here in Formo a man of some power in time to come. I wonder much if 'twill be a son that Ramborg will bear in spring after I am gone — I had been fain to live so long that I had seen two sons in my house — "

Kristin said she had sent word south to Dyfrin of his having fallen so sick. Gaute — that very morning he had set forth —

"You sent not the child to ride that road alone?" asked Simon, in alarm.

She had had none at hand that she deemed could keep pace with Gaute on Rauden, answered she. Simon said 'twas like to be a hard road for Ramborg — and if only she did not journey more hastily than was fit for her. "But my children, sure enough, I would fain see again — "

A while after, he began again to speak of his children. He talked of Arngjerd — of whether he had done wrong not to fall in with that proffer from the folk at Eiken. But the man seemed to him full old — and he had been fearful, for that Grunde had the name of being somewhat ungoverned when he was in drink. Arngjerd — her in especial he would fain have seen settled in full security. Now 'twould be for Gyrd and Gudmund to find a husband for her. "Tell my brothers, Kristin — I sent them greetings and prayed that they would look well before them in this matter. Would you take her away with you to Jörundgaard for a while, I would be thankful to you, where I lie. And should Ramborg wed again ere Arngjerd is cared for, then must you take her to you, Kristin. Nay, you must not deem aught else than that Ramborg has been good to her at all times — but were she to have both step-mother and step-father, I fear me she might be looked on more as a serving-wench than as — you mind, I was wed with Halfrid when I became her father — "

Kristin laid her hand gently on Simon's, and gave her promise that she would do for the maid all that lay in her power. She remembered all she had seen — things were hard for the children that had a man of worship for father, and they born out of wedlock. Orm and Margret, Ulf Haldorssön — She stroked and stroked Simon's hand.

"But 'tis not so sure, either, that you will die this time, brother-in-law," she said, smiling a little. Even yet, at times, there would pass as 'twere a shadow of the young maid's sweet, gentle smile over the thin, stern face of the woman. Thou sweet, young Kristin — !

Simon's fever was not so high this evening, and the pains were less, he said. When Kristin changed the ban-dages on his arm, 'twas not so swollen; the flesh was softer, the marks of her fingers stayed a while when she pressed it warily.

Kristin sent the serving-folk to bed. Jon Daalk, whom naught would serve but that he should watch over his master, she let lie down over on the bench. The box bench with the carven back she had drawn up before the bed, and she sat there, leaning in a corner. Simon dozed and slept — once, when he woke, he saw that she had got her-self a spindle. She sat so straight; she had stuck the staff with the tuft of wool under her left arm, her fingers twisted the yarn, the staff sank and sank alongside her long, slender lap — then she wound up the thread, twisted again, the staff sank and sank — he drowsed off with watching it —

When he waked again, towards morning, she still sat there as before, spinning. The light from the taper she had placed so that the bed-hanging shaded him, fell straight upon her face. It was so pale and still; the full, soft mouth had grown thin-lipped and firmly shut; she sat with downcast eyes, spinning. She could not see that he lay awake, gazing at her from the shelter of the bed-tent. She seemed so deathly sad, that Simon felt as though his heart bled within him as he lay there and gazed at her.

She rose, went over and saw to the fire. So noiselessly!
When she came back she peered in behind the bed-tent —
met his open eyes looking from the dark.

"How is't with you now, Simon?" she asked, softly.

"Well — 'tis with me now."

But he deemed he felt now a tenderness up under his
left arm, too — and under his chin when he moved his
head. Oh, no, 'twas naught but fancy, belike —

— Ah, sure it was she would never deem she had lost
aught when she cast away his love — so far as that went,
he might well tell her of it. 'Twas impossible *that* should
make her more heavy-hearted. He *would* tell her, before
he died — *once* only: I have loved you all these years —

The fever waxed again. And there *was* pain in the left
arm —

"You must try if you can sleep again, Simon. Maybe
you will mend now quickly," she said, low.

"I have slept much to-night — " He began speaking of
his children again — the three he had and loved so dearly
— and the one unborn. Then silence fell upon him — the
pains took him again so sorely. "Lie down a little now,
Kristin. Jon can sit up a while, I trow, if you deem 'tis
needful that one keep watch."

In the morning, when she loosed the bandages, Simon
looked up calmly into her despairing face: "Ah, no, Kristin, there was overmuch foulness and poisonous stuff in the
arm already — and freezing cold had I been too — ere I
came into your hands. 'Tis as I said — me you cannot heal.
Be not so sorrowful for this, Kristin."

"You should not have journeyed all that long way," she
said, in a weak voice.

"No man outlives his fated day," answered Simon, as
before. "I was set on getting home, you see — There is
one thing and another to speak about — how things shall
be ordered when I am gone."

He laughed a little:

"All fires burn out at last."

Kristin looked at him with tea-bright eyes. He had ever
had a by-word in his mouth. She looked down at his red-
flecked face. The heavy cheeks, the folds below the chin,
seemed as 'twere sunken — lay in deep layers. His eyes
looked both dull and glittering — then again they cleared

and thought came back to them; he looked up at her with the steadfast, searching look which most oft had been in his small, sharp, steel-grey eyes.

When broad daylight came in the room, Kristin saw that Simon's face was grown thin about the nose — a strip of white ran down on either side to the corners of his mouth.

She went over to the little glass pane, stood there, and swallowed down her tears. The thick coating of rime on the window glittered and shone a golden green. Without must still be such fair winter weather as had been all the week —

—'Twas the mark of death, she knew —

She came back, and passed her hand in under the coverlid — he was swollen around the ankles, and up along the legs.

"Would you — would you that we should send for Sira Eirik now?" she said softly.

"Ay, to-night," answered Simon.

He must speak of it *before* he confessed and took the sacrament. Afterward he must try and turn his thoughts another way.

"Strange it is that 'tis like to be you that will lay out my body," said Simon. " — And a fair corpse I fear me I shall not be."

Kristin choked down a sob. She went away and made ready a cooling draught again. But Simon said:

"I like not these drinks of yours, Kristin — a man's thoughts grow so unclear after them."

Yet, after a while, he begged that she would give him a little. "But put not overmuch in it of the drowsy stuff. I must speak with you of a matter."

He drank, and lay waiting for the pains to abate so much that he could talk with her clearly and calmly.

"Would you not that we should fetch Sira Eirik — that he might speak such words as would bring you solace at this pass?"

"Yes, soon. But there is somewhat I must get said to you first."

He lay a little. Then he said:

"Say to Erlend Nikulaussön, that the words I spoke when last we parted, those words have I repented each day since. Unmanly and little-minded did I show me to my brother-in-law that night — Greet him and say — pray him to forgive it me."

Kristin sat with bowed head — Simon saw she flushed blood-red to the very brows.

"You will bear this message to your husband?" he asked. She nodded a little. Then Simon said again:

"If Erlend come not to my grave-ale, then must you seek him out, Kristin, and tell him this."

Kristin sat silent, with face dark flushed.

"You will not deny me this that I beg of you, now that I am to die?" asked Simon Andressön.

"No," whispered the woman, "I will — do it — "

" 'Tis ill for your sons, Kristin, that there is unfriendliness 'twixt their father and mother," Simon began again. "I marvel if you have seen how much it troubles them. Hard is it for the brave lads to know that their parents are the common talk of the parish."

Kristin answered, in a low, hard voice:

"Erlend forsook our sons — not I. First my sons lost their foothold in the country-side where they were born to rank and udal lands. If now they must suffer that their home here in the Dale, my home, is matter of parish talk — 'tis not I that have wrought it."

Simon lay for a little in silence. Then he said:

"I have not forgot it, Kristin — much rightful cause have you to plain — ill has Erlend ordered things for his own. But you should remember — had this his plan gone forward, his sons' lot were now secure, and he himself had stood amid the mightiest knights of this realm. Traitor is he called who fails in such a venture — but if he wins, folk talk far otherwise. Half Norway thought with Erlend then — that we were ill served with sharing a king with the Swedes, and that in Knut Porse's son we might look to find other metal than in this weakling — could we have got Prince Haakon hither to us in his tender years. Many stood behind Erlend then and pulled the rope with him — they dropped it and crept to shelter when the matter came to light — so did my brothers and many others whom folk call now good knights and esquires-at-arms. Erlend alone went down — And in that pinch, Kristin, your husband showed him a bold and manful fellow — howsoever he may have borne him before and since — "

Kristin sat quiet, trembling.

"I hold, Kristin, if 'tis by reason of this matter you have spoken to your husband bitter words, then must you eat them again. Surely you can bring you to do that, Kristin — once on a time you held to Erlend fast enough — would not hear a true word said of his dealings with you, when he had done such deeds as I could never have deemed an honest man, not to say a high-born knight and a *kurteis* gentleman-at-arms — mind you where I came upon you two in Oslo? *That* you could forgive Erlend, both then and since — "

Kristin answered low:

"I had cast in my lot with his then — what would have become of me afterwards, had I parted my life from Erlend's?"

"Look on me, Kristin," said Simon Darre, "and answer me true. Had I held your father fast to the word he had given — chosen to take you, even as you were — had I said to you that never should you be minded of your shame by me, but that loose you I would not — what had you then done?"

"I know not."

Simon laughed a hard laugh:

"Had I forced you to drink the bride-ale with me — I trow, you had scarce taken me to your arms willingly, Kristin, my fair one — "

Her face was white now. She sat looking down, answering naught. He laughed as before:

"I trow you had scarce welcomed me kindly, when I mounted the wedding-bed beside you — "

"Methinks I had taken a knife with me to bed," she said in a half-choked whisper.

"I hear you know the ballad of Knut of Borg" — Simon smiled grimly. "That such a thing has happed 'twixt living folk I have never heard. But God knows whether *you* had not done it!"

A little after he spoke again:

" 'Tis unheard of, too, among Christian men, for lawfully wedded folk to part them of their own wills, as you have done — without lawful cause and the bishop's leave. Are you not ashamed, you two — ? You trod all underfoot and braved all that you might come together; that time Erlend was in peril of life, you thought of naught but of saving him, and he thought more on you than on his seven sons and his name and his goods. But so soon as you can possess each other in peace and safety, then you throw seemliness and peace to the winds — wrangling and miscontent were betwixt you at Husaby, too; that saw I myself, Kristin —

"— I tell you, for your sons' sakes, you must seek atonement with your husband. If you be least in the wrong, then belike 'tis the easier too for you to proffer Erlend your hand," said he, more gently.

" — 'Tis easier for you than for Erlend Nikulaussön, sitting up there at Haugen in poverty," said Simon again.

" 'Tis not easy for me," she whispered. "Meseems I have shown that, for my children, I can do a little. — I have striven and striven for them — "

"It is so," said Simon. Then he asked: "Mind you the day we met on the road by Nidaros? You sat in the grass giving Naakkve suck — "

Kristin nodded.

"Could you have done for the child at your breast what my sister did for her son — given him from you to those better able to care for him?"

Kristin shook her head.

"But pray his father to forget what you may have said to him in anger — think you not you could do that for him and six fair sons besides — say to your man, 'tis needful for the young lads' sakes that he come home to them and to his manor — ?"

"I will do as you would have me, Simon," said Kristin, low. "Hard are the words you have spoken to me," she said a little after. "Before now, too, you have chidden me more harshly than any other layman — "

"Ay, but now can I promise you 'twill be the last time" — his voice took on the teasing, mirthful ring of old days. "Nay, weep not so, Kristin — but remember, sister mine, this have you promised to a dying man." Once more the old, wicked gleam came to his eyes:

"You know well, Kristin — before now I have had cause to know you were not one to put full trust on!"

"Be still now, dear one," he begged a little later; he had lain listening to her broken, sore weeping. "Be sure I remember that you were to us a good and faithful sister. We were friends at the last in spite of all, my Kristin — "

Towards evening he prayed that they would fetch the

priest to him. Sira Eirik came, shrived him, and gave him
the last oil and viaticum. He took leave of his serving-folk
and of the Erlendssöns, the five who were at home —
Naakkve, Kristin had sent to Kruke — Simon had begged
to see Kristin's children that he might say farewell to them.

This night, too, Kristin watched over the dying man.
Towards morning she fell asleep for a moment. She was
wakened by a strange sound — Simon lay moaning a little,
softly. It shook her fearfully, when she heard it — that *he*
should bemoan himself, quietly and bitterly, like a poor,
forsaken child, now when, belike, he thought that none
would hear it. She bent down and kissed him many times
upon the face. A sickening, deathly smell came already
from his breath and his body. But, as the day grew light,
she saw that his eyes were alive and clear and steadfast
as ever.

He suffered fearful pain, she saw, when Jon and Sigurd
lifted him in a sheet while she put his bed aright and made
it as soft and easy as she could. Food he had taken none
for a whole day and night, but he had a great thirst.

When she had settled him aright, he begged that she
would make the sign of the cross over him: "I cannot
move the left arm either now."

— But when we cross ourselves, or mark with the cross
anything that we would guard, then shall we bear in mind
why the cross was made holy and what it means, and remember that 'twas by the pains and death of the Lord
that his sign came to honour and power —

Simon remembered, this had he heard one read aloud.
Sure enough he had been little wont to think much when
he crossed his breast, or set the cross upon his houses and
his goods. — He felt him unready and ill beseen to fare
forth from this earthly home — he must comfort himself by thinking that he had made him ready with shrift
as well as could be in the time, and that he had been given
the last offices. Ramborg — but she was so young, maybe
she would live much happier with another man. His
children, God must take them in His ward — and Gyrd
would care for their welfare faithfully and wisely. And
for the rest he must put his trust in God, who judges a
man, not according to his worth, but of His own grace —

On in the day came Sigrid Andresdatter and Geirmund
of Kruke. Thereupon Simon would have it that Kristin

must go out and rest, so long she had watched and tended him now. "And soon 'twill be irksome to be near me," said he, smiling a little. At that, for a moment, she broke into loud sobs — then she bent down and kissed again the poor body that was already begun to decay.

Thereafter Simon lay still. The fever and the pains were now less sore. He lay thinking, sure now it could not be long before he was set free.

He marvelled himself that he had spoken to Kristin as he had done. 'Twas not this that he had meant to say to her. But he had not been able to speak otherwise. At times he was well-nigh vexed about it.

But now the poison must have worked inward to his heart. A man's heart is the first thing to quicken in his mother's womb, and the last to grow still in him. But in him now it sure must soon come to rest.

In the evening he lay wandering. More than once he groaned aloud, so that 'twas fearsome to hear it. But at other times he lay laughing softly, and speaking his own name, as Kristin thought — but Sigrid, who sat bent over him, whispered to her, she deemed he was talking of a boy, their cousin, with whom he had been good friends in childhood. Towards midnight he grew still and seemed to sleep. Then Sigrid prevailed with Kristin to lie down a little upon the other bed in the room.

She was waked by a noise in the room — 'twas a little before dawn — and then she heard that the death-throes had begun. Simon was past speech, but he knew her yet; she could see it by his eyes. Then it seemed as though a spring snapped within them — they turned up under the eyelids. But yet a while he lay, the rattle in his throat, still living. The priest was come, he read the prayers for the dying; the two women sat by the bed, and the whole household were come into the room. At last, a while before midday, he drew his last breath.

The day after, Gyrd Darre came riding in to the Formo courtyard. He had broken down a horse on the way. Down by Breidin he had heard of his brother's death, so that he was calm enough at first. But when his sister threw herself weeping into his arms, he pressed her to him, and he too wept like a child.

Ramborg Lavransdatter, he told them, lay at Dyfrin

with a new-born son. When Gaute Erlendssön came with the message, she had shrieked aloud straightway that she knew 'twould be Simon's death. Then she had fallen upon the floor in a fit. The child had come six weeks before its time, but they hoped 'twould live.

A goodly grave-ale was held for Simon Andressön, and he was buried close up to the choir by the Olav's Church. The parish folk were well pleased that he had chosen his resting-place there. The old Formo stock, that died out on the spear side with Simon Sæmundssön, had been a mighty and a gallant line; Astrid Simonsdatter wed richly; her sons bore the knightly name and sat in the King's council, but came home but seldom to their mother's udal lands. When, therefore, her grandson took up his abode upon the manor, folk deemed 'twas well-nigh as though the old race was set in their seat again; soon they forgot to account Simon Andressön a stranger, and they sorrowed much that he must die so young; for at his death he was but two-and-forty winters old.

5

Week after week went by, and Kristin made ready in her heart to bear to Erlend the dead man's message. Do it she would for sure — but she deemed it a hard matter. And meanwhile there was so much that must be done at home upon the manor. From day to day she put herself off with fresh pleas for delay —

At Whitsuntide Ramborg Lavransdatter came back to Formo. The children she had left behind at Dyfrin. They were well, she answered, when Kristin asked after them. The two young maids had wept bitterly and sorrowed over their father. Andres was too young to understand. The youngest, Simon Simonssön, throve well, and there was good hope that in time he would grow big and strong.

Ramborg came once or twice to the church, and to her husband's grave; else she stirred not from her home. But Kristin went south to her often as she could. She wished now from her heart that she had known more of her young sister. The widow looked most childlike in her weeds — frail and undergrown her body seemed in the

heavy, dark-blue habit; the little, three-cornered face
showed sallow and thin among the linen bands, under the
black woollen veil falling in stiff folds from the crown of
her head almost to the hem of her skirt. And she had dark
rings under her big eyes, where the pupils ever gazed out
now, wide and coal-black.

At the hay harvest there came a week when Kristin
could not go to see her sister. From her hay-making folk
she heard there was a guest with Ramborg at Formo —
Jammælt Halvardssön. Kristin remembered that Simon had
spoken of this man; he owned a great manor not far from
Dyfrin, and he and Simon had been friends from childhood up.

A week on in the harvesting it set in rain; and Kristin
rode down the Dale to her sister. Kristin sat talking of the
untoward weather and of the hay, and asked how things
went here on Formo — when Ramborg said of a sudden:

" 'Twill be for Jon now to see to all that — I am faring
south a few days hence, Kristin."

"Ay, poor soul, you long for your children, I can well
believe," said Kristin.

Ramborg rose and walked to and fro in the room.

"You shall hear somewhat that will make you wonder,"
the young woman said in a little. "Soon will you and your
sons be bidden to a betrothal-ale at Dyfrin. I gave Jammælt my yea ere he went from here, and Gyrd will hold
my betrothal feast."

Kristin sat dumb. Her sister stood, black-eyed and pale,
gazing fixedly at her. At length the elder said:

"I see, then, not for long will Simon have left you
widowed — I had deemed you grieved for him so sorely.
— But 'tis true you are your own mistress now — "

Ramborg made no answer; then, in a little, Kristin asked:

"Gyrd Darre knows that you are minded to wed again
so soon?"

"Ay." Ramborg walked to and fro again. "Helga counsels it — Jammælt is rich." She laughed. "And Gyrd is so
clear-sighted a man, I trow he has seen long since how
wretchedly we lived together, Simon and I."

"What is't you say?" cried Kristin — "None else knew,
for sure, that you lived unhappily together," she said a
little after. "I wot not that any has seen other than friendship and goodwill betwixt you. Simon gave you your way

in all things, gave you all your heart desired, ever kept your youth in mind and was heedful that you should have joy of it, and be spared all toil and trouble. His children he loved, and showed you day by day his thankfulness for that you bore him those two — "

Ramborg smiled scornfully.

Kristin answered vehemently:

"Ay, if so it be that you have aught reason to say you lived ill together, then for sure 'tis not Simon that bears the blame — "

"No," said Ramborg. "I will take the blame — if *you* dare not."

Kristin sat in amaze.

"I trow you know not yourself what you say, sister," said she at length.

"Yes, in sooth," answered Ramborg. "But full well I trow that *you* know it not. So little have you thought on Simon that I well believe 'tis news for you. You counted him good enough to turn to when there was need of a helper that had gladly borne red-hot iron for your sake — but never did you fling so much thought Simon Andressön's way as to ask how much it cost him — I was left free to joy in my youth, ay — blithely and gently Simon lifted me into the saddle and sent me forth from him a-visiting and junketing; even as blithely and gently he welcomed me again when I came home — he patted me as he patted his dog and his horse — he felt no lack of me, wheresoever I went — "

Kristin had risen — she stood by the board moveless. Ramborg wrung her hands so that the joints cracked, going and coming, going and coming through the room:

"Jammælt — " she said, something more calmly. "I have known for long what *he* thought of me. I saw it even while his wife still lived. Not that he knows that he has betrayed him in word or deed — believe not that! He grieved so himself over Simon — came to me time and again and would have comforted me — 'tis true! 'Twas Helga who said to us both she deemed that now it were fitting if we —

" — And I wot not what I should wait for. Never shall I be more comforted or less than now I am — Now I have a mind to try how 'tis to live with a man who has kept silence and has thought on *me* for long, long years. I

know all too well how 'tis to live with one who keeps
silence and is ever thinking on another — "

Kristin stood as before. Ramborg stopped before her,
with flashing eyes:

"You know 'tis true, what I have said!"

Kristin went forth from the room, quietly, with bowed
head. While she stood in the rain in the courtyard waiting
for the serving-man to lead forth her horse, Ramborg
came to the door of the hall — she gazed at her elder
sister with black, hostile eyes.

'Twas not till the next day that Kristin called to mind
what she had promised Simon if Ramborg should wed
again. So she rode to Formo once more. This seemed to
her no easy thing to do. And the worst was that she knew
she could not say aught that would be a help or comfort
to her young sister. To her this match with Jammælt of
Ælin seemed rashly made — with Ramborg in the mind
she now was in. But Kristin was 'twould be of no avail
for her to gainsay it.

Ramborg was sullen and peevish and would scarce answer the other. She would in no wise consent that her
step-daughter should come to Jörundgaard. "Nor methinks are things so ordered at your manor that 'twere
wise to send a young maid thither." Kristin answered
mildly that herein Ramborg might mayhap be right. But
she had given Simon her word to make this proffer —

"Ay, and if so be Simon, in his fever-wanderings, understood not that 'twas an affront to me to ask you this, you,
at least, must know that 'tis an affront to tell me of it,"
answered Ramborg; and Kristin was fain to turn her
home from her fruitless errand.

Next morning promised fair weather. But when her sons
came in to the morning meal, Kristin said they must get in
the hay without her; she was setting forth on a journey,
and mayhap she would be gone some days.

"I think to go north to Dovre to seek out your father,"
said she. "'Tis in my mind to pray him to forget the
troubles that have been between us — to ask when he will
come home to us."

The sons flushed red; they scarce dared look up, but she
marked well how glad they were. She drew Munan to her
and bent her face over him:

"You scarce remember your father, I trow, little one?"

The boy nodded, dumbly, with shining eyes. One after another the other sons looked over at their mother: she was younger of face and fairer than they had seen her for many years.

She came out into the courtyard a little after, clad for the journey in her church-going clothes: a black woollen habit broidered with blue and silver about the neck and sleeves, and black, sleeveless, hooded cloak, since 'twas high summer. Naakkve and Gaute had saddled her horse and their own; they would go with their mother. She said naught against it. But she spoke little with her sons as they rode north across the gorge and up into Dovre. For the most she was silent and lost in thought, and if she talked with the young lads, 'twas of other things than of her errand.

When they were come so far that they could see up the hill-side and had sight of the house roofs of Haugen against the sky, she bade the lads turn back.

"You can understand well that your father and I may have much to say one to the other that we can best speak of alone."

The brothers nodded; they bade their mother farewell and turned their horses homewards.

The wind from the mountains swept, cool and fresh, against her hot cheeks as she came up over the last rise. The sun shone golden upon the small grey houses, casting long shadows across the courtyard. The corn up here would soon be earing — it showed fairly upon the small plots, shimmering and swaying in the wind. On all the stone heaps and over the hillocks tall waving willow-herb blossomed red, and in between were little haycocks. But on the farm was no living thing to be seen — not even a dog came forth to give warning.

Kristin unsaddled her horse and led it to the water-trough. She had no mind to turn it loose up here — so she took it into the stable. The sun shone in through a great hole in the roof — roof-turves hung down in tatters from the beams. And there was no sign that any horse had stood there for many a long day. Kristin saw to her beast, and betook her out into the courtyard again.

She looked into the byre. It was dark and empty — she knew by the smell that it must have stood long deserted.

Some skins of beasts were stretched upon the house wall to dry — a swarm of blue-flies flew up, buzzing, as she drew near. At the north end of the house earth had been heaped up and turf spread over it so that the house timbers were quite hidden. He had done it for warmth, belike —

She looked for naught else but that the house would be lock-fast, but the door flew open when she laid hand upon the latch. Erlend had not even barred his house.

An air noisome past bearing met her when she stepped in — the strong, rank smell of skins and of the stable. The first feeling that rushed over her as she stood within his house was heart-breaking remorse and pity. This dwelling seemed to her most like a bear's winter lair —

O ay, ay, ay, Simon — you were right!

Small the room was, but 'twas choicely wrought and had once been fine. The fire-place had even a masoned chimney above it, so that it should not smoke out into the room, like the fire-places in the hall-house at home. But when she would have opened the damper to clear the foul air a little, she saw the pipe had been blocked with slabs of stone. The glass pane in the window to the penthouse was broken, and had been stopped up with cloths. The whole room was floored with wood, but so thick with dirt was the floor that the planks could scarce be seen. Not a cushion was there upon the benches, but weapons, furs, and old clothes lay strewn about; the filthy board was littered with orts of food. And flies buzzed high and low.

She started — stood trembling — breathless, with thumping heart. In the farther bed — in yonder bed where *it* had lain when last she was here — lay somewhat covered with a wadmal cloth. She knew not herself what she thought —

Then she set her teeth, forced herself to go across and lift the cloth. 'Twas but Erlend's coat of mail, his helm and shield. They lay covered up upon the bare bed-boards.

She looked towards the other bed. 'Twas there they had found Björn and Aashild. 'Twas there Erlend slept now — Belike she herself would lie there this night —

But what must it have been for him to dwell in this house, to sleep here — ? Again all else that she felt was drowned in pity. She went over to the bed — she saw it had not been made for many days. The hay under the sheet of hide had been lain upon till 'twas hard as stone. There was nothing in the bed save some sheep-skins, and a pair of wadmal-covered pillows, so foul that they stank. Dust and trash showered from the bed-gear when she handled it. Erlend's resting-place was no whit better than a horse-boy's in a stable.

Erlend, who could never have bravery enough about him; Erlend, who would don a silken shirt, velvet and fine furs, on the least pretext — who chafed because she suffered his children to go clad in home-spun wadmal on workdays, and never could abide that she herself should suckle them and take a hand herself with her serving-women in the housework — like a cottar's wife, he said — Jesus — and 'twas he himself that had brought things to this —

— No, I will not say a word — I will take back all that I have said — Simon. You were right — he shall not bide on here, the father of my sons. I will proffer him my hand and my mouth and pray him for forgiveness —

'Tis not easy, Simon. But you were right — She remembered the sharp grey eyes — their look, steadfast as ever, well-nigh to the end. From out the poor body, already beginning to waste away, there shone through his eyes his pure and shining spirit, until his soul was taken home like a blade withdrawn. She knew 'twas as Ramborg had said. He had loved her all these years.

No day had gone by in these months since his death but she must think on him, and now it seemed to her that she had known it all ere ever Ramborg spoke. She had been driven in this time to turn over again every memory she had of him for as long as she had known Simon Darre. All these years she had borne within her false memories of him who had been her hand-fasted man; she had tampered with these memories as a bad ruler tampers with money, mixing base metal with the silver. When he set her free and took upon himself the blame for the breach of troth-plight — she had told herself, and believed, that Simon Andressön turned from her with scorn in the moment he knew of her dishonour. She had forgotten that when he freed her, that day in the nun's garden — then for sure he thought not aught else of her but that she was unstained and pure. But even then he was willing to bear the shame of her changefulness and revolt — craved only that her father should know 'twas not he who had willed the breach —

And *this*, too, she knew now: when he had learned the worst, and had stood up to save for her a semblance of honour in the world's eyes — had she been able to turn to him then, Simon would have taken her even then at the church door to be his wife, and he would have striven so to live with her that she should never have felt he had kept the memory of her shame.

And none the less she knew: never could she have loved him. Never could she have loved Simon Andressön — Yet — all that Erlend was not and that she had raged to find he was not, Simon was. But then must she herself be a pitiable woman, to murmur at her lot —

Simon had given, with a measureless bounty, to her he loved. And she had deemed surely that she too did the like —

But when she took gifts at his hands, unthinking and unthankful, he had but smiled. She understood now that often when they were together he had been heavy of heart. She knew now that behind that strangely steadfast mien he had hidden sorrow — then, flinging out a few jesting words, he would thrust all aside, and stand ready once more to guard, to help, and to give —

She herself had raged, had stored up and brooded over every hurt — when she reached forth her gifts and Erlend saw them not —

Here, in this room, she had stood and spoken such brave words: "I went astray of my own will — never will I cast blame on Erlend, should the path lead o'er the cliff edge." She had said it to the woman she drove to death to make way for her love.

Kristin moaned aloud, clasped her hands before her breast, and stood, rocking. Ay — she had said so proudly, she would cast no blame on Erlend Nikulaussön if he grew weary of her, betrayed her, forsook her even —

Ay — and if Erlend had done *that* — it seemed to her she could have stood to her word. If he had betrayed her once for all — and there had been an end. But he had not betrayed her — only failed her, failed her, and made her live ever fearful and unsure — no, never had he played her false, but never had he sustained her — and she could see no end to it: here she stood now, come to beg him to turn back to her, to fill her cup each day to the brim with unsureness and disquiet, with vain expectancy, with longings and fears, and hope that broke in sunder —

And it seemed to her she was worn out by him now. She had not the youth and courage to live with him any more — and belike she would never grow so old that Erlend could not play upon her fondness. Never so young that she could live with him in gladness, never so old that she could bear with him in patience. A little, weak woman was she grown — belike had ever been. Simon was in the right —

Simon — and her father. They had been constant ever in one in faithful love to her, for all she had trodden them down for the sake of this man she herself could bear with now no longer —

Oh, Simon, I know well, never have you wished for vengeance on me at any time. But I marvel, Simon, if, where you lie, you know not that now you are well avenged —

Nay, she must busy herself with somewhat, else she could not bear it. She set the bed in order; sought for a mop and a broom, but it seemed no such thing was in the house. She looked into the closet — now she saw whence came the smell of the stable. Erlend had made his horse's stall in there. But here the floor was swept and clean. The saddle and the gear that hung upon the wall were well kept and greased; their rents were mended.

Pity again drove all other thoughts away. Had he brought Soten in there because he could not bear to be all alone in the house — ?

Kristin heard steps in the penthouse. She stepped over to the glass pane — 'twas thick with dust and cobweb, but she thought she could dimly see a woman. She pulled out the cloth and peeped. Out there a woman was setting down a milk-can and a small cheese. She was oldish, lame, ugly, and poorly clad. Kristin scarce knew herself how much freer she drew breath.

She set the room in order as best she could. She found the writing that Björn Gunnarssön had carved upon a log of the long wall — it was in Latin, and she could not read it all, but he named himself both *dominus* and *miles*, and

she made out the name of his fathers' seat in Elvesyssel
that he had lost for Aashild Gautesdatter's sake. Amidst
the fine carvings on the high-seat was his shield, bearing
its device of the unicorn and the lily-star leaves.

A while after Kristin thought she heard a horse somewhere without. She went to the outer room and peered
forth.

Down from the wooded slope above the farm-stead
came a tall black horse harnessed to a load of firewood.
Erlend walked by its side, driving. One dog sat atop of
the wood; some others ran about the sleigh.

Soten, the Castilian, strained at his collar and dragged
the wood-sleigh forward over the courtyard sward. One
of the dogs dashed down the slope barking — Erlend, who
had begun to unharness, marked now by the flurry among
the dogs that something must be afoot. He took the wood-
axe from the load and walked toward the dwelling-
house —

Kristin fled in again, dropping the latch behind her. She
shrank in to the wall of the fire-place, and stood trembling
and waiting.

Erlend strode in, with the wood-axe in his hand and the
dogs tumbling over the threshold before and after him.
They found the stranger forthwith, and greeted her with
a storm of barking —

The first she saw was the wave of young, red blood that
rushed over his face — the fluttering quiver about his fine,
weak mouth, the great eyes deep in the shadow of the
brows —

The sight of him took away her breath. She saw, indeed,
the old growth of stubble upon his lower face, she saw
that his unkempt hair was iron-grey — but the colour
came and went in his cheeks in hasty pulses, as when they
were young — he was so young and so comely, 'twas as
though naught had availed to quell him —

He was miserably clad — his blue shirt dirty and ragged;
over it he wore a leathern jerkin, scarred and rubbed and
rent at the laceholes, but fitting closely and pliant to the
body's strong and gracious motions. His tight leathern
breeches had a rent over the one knee, and the seam behind
the other leg was burst. Yet never, more than now, had he
seemed the son of chiefs and nobles. So fairly and easily

he bore his tall slim form, with the broad shoulders somewhat stooped, the long, fine limbs — he stood there, resting a little on one foot, one hand laid on the belt about his
slender waist, the other, with the axe in it, hanging at his
side.

He had called the dogs back to him — stood looking at
her — went red and pale and said no word. For a good
while they both stood dumb. At last the man spoke, in a
voice that wavered a little:

"Are you come hither, Kristin?"

"I was fain to see how it fared with you," answered she.

"Ay, you have seen it, then." He cast a glance about the
room. "You see things are passably well with me here —
'tis good you chanced on a day when my house is trim
and in order — " He grew ware of the shadow of a smile
upon her face. " — Or maybe 'tis you who set it in order,"
said he, laughing low.

Erlend laid aside the axe and sat him down on the outer
bench, with his back leaned against the board. Of a sudden he grew grave:

"You stand there so — is aught amiss at home — at
Jörundgaard, I mean — with the lads?"

"No." Now was her time to bring out what she had to
say: "Our sons are thriving and doing well. But they long
so for you, Erlend. This was my errand — I came hither,
husband, to beg you to come home to us. We miss you,
all of us — " She cast down her eyes.

"You look well, none the less, Kristin — " Erlend looked
at her with a little smile.

Red, as though he had struck her, Kristin stood:

" 'Tis not for that — "

"Nay, I know 'tis not because you deem you too young
and fresh to live as a widow woman," Erlend went on,
when she stopped short. "I trow but little good would
come of it should I come back home, Kristin," said he,
more soberly. "In your hands all goes well on Jörundgaard, that know I — you have fortune with you in your
doings. And I am well content with the life I live here."

" 'Tis not well for the boys — that we should be at
odds," she answered in a low voice.

"Oh — " Erlend lingered on the word. "They are so
young, I can scarce believe they take it so to heart that
they will not forget it when they leave their childhood

behind. I care not if I tell you," he said with a little smile,
"I meet them now and again — "

She knew it — but she felt as though it humbled her,
and felt as 'twere so he had meant it — he had deemed
she knew it not. The sons had never known that she knew.
But she answered gravely:

"Then you know also that much on Jörundgaard is not
as it should be — "

"We never talk of such-like things," said he, smiling as
before. "We go a-hunting together — but you must be
hungry and thirsty" — he leapt up. "And you are standing too — nay, set you up in the high-seat, Kristin — ay,
do so, sweetheart! You shall have it to yourself — "

He fetched in the milk and the cheese, and brought out
bread, butter, and dried meat. Kristin was hungry and yet
more thirsty; but she found it hard to swallow down the
food. Erlend ate hastily and slovenly, as had always been
his wont when he was not with strangers — but he was
soon done.

He talked of himself the while. The folk down the hill
here tilled his land and brought him milk and a little food
— for the most part he lay out on the fells hunting game
and fishing. Howsoever, he said on a sudden, he had
thoughts now of faring from the land. Seeking service with
some outland chieftain —

"Oh, no, Erlend!"

He looked at her quickly and searchingly. But she said
no more. It began to grow dusk in the room — her face
and head-linen shone palely against the dark wall. Erlend
rose and made a fire in the fire-place. Then he sat him
down aslant on the outer bench, turned towards her; the
red glare from the fire flickered over his form.

But that he could even think of such a thing! He was
nigh as old as had been her father when he died. And yet
'twas believable enough that he would do it one day —
run after some such whimsy, off to seek for new adven-
tures —

"Deem you 'tis not enough," said the wife vehemently,
"'tis not enough that you have forsaken the parish and
your sons and me — would you flee the land from us
now?"

"Had I known your thoughts of me, Kristin," said Erlend gravely, "then had I gone forth from *your* manor

long ago. But I understand now that you have had to bear *much* from me — "

"You know full well, Erlend — you say *my* manor, but you have a husband's right over all that is mine." She heard herself how faint of voice she grew.

"Ay," answered Erlend. "But I know myself I was an ill husband of my own good." He was silent a while. "Naakkve — I mind the time he was unborn — you spoke of him that you bore beneath your girdle, that was to mount into my high-seat after me. I see now, Kristin — 'twas hard for you — best let things be as they are. And I thrive full well in his life — "

Kristin looked around her in the darkening room, shuddering — the shadows filled every corner now, and the fire-light danced —

"I understand not," she said, nigh sinking with heaviness, "that you can abide this house. Naught have you to do, none to bear you company — at the least you might get you a house-carl, I trow — "

"You mean that I should work the farm myself — ?" Erlend laughed. "Oh no, Kristin, sure you must know how little fit I am to play the farmer. I cannot sit quiet — "

"Quiet — Here surely you sit quiet enough — the long winter through — "

Erlend smiled to himself, his eyes far off and strange:

"Ay, when 'tis in that way — When I need not to think of aught but what runs in my head — can go and come as I like — And you know well — it has ever been so with me, that when there's naught to wake for, I can sleep — I sleep like a bear in its winter lair when 'tis not weather for the fells — "

"Are you never afraid to be alone here?" whispered Kristin.

At first he looked at her as though he understood not. Then he laughed:

"Because folks say 'tis haunted? Never have I marked aught. Sometimes I had been fain that my kinsman Björn *would* visit me. Mind you that he said once he deemed I would ill abide to feel the knife-edge at my throat. I could e'en have a mind to answer the knight now that I was not greatly feared when I had the rope about my neck — "

A long shudder passed through the woman's body. She sat there dumb.

Erlend rose.

"I trow 'tis time we went to rest now, Kristin."

Stiff and cold, she watched Erlend take the covering that lay over his armour, spread it on the bed, and turn it down over the dirty pillows. " 'Tis the best I have," said he.

"Erlend!" She clasped her hands beneath her breast. She sought for something she might say to gain a little time yet — she was so afraid. Then she remembered the errand she was to fulfil:

"Erlend — I was given a message to bear to you. Simon prayed me, when he lay dying, that I would greet you from him and say he had repented him each day of the words he said to you when last you parted. Unmanly he called them himself — and he begged that you would forgive him for them."

"Simon." Erlend stood holding the bedpost with one hand, gazing down at the floor. "He is the man I am least fain to be remembered of."

"I know not what has been between you," said Kristin. Strangely heartless these words of Erlend's seemed to her. "But 'twere strange and unlike Simon if it were as he said, that he had shown him little-minded in his dealings with you. If so it be — I trow the blame was not all his."

Erlend shook his head: "He stood by me like a brother when my need was greatest," he said low. "And I took help and friendship at his hands, and I knew not that all the time he could scarce endure me —

" — Methinks it must have been easier to live in the old world, when two such fellows as he and I met together hand to hand — met on a holm and put it to the trial of arms which should win the fair-haired maid — "

He took an old cloak from the bench and flung it over his arm:

"Maybe you would have the dogs beside you to-night?"

Kristin had risen:

"Whither go you, Erlend?"

"Out to the barn to lie there — "

"No — !" Erlend stopped — he stood there, straight and slender and young in the dim red light of the waning embers. "I dare not lie alone here in this house — I dare not — "

"Dare you lie in my arms then?" She half saw his smile

through the dusk, and drooped beneath it. "Are you not afraid I should crush you to death, Kristin — ?"

"Would that you might — !" She sank into his arms.

When she awoke, she saw by the pane of glass that it must be day without. Something lay crushingly heavy on her breast — Erlend slept with his head upon her shoulder; he had laid one arm over her and his hand was around her left arm.

She looked at the man's iron-grey hair. She saw her own small, shrunken breasts — above and below them the high-arched curves of her ribs showed under the thin covering of flesh. A kind of terror came over her, while memory after memory arose from this night. In this house — they two, young no longer — Disquiet and shame took hold on her when she saw the livid patches upon her work-worn, mother's arms, on her shrunken bosom. Wildly she caught at the coverlid and would have covered herself —

Erlend awoke, started up on his elbow, stared into her face — his eyes were coal-black from sleep:

"Methought — " He threw himself down beside her again; a deep wild tremor went through her whole being at the rejoicing and the fear in his voice. " — Methought I had dreamed again — "

She pressed her open lips upon his mouth and twined her arms about his neck. Never, never had it been so blessed —

Late in the afternoon, when the sunshine was yellow already and the shadows lay long over the green court-yard, they set out down to the beck to fetch water. Erlend bore the two great pails. Kristin walked by his side, slender, straight, and lissom. Her headlinen had slipped down, and lay around her shoulders; her hair shone bare and brown in the sunlight. She felt it herself, when she shut her eyes and lifted her face against the light — she had grown red in the cheeks; the lines of her face had softened. Each time she glanced at him, she sank her gaze, overcome — when she saw in Erlend's face how young she was.

Erlend bethought him that he would bathe. While he went a little farther down, Kristin sat on the greensward, leaning her back against a stone. The fell beck trilled and

gurgled her into a doze — now and then, when the midges
and gnats touched her skin, she opened her eyes a little
and brushed them off. Down among the sallows around
about the pool she caught a glimpse of Erlend's white
body — he stood with a foot upon a stone, rubbing himself with whisps of grass. She closed her eyes again and
smiled, in happy weariness. She was strengthless as ever
against him —

The man came and flung himself on the grass before
her — with dripping hair, the chill of the water upon his
red mouth when he pressed it into the palm of her hand.
He had shaved and found a better shirt — but this one
even was none too brave. Laughing, he took hold on it up
under the arm-pits, where it was tattered:

"You might as lief have brought me a shirt when you
did come north here at the last."

"I shall set about sewing and hemming a shirt for you
soon as I come home, Erlend," she answered smiling, and
passed her hand across his brow. He grasped it:

"Never shall you go from here again, my Kristin — "

The woman did but smile and answered naught. Erlend
dragged himself a little way, as he lay on his belly. Under
the bushes in the damp shade grew a cluster of small, white
starry flowers. The flower-leaves were veined with blue
like a woman's breast; in the midst of each blossom was
a little, blue-brown boss. Erlend plucked them one and
all:

"You that have lore of such things, Kristin, I trow you
know a name for these?"

" 'Tis Friggja-grass * — nay, Erlend — " She flushed and
put away his hand as he would have stuffed the blooms
into her bosom.

Erlend laughed and lightly bit the white petals one by
one. Then he laid all the blossoms in her open hand and
closed up her fingers over them:

"Do you mind when we walked in the garden of the
Hofvin Spital — you gave me a rose?"

Kristin shook her head slowly, smiling a little:

"No. But you took a rose from out my hand."

---

* See Note 4.

"And you suffered me to take it. And 'twas so you suffered me to take you, Kristin — as meek and gentle as a rose — afterwards you pricked me sometimes till the blood came, my sweet." He threw himself forward into her lap and laid his arms about her waist: "Last night, Kristin — 'twas of no avail — you did not get off by sitting meekly waiting — "

Kristin bent her head and hid her face against his shoulder.

On the fouth day they had taken harbour in the birch wood among the hillocks above the farm. For on that day the tenant was carrying the hay. And, without having spoken of it, Kristin and Erlend were at one that none need know she was with him. He went down to the houses once or twice to fetch food and drink, but she sat on in the heather up among the stunted birches. From where they sat they could see the man and woman toiling home, bearing the loads of hay upon their backs.

"Mind you," asked Erlend, "that time you promised me that, when I ended as a crofter away among the fells, then would you come and keep house for me? You will keep two cows here belike, and a few sheep and goats — ?"

Kristin laughed low, playing with his hair.

"What think you your sons would say, Erlend — if their mother fled the parish and forsook them in that wise — ?"

"I trow they would be fain enough to be their own masters on Jörundgaard," said Erlend, laughing. "They are old enough for it. You wot well Gaute is a full good farmer, young as he is. And Naakkve is well-nigh a man."

"O no." The mother laughed quietly. " 'Tis true he thinks so himself — ay, they think so, all five, I trow — but the lad lacks somewhat yet of a man's wit — "

"If 'tis after his father he takes, maybe 'twill come to him late or never," answered Erlend. He smiled slyly: "You deem you can still hide your children behind your skirts, Kristin — Naakkve had a son fathered on him up here this summer — you know not that, I trow — ?"

"No — !" Kristin sat there red and aghast.

"Ay, 'twas still-born — and I trow the boy will think twice ere he come thither any more — 'twas the widow

of Paal's son, here at Haugsbrekken; she said 'twas his,
and sackless, I trow, he was not, howsoever the matter
stood. Ay, such old folk are we now, you and I — "

"Can you talk so, when your son has brought on him
trouble and shame?" It cut her to the heart that the man
could talk so lightly — and that it seemed to be a jest in
his eyes that she had known naught of this.

"Ay, what would you have me say?" asked Erlend as
before. "The lad is eighteen winters old. You see yourself
now, it avails not much for you to go about keeping watch
on your sons as though they were children. When you
come up hither to me, we must see to getting him wed — "

"Think you 'twill be a light thing for us to find Naakkve
an equal match — ? No, husband, after this bethinks you
must come home with me and help to guide the lads."

Erlend raised himself sharply on his elbow:

"That will I not do, Kristin. A stranger in your country
I am and ever will be — no man there minds aught of me
but that I was doomed a traitor to king and country.
Thought you never in those years I lived on Jörundgaard
that I lived ill at ease — at home in Skaun I was wont to
count for something more 'mongst folk. Even at that time
— in my youth — when the tale of my evil life was buzzed
abroad, when I lay under the Church's ban — none the less
was I Erlend Nikulaussön of Husaby! Then came the time,
Kristin — I had the fortune to show the folk yonder, north
of the fells, that wholly unworthy of my forefathers I
was not — No, I tell you! Here, on this little croft, I am a
free man — none gape after my doings or talk behind my
back. Hearken to me, Kristin, my only love — stay with
me! Never shall you have cause to repent it. Here is better
dwelling than was at Husaby on any day. I wot not how
it is, Kristin — I was never glad or light of heart there,
not when I was a child, and never since. 'Twas hell while
I had Eline with me, and never were you and I glad at
heart together there — Yet God the Almighty knows I
have loved you each day and each hour I have known
you. Bewitched, I trow, the manor was — mother was
wrung to death there, and my father was ever an unglad
man. Here 'tis good to be, Kristin — if only you will be
with me. Kristin — as true God died for us upon the cross,
I hold you as dear to-day as that night you slept beneath

my cloak — the night after Margaret's Mass — and I sat and looked on you, pure and fresh and young and untouched blossom that you were."

Kristin answered low:

"Mind you, Erlend, too, you prayed that night that I should never have to weep a tear for your sake — "

"Ay — and God and all the saints in heaven know that I meant it! 'Tis true it fell out otherwise — maybe it had to — belike it ever so befalls while we dwell in this earthly home. But I loved you when I wrought you evil and when I wrought you good. Bide here, Kristin — "

"Have you never thought on this," she asked, gently as before, "that it might well make your sons' lot hard to have their father talked of so as you say? Flee to the hills from the parish talk, they cannot, all the seven — "

Erlend looked down:

"They are young," said he, "comely and gallant lads — They will make a way for themselves yet — We, Kristin, we have not so many years before us, ere we grow old and grey — will you waste the time while yet you are fair and fresh and fit to joy in life? Kristin — ?"

She cast down her eyes before the giddy gleam in his. In a little while she said:

"Have you forgot, Erlend, that two of our sons are little children yet? What deem you I were worth if I forsook Lavrans and Munan — "

"You must bring them up hither, then — if Lavrans would not rather bide with his brothers. So little a boy he is not neither. — Is Munan comely as ever?" the father asked, smiling.

"Ay," said the mother, "he is a fair child."

Thereafter they sat long silent. And when again they spoke, it was of other things.

She woke in the grey of dawn next morning, as she had waked each morning up here — lay and heard the horses stamping without the house wall. She had Erlend's head fast in her arms. The other mornings when she awoke in this grey and early hour she had been gripped by the same fear and shame as on the first — she had striven to stifle them. Were they not a wedded pair at odds who had now made up their quarrel? Could aught better befall the chil-

dren than that their father and mother should make friends
again?

But this morning she lay striving to remember her sons.
For 'twas as though a spell was on her — and straight from
the wood at Gerdarud, where first he had taken her to his
arms, Erlend had borne her with him hither. They were
so young — it could not be true that already she had
borne this man seven sons, that she was mother to tall,
grown men — It seemed as though she must have lain here
in his arms and but dreamed of the long years they had
lived as man and wife at Husaby — All his reckless words
lured her and echoed in her — giddy with fear, she felt
as though Erlend had swept from off her the seven-fold
burden of her charge — thus must it be with a young mare
when she stands unsaddled upon the sæter pasture-ground
— pack and saddle and head-gear are gone from her;
against her blow the winds and the airs of the uplands; she
is set free to graze the tender mountain grass, free to run
far as she will over all the upland wastes.

And at the same time she longed already, sweetly and
yearningly, right willing to bear a new burden. Already
she yearned with a little tender dizziness towards him who
should abide next to her heart for nine long months. She
had known full surely from the first morning she awoke
up here in Erlend's arms. Along with the hard, dry,
scorching fever in her mind, barrenness had passed away
from her. She bore Erlend's child in her womb, and, with
a strangely tender impatience, her soul stretched forward
towards the hour when it should be brought forth to day.

Those great sons of mine have no need of me, she
thought. To them I seem but doting and troublesome. We
shall but stand in their way, the little one and I. No. I
cannot part from here — we must bide here with Erlend.
I cannot go —

Yet, none the less, as they sat together at their morning
meal, she let fall that she must get her home now to her
children.

'Twas of Lavrans and Munan she thought. They were
so old now, that she was abashed when she thought of
them dwelling up here with Erlend and her, and mayhap
looking with wondering eyes at their father and mother,
grown so young again. But do without her those two
could not.

Erlend sat gazing at her while she spoke of her journey home. At last he spoke with a flitting smile.

"Ay — if so be you will, you must even go!"

He made ready to bear her company on her way. And he rode with her right down through the gorge into Sil, until he caught a glimpse of the church roof over the pine-tops. Then he bade her farewell. At the last he was still smiling, a roguishly secure smile.

"Ay, you know well, Kristin — whether you come by night or by day — whether I wait for you short or long — I shall welcome you as you were the Queen of Heaven come down to my croft from the skies — "

She laughed:

"Ay, with such great matters *I* dare not meddle. But I trow you know now, love, that great will be the joy in your house the day the master comes home to his own."

He shook his head, laughing a little. Smiling, they made their farewells; smiling, Erlend leaned over, as they sat a-horseback side by side, and kissed her many, many times, and between the kisses he looked at her with his laughing eyes:

"We must see, then," he said at last, "which of us two is the more stubborn, my sweet Kristin. This will not be our last meeting — that know we well, both you and I!"

As she rode by the church a little shudder ran through her. 'Twas as though she were coming home from the Mountain King's Hall; as though Erlend were the Mountain King himself, and could not pass the church and the cross on the green.

She drew rein — was well-nigh minded to turn about and ride after him —

Then she looked out over the green grassy slopes, down upon her own fair manor with meadows and tilled fields, and the river sweeping in shining loops down through the Dale. The mountains rose in a warm blue haze — the heavens were full of bellying summer clouds. 'Twas madness. There, at home with their sons, was his place. He was no knight of faerie — but a Christian man, full as he was of mad-brained moods and thoughtless whims; her wedded husband, with whom she had borne both good and ill — dear, dear, sorely as he had tormented her with his wayward fancies. She must bear with him; since she

could not live without him, she must strive on and suffer
dread and insecurity as best she might. Long, she deemed,
it would not be till he came after — now that again they
had been together.

6

To her sons she said, their father must take order with
one thing and another at Haugen ere he came home. Most
like he would come down in early autumn.

At home she went about the manor, young, rosy-
cheeked, her face soft and gentle, quicker at all her work
— yet she made not such good speed as when she worked
in her wonted quiet and ordered fashion. She took not her
sons to task sharply, as had been her wont, when they did
amiss or she had cause for miscontent with them. Now
she spoke to them jestingly, or let it pass without saying
aught.

Lavrans was now for sleeping in the loft with his big
brothers.

"Ay, maybe we must reckon you among the grown
lads now, my son." She ran her fingers through the boy's
thick, yellow-brown hair, and drew him to her — he was
as high already as her mid-breast. "And you, Munan, will
you let your mother count you for a child a little while
longer?" — Of an evening when the boy had gone to rest
in the hall, he still liked that his mother should sit her
down on the bedside and fondle him a little; he lay with
his head in her lap, and prattled in more childish fashion
than he would in the day, when his brothers could hear
him. The two talked of the time when father would
come home.

Then he would move over to the wall, and his mother
would draw the covers over him. Kristin lit the candle,
took her sons' garments that were to mend, and set herself
to sew.

She unclasped the brooch over her bosom, and felt with
her hand about her breasts. They were round and firm
as a quite young woman's. She pushed her sleeve right
up to the shoulder, and looked on her naked arm in the
light. It was grown whiter and fuller. Then she rose and

walked — felt how softly she trod in the supple within-door shoes — passed her hand down over her slim hips: no longer were they sharp and hard as a man's. The blood flowed through her body as in spring-time the sap flows in the trees. 'Twas youth burgeoning within her.

She was busy with Frida in the brew-house, pouring warm water upon the grain for the Yule malt. Frida had forgot to see to it in time; it had been suffered to go bone dry while yet swelling. But Kristin did not chide the woman — with a half-smile she listened to the other excusing herself. For the first time it had befallen that Kristin had forgot to look to it herself.

By Yule-tide she would have Erlend at home with her. When she sent him these tidings, he would come home at once, for sure. So mad the man could not be as not to give way now — he must see 'twas not possible she could go up to Haugen, far from all folk, when she bore another life with her. But she would tarry a little yet before she sent him this message — though 'twas sure enough — maybe even till she had felt it quicken — The second autumn they dwelt on Jörundgaard she had had to go out of the way, as folk say. She had taken comfort quickly enough then. She was not afraid that 'twould fall out so this time — it *could* not be. Nevertheless —

She felt as though she must bend all her being to the shielding of this tiny, tender life that she bore beneath her heart — as one bends one's hands to guard a little, new-lit flame —

One day late in autumn Ivar and Skule came and said they were for riding up to their father — 'twas rare and fine now in the fells; they would ask leave to go a-hunting with him, now 'twas clear black frost.

Naakkve and Björgulf were sitting at the chess-board; they stopped and listened.

"I know not," said Kristin. She had not thought on it before — whom she should send with the tidings. She looked at her two half-grown sons. Foolish, she herself deemed it, but to tell them she could not bring herself. She might say they must take Lavrans with them, and tell him to speak with his father alone. He was so young he would not wonder. And yet —

"You wot well your father is coming hither soon," she

said. "Like enough you would but be in his way. Soon, too,
I shall have a message to send him myself."

The twins grumbled. Naakkve looked up from the
chess-board and said shortly: "Do as our mother bids,
boys."

When Yule was nigh she sent Naakkve north to Erlend. " — You must tell him, son, I begin now to long for
his coming — and, so, I trow, do all of you!" She spoke
not of the new reason there was now — 'twas most like,
she deemed, that the grown lad had seen it for himself;
he should judge himself whether he would tell his father
of it.

Naakkve came back — he had not found his father. Erlend was gone to Raumsdal; he had had word, it seemed,
that his daughter and her husband were now to flit to
Björgvin, and that Margret was wishful to meet her father
at Veöy.

'Twas but reason, this — Kristin lay awake of nights —
now and again she would stroke Munan's face as he slept
there by her side. It grieved her that Erlend came not for
Yule. But 'twas but reason that he would fain see his
daughter when the chance offered. She wiped away the
tears as they stole down her cheek. She wept so easily
again now, even as when she was young.

Just after Yule-tide Sira Eirik died. Kristin had been to
him at Romundgaard more than once in the autumn while
he lay bed-ridden; and she was at his grave-ale. Else she
never came out among folks now. She deemed it great loss
that their old parish priest was gone.

At the grave-ale she heard that someone had met Erlend north at Lesja; he was on his way home then. So he
would soon come, for sure —

In the days that followed, sitting on the bench under
the little window, with her hand-mirror, that she had
sought out, in her hand, she would breathe on it, and rub
it bright, and scan her face in it.

She had been sunburned as a cottar's wife these last
years, but all trace of that was gone now. Her skin was
white, with round, clear red roses on her cheeks like some
painted picture. So fair of face she had not been since she

was a young maid — Kristin sat and held her breath with
wondering joy.

So, at length, they would have the daughter Erlend
had wished so much — if it fell out as the wise women
say. Magnhild. They must break with the custom this
time and give the first daughter her father's mother's
name —

There hovered before her some memory of a fairy-tale
she had once heard told. Of seven sons who were outlawed
and hunted into the wilds for a little unborn sister's sake.
Then she laughed at herself — how she had come to think
on it she understood not.

Out from her sewing-chair she took the shirt of finest
white linen that she sewed upon when she was alone. She
pulled out threads of the linen and sewed birds and beasts
on a glassy drawn-work ground — 'twas many and many
a day since she had done such fine work. — Oh, would
that Erlend might come *now* — while as yet this had but
made her fair, young and straight, rosy and blooming —

When Gregory's Mass * was but just gone by, the
weather grew so fair 'twas right spring-like. The snow was
melting — it shone like silver; already there were brown
patches on the slopes that took the sun; a blue haze lay
upon the mountains.

Gaute stood in the courtyard one day mending a broken
sledge. Naakkve stood leaning against the wood-shed wall
watching his brother at his work, when Kristin came from
the kitchen-house bearing in both arms a great trough of
new-baked brown bread.

Gaute looked up at his mother. Then he laid axe and
auger down upon the sledge, ran after her, and took the
trough; he bore it over to the storehouse.

Kristin had stopped still; her cheeks were red. When
Gaute came back, she went over to her sons:

"You must ride up to your father one of these days, I
trow — say that now is there great need of him here at
home, to take the care of things from off my shoulders.
I can do so little now — and 'twill be in the very midst of
the spring work, too, that I shall have to lie in — "

---

* 12th March.

The young lads listened to her; they too flushed, but she saw they were full glad at heart. Naakkve said, with a show of carelessness:

" 'Twere as well we rode to-day — towards nones — what think you, brother?"

It was but the next day at noon when Kristin heard horsemen in the courtyard. She went out — 'twas Naakkve and Gaute — they were alone. They stood by their horses, looked down, and said naught.

"What answered your father?" asked the mother.

Gaute stood leaning on his spear — he still looked on the ground. On that Naakkve spoke:

"Father bade us say to you that he had looked each day, all winter, that you should come up to him. And he said you would be no less welcome than when last you went to visit him."

The colour came and went in Kristin's face:

"Said you not then to your father — that things stood thus with me — that 'twill not be long ere I shall have a child again — ?"

Gaute answered without looking up:

"It seemed as though father deemed *that* no reason — thought not that because of that you should not be able to remove to Haugen."

Kristin stood a little silent:

"What said he?" she asked, in a low harsh voice.

Naakkve would have spoken. Gaute lifted his hand a little, and looked up quickly, beseechingly, at his brother. But the eldest son spoke out his message:

"Father bade us say this: you knew when the child was begot how rich a man he was. And if he be not grown richer since, neither is he grown poorer."

Kristin turned away from her sons and went slowly towards the hall-house. Heavily and wearily she sat her down on the bench under the little window, from which the spring sun had melted the ice and rime already.

— It *was* so. 'Twas she had prayed to be suffered to lie in his arms — first. But 'twas not well done of him to mind her of that now. She deemed 'twas not well done of Erlend to send her this answer by their sons —

The spring weather held. There came a week's south wind, with rain — the river rose, waxed great and loud.

Down the hill-sides the waters gushed noisily; there were sounds of snow-slides from the mountain valleys. Then came sunshine again.

Kristin stood without, behind the house, in the grey-blue evening. The thicket below the field was full of the singing of birds. Gaute and the twins were gone up to the sæter — they were after black-cock. Even down to the manor the drumming of the game-birds came from all the hill-sides in the mornings.

She pressed her clenched hands beneath her bosom. 'Twas but a short time now — she must bear it with patience to the end. Often, doubtless, she had been way-ward and hard to live with, she too — Ill-judging in her endless carefulness for the children — ill-timed, as Erlend had said. It seemed to her, none the less, that now he was hard. But now the time would soon be here when he *must* come to her — that he too knew, for sure.

Sunshine and showers followed one another. One after-noon her sons called to her. They were standing without in the courtyard, all seven, with the whole household. Right across the Dale stretched three rainbows; the inner-most rested a foot upon the Formo houses; 'twas quite unbroken, and the colours shone strong and bright; the two outer ones were fainter and faded away above —

Even while they stood gazing at this strange and lovely sign, the air grew grey and dark. From the south a snow-squall came sweeping. It snowed till in a little while all the world was white.

Kristin sat in the evening and told Munan of King Snow and his fair white daughter — Mjöll * was her name — and of King Harold Luva,† who was fostered by Giant Dovre. She felt a pang of sorrow when she remembered 'twas years now since she had sat thus and told tales to her children — 'twas pity of Lavrans and Munan that she had given them so little of this joy. And now they would soon be great boys. While the others were small, at home at Husaby, she had sat telling them fairy-tales of an eve-ning — so often, so often.

She saw that the grown sons sat listening — she flushed

---

* Mjöll = Powdery snow.

† Luv = Snow-cap; e.g. on trees.

red and stopped short. Munan begged her to tell more. Naakkve rose and drew near:

"Mind you, mother, Torstein Uksafot * and the trolls of Höiland's forest — tell us that one!"

While she told the tale, her mind went back. They lay resting in the birch grove down by the river, having a bite of food, her father and his harvest-folk, men and women. Her father lay upon his belly; she sat astride the small of his back, kicking his sides with her heels — 'twas a hot day, and she had got leave to go barefoot, as did the grown women. Her father reeled off the tale of the kindred of the Höiland trolls: Jernskjold † had Skjoldvor; their daughters were Skjolddis and Skjoldgjerd, that Torstein Uksafot slew. Skjoldgjerd had been wed to Skjoldketil; their sons were Skjoldbjörn and Skjoldhedin and Valskjold, who owned Skjoldskjessa; they begot Skjoldulf and Skjoldorm; Skjoldulf got Skjoldkatla, and begot on her Skjold and Skjoldketil —

Nay, he had named that name already, cried Kolbjörn laughing. For Lavrans had boasted that he could teach them two dozen troll names, but he had not even filled the first full dozen. Lavrans laughed too: "Ay, but sure you know the trolls, too, call their children for their fathers that are gone!" But the work-folk would not let it pass; they doomed him to pay them a drink of mead as fine. Ay, then, said the master, they must have it — to-night, when they came home. But the folk would have it now, at once — and at length Tordis was sent up for the mead.

They stood up in a ring, and the great horn went the round. They they took their scythes and rakes and went to the meadows again. Kristin was sent home with the empty horn. She held it before her in both hands as she ran barefoot in the sunshine on the green path up towards the manor. Between-whiles she stopped, when a drop of mead had gathered in the toe of the horn — then she tilted it over her little face and licked the gilded edge within and without, and then her fingers to catch the sweetness.

Kristin Lavransdatter sat still, gazing before her. Father!

---

* = Ox-foot.
† = Iron-shield.

She remembered a shiver passing over his face, a whitening, as the wooded hill-sides grow white when a storm-gust turns the leaves upon the trees — a clang of cold, harsh scorn in his voice, a gleam in his grey eyes like the flash of a half-drawn sword. A moment, then it passed away — in merry, kindly jest while he was young; oftener and oftener, as he grew older, in a gentleness quiet and something sad. In her father's soul there had dwelt somewhat else besides that deep, tender sweetness. She had learned, with the years, to understand it — her father's wondrous gentleness came not therefrom that he saw not clear enough the faults and the vileness of mankind, but that he was ever searching his own heart before his God and bruising it with repentance for his own sins.

No, father, I will not be impatient. Much have I sinned against my husband, I too —

On the eve of Cross-Mass * day, Kristin sat at the board with the house-folk, and seemed not other than her wont. But when her sons had gone up to rest in the upper hall, she called Ulf Haldorssön softly to her. She asked him to go down to Isrid at the farm, and pray her to come up to the mistress in the old weaving-house.

Ulf said: "You must send word to Ranveig of Ulvs-volden and to Haldis, the priest's sister, Kristin — and most fitting 'twere if you could send to fetch Astrid and Ingebjörg of Loptsgaard to take the charge of the room — "

"There is no time," said Kristin. "I felt the first pains already before nones. Do as I say, Ulf — I will have none but my own women and Isrid with me."

"Kristin," said Ulf gravely, "see you not that much evil talk may come of it, if you should creep into hiding this night — "

Kristin let her arms fall heavily across the board. She shut her eyes.

"Then they must talk who will! I *cannot* bear to see these strange women around me to-night — "

Next morning the big sons sat silent — with eyes cast down; while Munan prattled and prattled of the little

---

* 3rd May.

brother he had seen in his mother's arms down in the
weaving-house. At last Björgulf said he had best talk no
more now of *that*.

Kristin did naught but lie and listen — it seemed to her
she never slept so sound that she was not listening, and
waiting.

She rose from her bed the eighth day, but the women
about her knew 'twas not well with her. She shivered and
felt waves of heat; one day the milk would stream from
her breasts so that her clothes were wet through; the next
day she would not have enough to give the child its fill.
But she would not lie down again. She would not let the
child out of her arms — she never laid it in the cradle; of
nights she had it with her in the bed; in the day she went
about bearing it in her arms, sat with it by the hearth, sat
with it on her bed, listened and waited, and gazed on it;
yet for hours she seemed neither to see it nor to hear its
wailing. Then she would seem to wake — she took up
the boy, walked and walked the floor with him; with her
cheek bent down to his she crooned and crooned to him
low and softly; then sat her down and held him to her
breast; sat gazing on him as before, her face set as stone —

When the boy was near six weeks old — and the mother
had not yet been over the weaving-house threshold — Ulf
Haldorssön and Skule came in thither one day. They were
clad for the road.

"Ay, now are we riding north to Haugen, Kristin,"
said Ulf. "There must be an end to these matters now — "

Kristin sat silent and stiff, with the boy at her breast.
At first she seemed not to understand. All at once she
started up, flushed blood-red in the face:

"Do as you will. If you long to go back to your right
master, I will not hinder you. 'Twere best you took your
wage — then you will not need to seek us down here
again."

Ulf half uttered a savage oath. Then he looked at the
woman standing there with the little child clutched to her
breast. He pressed his lips together and held his peace.

But Skule took a step forward:

"Yes, mother mine — I ride now up to father — if so be
you forget that Ulf has been foster-father to all us
brothers, you must mind at least that me you cannot bid

and forbid as though I were a serving-wench or a sucking child — "

"Can I not?" His mother struck him on the ear, so that the boy staggered: "Methinks I shall bid and you shall all do my bidding so long as I feed and clothe you — Get you out!" she shrieked, stamping with her foot.

Skule was wild with rage. But Ulf said below his breath: " 'Tis better so, boy — better that she be wild and head-strong than to see her sitting staring as though she had grieved her wits away — "

Gunhild, the house-wench, came running after them. They were to come at once down to the weaving-house to the mistress — she would speak with them and with all her sons. Curtly and harshly Kristin bade Ulf ride down to Breidin and talk with a man who had hired two cows of her; the twins he should take with him, and they need not come home before the morrow. Naakkve and Gaute she sent up to the sæter — she bade them go up the Illmand dale, and see how it stood with the horse-shelter there — and on the way up they were to look in on the tar-burner, Björn, Isrid's son, and pray him to come to the manor that evening. 'Twas of no avail that they tried to make excuse, saying that the morrow was Mass-day —

Next morning, when the bells began to ring, the mistress set forth from Jörundgaard, followed by Björn, and by Isrid, who bore the child. She had given them good and seemly clothes — but Kristin herself was so decked out with gold for her churching that all might see she was the mistress and the other two her servants.

Proud and defiant, she faced the wonderment and ill-will that she felt look out on her from the eyes of the folk on the church-green. Oh, ay, another kind of churching had been hers ere now — with the highest ladies in her train. Sira Solmund looked at her with ungentle eyes, when she stood before the church door with the taper in her hand — but he gave her entrance in the wonted way.

Isrid was nigh to her second childhood now, and under-stood but little; Björn was a strange, tongue-tied man, who never troubled his head with other folks' affairs. These two were godmother and godfather.

Isrid named the child's name to the priest. He started —

he faltered a moment — then he gave it out so that it rang down the nave to all the folks:

"Erlend — in the name of the Father, the Son, and the Holy Ghost — "

A shock seemed to run through the whole congregation. And Kristin felt a wild, revengeful joy.

The child had seemed strong enough when 'twas born. But even from the first week Kristin had seemed to know it would not thrive as it should with her. She herself had felt at the moment of her delivery — as though her heart fell to pieces now like a burnt-out cinder. And when Isrid showed her the new-born boy, she misdoubted that the spark of life had but a slender hold on this child. But she drove the thought from her — for untold times ere now she had felt as her heart were broken within her. And the child was big enough and looked not weakly —

But her disquiet for the boy grew from day to day. He was peevish and had but little stomach for food — she might sit trying for a long while ere she could bring him to take the breast. And when at last she had coaxed him to suck, he would fall asleep well-nigh at once. — She could not see that he grew —

In unspeakable fear and torment of heart, she seemed to mark that, from the day he had been christened and had got his father's name, little Erlend faded more and more.

None, no, none of her children had she loved as she loved this little child of sorrow. None had she conceived in such sweet, wild joy; none had she borne within her with such happy hope. Her thoughts went again over the past nine months; at the end there had been naught for her but to fight with all her might to hold fast to hope and faith. She *could* not lose this child — and she could not save it —

Almighty God, Queen of Mercy, Holy Olav — she felt herself this time it availed not that she threw herself down and begged for the life of the child —

Forgive us our trespasses, as we forgive them that trespass against us —

She went to church each Mass-day as she was wont to do. She kissed the doorpost, sprinkled herself with holy water, bent her knee before the ancient crucifix above the choir arch. The Saviour looked down, sorrowful and gentle, in the anguish of death. Christ died to save His murderers. Holy Olav stands before His face, in everlasting

supplication for the folk that drove him into outlawry and
slew him —

As we forgive them that trespass against us.

Blessed Mary — my child dies! Know you not, Kristin,
rather had I borne His cross and suffered His death than
have stood under my Son's cross and seen Him die — But,
since I knew that this must be, for the salvation of sinners, I gave consent in my heart — I gave consent when
my Son prayed: Father, forgive them, for they know not
what they do —

— As we forgive them that trespass against us —

The cry of your heart is no prayer until you have said
your Paternoster without guile —

Forgive us our trespasses — Mind you how oft your
trespasses were forgiven. — Behold, yonder, your sons
among the men. Behold him who stands foremost, the
chief of this fair troop of youths. The fruit of your sin —
for nigh twenty years have you seen God add to his comeliness, his understanding, and his manhood. Behold His
mercy — where is your mercy towards your youngest
son at home — ?

Remember you your father; remember you Simon
Darre —

— But in the depths of her heart she felt not that she had
forgiven Erlend. She could not, for she would not. She
clung to her cup of love, would not let it go, even now
when it held naught but the last bitter dregs. In the hour
when she could forgive Erlend, could even think of him
without this gnawing bitterness — then would all that had
been between them be at an end.

'Twas thus she stood throughout the Mass, knowing
that it profited her nothing. She tried to pray: Holy Olav,
help me; work a miracle in my heart, that I may say my
prayer without deceit or guile — may think of Erlend
with god-fearing peace in my soul. But she knew she
wished not herself that this prayer be heard. And so she
felt 'twas of no avail when she prayed that she might have
grace to keep the child. Young Erlend was lent her of God
— on one condition only might she have leave to keep
him, and that condition she would not fulfil. And to Saint
Olav is availed not to lie —

* * *

So she sat over the sick child. Her tears flowed without ceasing; she wept without a sound, and without moving a muscle of her face; her whole face was grey and hard as stone; only little by little her eyes and her eyelids grew red as blood. If someone came in to her, she dried her face in haste and sat dumb and stark.

— Yet but little was needed to thaw her. If it chanced that one of the big sons came in, cast a look on the little child, and said a gentle, pitying word to it, the mother could scarce refrain her from sobbing aloud. Could she have spoken with her grown-up sons of her fears for the little one, she knew her heart would sure be melted. But they were grown shy of her now. Since the day they came home and heard what name she had given their youngest brother, the lads seemed to have drawn yet closer together, and stood, as it were, so far away from her. But one day, as Naakkve stood looking at the child, he said:

"Mother, give me leave — let me seek out father and tell him how it is with this boy — "

"Naught will avail now any more," answered the mother, hopelessly.

Munan understood it not. He brought his playthings to his little brother, was overjoyed when he had leave to hold him and deemed that he had got the child to smile. Munan talked of the time when father would come home, and wondered how he would like this new son. Kristin sat silent and grey of face, letting the boy's prattle cut her to the heart.

The babe was thin now, and wrinkled as an old man; his eyes were over large and bright. Yet had he begun to smile at his mother — she moaned softly when she saw it. Kristin fondled the small thin limbs, took his feet into her hand — never would this child lie clutching in wonder at the strange, sweet, pinky things dancing in the air above him, which he knew not were his own feet. Never would these little feet tread the earth.

When she had sat through all the weary week's workdays to the end, watching the dying child, she would think, while she dressed for church-going — nay, now was she humble enough for sure. She had forgiven Erlend — she cared about him no more; if only she might have leave

to keep her sweetest, her most dearest treasure, gladly
would she forgive the man.

But when before the cross she whispered out the Paternoster and came to the words: "*sicut et nos dimittimus
debitoribus nostris*," then felt she her heart harden like a
hand that clenches for a blow. No!

Hopeless and soul-sick, she wept, for *will* it she could
not.

And so died Erlend Erlendssön, the day before Mary
Magdalene's Feast,* something less than three months old.

7

THIS autumn Bishop Halvard came on visitation north
through the Dale. To Sil he came the day before Matthew's
Mass.† 'Twas more than two years since the bishop had
been so far north, so there were many children to be confirmed this time. Munan Erlendssön was amongst them;
he was now eight years old.

Kristin prayed Ulf Haldorssön to take the boy up for
the laying on of hands — not a friend had she now in her
home parish of whom she would ask this. Ulf seemed glad
when she spoke to him of it. When the bells rang for
Mass, then, these three, Kristin, Ulf, and the boy, went up
churchward. The other sons had been at early Mass, all but
Lavrans, who lay abed with fever; to this Mass they had
no mind to go, the throng in the church would be so great.

As they passed by the steward's house, Kristin saw that
many strange horses stood tied outside the fence. A little
up the road they were overtaken by Jardtrud, who came
riding with a great following and passed them by. Ulf
made as if he saw not his wife and her kinsfolk.

Kristin knew for sure that Ulf had not set foot inside
his own threshold since just after the new year. 'Twas
said that, at that time, things had gone even worse than
their wont betwixt him and his wife; and thereafter he had
shifted his clothes-chest and his weapons up into the upper-

---

* 22nd July.
† 21st September.

hall, and abode there with the lads. Once, early in spring, Kristin had said to him 'twas an ill thing that he and his wife were so sorely at odds — on that he had looked at her, and laughed in such wise that she said no more.

'Twas sunshine and fair weather. Away over the Dale the air lay blue between the fells. The yellow leafage of the birch-clad slopes was beginning to grow thin, and in the parish most of the corn was cut, but here and there by the farms a pale barley-field still waved, and the after-math stood green and dew-wet on the meadows. There were many folk at the church, and much nickering and neighing of stallions, for the church stables were full, and many had been fain to bind their steeds without.

A kind of smothered, hostile air ran through the throng, whithersoever Kristin and her companions went. A young fellow slapped his thigh and laughed, but was sharply hushed by elder folk. Kristin walked, with measured pace and head held high, over the green into the churchyard. She tarried first for a while by the child's grave, and then by Simon Andressön's. A flat grey slab of stone was laid upon it — thereon was graven the likeness of a man, in visored helm and coat of scale armour, resting his hands upon his great three-cornered shield with its device. About the stone's rim stood carven:

In pace. Simon Armiger. Proles Dom. Andreæ Filii Gudmundi Militis Pater Noster.

Ulf stood without the south door; he had put off his sword in the cloister-way.

Then came Jardtrud into the churchyard with four men in her company — they were her two brothers and two old farmers; one was Kolbein Jonssön, that had been arms-bearer to Lavrans Björgulfsön for many years. They went towards the priest's door, south of the choir.

Ulf Haldorssön sprang down and set himself in their way. Kristin heard quick hot speech from where they stood. Ulf would have hindered his wife and her follow-ing from going farther. Folk in the churchyard drew near; Kristin, too, went over thither. Then Ulf sprang upon the stone base that bore the cloister arches, bent in through an arch, and seized the first axe he could lay hands on; and when one of Jardtrud's brothers would have pulled him down, Ulf leapt forward and flung up the axe. The blow struck his brother-in-law on the shoulder, and now folk ran up and laid hands on Ulf. He struggled to tear himself free — Kristin saw that his face was darkly flushed, writhen, and desperate.

Then came Sira Solmund and a clerk of the bishop's train to the priest's door. They spoke a few words with the farmers. Straightway three jackmen, who bore the bishop's white shield on their livery, took Ulf in charge and led him forth from the graveyard; but his wife and her following went into the church after the two priests.

Kristin stepped forward to the knot of farmers:

"What is it?" she asked sharply. "Wherefore took you Ulf in charge?"

"You saw, I trow, that he smote a man in the churchyard," answered one as sharply. All the folk drew away from her, so that she was left standing alone with her boy by the church door.

Kristin deemed she understood — Ulf's wife would make complaint of him before the bishop. And by forgetting himself and breaking the churchyard peace he had got him into ill case. When a stranger reading-deacon came to the door and looked out, she went forward to him, named her name, and asked that she might be brought before the bishop.

Within the church all its treasures were set forth, but the candles on the altar were not yet lit. A little sunlight came in through the small round windows high up, and streamed down amongst the dark-brown pillars. A part of the congregation was already come into the nave, and had sat them down on the bench that ran along the wall. In the choir before the bishop's throne stood a little knot of folk, Jardtrud Herbrandsdatter and her two brothers — Geirulv with his arm bound up — Kolbein Jonssön, Sigurd Geitung, and Tore Borghildssön. Behind and round about the carven chair stood two young priests from Hamar, some other men of the bishop's following, and Sira Solmund.

All these stared hard when the mistress of Jörundgaard stepped forward and made low obeisance before the bishop.

Sir Halvard was a tall, stout man of exceeding venerable mien. Beneath his red silk cap his hair shone snow-white on the temples, and his plump oval face glowed large and red; he had a strong, crooked nose, and a heavy chin; and his mouth, narrow as a slit, and all but lipless, ran straight across his face, on which closely shaven stubble showed greyish-white — but the bushy eyebrows, over his sparkling coal-black eyes, were still dark.

"God be with you, Kristin Lavransdatter," said Sir Halvard. He looked ponderingly at the woman from under his heavy brows. One of the old man's large, white hands clasped the gold cross on his breast; in the other, resting on the lap of his dark violet robe, he held a wax tablet.

"What moves you to seek me here, Mistress Kristin?" asked the bishop again. "Deem you not 'twere more fitting that you tarried till after noon, and came to me at Romundgaard to say what lies upon your heart?"

"Jardtrud Herbrandsdatter has sought you here, reverend father," answered Kristin. "Now hath Ulf Haldorssön been with my husband these five-and-thirty years; he was ever our true friend and helper and good kinsman — methought, perchance, I might help him in some wise — "

Jardtrud gave a low cry of scorn or rage — all the others stared at Kristin, the parish folk with bitter looks, the bishop's train keenly and curiously. Sir Halvard looked about him sternly; then he said to Kristin:

"Stands it so that you would essay to make Ulf Haldorssön's defence? You know, mayhap," he said quickly, raising a hand, as she would have answered, "none has the right to call on you to speak in this matter — saving your husband — if your own conscience drive you not thereto. Bethink you first — "

"I thought most of this, Lord Bishop, that Ulf had let anger carry him away and laid hand on his weapon at the church door — and whether I might help him at all by standing bail. Or else," she brought out painfully, "full sure I am my husband will do all he can in this matter to help his friend and kinsman — "

The bishop turned impatiently to the bystanders, who all seemed much wrought up:

"The woman need not tarry here. Her spokesman may have leave to wait out in the nave — go down thither all of you, while I speak with the lady — and send the folk outside for a while — and Jardtrud Herbrandsdatter with them."

One of the young priests had been busy laying out the

bishop's vestments. Now, with heedful care, he laid the
mitre with its golden cross down on the outspread folds
of the cope, and went down and spoke a little with the
folk in the nave. The others followed him down thither.
The congregation went out, and with them Jardtrud, and
the sacristan barred the doors.

"You spake of your husband," said the bishop, looking
at her as before. "Is it sooth that last summer you sought
atonement with him?"

"Ay, my lord."

"But you came not to an accord?"

"My lord — forgive me if I say it — but of my husband I have made no plaint. I sought you that I might
speak of Ulf Haldorssön's matter — "

"Knew your husband of this — that you were with
child?" asked Sir Halvard; he seemed to be wroth at her
demurring thus.

"Ay, my lord," she said, very low.

"And how took Erlend Nikulaussön that tidings?" asked
the bishop.

Kristin stood with downcast eyes, twisting between her
fingers the fall of her linen coif.

"He would not be reconciled with you when he heard
it?"

"My lord, forgive me — " Kristin was grown very red.
"Whether my lord Erlend have been thus or thus towards
me — if it can help Ulf's cause aught that he come hither,
I wot well that Erlend will hasten hither to him."

The bishop knit his brows, as he looked upon her:

"Mean you, out of friendship for this man Ulf — or,
since the matter is now come to light — will Erlend now,
after all, own the child you bore last spring?"

Kristin lifted her head — she gazed at the bishop with
wide-open eyes and lips half parted. 'Twas as though
now, little by little, the meaning of his words were coming
home to her. Sir Halvard looked on her gravely:

"True it is, woman, that none but your spouse has the
right to charge you with this offence. But you understand,
belike, that both he and you were guilty of great sin if
he took on himself the fatherhood of another's child to
shield Ulf. Far better for you all, if you have sinned, that
the sin be confessed and atoned for."

The colour came and went in Kristin's face:

"Has any said that 'twas not my husband — 'twas not his child — ?"

The bishop asked slowly:

"Would you, Kristin, I should believe you have not even known what folk say of you and your steward — ?"

"I have not." She drew herself up — stood with her head thrown back a little, white of face under her flowing head-linen. "Now do I pray you, my reverend lord and father — if any have defamed me behind my back, that you charge them to make it good before my face!"

"No name has been named," answered the bishop. "'Tis against the law. But Jardtrud Herbrandsdatter has craved leave to part her from her husband and betake her home with her kinsmen, laying to his charge that he has lived with another woman, a wedded wife, and begotten a child with her."

For a while both were silent. Then Kristin spoke again:

"My lord — I pray you, do me so much grace, and demand of these men that they say in my hearing — that *I* am that woman."

Bishop Halvard looked at the lady sharply and searchingly. Then he beckoned — the men in the nave came up and stood about his chair. Sir Halvard spoke:

"You good men of Sil have come to me at an unbefitting time, and laid before me a complaint which rightly should first have come before my deputy. I fell in with this but now, for that I knew you can scarce have full skill in the law. But here is this woman, Mistress Kristin Lavransdatter of Jörundgaard, come to me with a strange prayer — she prays me to ask you if you dare to say to her, face to face, that word has gone about the parish that her husband, Erlend Nikulaussön, was not father to the child she bore in spring?"

Sira Solmund answered:

"It has been said in every manor and every cot in this our parish, that the child was begotten in whoredom and in incest 'twixt the mistress and her steward. And to us it seems not to be believed that the woman herself should not know such was the rumour."

The bishop would have spoken, but Kristin said, loud and firmly:

"So help me God Almighty, Mary Maid, and Saint

Olav, and Saint Thomas Archbishop — I have never known that this lie was told of us."

" 'Tis not easy then to understand — wherefore deemed you then that you need hide so heedfully that you went with child," asked the priest. "You hid yourself from all folk, and scarce came forth from your house the winter through."

" 'Tis long since I had friends amongst the people of this parish — little company have I kept with folk hereabout in these last years. Though I knew not, as now it seems, that all were my foes. But I came to church each Mass-day," said the woman.

"Ay — and you wrapped you in thick cloaks, and clothed you so that none might see you grew big beneath your belt — "

"So does every woman — she would fain look seemly when among folk," answered Kristin curtly.

The priest spoke again:

"Had it been your husband's child, as you say — I trow that then you had not tended it so ill that you wrought its death with your ill guidance."

One of the young Hamar priests stepped forth and put his arm about Kristin quickly. A moment after, she stood as before, pale and straight — she thanked the priest with a reverence.

Sira Solmund went on vehemently:

"The serving-women at Jörundgaard said it — my sister, who comes about the manor, saw it too — the woman went there, and the milk was spurting from her breasts so that her clothing was wet through — yet every woman that saw the boy's body can bear witness he died of hunger — "

Bishop Halvard struck out sidewise with his hand:

"Enough, Sira Solmund. We must keep to the matter before us, and that is whether Jardtrud Herbrandsdatter had naught else to go upon, when she made plaint against her husband, than that she had heard tales which the mistress here says are lies — and whether Kristin can prove these untrue. — None says, I trow, that she has laid hands upon her child — "

But Kristin stood pale and said no word.

The bishop turned to the parish priest:

"But you, Sira Solmund, 'twas your bounden duty to speak with the woman here and let her know what folks were saying. Did you this?"

The priest turned red:

"I have prayed from my heart for this woman, that she might of her own accord turn from her stiff-neckedness, repent her, and do penance. — *My* friend her father was not," said the priest vehemently. "But yet I know, too, that Lavrans of Jörundgaard was a righteous man and strong in the faith. True it is he had been worthy a better child — but this daughter of his has heaped on him shame upon shame. Scarce was she grown maid when, by her wantonness, she brought two good lads of the parish here to their death. Then she broke her faith and troth with a bold and gallant esquire that her father had chosen to be her husband, gained her end in dishonourable wise, and got this man, who you, my lord, know well was doomed outlaw and traitor. But methought at last, for sure, her heart must be softened, when she saw that she dwelt here hated and scorned and of the worst repute, she and all hers, at Jörundgaard — where her father and Ragnfrid Ivarsdatter lived with all men's love and reverence —

"But 'twas too much when she came hither at this time with her son to confirmation — and that man was to lead the boy before you whom all the parish know she had lived with in twofold adultery and incest — "

The bishop made a sign to the other to be silent:

"How near of kin to your husband is Ulf Haldorssön?" he said to Kristin.

"Ulf's true father was Sir Baard Peterssön of Hestnæs. He was brother, by the same mother, of Gaute Erlendssön of Skogheim, Erlend Nikulaussön's mother's father."

Sir Halvard turned to Sira Solmund impatiently:

"Incest 'tis not — her mother-in-law and Ulf are cousins — 'tis breach of kinship's dues and grievous sin, if it be true — no need to make it worse."

"Ulf Haldorssön is godfather to this woman's eldest son," said Sira Solmund.

The bishop looked at her, and Kristin answered:

"Ay, my lord."

Sir Halvard sat a while in silence.

"God help you, Kristin Lavransdatter," he said sorrowfully.

"I knew your father of old — I was his guest at Jörund-gaard in my youth. I mind you well when you were a fair and sinless child. Had Lavrans Björgulfsön lived, then had this not befallen. Think on your father, Kristin — for his sake you must cast off this shameful charge, and clear you, if you can — "

Like a lightning-flash it came to her — she knew the bishop again. A winter's day at the sunset hour — a rear-ing, red young stallion in the courtyard, and a priest with a black ring of hair round his fiery red face; hanging to the halter-rope, spattered with foam, striving to master the unruly beast and mount him bare-backed. Clusters of drunken, laughing Yule-guests hovering about, her father among them, red of face from drink and cold, shouting, dizzily merry —

She turned to Kolbein Jonssön:

"Kolbein! You that have known me from my cradle up — you that knew me and my sisters in our father's and mother's home — I know you so loved my father that — Kolbein — believe *you* this of me?"

Farmer Kolbein looked on her, hard and sorrowful of face:

"We loved your father, say you — Ay, all we house-carls of his, poor serving-men and common folk who loved Lavrans of Jörundgaard and deemed him such an one as God would have a chieftain to be —

"Ask not us, Kristin Lavransdatter, who saw how your father loved you, and how you rewarded his love — ask not us what we deem is too evil for you to do!"

Kristin bowed her head upon her breast. The bishop could draw from her no further word — she answered his questions no longer.

Then Sir Halvard rose. By the side of the high altar was a little door that led to the closed-in cloister-way behind the apse. A part of this served as sacristy, and in part had been pierced some small openings, through which the lep-rous might receive the host when they stood without there and heard Mass apart from the rest of the congregation. But now, for many years, none in the parish had been sick of leprosy.

"Mayhap 'twere best you waited out there, Kristin, till the folk are come in to the service. I will speak with you afterwards — but now must you go home to your own place."

Kristin curtsied before the bishop.

"I would liefer go home straightway, reverend sir, if so be you give me leave."

"As you will, Kristin Lavransdatter. God be your shield, mistress — if you be guiltless, be sure they will work your assoilment, God Himself and His blood-witnesses who are this church's lords, Saint Olav and Saint Thomas, who died for righteousness' sake."

Kristin curtsied again before the bishop. Then she went through the priest's door out into the churchyard.

A little stripling in a new red habit stood there all alone, stiff and straight. For a moment Munan turned his pale child's-face up towards his mother; his eyes were big and frightened.

Her sons — she had not thought of them before. As in a flash she saw her troop of boys — as they had stood on the outskirts of her life this last year, thronging together like a herd of horses in a thunder-storm, at gaze, affrighted — far off from her, while she struggled in the last death-throes of her love. What had they seen, what had they thought, what had they suffered, while she tossed and writhed in her madness — ? What would become of them now — ?

She held Munan's little rough fist in her hand. The child stared straight out before him — his mouth quivered a little, but he held himself upright.

Hand in hand with her son, Kristin Lavransdatter went across the graveyard, out on to the church-green. She thought of her sons, and it seemed as though she must wholly break and sink to the earth. The throng of folk was drawing towards the church doors, while in the belfry all the bells were ringing.

She had heard a saga once of a slain man that could not fall to earth for the many spears stuck fast in him. She, as she walked there, could not drop down for all the eyes that stabbed her through.

The mother and the child came in to the upper hall. The sons stood in a cluster round Björgulf, who sat at the board. Naakkve's head towered high above his brothers', where he stood with one hand on the half-blind boy's shoulder. Kristin saw her first-born's narrow, dark, blue-eyed face, the soft, dark down about his red mouth.

"You know it?" she asked calmly, as she came forward towards the group of lads.

"Ay." Naakkve answered for them all. "Gunhild was at the church."

Kristin stood a little. The lads had turned again to their eldest brother, until the mother spoke:

"Have any of you known that such things were whispered in the parish — of Ulf and me?"

At that Ivar Erlendssön turned to her suddenly:

"Think you, mother, that, had we known, you had heard no tidings of *our* doings? 'Tis not *I* who had sat still and let my mother be miscalled for an adultress — not if I knew 'twas true she *were* one!"

Kristin said sorrowfully:

"I marvel now, my sons, what you have thought of all this that has befallen in this last year."

The lads stood silent. Then Björgulf lifted his face, and looked up at his mother with his ailing eyes:

"Jesus Christus, mother — what should we think — this year — and all the years that went before? Trow you 'twas easy for us to know what we should think?"

Naakkve said:

"O ay, mother — it may be I should have spoken to you — but you bore you in such wise that we could not. And when you had our youngest brother christened as though you would give out our father for a dead man — " He broke off with a vehement gesture.

Björgulf spoke again:

"Of naught did you think, father and you, but of this strife of yours — No thought had you that we were growing to manhood the while. Never did you take heed who might come between your weapons and be dealt bleeding wounds — "

He had sprung up. Naakkve laid a hand upon his shoulder. Kristin saw 'twas true — these two were grown men. It seemed as though she stood naked before them, as though she herself had stripped her shamelessly before her children — "

'Twas this they had seen, more than aught else, in their upgrowing — that their father and mother had come to be old folk — and the heats of youth pitiably misbecame them — and yet they had not been able to grow old in honour and reverence —

Then the child's voice cut through the silence. Munan broke out into wild lamentation:

"Mother — are they coming to take you to prison, mother? Are they coming now to take mother away from us — ?"

He flung his arms about her, and pressed his face up under her bosom. Kristin drew him to her, sank down upon the bench, and gathered the little weeping boy into her arms; she tried to soothe him:

"Little son, little son, weep not so — "

"None can take our mother from us." Gaute went and laid hold of his little brother. "Weep not so — they cannot harm her. Now must you be still, Munan — you sure must know, boy, we shall guard our mother!"

Kristin sat with the child crushed close to her — 'twas as though the little one had saved her by his tears.

Then Lavrans said — he sat up with the flush of fever on his cheeks:

"Ay — what will you do, brothers?"

"When Mass is sung to an end," said Naakkve, "we will go to the parsonage and proffer bail for our foster-father. That is the first thing we shall do — think you not so, good fellows?"

Björgulf, Gaute, Ivar, and Skule answered ay. Kristin said:

"Ulf has borne arms against a man in the churchyard. And somewhat must I do to free him and myself of these slanders. These are such grave matters, my sons, meseems you young lads must take counsel of someone how to deal with them."

"Whom think you we should pray for counsel?" asked Naakkve, with a touch of scorn.

"Sir Sigurd of Sundbu is my mother's sister's son," answered his mother, faltering a little.

"Since he has not bethought him of it ere now," said the young man as before, "methinks 'tis not like that we Erlendssöns will go a-begging to him now that a pinch has come. What say you, brothers? If we be not of full age, yet are we of age to bear arms, the five of us — "

"Boys," said Kristin. "In this matter you will make no speed with arms."

"You must leave us to judge, mother," answered Naak-kve curtly. "But now, mother, 'twere well you let us have some food. And seat you in your wonted place — for the house-folk's sake," said he, as one giving command.

'Twas but little she could eat. She sat, thinking — she dared not ask if now they would send after their father. And she thought — in what wise would this matter go forward? She knew but little of the law in such things — maybe she must clear herself of the slander by oath with compurgators.* If so it were, 'twould most like be at the head church at Ullinsyn in Vaagaa — There she had kin on her mother's side well-nigh on every great manor. And if her oath fell to the ground — and she should stand be-fore their eyes unable to free herself of this shameful charge! Bring shame upon her father — He had been a stranger here in the Dale. He had been able to make good his place; him all had honoured. Those times when Lav-rans Björgulfsön took up a cause at Thing or moot, he had ever had a full following. But she knew her shame would strike back at him. She saw now, all at once, how lonely her father had stood — in spite of all, alone and a stranger amid the folk here, when time after time she loaded him with a burthen of shame and sorrow and ill repute.

She had not thought she could feel the like of this any more — again and again it had seemed to her that her heart must break into bleeding shards — and now once more 'twas as though it were bursting.

Gaute went out upon the balcony and looked north-wards:

"The folk are coming out now from the church," said he. "Shall we tarry till they have gone a little on their way?"

"No," answered Naakkve. "They may as lief see that the Erlendssöns are out. We must busk us now, boys. 'Twere well you took your morions on."

Only Naakkve owned right harness. His coat of mail he left, but set his helm on, and took shield and sword and a long halberd. Björgulf and Gaute put on the old iron casques the boys wore when they practised them in sword-

---

* See Note 5.

play, but Ivar and Skule were fain to rest content with small steel caps, such as the yeoman levies still used. Their mother looked on. She felt a strange tightening in her breast:

"Meseems 'tis ill bethought, my sons, to arm yourselves thus to go to the priest's manor," said she, uneasily. "Take heed you forget not the holy-day peace and the bishop's reverence."

Naakkve answered:

"There is dearth of honour here on Jörundgaard now, mother — we must buy it at what price we may."

"Not you, Björgulf," begged the mother, fearfully, for the weak-sighted boy had taken up a great battle-axe. "Remember, son, you can see but little!"

"Oh, as far as this reaches, I still can see," answered Björgulf, weighing the axe in his hand.

Gaute went over to young Lavrans' bed and took down his grandfather's great battle sword, which the boy would ever have hanging on the wall above his couch. He drew it from its sheath and looked on it:

"You must lend me your sword, kinsman — I deem that our grandsire would like full well that it should go with us on this journey."

Kristin wrung her hands where she sat. It seemed as though she must cry out — in agony and utmost horror, urged too by a power stronger than agony or horror — as she had cried out when she gave these men birth. Wounds and wounds and wounds without number had been dealt her throughout her life, but now she knew they were all healed over — the scars were tender as raw flesh — but bleed to death she knew she could not — never had she been more alive than now —

Blossom and leaf were worn from off her, but her branches were not lopped, and felled she was not. For the first time since she had borne Erlend Nikulaussön's child, she forgot the father quite and saw naught but his sons —

But the sons looked not at their mother, sitting white, with fixed, wide eyes. Munan still lay across her lap — he had not unclasped her all this time. The five lads went forth from the loft.

Kristin stood up and stepped out upon the balcony. Now they came forth from behind the storehouses and, one behind the other, went up the path to Romundgaard between the pale, waving barley-fields. The morions and steel caps gleamed dully, but the sunlight glittered on Naakkve's glaive and on the twins' spearheads. She stood there looking after the five young men. She was mother to them all —

Within the room she sank down before the chest, below where Mary Virgin's picture hung. Her sobs and weeping seemed to tear her in sunder. Munan, sobbing too, nestled close to his mother; Lavrans sprang from his bed and cast himself down on his knees at her other side. She flung her arms about her two youngest sons —

Since the little one died — she had thought: what was there to pray for? Hard, cold, heavy as stone, she had felt her falling toward hell's gaping jaws. But now prayer burst from her lips resistlessly — without her conscious will her soul poured itself out to Mary, maid and mother, Queen of heaven and earth, cries of dread, of praise, of thanksgiving — Mary, Mary, I own so much, still have I endless treasures that may be reft from me. — Mother of Mercy, take them in thy ward — !

There were many folk in the courtyard at Romund-gaard. When the Erlendssöns came in, some yeomen asked what they would.

"Of you we would naught — as yet," said Naakkve, with a galling smile. "We have an errand to the bishop to-day, Magnus. Afterward, mayhap, we brothers may deem we have somewhat to say to you folks too. But to-day you need not fear us."

There arose some cries and commotion. Sira Solmund came out and would have bidden the lads begone from there; but now some farmers spoke up: the boys should have leave, they said, to make inquiry concerning this charge against their mother. The bishop's servants came out and said to the Erlendssöns: they must go now; folk here were sitting down to meat, and none had time now to listen to them. But this the farmers liked not.

"What is this, good folk?" asked a loud voice above them. No one had marked that Sir Halvard himself was come out on the loft balcony. There he stood now in his violet robe, the red silk cap upon his white hair, tall, broadly built, chieftain-like. "Who are these young men?"

He was answered that these were Kristin of Jörund-gaard's sons.

"Are you the eldest?" asked the bishop of Naakkve. "Then will I speak with you. These others must bide here in the courtyard the while."

Naakkve went up the stairs of the upper hall and followed the bishop into the room. Sir Halvard sat him down in the high-seat and looked at the young man, who stood before him leaning on the great halberd.

"What is your name?"

"Nikulaus Erlendssön, my lord."

"Think you 'tis needful to be so well armed, Nikulaus Erlendssön," said the other, smiling a little, "when you go to have speech with your bishop?"

Nikulaus flushed deep. He went over to the corner, laid aside his weapons and head-piece, and came back. He stood up before the bishop, his bared head bowed, one hand clasped about the other wrist, with an easy, yet seemly and reverent, bearing.

Sir Halvard thought: this young man had not lacked teaching in *kurteisi* and mannerly bearing. 'Twas true he could not have been so young a child when his father fell from wealth and honourable estate — he remembered, for sure, the time he was heir to Husaby. A comely fellow he was, too — 'twas great pity of him, the bishop thought.

"Were they your brothers, all those who were in your company? How many are you Erlendssöns?"

"We are seven, my lord, living."

— So many young lives entangled in this broil. Unwittingly the bishop heaved a sigh.

"Be seated, Nikulaus — you would speak with me, belike, of these rumours that have gone abroad about your mother and her steward?"

"Thanks, reverend sir, I would liefer stand before you."

The bishop gazed thoughtfully at the young man. Then he said, slowly:

"The thing stands thus, Nikulaus; methinks 'tis hard to believe that this that is said of Kristin Lavransdatter can be true. And right to impeach her of adultery has none save her husband. But there is, besides, the kinship 'twixt your father and this Ulf, and this, too, that he is your godfather — And Jardtrud has made her plaint in such

wise that it must be read as importing your mother's dishonour. — Wot you if 'tis as she says, that her husband
has beat her often, and that he has shunned her bed close
on a year?"

"Ulf and Jardtrud lived not well together — our foster-
father was not young when he wed, and something harsh
and hasty he can be. Towards us brothers and to our father
and mother he has ever been the most trusty friend and
kinsman. 'Twas the first prayer I had thought to lay before you, dear my lord: that if 'twere in any wise possible,
you would be pleased to let Ulf go free against bail."

"You are not of age yet?" asked the bishop.

"No, my lord. But our mother is willing to proffer whatever bail you may demand."

The bishop shook his head.

"My father will be of the same mind, that know I full
surely. 'Tis my intent now to ride from here straightway
up to him, and make known what has here befallen. If,
then, you would grant him a hearing to-morrow — "

The bishop put his hand about his chin, and sat, rubbing
his thumb softly over the stiff hairs with a little rasping
noise.

"Be seated, Nikulaus," he said; "we can talk the better
so." Naakkve bowed in thanks and sat him down. " — But
it is true then that Ulf has denied to live with his wife?"
he asked, as though he had just bethought himself of this
again.

"Ay, my lord. So far as my knowledge goes — " A smile
crossed the bishop's face, and at that the young man smiled
a little too. "Ulf has slept in the loft with us brothers since
Yule that is overpast."

The bishop sat silent for a while again: "And his food
— where got he his food?"

"He had his wife give him his victuals out, when he had
to go to the forest or the like." Naakkve faltered a little.
"There was some trouble in the matter — mother deemed
'twere best he had his board with us again, as he had had
before he wed. Ulf would not have this, for he said there
would be so much talk if now they changed the bargain
he and father struck, about the goods he was to have from
the manor for his dwelling when he set up house — and
he deemed it not just that mother should take him to board

again without abatement of those supplies. But mother had
her way — Ulf had his food with us — and the rest was to
be settled hereafter."

"Hm. Your mother has else the name of one that looks
narrowly to her goods, and is a most notable and thrifty
housewife — "

"Not with food," said Naakkve eagerly. "To that every
soul can bear witness, every carl and every woman that
has served on our manor — with food is mother the most
free-handed woman. In that way she is no otherwise now
than when we were rich folk — never gladder than when
she can set on her board some dainty dish — and she
purveys such full measure that each serving-man and
woman, down to the swineherd and the bedesfolk, get their
share of the good things."

"Hm." The bishop sat in thought. "You said you were
minded to fetch your father?"

"Ay, my lord. Surely aught else were against reason?"
The bishop made no answer, and Naakkve went on: "We
spoke with father in the winter, my brother Gaute and I
— we told him, too, these tidings, that our mother was
with child. But we saw no sign and we heard no word
from his mouth which we could take to mean he doubted
mother was true to him as gold, or that he marvelled. But
father has never felt at ease in Sil; he was minded to dwell
on his own farm in Dovre, and mother was there a while
last summer. He was wroth because she would not bide
there and keep his house — his will was that she should
let Gaute and me have the care of Jörundgaard, and should
move herself to Haugen — "

Bishop Halvard rubbed and rubbed his chin and gazed
at the young man.

— What kind of man soever Erlend Nikulaussön might
be — so base he could scarce be as to have charged his wife
with whoredom before their young sons.

Though much seemed to tell against Kristin Lavransdatter — nevertheless he believed not the charge. He
deemed he had seen that she spoke truth when she denied
knowing that she was suspect with Ulf Haldorssön. Yet
he remembered this woman had been weak before when
fleshly lusts had lured — with ugly tricks had they forced
Lavrans' consent from him, she and this man whom she
lived now at strife —

When the matter of the child's death came up, he saw at once that conscience smote her. But even if she had been neglectful of her child, she could not for that be haled before an earthly court. For that she must atone to God according to her father confessor's bidding. And the child *might* be the husband's none the less, even though she had tended it but ill. Glad she could scarce have been to have a babe on her hands again, well on in years as she was, forsaken of her husband, with seven sons already to nuture, with narrowed means by far than they were born to. 'Twould be against reason to look that she should love that child overmuch.

He believed not she was an unfaithful wife. Though God alone knew what things he had heard and seen in the two score years he had been priest and heard confession. But he believed her —

But Erlend Nikulaussön's doings in this matter he could not understand save in one way. He had not come near his wife while she was with child, nor when the child was born, nor when it died. *He* must needs believe he was not the father —

Now 'twas to be thought on how the man would act. Whether, notwithstanding, he would stand forth and shield his wife for their seven sons' sake — 'twere thus a man of honour would bear him. Or would he, now these tales were noised abroad, make plaint against her. From what the bishop had heard of Erlend of Husaby, he deemed he could not be sure the man might not do this.

"Who are your mother's nearest kin by blood and marriage?" he asked again.

"Jammælt Halvardssön of Ælin is wed with her sister, widow of Simon Darre of Formo. Then has she two cousins on the father's side, Ketil Aasmundssön of Skog and his sister Ragna, wife to Sigurd Kyrning. Ivar Gjesling of Ringheim and his brother Haavard Trondssön are her mother's brother's sons. But they all dwell far away — "

"But Sir Sigurd Eldjarn of Sundbu — your mother and he are sisters' children. In such a cause the knight must stand forth and defend his kinswoman, Nikulaus! You must ride thither to him even now — to-day — and bring him word of this, friend!"

Hesitating a little, Naakkve answered:

"Reverend sir — there has been little fellowship 'twixt him and us. And I believe not, my lord, 'twould vantage my mother's cause if that man stood forth in her defence. Erlend Eldjarn's house are little liked in this country-side. Naught harmed my father more in folk's esteem than this, that the Gjeslings had bound them to him in that emprise that cost us Husaby, and whereby they lost Sundbu."

"Ay, Erlend Eldjarn"; the bishop laughed a little. "Ay, he had the knack of falling at odds with folk — he quarrelled with all his brothers-in-law here in the north. Your mother's father, that was a godly man, and not afraid to bend if peace and concord 'twixt kinsmen could thereby be furthered — he fared no better than the rest; he and Erlend Eldjarn came to be the bitterest unfriends."

"Ay"; Naakkve began to laugh a little. "And 'twas not over any such great matters either — two sheets with fringes and a blue-bordered towel; 'twas valued at two marks in money, the whole matter. But mother's mother had been so urgent that her husband must get just these very things at the parting of the heritage, and Gudrun Ivarsdatter had spoken of them to her man also. In the end Erlend took them and hid them in his travelling bags, but Lavrans took them out again — he deemed he had most right to them, for 'twas Ragnfrid who had worked these things when she was a young maid at home on Sundbu. But when Erlend grew ware of this, he struck grandfather in the face, and then my grandfather laid hold on him and threw him three times and shook him like a pelt. After that they never changed a word again — and 'twas all for the sake of these trumpery rags — mother has them at home in her chest — "

The bishop laughed heartily. He knew this tale full well already — it had made much merriment for folks in its day — of how the husbands of Ivar's daughters were so zealous to please their wives. But he had gained his end — the young man's face had melted into a smile; the watchful, fearful look was driven for a while from the comely, blue-grey eyes. Then Sir Halvard laughed yet louder:

"Ay, but, Nikulaus, they spoke together once again, and I stood by. 'Twas in Oslo, at the Yule-tide feasting, the year before the Queen, the Lady Eufemia, died. Our lord, King Haakon of blessed memory, spoke with Lavrans —

he had come south to greet his master and lay before him his faithful service — the King spoke of how 'twas unchristian and churl-like, this enmity 'twixt the husbands of two sisters. Lavrans went over to where Erlend stood with some gentlemen of the guard, prayed him lovingly to forgive his over-hastiness, and proffered to send the things to Lady Gudrun with loving greetings from her brother and sister. Erlend answered: he would make up the quarrel if Lavrans would own, before the men who stood there, that he had borne him like a thief and a robber at the parting of their father-in-law's goods. Lavrans turned upon his heel and walked away — and *that*, I trow, was the last time Ivar Gjesling's sons-in-law met on earth," the bishop ended, laughing.

"But hearken to me now, Nikulaus Erlendssön," he said, folding his hands together. "I know not if 'tis wise to make such haste to bring your father down hither — or to set this Ulf Haldorssön free. Clear herself your mother *must*, meseems — seeing how loud has been the talk of her having done amiss. But, as matters now stand, think you 'twill be easy for Kristin to find the matrons who will join with her in making oath?"

Nikulaus looked up at the bishop — his eyes grew doubtful and afraid.

"Wait but a few days, Nikulaus! Your father and Ulf are men from outland parishes and little liked — Kristin and Jardtrud are both from the Dale here — but Jardtrud, you wot, is from far farther south, and your mother is one of these folks' own. And I have marked well that Lavrans Björgulfsön is not forgotten of the people. Well-nigh it seems as though they had meant to chasten her because they deemed she had been a bad daughter — but I can tell already that many see they served the father but ill by raising such a cry against his child — they are vexed and repentant, and soon they will wish for naught so much as that Kristin may be able to clear herself. And, mayhap, 'twill be little enough that Jardtrud has to show, when we come to look into her wallet. Another matter would it be if her husband were to go about, chafing the folk and setting them against him — "

"My lord," said Naakkve, looking up at the bishop: "forgive me that I say it, but 'tis little to my mind — that we should do naught for our foster-father, and that we should not fetch my father to stand at this time by mother's side — "

"Nevertheless I pray you, my son," said Bishop Halvard, "to take my counsel. Press not on over-hastily by bringing Erlend Nikulaussön hither. Meanwhile will I have a letter written to Sir Sigurd of Sundbu, praying him to come forthwith and meet me — what is this?" He stood up and went out on the balcony.

Their backs against the storehouse wall, Gaute and Björgulf Erlendssöns stood, holding off a knot of the bishop's men, who made at them with uplifted weapons. Björgulf felled a man to the earth with a blow of his axe at the moment the bishop and Naakkve came out. Gaute was parrying blows with his sword. Some farmers held Ivar and Skule fast, while others led away a wounded man. Sira Solmund stood a little way off, bleeding from mouth and nose.

"Hold there," cried Sir Halvard. "Down with your arms, you Erlendssöns — " He went down into the courtyard, and up to the young men, who had obeyed straightway. "What is this?"

Sira Solmund came forward, bent him before the bishop, and said:

"Thus it is, reverend father; Gaute Erlendssön has broken the holy-day peace, and smitten me, his parish priest, even as you see!"

At the same moment one of the elder farmers stepped forth, made obeisance to the bishop, and spoke:

"Reverend sir, the boy was sorely wrought on. The priest there spoke of his mother in such wise, that one could scarce look that Gaute should brook his words tamely."

"Hold your peace, Sira — I cannot hearken to more than one of you at a time," said Sir Halvard impatiently. "Speak, Olav Trondssön."

Olav Trondssön spoke:

"The priest sought to stir up the Erlendssöns, but Björgulf and Gaute answered him back, soberly enough. Gaute said, too, what we all know is true, that Kristin lived with her husband at Dovre a while last summer, and 'twas then he was smithied — the poor little soul there is all this stir about. But at that the priest says, since folk on Jörund-gaard have ever been so book-learned — 'twas like she knew the saga of King David and Lady Bath-sheba — but Erlend Nikulaussön had mayhap been as sleepy-headed as the knight Urias."

The bishop's face flushed as purple as his own robe; his black eyes flashed. He looked at Sira Solmund for a space. But 'twas not to him he spoke:

"You know, I trow, Gaute Erlendssön, that by this deed you have brought on you the Church's ban?" he said. Then he bade that the Erlendssöns be carried home to Jörundgaard; two of his henchmen, and four farmers whom the bishop chose as men of worth and of good wit, he sent with them to keep guard on them.

"You must go with them, too, Nikulaus," he said to Naakkve, "and keep you quiet. Your brothers have done their mother no good service, but I see well that they were sore provoked."

In his heart the Hamar bishop scarce deemed that Kris-tin's sons had harmed her cause. He had seen that already there were many who had other thoughts of the mistress of Jörundgaard than had been theirs that morning, when she had made the cup to overflow by coming to the church with Ulf Haldorssön to be sponsor for her son. One of these was Kolbein Jonssön — and him, therefore, Sir Halvard set over the guard.

Naakkve went the first into the upper hall, where Kris-tin was sitting on the edge of Lavrans' bed, with Munan on her lap. He told her what had befallen, but laid much weight thereon that the bishop held her to be guiltless, and thought, too, that the younger brothers had been sorely baited ere they broke the peace. He counselled his mother not to go herself and seek speech of the bishop.

The four brothers were led in now. Their mother gazed at them; she was pale and strange-eyed. In the midst of her deep despair and dread, her heart seemed to swell again to bursting. Yet she spoke calmly to Gaute:

"Ill have you borne you, son, in this matter — and 'twas little honour for Lavrans Björgulfsön's sword that you should draw it against a herd of tale-mongering boors — "

"Faith, I drew it first against the bishop's jackmen," said

Gaute, angrily. "But true it is, 'twas small honour for our grandfather that we should need to take up arms in such a cause—"

Kristin looked at her son. Then she had perforce to turn her head away. Sorely as his words hurt her, she could not but smile — 'twas as when a child bites with its milk-teeth into its mother's nipple, she thought.

"Mother," said Naakkve, "methinks 'twere best you went now, and took Munan with you. — You must not leave him alone at all, till things are better with him," he said low. "Keep him within the house, so he see not that his brothers are in durance."

Kristin stood up:

"My sons — if you deem not that I am unworthy, I would pray you kiss me ere I go from here."

Naakkve, Björgulf, Ivar, and Skule went one by one and kissed her. The outlaw gazed sorrowfully upon his mother — when she held out her hand to him, he took up a fold of her sleeve and kissed it. All these five, save Gaute, were taller now than she, Kristin saw. She tarried a little, setting Lavrans' bed in order, and then went out with Munan.

There were four loft-houses on Jörundgaard: the great hall; the new storehouse, that had been the summer dwelling in Kristin's childhood, before Lavrans built the great house; the old storehouse; and the salt-store — it had a loft where the women servants slept in summer.

Kristin went up to the new storehouse loft with Munan; they two had slept there since the little child's death. There she was pacing the floor to and fro, when Frida and Gunhild came with the evening porridge. Kristin bade Frida see to it that the watch were served with ale and meat. The woman answered she had done so already — at Naakkve's behest — but the men had said they would take naught at the mistress's hands, since they were at her manor on such an errand. They had gotten meat and drink from elsewhere.

"Nevertheless, see to it that an ale-keg is borne in to them," said Kristin.

Gunhild, the young serving-wench, was all red-eyed with weeping:

"There are none of us, your house-folk, that believe

this of you, Kristin Lavransdatter, trust me — we ever said we knew for sure 'twas all lies."

"You have heard this talk then," said the mistress. "Better had it been had you told me of it — "

"We dared not, for fear of Ulf," said Frida, and Gunhild went on, weeping:

"He forced us to hold our peace with his threats — often I thought I should have told you, and begged you to be more wary — when you stayed behind talking with Ulf far into the night."

"Ulf — he knew of it too, then?" asked Kristin, low.

"Jardtrud has long been throwing it in his teeth — 'twas ever for that he beat her, I trow. And one night this last Yule-tide, about the time you began to grow big — we sat drinking with them over at the steward's house — Solveig and Öivind were there, and some folk from south in the parish — Jardtrud said to him then that 'twas his doing. Ulf struck her with his belt so that the buckle drew blood. But thereafter Jardtrud went about saying that Ulf had not spoken one word in denial — "

"And afterward there was talk of this in the parish?" asked the mistress.

"Ay. But we house-folk of yours have ever stood out against it," said Gunhild, tearfully.

To quiet Munan, Kristin was forced to lay her down with the child and take him in her arms; but she put not off her clothing, and no sleep came to her that night.

Meanwhile in the upper-hall young Lavrans had arisen and donned his clothes. And later, towards evening, when Naakkve had gone down to help with the cattle, the boy went forth and down to the stable. He saddled the red gelding that Gaute owned; 'twas the best horse there, next to the stallion, and that he ventured not to back.

Some of the men on guard at the manor came out and asked the boy whither he would go.

"I wot not that *I* am a prisoner," answered young Lavrans. "But I care not if I let you know it — you cannot hinder me from riding to Sundbu to fetch the knight hither to stand by his kinswoman — "

" 'Twill soon be dark, boy," said Kolbein Jonssön "This child cannot be suffered to ride the Vaage Gorge by night. We must speak with his mother."

"No, do not so," said Lavrans. His mouth trembled a little. "I ride on such an errand that I put my trust in God and Mary Virgin — they will watch over my goings, if mother be guiltless. And else, naught matters — " He broke off, for he was nigh to tears.

The men stood silent for a little. Kolbein gazed at the comely, fair-haired child:

"Ride then — and God be with you, Lavrans Erlendssön," said he, and would have helped the boy into the saddle.

But Lavrans led forth the horse, so that the men must needs give way. At the great stone near the manor gate he climbed up and threw himself on Rauden's back, then galloped westward on the road to Vaagaa.

8

LAVRANS had ridden his horse into a lather of sweat when he came to the spot whence he knew there went a path up through the screes and among the cliffs that everywhere rise sheerly on the north side of Silsaa dale. He must be up on the uplands, he knew, ere it grew dark. He was not at home in these fells between Vaagaa, Sil, and Dovre; but the gelding had been here to grass one summer, and had borne Gaute to Haugen many a time, though 'twas by other paths. Young Lavrans lay forward along the horse's neck and patted him.

"You must find your way to Haugen, Raud, my son. You must bear me up to father to-night; ay, good nag!"

Scarce was he come up on to the brow of the fell and could sit in the saddle again, when darkness came hastily on. He rode on through a shallow marshy glen, betwixt low crags in endless line against a sky that grew ever darker. There were birch brakes on the dale-sides, and the tree-stems shone white; time and again wet leaf clusters brushed against the horse's chest and the boy's face. Stones loosened underfoot and went rolling down into the beck in the dale-bottom — then the horse's hoofs would plash in deep mire. Rauden picked out his way in the dark, up and down the slopes, so that the gurgle of the beck now sounded near and loud, now dwindled away. Once some beast yelped, away in the night, but Lavrans knew not what it was — and the soughing and singing of the wind rose and fell.

The child held his spear along above the horse's neck so that the point stood out twixt the beast's ears. 'Twas the very haunt of bears, this dale. He wondered when it would end. Very softly he began to croon out into the dark: "*Kyrie, eleison, Christeleison, Kyrieleison, Christeleison* — "

Rauden plashed through a shallow place in a mountain stream. The star-strewn skies grew wider about him — the hill-tops stood farther off against the gloom, and the wind sang with another note in the open spaces. The boy let the horse go as it list, and hummed all he could call to mind of the hymn, *Jesus Redemptor omnium* — *Tu lumen et splendor patris* — and ever and anon *Kyrie eleison*. He was riding now almost due south, he could see by the stars; but he dared not do aught but trust to the horse and let it follow its own counsel. Now they were riding over rocky slabs, where the reindeer-moss beneath him showed palely upon the stones. Rauden stood a little, panting, and peered into the night. Lavrans saw that the sky in the east grew lighter; clouds were lifting yonder, silver-edged beneath. The horse went on again, straight now towards the rising moon. There must be an hour yet till midnight, or thereabouts, by the boy's reckoning.

When the moon shot up clear of the far-off hills, and her light shone in on the new snow on peaks and domes, and whitened the mist wreaths drifting by cleft and hilltop, then Lavrans knew where he was come to in the fells. He was upon the marish grounds below the Blaahöer.

Soon after, he found a path that led down into the upland dale. And three hours later Rauden limped into the moon-blanched courtyard at Haugen.

When Erlend opened the door, the boy sank forward swooning on the penthouse floor.

Some while after, Lavrans woke in bed, under filthy, sour-smelling fur coverings. Light came from a pine-root brand stuck in a crack of the wall near by. His father stood over him, damping his face with somewhat; his father was but half clad, and the boy saw by the flickering light that his hair was wholly grey.

"Mother — " said young Lavrans, looking up.

Erlend turned, so that his son could not see his face. "Ay," he said in a little, so low he could scarce be heard. "Is your mother — has she — is your mother — sick?"

"You must come home straightway, father, and save her — they are laying the worst of things to her charge — they have prisoned Ulf and her and my brothers, father!"

Erlend felt the boy's hot face and hands; the fever had mounted again. "What is't you say — ?" But Lavrans sat up and told clearly enough of all that had befallen at home the day before. His father listened in silence, but a little on in the boy's tale he began to finish his dressing; he drew on his boots and buckled spurs on them. Then he fetched some milk and food and brought them to the child.

"But you cannot bide alone in the house here, my son — I must take you to Aslaug at Brekken here hard by, ere I ride downward."

"Father — " Lavrans caught him by the arm; "No — I must go with you home — "

"You are sick, little son," said Erlend; and never before in the boy's memory had he heard such a tender tone in his father's voice.

"Nay, father — indeed, indeed I would go home with you to mother — I would home to my mother — " He wept now like a little child.

"But Rauden is lame, boy — " Erlend took his son on his lap, but he could not stay the child's weeping. "And you so weary — Well, well," he said at length, "Soten can bear us both, belike — "

"You must mind, if you can," he said — when he had led the Castilian out, put Rauden in his place, and cared for him — "to see that someone comes north hither to look to your horse — and my gear — "

"Will you stay at home now, father?" asked Lavrans joyfully.

Erlend gazed out before him.

"I know not — but 'tis in my mind that hither I shall come no more."

"Should you not be better armed, father?" asked the boy again, for Erlend, beside his sword, had taken but a small light axe, and he was making to leave the house. "Will you not take your shield at least?"

Erlend looked upon his shield. The oxhide was so scarred and torn that the red lion on the white field was all but blotted out. He laid it down again and spread the covering over it.

"I am armed well enough to drive a herd of peasants from my manor," he said. He went out, locked the house door, mounted his horse, and helped the boy up behind him.

The sky clouded up more and more; when they were come a little down the hill-side, where the woods grew thick, they rode in darkness. Erlend marked that his son was so weary he could scarce keep himself from falling off; and on that he made Lavrans sit before him and put his arm about the lad. The young fair-haired boyish head against his breast — Lavrans was of all the children the likest to his mother. Erlend kissed the crown of his head as he drew the hood around it.

"Did she sorrow much, your mother, when the little child died in summer?" he asked once, very low.

Young Lavrans answered:

"She wept not after he was dead. But she went up to the graveyard gate each night — Gaute and Naakkve used to follow when she went out, but they dared not speak to her, nor durst they let mother see they watched her — "

A little after, Erlend said:

"She wept not — ? I mind me, the time your mother was young, she wept as easily as the dew drops from the willow twigs by the beck. She was so mild and soft, Kristin, when she was amid those she deemed wished her well. Afterward she had to learn to be harder — and most often, I trow, 'twas my doing."

"Gunhild and Frida say that all the time our youngest brother lived, she wept each hour and each moment, when she thought that none could see it."

"God help me," said Erlend, softly. "I have been an unwise man."

They were riding now in the dale-bottom, with the cold draught from the river at their backs. Erlend wrapped his cloak about the boy as closely as he could. Lavrans, as he dozed and was near dropping off to sleep, marked that his father's body smelt like a poor man's. Dimly he remembered from his early childhood, while they were yet at Husaby, when his father came from the bath-house of a Saturday, he was wont to have some little balls that he held within his hand. They smelt so daintily, and their fine, sweet scent hung about the palms of his hands and in his clothes all the holy-day.

Erlend rode at an even quick pace; here, down on the flats, it was quite dark. Without thinking on it, he knew at each moment where he was — he knew, by the changing tone of the river's roar, where the Laagen ran in rapids and where in headlong falls. Now the path led over flat rocks, where the sparks flew from under the horse's hoofs; now Soten picked his way surely and easily mid twisted fir roots, where the road passed through thick forest; now there came sucking, sobbing sounds, as he rode over spongy green slopes, where some rill from the mountains trickled. He would be home by break of day — and that would fit in pat —

— All the time there ran in his mind that far-away night of frost and pale-blue moonlight when he had driven a sledge down through this dale — Björn Gunnarssön sat behind, holding a dead woman in his arms. But the memory was faint and far off, and far off and unreal was all this that the child had told — this that they said had happed down in the parish, and the crazy tales about Kristin — 'Twas as though he could not get all this into his head. When he got home, there would be time enough, belike, to think what he should do. Naught was real save the strain and the fear — soon, now, he would meet Kristin.

He had waited and watched for her so. And never had he doubted but she would come at last — until he heard what name she had given the child —

In the grey dawn, folk who had been hearing one of the Hamar priests say early Mass came forth from the church. Those who came first saw Erlend Nikulaussön ride by towards his home, and told the others. There was some uneasiness and much talk; folk drew slowly down and stood in clusters where the way to Jörundgaard left the highway.

Erlend rode into the courtyard as the waning moon was sinking down between a cloud rim and the mountain crest, pale in the breaking day.

Without the steward's house stood a knot of folk — Jardtrud's kinsfolk and her friends who had been with her for the night. And at the sound of hoof-falls in the courtyard came out the men who had been on guard in the room below the upper hall.

Erlend drew up his horse. He looked out over the farmers' heads and spoke, loud and scornfully:

"Is a feast towards on my manor — and I know not of it — or wherefore are all you good folks gathered here in the morning so early?"

Dark and angry looks met him from every side. Erlend sat tall and slim on the long-legged, outlandish stallion. Soten had had a cropped mane, but now it was ragged and unclipped; the horse was ill groomed, and its head showed grey hairs, but there was a dangerous glitter in the beast's eyes, and it stamped and fidgeted restlessly, laid back its ears, and tossed its fine, small head so that the foam flakes bespattered its chest and shoulders and the rider on its back. The riding-gear had once been red, and the saddle stamped with gold; now it was worn and broken and patched. And the man was clothed much like a beggar; the hair that surged out from under a coarse black woollen hat was a whitish-grey, a grey stubble grew upon the pale, lined, big-nosed face. But he sat erect, and he smiled haughtily down at the crowd of peasants; young he looked, in despite of all, and like a chieftain — and hate rose hot against this stranger man at halt there, bearing his head high and unabashed — after all the sorrow and shame and misery he had brought down upon them that these peasant folk deemed their own chiefs.

Yet he spoke soberly enough, the farmer who answered Erlend first:

"I see you have found your son, Erlend — so methinks you know we are not gathered here for feasting — and strange it is that you would jest with such a matter."

Erlend looked down at the child, who was still asleep — his voice grew softer:

"The boy is sick, as you may see. The tidings he brought me from the parish here seemed so unbelievable, almost I thought he spoke in fever wanderings —

" — Some at least of what he told is empty talk, I see — " Erlend looked toward the stable door with a puckered brow. Ulf Haldorssön and a couple of men, a brother-in-law of his amongst them, were leading out some horses.

Ulf let go his horse and went up to his master quickly:

"Are you come at last, Erlend? — and there is the boy — praised be Christ and Mary Virgin! His mother knows not he has been gone. We were setting forth to seek for him — the bishop set me free upon my oath, when he heard the child had ridden alone to Vaagaa — how is't with Lavrans?" he asked, fearfully.

"Nay, God be praised that you have found the boy," said Jardtrud, weeping; she was come out into the court-yard.

"Is't you that are there, Jardtrud?" said Erlend. "'Tis the first thing I must see to, I trow, that you get you gone from my manor, you and your tribe. This slanderous hussy will we send packing first of all — and after, they that have lied about my wife shall have their deserts, one and all — "

"So it cannot be, Erlend," said Ulf Haldorssön. "Jard-trud is my wedded wife. I trow that she and I have little mind to hold together, but from my house she goes not ere I have made over to her brothers all her goods, her dowry and her extra-gift and morning-gift — "

"Is it I who am master on this manor?" asked Erlend, furiously.

"That you must ask of Kristin Lavransdatter," said Ulf. "Here she comes."

The mistress was standing up on the new storehouse balcony. Now she came slowly down the steps. Unwittingly she drew her coif forward over her head — it had slipped back — and smoothed the church-going dress that she had worn since the day before. But her face was set hard as stone.

Erlend rode to meet her, foot by foot — bending forward a little he gazed fearfully, despairingly, into his wife's grey, lifeless face.

"Kristin," he begged, "my Kristin — I am come home to you."

She seemed neither to hear nor see. Then Lavrans, who had sat in his father's arms and waked up little by little, slid down to the ground. As he touched the sward with his feet, the boy sank down and lay in a heap.

A quiver passed over the mother's face. She bowed her down and lifted the great boy up in her arms, laid his head close against her neck, as though he had been a little child — but his long legs hung limply down in front of her.

"Kristin, my dearest love," begged Erlend desperately, "oh, Kristin, I know 'tis all too late that I am come to you —"

Again a quiver ran across the woman's face:

"Too late 'tis not," she said in a low, hard voice. She gazed down at her son lying swooning in her arms. "Our last child lies in the earth already — and now 'tis Lavrans. On Gaute is the Church's ban — and our other sons — we two still have much that can be laid in ruin, Erlend!"

She turned away from him, and began to cross the court-yard with the child. Erlend rode after, keeping by her side:

"Kristin — Jesus, what shall I do for you? — Kristin, would you not, then, that I should bide here with you now — ?"

"No longer need I now that you should do aught for me," said the wife, as before. "Me you cannot help, whether you abide here or make your bed in Laagen — "

Erlend's sons were come out upon the balcony of the upper hall; Gaute ran down now, sprang towards his mother, and would have stayed her.

"Mother," he prayed her. Then she looked at him, and he stood still, helpless.

By the foot of the hall stairs stood some peasants.

"Make room men," said the mistress, and would have passed with her burden.

Soten tossed his head and danced restively; Erlend wheeled him half round, and Kolbein Jonssön caught hold of the bridle. Kristin had not rightly seen what was afoot — now she turned somewhat and said over her shoulder:

"Let the horse go, Kolbein — if he would ride forth, even let him ride — "

Kolbein took faster hold and answered:

"Understand you not, Kristin, that 'tis time the master stayed at home on the farm? *You* at least ought to under-stand it," he said to Erlend.

But Erlend struck the other over the hand and drove the stallion on so that the old man reeled. A couple of men sprang forward. Erlend shouted:

"Away with you! Naught have you to do with my affairs and my wife's — and I am no master of a farm; never will I be bound to any stead like a steer in its stall.

If I own not the manor here, at least the manor owns not me — !"

Kristin turned full round upon the man and shrieked:

"Ay, ride! Ride, ride to the devil, whither you have driven me and flung all you have ever owned or laid your hands on — "

What now befell came so swiftly that none rightly saw or could have hindered it. Tore Borghildssön and another farmer caught the woman by the arms:

"Kristin, speak not so to your husband now — "

Erlend rode at them:

"Would you dare lay hands upon my wife — ?" He swung his axe and smote at Tore Borghildssön. The blow fell betwixt his shoulder-blades, and the man dropped. Erlend lifted the axe anew, but at the moment he rose in his stirrups, a man thrust a spear into his side — it pierced his groin. 'Twas Tore Borghildssön's son that did it.

Soten reared and struck out with his forefeet. Erlend pressed his knees into the horse's sides, bending forward somewhat, while he wound the reins about his left hand and again raised the axe. But at once almost he lost one of his stirrups, and down his left thigh blood ran in streams. Some arrows and javelins whizzed across the courtyard — Ulf and Erlend's sons ran into the crowd with uplifted axes and drawn swords — then a man stabbed the stallion under Erlend, and it fell forward on its knees, neighing wildly and shrilly, so that the horses answered from their stalls.

Erlend stood up, astride the beast. He clutched Björgulf's shoulder and stepped clear of the horse. Gaute came up and grasped his father under the other arm.

"Kill him," said he, pointing to the horse; it had fallen over now on its side, and lay with outstretched neck, frothing blood at the mouth and kicking with its mighty hoofs. Ulf Haldorssön did it.

The farmers had drawn aside. Two men bore Tore Borghildssön towards the steward's house, and one of the bishop's men led off his comrade, who was wounded.

Kristin had put down Lavrans, who had come to himself now; they stood, clinging fast to one another. She did not seem to understand what had befallen — the thing indeed had come about too quickly.

The sons would have led their father to the hall-house, but Erlend said:

"I will not thither — I will not die there, where Lavrans died — "

Kristin ran forward and flung her arms about her husband's neck. Her frozen mask broke up before a rush of weeping, as ice is splintered under the dint of a stone: "Erlend, Erlend!"

Erlend bowed his head so that his cheek brushed hers — he stood thus a moment.

"Help me up to the old storehouse, boys," he said. "I would liefest lie there — "

In haste the mother and the sons made ready the bed in the old storehouse loft, and put off Erlend's clothes. Kristin bound up his wounds. The blood welled in gushes from the spear-thrust in his groin, and he had got an arrow-wound low on the side of the left breast; but that bled not much.

Erlend passed his hand over his wife's head:

"Me you cannot heal, I trow, my Kristin — "

She looked up in despair — a deep shudder ran through all her frame. She remembered, Simon, too, had said this — and it seemed to her a forewarning of the worst, that Erlend should now say these same words.

He lay in the bed, propped up high with pillows and cushions, and with the left leg bent up to stop the bleeding from the groin wound. Kristin sat bending over him, and he took her hand:

"Mind you the first night we slept together in this bed, my sweet — ? I knew not that even then you bore a secret sorrow that I had wrought you. And 'twas not the first sorrow, either, you had had to bear for my sake, Kristin — "

She took his hand in both of hers. Its skin was cracked, and 'twas ingrained black about the narrow, scored nails and in the creases of each joint of the long fingers. Kristin lifted it to her breast and to her lips; her tears streamed down upon it.

"So hot as your lips are!" said Erlend in a low voice. "I waited and I waited for you — I thought so long — At last I thought *I* would give way — come down hither to you — but then I heard — Methought, when I heard that he was dead, 'twas too late, belike, for me to come to you — "

Kristin answered, sobbing:

"I looked for you still, Erlend. I thought, for sure, some time you must come to the boy's grave."

"You had scarce greeted me then as your friend, I trow," said Erlend. "And God knows you had no cause either. — So sweet and lovely as you were, my Kristin," he whispered, and closed his eyes.

She sobbed, low and piteously.

"Now is there nothing left," said the man, as before, "save that we try to forgive one another like Christian wedded folk — if you can — "

"Erlend, Erlend — " She bent down over him and kissed the white face. "You must not speak so much, my Erlend — "

"Rather must I make haste and say what I have to say," answered the man. "Where is Naakkve?" he asked uneasily.

They answered that yestereve, when Naakkve heard that his young brother had taken the road for Sundbu, he had ridden after as fast as horse could bear him. He would be clean beside himself, for sure, since he had not found the child. Erlend sighed and moved his hands restlessly on the coverlid.

The six sons came forward to his bed.

"Ay, by you I have not done well, my sons," said their father. He coughed a strange, guarded cough — a bloody froth came oozing over his lips. Kristin wiped it away with her coif. Erlend lay quiet a little:

"You must forgive it me now, if you deem you can. Never forget, good lads, that your mother has striven for you each day of all the years she and I were together — there never was ill blood between us but what I wrought, by thinking too little on your welfare — but *she* loved you more than her own life — "

"We shall not forget," answered Gaute, weeping, "that you, father, seemed to us all our days the most manful of men and the foremost of chieftains. Proud we were to be called your sons, no less when fortune forsook you than in your days of power."

"You speak so, knowing no better," answered Erlend; he laughed a little broken, coughing laugh. "And give not your mother the sorrow to see you follow in my foot-steps — enough affliction has she had to suffer since she got me — "

"Erlend, Erlend," sobbed Kristin.

The sons kissed their father on hand and cheek; weeping they went away and sat them down by the wall. Gaute put his arm about Munan and drew the child to him; the twins sat hand in hand. Erlend laid his hand in Kristin's again. His was cold; and she drew the coverlids over him right to his chin, but sat clasping his hand in hers beneath the coverings.

"Erlend," said she, weeping. "God have mercy on us — we must fetch a priest now to you — "

"Ay," said Erlend, weakly. "Someone must ride up to Dovre, and fetch Sira Guttorm, my parish priest — "

"Erlend — he will not come in time," she said, in dismay.

"Yes," said Erlend, vehemently. "If so be God will be gracious to me — for the last office I will not take from this priest that spread lying tales of you — "

"Erlend — for Jesus' sake — you must not talk so — "

Ulf Haldorssön stepped forward, and leaned over the dying man.

"I, Erlend, will ride to Dovre — "

"Mind you, Ulf," said Erlend — his voice began now to grow weak and unclear — "the time we set forth from Hestnæs, you and I — " He laughed a little. "Ay, I promised then to stand by you all our days as your trusty kinsman — God mend us all, friend Ulf — oftenest 'twas you and not I — of us two — that showed a kinsman's faith and truth — I must — thank you then — kinsman."

Ulf bowed down and kissed the other's bloody lips:

"Thanks to *you*, Erlend Nikulaussön — "

He lit a candle, set it near the dying man's couch, and went his way.

Erlend's eyes had fallen shut again. Kristin sat staring at his white face — she passed her hand over it now and again. She deemed she saw that he began to sink towards death.

"Erlend," she begged, softly. "For Jesus' sake — let us fetch Sira Solmund to you. God is God, whatever priest may bear him to us — "

"No!" The man sat up in bed, so that the coverings slid down from his naked, yellow body. The bandages over his breast and belly were stained anew in bright red patches by the fresh blood that welled forth. "A sinful man I am — God in His mercy grant me what forgiveness He will; but I feel — " He fell back on the pillows — whispered so that he could scarce be heard: "not long enough shall I live to grow — so old — and so meek — that I can suffer — stay quiet in one room with him that lied of you — "

"Erlend, Erlend— think on your soul!"

The man shook his head as it lay on the pillows. His eyelids had drooped close again.

"Erlend!" She clasped her hands; she cried aloud in utmost need. "Erlend — see you not that, so as you had borne you towards me, this *must* needs be said!"

Erlend opened his great eyes. His lips were leaden — but a shadow of his young smile flitted over the sunken face:

"Kiss me, Kristin," he whispered. There was somewhat like a shade of laughter in his voice. "There has been too much else 'twixt you and me, I trow — beside Christendom and wedlock — for us easily — to forgive each other — as Christian man and wife — "

She called and called his name after him; but he lay with shut eyes, his face wan as new-cloven wood under his grey hair. A little blood oozed from the corners of his mouth; she wiped it away, whispering imploring words to him — when she moved she felt her clothing clinging cold and wet from the blood she had got upon her when she led him in and laid him in the bed. Now and again there was a gurgling sound in Erlend's breast, and he seemed to draw breath painfully — but he heard no more, and most like felt nothing, as he sank steadily and surely towards the sleep of death.

The hall door was opened suddenly; Naakkve rushed in, flung himself down before the bed, and grasped his father's hand, calling on his name.

Behind him came a tall and heavy man in a travelling-cloak. He bowed him before Kristin:

"Had I known, my kinswoman, that you stood in need of your kinsmen's help — " He broke off when he saw that the man was dying, crossed himself, and moved away to the farthest corner of the room. In a low voice the knight of Sundbu began to say the prayers for the dying

— but Kristin seemed not even to have marked Sir Sigurd's coming.

Naakkve was upon his knees, bent over the bed:

"Father! Father! Know you not me, father?" He laid his face on the hand that Kristin sat holding; the youth's tears and kisses rained upon both his parents' hands.

Kristin thrust her son's head a little aside — as though half awaked:

"You trouble us," she said impatiently; "get you away from here — "

Naakkve rose upon his knees:

"Go — ? But, mother?"

"Ay — set you down by your brothers yonder — "

Naakkve lifted his young face — wet with tears and drawn with sorrow — but his mother's eyes saw naught. Then he went over to the bench where his six brothers sat already. Kristin marked it not — she did but stare, with wild eyes, at Erlend's face, that now shone snow-white in the light of the taper.

A little after, the door was opened again. With candles and the ringing of a silver bell, deacons and a priest came with Sir Halvard, the bishop, into the hall. Ulf Haldorssön came in last. Erlend's sons and Sir Sigurd rose, and fell to their knees before the Lord's body. But Kristin only lifted her head a little — turned for a moment her tear-blind, unseeing eyes towards the comers. Then she laid her down again, as she had lain, stretched forward over Erlend's corpse.

THE CROSS

PART THREE

THE CROSS

I

ALL fires burn out at last.

There came a time when these words of Simon Darre's rang again in Kristin's heart.

It was the summer of the fourth year after Erlend Nikulaussön's death, and of her flock of sons only Gaute and Lavrans were left with their mother at Jörundgaard.

Two years before, the old smithy had burned down, and Gaute had built a new one north of the manor up by the high-road. The old smithy had lain south of the houses, down towards the river, in a hollow between Jörundsbarrow and some mighty heaps of stones that they said had been cleared from off the fields in ancient days. Well-nigh every year at flood-time the water had come right up to the smithy.

Now naught was left to mark the spot but the heavy, fire-cracked slabs of stone that showed where the door had been, and the masoned fire-place. Fine, soft, pale-green grass sprouted up now from the black, charcoal-covered ground.

Kristin Lavransdatter had a plot of flax this year close to the old smithy-ground; Gaute would have corn now on the fields nearer the manor, where the mistresses of Jörundgaard time out of mind had been wont to sow flax and raise onions. And Kristin often had errands that took her that way besides looking to her flax. On Thursday evenings she bore her gift of ale and meat to the Old Man of the barrow; on bright summer eves the lonely hearth in the meadow would look then like some age-old heathen altar, glimmering there amidst the grass, greyish-white and streaked with soot. On scorching, hot summer days she would go with her basket to the stone heaps at noontide, to pluck raspberries, or gather the willow-herb leaves that are so good for brewing cooling drinks against the fever-sickness.

The last notes of the church bells' midday greeting to

God's mother died away in the light-drenched air between the mountains. The country-side seemed to lay itself to rest under the flooding white sunshine. Since dewy dawn the song of the scythes in the flowery meadows, the ring of whetstones on iron, and voices calling, had sounded from the farms far and near. Now all sounds of toil were hushed; the midday rest sank over all. Kristin sat on the stone heap, listening. Only the rush of the river could be heard now, and the faint rustling of the leaves in the grove; the thin buzz and muted hum of flies and gnats above the meadow; the clink of a lonely cow-bell somewhere far away. A bird winged its way, swift and silent, along the edge of the alder thicket; a bird rose from the meadow tussocks and flew with a shrill twitter to light on a thistle-stalk.

But the drifting blue shadows along the hill-side, the fair-weather clouds that piled up over the edge of the fells and melted in the blue summer sky, the glitter of the Laagen's water between the tree-trunks, the white gleam of the sunlight on all the leaf-trees — these things she was ware of as the voice of the stillness heard by an inner ear, rather than as seen by the eye. With her coif drawn over her brow to ward off the sun, Kristin sat listening to the play of light and of shadows over the Dale.

— All fires burn out at last —

In the alder wood along the marshy river-bank, pools of water glittered in the darkness between the thick-growing sallows. Sedge grew there and tufts of cotton-grass, and thick as a carpet the marsh cinquefoil covered the ground with its grey-green, five-fingered leaves and red-brown blossoms. Kristin had plucked a heavy bunch of them. Often had she wondered whether this herb might not have in it some useful virtue; she had dried it and seethed it and added it to ale and mead. But it seemed to stand in no stead. Yet could Kristin never forbear to go out into the marsh and wet her shoes to gather it.

Now she stripped all the leaves from the stems and wove a wreath of the dark flower-heads. They were like both red wine and brown mead in hue; they were moist, as with honey, at the base of the red bunches of filaments. Sometimes Kristin would weave a wreath for the picture

of Mary Virgin in the upper hall — such was their wont
in southern lands, she had heard from priests who had
been there.

Else had she none now to make wreaths for. Here in
the Dale 'twas not the young men's use to deck themselves
with wreaths when they went to dance on the green. In
the Trondheim country, the men who came home from
serving in the body-guard had brought the custom with
them to some places. The mother thought this thick, dark-
red wreath had gone passing well with Gaute's light-hued
face and flaxen-yellow hair — or with Lavrans' nut-brown
mane.

— 'Twas an endless age since the time when she was
wont to walk with all her little sons and their foster-
mothers in the pasture above Husaby, those long, fair
summer days. Then she and Frida could not make wreaths
fast enough for all the impatient little ones. She remembered when she had Lavrans at her breast still, and Ivar
and Skule had deemed the suckling child too should have
a wreath — but it must be of quite little flowers, said the
four-year-olds —

Now she had only grown-up children.

Young Lavrans was fifteen winters old; he should not
be counted as full-grown yet, maybe. But, as time went
on, the mother had grown ware that this son stood farthest
from her of all her children. He did not hold himself
aloof from her of set purpose, as Björgulf had done; he
was not self-wrapped, nor seemed he close-lipped like the
blind boy — but 'twas like he was yet more silent than
he by nature — only none had marked it when all the
brothers were at home: he was bright and fresh, and
seemed ever glad and well-humoured, and all were fond of
the winsome child, and never gave it a thought that
Lavrans well-nigh always went alone and spoke but little.

He was held to be the fairest of all Kristin of Jörundgaard's fair sons. Their mother always deemed the one
that at the moment she thought on to be perhaps the
fairest, but she felt, she too, how Lavrans Erlendssön
seemed to give out brightness. His light-brown hair and
apple-fresh cheeks seemed, as 'twere, gilded, full-filled with
sunshine; his great dark-grey eyes, too, seemed sown full
of yellow sparks — he was much like what she herself had
been in her youth, with her bright skin hue veiled, as it

were, with sun-browning. And he was big and strong for his age, stout and handy at all work he was put to, biddable with his mother and elder brothers, cheerful, kind, and friendly. But withal there was this strange aloofness about the boy.

On winter evenings, when the household gathered in the weaving-house and passed the time with jest and gossip, while each one had his work to keep him busy, Lavrans would sit as in a dream. Many a summer evening, when the day's work on the manor was done, Kristin would go out and set her down by this boy, where he lay on the green, chewing resin or rolling a sprig of sorrel in the corner of his mouth. She marked his eyes as she talked with him — 'twas as though he fetched his thoughts home from afar off. Then he would smile up into his mother's face, answer her clearly and with understanding; often would they two sit out on the bank for hours in close and easy talk. But no sooner did she rise to go in than 'twould seem as though Lavrans let his thoughts wander far afield again.

And 'twas impossible for her to make out what it was the boy thought so deeply on. He was good enough at sports and with his weapons — yet he was much less keenly set on such things than had been her other sons, and he never went off alone a-hunting, though he was glad when Gaute took him out along with him. So far, at any rate, he did not seem to mark that women looked upon his fair youth with kind eyes. He had no mind at all to book-learning, and to all the talk of his elder brothers' purpose to go into a cloister the youngest seemed to pay little heed. Kristin could not mark that the lad looked for any other lot than to stay here at home all his days, helping Gaute with the farming, even as now he did —

Sometimes Kristin deemed that these strange, absent ways of Lavrans's put her in mind somewhat of his father — but Erlend's soft, drowsy ways had often given place to wild wantonness; and Lavrans lacked altogether his father's hasty, vehement moods. Erlend had never been *so* far away from what went on about him —

Lavrans was the youngest now. Soon now 'twould be a long time that Munan had slept in the graveyard beside his father and his little brother. He died early in spring the year after Erlend was slain.

The widow had gone about after her husband's death as though she neither heard nor saw. More than pain and sorrow, she felt a numbing chill, a dull nervelessness in body and soul, as if she herself were still bleeding to death from his death-wounds.

The whole of her life had lain within his arms, since that thunder-fraught midday hour in the out-barn at Skog, when for the first time she gave herself to Erlend Nikulaussön. Then was she so young and so unweeting, and knew so little what she did, that she strove to hide that she was near weeping because he wrought her pain, while she smiled because she deemed she gave her lover the most precious gift. And whether, after all, it had been a good gift or no — at least she had given him herself, wholly and for ever. Her maidenhood, which God and His mercy had adorned with comeliness and health, when he caused her to be born to a safe and honourable lot, and which her parents had guarded with most loving strictness all the years she was in their care — with both hands she had given all to Erlend, and thereafter she had lived but in his arms.

How often, in the years that followed, had she suffered his caresses, hard and cold with anger, dutifully yielded to her husband's will, while she felt as though she must perish, worn out with weariness. She had thought with a kind of wrathful joy, when she looked on Erlend's fair face and sound and comely body: *that* could no longer blind her to the man's faults. Ay, he was young and fair as ever; he could still overpower her with his caresses, fiery as when she too was young. But *she* was aged, she thought — and with the thought came a kind of passion of victorious pride. Easy to keep their youth for them who will never learn a lesson, who list not to fit themselves to the fate life brings them, nor to strive to master fate by man's will.

But even when she met his kisses with hard, locked lips, and turned with all her being from him to the fight for her sons' future, she knew dimly 'twas with the fire this man had once for all kindled in her blood that she threw herself into the work. The years had chilled her, so she

deemed, for she no longer grew hot when Erlend's eyes
had that old gleam, and his voice that deep note which
had made her sink down, will-less and strengthless with
happiness, when first she knew him. But as then she had
longed to drown the heaviness and heart-ache of separa-
tion in her meetings with Erlend, so afterwards she longed,
dully yet feverishly, after a goal which would be reached
when, one day, a white-haired old woman, she saw her
sons' lot settled and secure. Then 'twas for Erlend's sons
that she suffered the old dread of the uncertainty that lay
before them. She was tormented still by a craving like
hunger and burning thirst — she must see her sons thrive
and flourish.

And as at first she had given herself wholly to Erlend,
so, afterwards, she gave herself wholly to the world that
had sprung up around their wedded life — flung herself
in the breach to answer every call that must be met, threw
herself into every work that must be done to safeguard
Erlend's and his children's welfare. She half understood
herself that she lived ever with Erlend; when she sat at
Husaby pondering with their priest over the papers in
her husband's chest; when she talked with his tenants and
working-folk; busied herself with her serving-wenches in
storehouse and kitchen; sat up in the horse-paddock with
the foster-mothers keeping watch on her children on fair
summer days. It seemed to herself as though 'twas against
Erlend she turned her wrath when aught went wrong in
the house and when the children crossed their mother's
will; 'twas to him her heart-felt joy went forth when they
got the hay in dry in summer, or did well with the corn
in autumn, when her calves throve, and when she heard
her boys shout and laugh in the courtyard. The thought
that she was his glowed hidden in her heart when she laid
aside, full finished, the last of the holy-day garments for
the seven sons, and stood joyful, looking at the pile of
goodly, well-wrought work done by her own hands
through the winter. It was of *him* she was sick and weary
when, of a spring evening, she went home from the
river with her women — and they had washed wool from
the last shearing, boiled water in a cauldron by the strand,
rinsed the wool in the stream — and the mistress herself
felt as though her back were broken across, and was coal-

black with wool-dirt high up her arms, and the smell of sheep and greasy filth had soaked into her clothes till it seemed three baths would not make her body clean again.

And now that he was gone, 'twas as though the widow could see no meaning any more in her life's restless busyness. *He* had been cut down, and so she must die, like a tree whose roots are severed. The young suckers that had shot up around her lap must grow now from their own roots. They were old enough for each of them to take order for his own lot. The thought flitted through Kristin's mind — if she had but understood this before, that time when Erlend said it. Shadow-like pictures of a life with Erlend up on his mountain croft drifted across her mind — they two, grown young again, the little child beside them. But 'twas not that she repented or grieved for what might have been. She herself could not have parted her life from her sons' lives — now death would part them soon, for without Erlend she had not strength to live. All that had befallen, and all that was yet to befall, was their doom — all things fall out as they are doomed to fall.

She grew grey of hair and skin, scarce cared to keep her trim or put her clothes on rightly. Of nights she lay and thought of her life with Erlend; in the day she went about as in a dream, never spoke with any till spoken to, seemed not even to hear when her little sons spoke to her. The watchful and hard-working housewife set her hand to no work. Love had underlain all her strivings with earthly things — Erlend had given her little thanks for it; 'twas not so that he listed to be loved. But she could do no otherwise; it was her nature to love with much toil and care.

At this time she seemed to be slipping down towards the trance of death. Then came a sickness that ran through all the parish, and laid her sons upon a sick-bed — and the mother awoke once more.

The sickness was more perilous for grown folk than for children. On Ivar it took such a hold that none looked that he should live. The young lad had a giant's strength in his fever fits; he roared, and struggled to get up and seize his weapons — his father's death seemed to run in his mind. 'Twas all Naakkve and Björgulf could do to hold him down by main force. Then Björgulf was laid low. Lavrans lay with his face so swollen with the breaking sores it scarce seemed his own — his eyes glittered dully through two small slits — seemed as though they must burn out in the glowing fever.

Their mother watched over these three in the loft. Naakkve and Gaute had had the sickness as small children, and Skule was much less sick than his brothers; Frida looked to him and Munan down below in the hall. None deemed that Munan was in any peril; but he had never been strong, and one evening, when they all believed he was near well, of a sudden he went off into a swoon. There was scarce time for Frida to warn his mother — Kristin ran down, and, a moment after, Munan breathed his last in her arms.

The child's death awoke her to a new, wide-eyed despair. Her wild sorrow for the suckling that died at its mother's breast had been, as it were, tinged red by the memory of all her slain dreams of happiness. The very storm in her heart had borne Kristin up in those days. And the fearful strain that had ended but when she saw her husband slain before her eyes, left behind it such a weariness of soul that Kristin herself deemed for sure she would soon die of grief for Erlend. But this surety had dulled the edge of sorrow. She had lived, feeling dusk and shadows thicken round her, while she waited for the door to be opened for her too —

But over Munan's little corpse the mother stood grey and wide awakened. The fair, sweet little boy had been her youngest child for so many years, the last little one that she still dared fondle and laugh at, when she should have been stern and grave and have corrected her son for his small misdeeds and giddinesses. And he had been so loving and so fond of his mother. It seemed to cut into her very flesh — so bound was she still to life; 'twas not so easy as she had thought for a woman to die, when she has poured her life's blood into so many new young hearts.

In cold, steadfast despair she passed to and fro betwixt the child that lay on the dead-straw and her sick sons. Munan lay in the old storehouse, where first the little babe and then the father had lain — three corpses in her home in less than one year. With a heart withered with dread, but stark and dumb, she waited for the next to die — she waited as for a relentless fate. She had never set store enough by the gift she had got when God granted her so many children. And the worst was that *understood* it she had in a fashion. But she had thought more on the troubles, the pangs, the fears and struggles — though she had learned over again and over again, through what she missed each time a child grew too great for her arms, through the delight each time a fresh one lay upon her bosom — that the joy was unspeakably greater than the labour and the pain. She had murmured because the children's father was so trustless a man, with little forethought for the line that should come after him. She forgot always that he had been no other, that time she broke God's law and trod her own kin beneath her feet to come to him.

Now he had been torn from her side. And now she looked to see her sons die, one by one. Perchance 'twas her lot to be left a childless mother at the last.

— There were so many things that before she had seen indeed, but not thought of much, what time she saw the whole world through the mist of her own love and Erlend's. She had seen, truly, that to Naakkve 'twas an earnest matter that he was the first-born and that 'twas his to be the head and leader of the band of brothers. She had seen, too, that he loved Munan dearly. Yet she was shaken, as by something unlooked for, when she saw his vehement sorrow at the youngest brother's death.

But the other sons grew well again, though but slowly. On Easter Sunday she was able to take to church four sons; but Björgulf lay abed still, and Ivar was too weak to come without the house. Lavrans had grown much in height while he lay on his sick-bed, and in other ways, too, 'twas as though this half-year's happenings had advanced him far beyond his age.

And so it seemed to Kristin that she was an old woman now. A woman must be held young, she deemed, so long as she had little children sleeping in her arms at night, playing about their mother in the day-time, and needing her care day and night. When her little ones have grown too great for this, a mother is an old woman.

Her new brother-in-law, Jammælt Halvardssön, spoke to her of the Erlendssöns' tender age, and of how she herself was but little over forty years; she would soon feel, mayhap, that she must wed again; she needed a husband to help her with the care of the estate and the nurture of the younger sons. He named more than one good man who he deemed might be a fitting match for Kristin — she must visit their home at Ælin in the fall, and he would see to it that she met them, and thereafter they could talk more nearly of this matter.

Kristin smiled wanly. Ay — she *was* no more than forty years of age. Had she heard of another woman that had been widowed with a flock of growing children, she had said as Jammælt said — she must wed again, seek the stay of a new husband; she might even have more children by him. — But she herself would not —

'Twas when the Easter holy-days were just gone by that Jammælt of Ælin came to Jörundgaard, and Kristin met her sister's new husband for the second time. They had gone neither to the betrothal at Dyfrin nor to the bride-ale at Ælin, she and her sons. The two feasts had been held with but short space between, that spring when she was heavy with her last child. As soon as Jammælt had heard of the slaying of Erlend Nikulaussön, he had hasted to Sil; with rede and deed he helped his wife's sister and sister's sons, ordered, as well as he might, all that must be done after the master's death, and took upon him the conduct of the charge against the man-slayers, since none of the Erlendssöns was yet of age. But at that time Kristin knew naught of what went on around her. Even the judgment on Gudmund Toressön, who was found to be Erlend's slayer, seemed to stir her little.

This time she spoke more with her brother-in-law, and he seemed to her a man to be liked. Young he was not — he and Simon Darre were of an age — a quiet and steady man, tall and big, of darker hue than common, comely of face, but somewhat stooped. He and Gaute were good friends at once. Naakkve and Björgulf, since their father's death, had held themselves yet closer together and apart from all the rest. But Ivar and Skule told their mother they liked Jammælt well — "Yet to us it seems, none the less, that Ramborg might well have done so much honour to Simon as to bide a widow something longer — this new husband of hers is no-ways the like of Simon." Kristin marked that these two madcaps of hers still remembered Simon Andressön: by him they had let them be guided, whether with sharp words or with kindly jest, though they would not suffer a word of correction from their own father and mother without their eyes flashing and their hands clenching with rage.

While Jammælt was at Jörundgaard, Munan Baardssön too came hither to visit Kristin. Not much was left now of Sir Dance Munan. He had been wide of girth and portly in the old days, and he had borne his heavy body not without grace, so that he looked taller and more stately than he was. Now the gout had crooked him, and the skin hung loosely on his shrunken frame; he looked most like a little hobgoblin, wholly bald but for a scant fringe of limp white tufts about his nape. Once a strong, blue-black beard had darkened his smooth, plump cheeks and chin, but now grey stubble grew rankly in all the flabby folds of his chin and neck, whither his razor found it hard to make its way. He was grown blear-eyed, drivelled a little — and was much plagued with a weak stomach.

With him he had his son Inge, whom folk called Fluga, after the mother; he was an oldish man already. The father had helped this son forward in the world right well; made a rich match for him, and got Bishop Halvard to lend Inge his countenance — Munan's wife Katrin had been the bishop's cousin, and therefore was Sir Halvard fain to help Inge to wealth, so that he should not trespass on the heritage of Lady Katrin's children. The bishop held the Hedemarken wardenship in fief, and he had made Inge Munanssön his deputy, so that he now owned no little land in Skaun and Ridabu. His mother too had bought her a manor in those parts; she was a most pious woman now, and did much good, and she had vowed to live a life of chastity till her death. "Ay, and she is none so old or so failing either," said Sir Munan, testily, when he saw Kristin smile. He would have been fain, indeed, to have so ordered things that Brynhild should come to him and keep house for him at his manor near Hamar, but that she would not do.

He had so little joy of his old days, Sir Munan complained. His children were so quarrelsome — the children of the same mother were at odds one with another, and fought and wrangled with their half-brothers and sisters. The worst was the youngest daughter; her he had got

with a paramour while he was a wedded man, so that he
could leave her no heritage, and therefore she plundered
her father of all she could lay hands on while yet he
lived. She was a widow, and had sat her down at Skogheim, the manor that was Sir Munan's proper seat; neither
her father nor her brothers and sisters could shift her
therefrom. Munan was sore afraid of her, but when he
tried to scape and live with any of his other children, he
was plagued there, too, with plaints of the others' greed
and dishonest dealings. He was happiest with the youngest
of his true-born daughters, who was a nun at Gimsöy;
he liked well to be in the hostel there for a while; at such
times he strove much to make his soul with penance and
prayers under his daughter's guidance, but he could not
put up with the life there for long at a time. Kristin was
not sure that Brynhild's sons were much kinder towards
their father than the other children, but this Munan
Baardssön would not own; he loved them best of all his
offspring.

But miserable as this kinsman of hers now was, 'twas
while he was with her that Kristin's stony sorrow first
seemed to melt a little. Sir Munan talked of Erlend early
and late — when he was not groaning over his own trials
he was ever speaking of his dead cousin and boasting of
Erlend's deeds — but most of all of his reckless youth:
Erlend's wild pranks when first he was let loose into the
world, away from his home at Husaby — where Lady
Magnhild evermore gloomed at his father and the father
gloomed at his eldest son — and from Hestnæs and his
grave, pious foster-father, Sir Baard. Sir Munan's prate
might have seemed strange comfort for Erlend's sorrowing
widow. But in his own way the knight had loved his
young kinsman, and had ever deemed that Erlend out-
shone all other men in comeliness and manhood — ay,
and in understanding as well, said Munan eagerly, only
that he list not to use it. And though Kristin deemed full
surely that 'twas not for Erlend's good that he had come
out and into the King's guard when but sixteen, with
this cousin of his for guide and teacher, she yet was fain
to smile sorrowfully and tenderly when Munan Baardssön
talked on and on, while the spittle ran out of the corners
of his mouth and the tears oozed from his old, red-rimmed
eyes — of Erlend's flashing joyous spirit in his boyish

years, ere unhappy chance had led him astray after Eline Ormsdatter and scorched him for his lifetime.

Jammælt Halvardssön, sitting in earnest talk with Gaute and Naakkve, looked across at his sister-in-law wonderingly. She had sat her down on the cross wall-bench with this unsavoury old man and Ulf Haldorssön — Ulf seemed to Jammælt to look somewhat moodily, but she smiled as she chatted with them and filled their beakers — he had not seen her smile before, but it became her well, and her little, low laughter was like a quite young maid's.

Jammælt spoke once of how 'twas not possible all these six brothers could stay at home, living on their mother's manor. None could look that any rich man of equal birth would give kinswoman of his to Nikulaus if his five brothers were to dwell with him, and maybe draw their livelihood from the manor when they wed. And they ought to look about for a wife for the young man now — he was twenty winters old already and seemed to be of a lusty habit. Therefore Jammælt was minded to take Ivar and Skule with him when he journeyed south again; doubtless he would find a way to their advancement. When Erlend Nikulaussön had met his end in such hapless wise, it had plainly appeared that the great nobles of the land bethought them now once more that the slain man had been one of their own peers, marked out by birth and blood to take his place among the foremost, of a winning nature, high-minded in many ways, in war a hardy and valiant chieftain — though fortune had not been with him. The men who had taken part in slaying the master on his own manor were dealt with most sternly. And Jammælt could tell of many who had asked him of Erlend's sons. The men of Sudrheim he had met at Yule, and they had let fall that these young lads were their own kin; Sir Jon had bidden him greet them, and say he would welcome Erlend Nikulaussön's sons as a kinsman and gladly keep any of them that would join his household. Jon Haftorssön was now to be wed with the Lady Elin, Erling Vidkunssön's eldest daughter, and the young bride had asked if the youths were like their father: she well remembered that Erlend had visited them in Björgvin when she was a child, and that he seemed to her the comeliest of all men. And her brother, Bjarne

Erlingssön, had said that all he could do for Erlend Nikulaussön's sons, that would he do with all his heart.

Kristin sat gazing at her twin sons while Jammælt talked. They grew more and more like their father: silky fine, soot-black hair clung close and smooth to their heads, but curled a little in their forelocks and down over their slim brown necks. They had narrow faces with high-bridged, outstanding noses, and fine small mouths with a knot of muscles at each corner. But they had shorter and broader chins and darker eyes than Erlend. And it was this most of all, his wife now thought, that had made Erlend so wondrous fair, that when his eyes looked up, light-blue and clear, out of that lean, dark face under the coal-black hair, they took one so unawares.

But there was a gleam of steel-blue in the young lads' eyes now as Skule answered his uncle (he was wont to be spokesman for the two):

"We thank you for this your good and kindly proffer, kinsman. But we have spoken already with Sir Munan and with Inge, and taken counsel of our eldest brother — and the upshot is that we have come to an accord with Inge and his father. These men are our near kindred on our father's side — and we are to bear Inge company when he rides south, and are minded to bide at his manor this summer, and for some further time — "

The boys came down to their mother in the hall that evening when she had gone to rest:

"Ay, we deem most like you understand this, mother," said Ivar.

"We will not claim kindred and beg for help and friendship from the men who sat dumb and looked on while our father suffered wrong," added Skule.

The mother nodded.

She deemed her sons did right. Jammælt was a prudent and right-minded man, she saw, and his proffer had been well meant — but she was well pleased that the lads were true to their father. Yet had she never thought of old that the day would come when her sons would serve Brynhild Fluga's son.

The twins set forth with Inge Fluga as soon as Ivar was strong enough to ride. The manor grew passing still when they were gone. The mother remembered — last year about this time she lay in the weaving-room with a

new-born babe — it seemed to her like a dream. So short
a time was it since she had felt her young, with her mind
stirred and shaken by a young woman's cares and yearnings, by hope and hate and love. — Now was her flock
shrunken to four sons, and in her mind naught stirred,
save disquietude for the grown young men. In this stillness which fell upon Jörundgaard after the going of the
twins, her smouldering fear for Björgulf broke out into
flame.

On the guests' coming, he and Naakkve had moved
down to the old hearth-room house. He rose from his
bed in the daytime, but he had not yet been without the
door. With deepest dread Kristin marked that Björgulf
sat ever in the same spot, never crossed the floor, and
scarce moved at all when she was in beside him. She
knew that his eyes were grown worse in this last sickness. Naakkve was most still and silent — but so he had
been ever since his father's death, and he seemed to hold
aloof from his mother all that he could.

At length one day she took heart of grace and questioned the eldest how it stood now with Björgulf's sight.
For long Naakkve turned off her questions. But at last
she called on her son to tell his mother the truth.

Naakkve said:

"Strong light he can still see dimly — " As he said it
the young man grew deadly pale, turned sharply, and
went from the room.

Late in the day, when the mother had wept her so
weary that she deemed now she might trust herself to
speak calmly with her son, she went over to the old house.

Björgulf lay upon the bed. Soon as she came and sat
her down by him on the bed's edge, she could see by his
face that he knew she had spoken with Naakkve:

"Mother. You must not weep, mother," he prayed,
fearfully.

She would fain have cast herself down over her son,
taken him in her arms, wept over him, and wailed his
hard lot. But she did but steal her hand into his under
the coverlid:

"Greatly does God try your manhood, my son," she
said, hoarsely.

The look on Björgulf's face changed, grew firm and
steadfast. But it was a little while ere he could speak:

"I have known for long, mother, that I was chosen out to suffer this. Already that time we were at Tautra — brother Aslak spoke to me of this, and said that, should it go thus with me, then —

" — As our Lord Jesus was tempted in the wilderness, said he — He said the true wilderness for a Christian man's soul was when sight and sense were barred — then followed he the Lord's footsteps out into the wilderness, even though his body were amidst his brethren and his kinsmen. He read of these things from the books of Saint Bernard. And if a soul but understand that him hath God chosen in especial for such a hard trial of manhood, then he need not fear that he cannot abide it. God knows my soul better than the soul knows itself — "

He went on speaking to his mother after this fashion, comforting her, with wisdom and strength of soul which seemed far beyond his years.

In the evening Naakkve came to Kristin and begged that he might speak with her alone. Thereupon he said that 'twas his intent and Björgulf's to enter a godly brotherhood and take the vows as monks at Tautra.

Kristin stood struck dumb, but Naakkve went on, calmly. They would wait till Gaute was of age and could see to their mother's and their younger brothers' affairs. They would go into the convent with goods in such measure as befitted the sons of Erlend Nikulaussön of Husaby, but they would have an eye also to their brothers' welfare. From their father the Erlendssöns had naught in heritage worth the speaking of, but the three who were born ere Gunnulf Nikulaussön went into the cloister owned some parcels of farms north of the fells — he had given gifts to his nephews when he made division of his wealth, though most of what he gave not to the Church and godly works he made over to his brother. And, said Naakkve, if he and Björgulf claimed not their full share of the heritage, 'twould be a help to Gaute too, who was now to be the head of the house and carry it onward, that they two should die to the world.

Kristin felt as though a blow had stunned her. Never had she dreamed that Naakkve would think of a monk's life. But she spoke naught against it — she was so overcome. And she dared not try to turn her son's mind from so fair and so profitable a purpose.

"Even while we were boys, dwelling together in the cloister there in the north, we two promised each other we would never part our company," said Naakkve.

His mother nodded; she knew it. But she had deemed 'twas so meant, that Björgulf should go on living with Naakkve, even when the eldest brother wed.

It seemed to Kristin well-nigh a miracle that Björgulf, so young as he was, could bear his ill-fortune so manfully. The times she spoke with him of it, throughout the spring, she heard naught from his lips but brave and god-fearing words. 'Twas scarce to be understood, it seemed to her — but it must surely be that he had known for many years already what would come of his dim-sightedness, and so, belike, he had been arming his soul with patience ever since the time he dwelt amongst the monks —

But since this was so, she could not but think how hard and heavy had been the lot of this luckless child of hers — and how little she had understood, standing by with mind filled full of her own concerns. And now Kristin Lavransdatter would steal, each moment she was alone, to kneel down before the likeness of Mary Virgin at home in the loft, and before her altar northward in the church as oft as it was opened. Grieving from the bottom of her heart, and with humble tears, she prayed the Redeemer's gentle mother to be to Björgulf in a mother's stead, and make good to him all that his mother in the flesh had left undone.

One summer night Kristin lay awake. Naakkve and Björgulf had gone back to the upper hall, but Gaute lay below with Lavrans, for the elder brothers had a mind to practise them in watching and praying, Naakkve had said. She was about to drop asleep at last, when she was roused by a noise of one moving stealthily up in the loft balcony. There were footfalls on the stairs — she knew the blind man's tread.

'Twas but that he had some errand, she thought — yet she got up and felt for her clothes. Then she heard the door above thrown open — someone cleared the steps in two or three bounds.

The mother ran to the outer room and threw open the door. The mist lay so thick without that the storehouses

across the courtyard were but dimly seen. Up by the
manor gate Björgulf was fighting furiously to free him
from his brother's hold:

"Will you lose aught," cried the blind man, "if you be
quit of me? — then were you free of all your vows —
and had no need to die to this earthly home — "

What Naakkve answered, Kristin could not hear. She
ran out barefoot into the dripping wet grass. Björgulf
had wrenched him free now — then he dropped, as though
felled by a blow, down over the great stone, and beat
upon it with his clenched fists.

Naakkve saw his mother, and came hastily some few
steps towards her:

"Go in, mother — I can deal best with this alone — you
shall go in, I say," he whispered urgently, then turned
and stood again bowed over his brother.

The mother stood watching a little way off. The sward
was soaking with wet; it dripped from all the roofs, and
drops trickled from every leaf — it had rained all the day,
but now the clouds were sunken low, in a thick, white
fog. When after a while her sons came down the path —
Naakkve had hold of Björgulf beneath the arm and led
him thus — Kristin shrank back within the outer-room
door.

She saw that Björgulf's face was bleeding; belike he had
struck it against the stone. Unwittingly, Kristin thrust her
hand within her mouth and bit into her own flesh.

On the stairs Björgulf tried once again to tear himself
from Naakkve — he stumbled against the wall, crying:

"I curse, I curse the day that I was born — !"

When she had heard Naakkve bar the door of the loft
behind them, their mother stole up after them and stood
in the balcony without. Long she heard Björgulf's voice
from within — he raged, shrieked, and cursed — one or
two of his wild words she could make out. Between-
whiles she heard that Naakkve spoke to him, but his
voice came to her as a muffled murmur only. At length
Björgulf fell into a loud and heart-rending sobbing.

The mother stood, shivering with cold and grief. She
had on her but a cloak flung over her shift; she stood
there so long that her loose-flowing hair was wetted by
the raw night air. At last silence fell within the loft.

When she was come into the room below, she went to

the bed where Gaute and Lavrans slept. They had heard naught. While her tears ran down, she put out her hand in the dark, felt the two warm faces, and listened to the boys' healthy breathing. It seemed to her that now were these two all she had left of her riches.

Shuddering with cold, she crept up into her own bed. One of the dogs that lay over by Gaute's bed pattered across the floor, jumped up beside her, and curled him up upon her feet. He was wont to do this of nights, and she scarce had the heart to drive him away, though he was heavy and weighed upon her legs so that they grew numb; but Erlend had owned the dog, and 'twas his favourite, a coal-black, ragged old bear-hound. To-night Kristin deemed 'twas good that it should lie there and thaw her frozen feet.

—She saw naught of Naakkve the next morning till the morning meal. Then he came in and sat him down in the high-seat; this place had been his since his father died.

He said not a word throughout the meal, and there were black rings about his eyes. His mother followed when he went out again.

"How is't with Björgulf now?" she asked, in a low voice.

Naakkve shunned her look, but he answered, as low, that Björgulf slept now.

"Has — has he been thus before?" she whispered, fearfully.

Naakkve nodded, turned from her, and went up to his brother again.

Naakkve watched over Björgulf late and early, and kept his mother from him all he could. But Kristin knew that the two young men had many a heavy hour together.

'Twas Nikulaus Erlendssön who should have been master at Jörundgaard now, but he could find no time to pay the least heed to the farming. It seemed too that, like his father, he had small mind to the work and small skill in it. So Kristin and Gaute had the whole charge upon their shoulders — for this summer Ulf Haldorssön, too, forsook her.

After the hapless doings that ended with Erlend Nikulaussön's slaying, Ulf's wife had gone home with her brother. Ulf stayed on at Jörundgaard — he said he would show folk he would not be driven out by lies and gossip.

But he hinted, none the less, that here his time was well-nigh spent; he thought maybe he would betake him north of the fells to his own farm in Skaun, when so much time had gone by that none might say he had fled from the slanders.

But then the bishop's deputy began to bring in question whether Ulf Haldorssön had put away his wife unlawfully. On this Ulf made ready to depart, fetched Jardtrud, and was now to set forth for the north ere the autumn storms made the roads across the mountains over toilsome. To Gaute he said that he would join company with his half-sister's husband, that was an armourer in Nidaros; his brother's son would still work his Skjoldvirkstad farm for him, and he would send Jardtrud to dwell there.

On the last night Kristin drank to Ulf from the silver-gilt beaker her father had had in heritage from his father's father, Sir Ketil the Swede. She prayed that he would take the beaker and keep it in memory of her; thereafter she set a gold ring that had been Erlend's upon his finger, and bade him wear it for his kinsman's sake.

Ulf kissed her in thanks: " 'Tis one of the dues of kin," said he, laughing. "You thought not, Kristin, for sure — when first we were acquaint, and I was the serving-man that came to fetch you and bring you to my master — that we should part in this wise?"

Kristin flushed crimson, for he was smiling at her with his old mocking smile — yet she deemed she saw in his eyes that he was sad. So she said:

"None the less, Ulf, I trow you think long till you are back in the Trondheim country, you who were born and bred there in the north. I long for the fjord there many a time, I who lived there but those few years." Ulf laughed as before; and then she said, low: "If, in my youth, I affronted you at any time by haughtiness or — I knew not then that you were near kinsmen, you and Erlend — you must forgive it me now!"

"Nay — and 'twas not Erlend who would not own the kinship. But I was so high and mighty when I was young — since my father had cast me out from among my kindred, beg me a place I would not — " He rose hastily, and went over to where Björgulf sat on the bench: "Understand you, Björgulf, my fosterling — your father — and Gunnulf — they showed me the hearts of kinsmen

from the time when first we met as lads — far otherwise
than my brothers and sisters at Hestnæs. Afterward —
never did I put me forward as Erlend's kinsman unless I
saw that thereby I could the better serve him — and his
wife — and you, my foster-sons. Understand you?" he
said, vehemently, and laid his hand over Björgulf's face,
hiding the sightless eyes.

"I understand." Björgulf's answer came half smothered
through the other's fingers; he nodded behind Ulf's hand.

"We understand, foster-father"; Nikulaus laid his hand
heavily on Ulf's shoulder, and Gaute drew closer to the
group.

A strange feeling came to Kristin — 'twas as though
they would speak of things she had no knowledge of.
Then she too went forward to the men, saying:

"Trust me, Ulf, kinsman, all of us understand — other
friend so trusty as you not Erlend nor any of us ever
had. God bless you!"

The next day Ulf Haldorssön set forth for the north.

As the winter went on, Björgulf grew more at peace,
so far as Kristin could see. He came again to the household meals and went to Mass with the folk, and he took
in willing and friendly wise at Kristin's hand the help and
service she was so fain to render to him.

And as the time went by, and Kristin never heard her
sons say aught more of the cloister, she felt herself how
unspeakably loath she was to give up her eldest son to
the convent life.

She could not but see that for Björgulf the cloister
would for sure be the best. But she knew not how she
could endure to lose Naakkve in this wise. It must be,
after all, that the first-born was in a way knit to the
mother's heart yet more closely than were the other sons.

Nor could she see that Naakkve was fitted to be a
monk. True enough, he had a passing good head for the
arts of learning and a love for godly exercises; yet, all
the same, he seemed not to his mother to be truly devout
of mind. He showed no zeal in attendance at his parish
church, missing the services often on slender grounds, and
she knew that neither he nor Björgulf made to their
parish priest aught but the common confession of sins. The
new priest, Sira Dag Rolfssön, was a son of Rolf of

Blakarsarv, who had been wed with Ragnfrid Ivarsdatter's cousin, and he came much to his kinswoman's manor; he was a young man of about thirty years, learned and a good clerk; but the two eldest sons met him with coldness. Howbeit with Gaute he was good friends straightway.

Gaute was the only one of the Erlendssöns who had made friends amongst the folk of Sil. But yet none of the others had kept himself so much a stranger in the parish as had Nikulaus. He never mixed with the other youths — if so be he went where the youth were met for dance or trysting, he would stand most often aside at the border of the green, and look on — with the mien of one who deemed himself too good to take part. But should the whim take him, he would join in the game unbidden — from vainglory folk said, to show off his powers: he was lusty, strong, and nimble, easily egged on to fight — and after he had set down two or three of the most renowned fighters of the parish, folk thought it best to put up with his manners. And if so were that he had a mind to dance with a maid, he paid no heed either to brothers or kinsmen, but danced with the girl and after sat alone with her — and never did it befall that a woman said no when Nikulaus Erlendssön proffered her his company. He was none the better liked for this.

Since his brother was grown quite blind, Naakkve seldom left him, but, if it chanced that he went out of an evening, he bore him no otherwise than he had ever done. He had given up too, for the most part, his long hunting-trips, but none the less this same autumn he had bought of the Warden a most costly white falcon, and he was zealous as ever to practise him in archery and sports. Björgulf had taught himself to play chess in despite of his blindness, and the brothers often spent whole days over the chess-board; they were both most eager players.

At this time Kristin heard that folk were talking of Naakkve and a young maid, Tordis Gunnarsdatter of Skjenne. The next year the girl lay up at the sæter the summer through; and Naakkve more than once was away from home by night. Kristin came to know that he had been with Tordis.

The mother's heart trembled, and turned hither and thither like an aspen-leaf on its stalk. Tordis was of an old and honourable kin — she herself was a good, inno-

cent child; 'twas impossible that Naakkve could have the
heart to wrong her. If the two young folk forgot themselves, then must he make this girl his wife. Sick with
dread and shame of her own thoughts, Kristin yet knew
in her heart that 'twould surely not grieve her overmuch
if so it turned out. But two years agone she would have
heard naught of it — that Tordis Gunnarsdatter should be
mistress of Jörundgaard after her. The maid's father's father
was still living, and dwelt on the manor with four married
sons; she herself had many brothers and sisters; she would
be a poorly dowered bride. And each woman of that
kindred had ever one witless child at the least. The
mountain-people either changed the children or cast a
spell on them — in despite of all they could do to guard
the lying-in women and make them safe, neither baptism
nor exorcism seemed to avail aught. There were two old
men now at Skjenne whom Sira Eirik had adjudged to be
changelings; two deaf-and-dumb children — and Tordis's
eldest brother the wood-elf had bewitched when he was
in his seventeenth year. Otherwise the Skjenne kindred
were a goodly tribe; they had luck with their cattle, and
they throve in all their doings; but there were so many
of them 'twas impossible they should lay up riches.

— God alone might know whether Naakkve could draw
back from his purpose without sin, if he had vowed him
already to Mary Virgin's service. But she knew that a
man must ever prove him for a year as novice in the
cloister ere he took the vows — he could draw back even
then, if he felt he was not called to serve God in this
wise. And she had heard how that a count's lady of
Valland, who was mother to the great doctor in religion
and preaching friar, Sir Thomas Aquinas, had shut her
son in with a fair and wanton woman, to shake his purpose
when he was minded to forsake the world. Kristin deemed
'twas the foulest deed she had heard on — and yet this
woman died at peace with God. So belike it could not be
so fearful a sin in her, if she thought now that she would
welcome Tordis of Skjenne with open arms as her sons's
wife.

In the autumn Jammælt Halvardssön came to Formo,
and from him they learned the truth of the rumours of
great tidings that had spread up through the Dale before
his coming. With consent of the foremost fathers of the

Church, and the knights and esquires of the Council of Norway's realm, Sir Magnus Eiriksson had resolved to part his kingdoms 'twixt the two sons he had got by his queen, the Lady Blanche. At the Diet at Varberg he had bestowed on the younger, Prince Haakon, the name of King in Norway; the chiefs of the realm, both clerks and laymen, had sworn upon the Lord's body to hold and guard the land for him. 'Twas said he was a fair and likely child of three years old, and was to be nurtured here in Norway, with four of the best Norse dames for foster-mothers, and two Church and two lay lords for foster-fathers, when King Magnus and Queen Blanche were in Sweden. Sir Erling Vidkunssön and the bishops of Björgvin and Oslo, 'twas said, had thought out this choice of king, and Bjarne Erlingssön had furthered the matter most with King Magnus; for of all men in Norway's land he loved Bjarne best. And all men deemed 'twould be of great gain to Norway's might and welfare, that now we should have a king again who made his home amongst us and would guard our laws and rights and the land's weal, instead of wasting his time and strength and the realm's wealth on emprises in other lands.

Kristin had heard of the choice of king, even as she had heard of the feuds with the German merchants in Björgvin and of the King's wars in Sweden and Denmark. But the tidings had touched her little — 'twas like the echoes of thunder-claps amidst the mountains when the storm passes over far-off country-sides. Her sons, she knew, had talked among them of these things. But by Jammælt's tale Erlend's sons were vehemently stirred. Björgulf sat with his forehead on his hand, hiding his blind eyes; Gaute listened with lips a little open, his hand clutching his dagger's hilt; Lavrans breathed quick and heavily, and kept ever looking from his aunt's husband over at Naakkve in the high-seat. The eldest son was pale of face and his eyes glowed.

"It has been the lot of many a man," said Naakkve, "that they who stood against him most stiffly in life went forward to victory on the road he showed them — when they had first laid him out as food for worms. When once his mouth is filled with mould, lesser men than he are fain enough to own his words true."

"Ay, maybe so, kinsman," said Jammælt, soothingly, "there is truth in what you say; your father, first of all men, thought of this way out of the slough — to put two brothers on the thrones here and in Sweden. A deep-thinking, wise and great-hearted knight was Erlend Nikulaussön, I wot. But be wary in your speech, Nikulaus; I trow well you would not have such words go abroad from you as might work harm to Skule — "

"Skule asked not my leave for this he has done," said Naakkve sharply.

"Nay, he remembered not, belike, that you are come of age now," answered Jammælt, as before, "and I thought not on it either — so 'twas with my consent and goodwill that he laid his hand on Bjarne's sword and swore — "

"I trow he remembered it — but the cub knew full well I had never given consent. And the Giske men stood in need, no doubt, of this salve for a pricking conscience — "

— Skule Erlendssön had taken service with Bjarne Erlingssön as his sworn follower. He had met the young noble at Yule-tide when a-visiting his mother's sister at Ælin, and Bjarne had made it clear to the boy that it was most through Sir Erling's pleadings and his own that Erlend's life had been pardoned — without their backing 'twas impossible Simon Andressön's errand to King Magnus could have sped. — Ivar was still with Inge Fluga.

Kristin knew that what Bjarne Erlingssön had said was not wholly untrue — it fitted in well enough with Simon's own tale of his journey to Tunsberg. Nevertheless she had all these years thought with great bitterness of Erling Vidkunssön; it seemed to her he must needs have had the power to help her husband to win better terms had he had the will. Bjarne, belike, counted for little at that time, being but a boy. Howsoever it was, she liked not over well that Skule had bound him to this man — and it took her breath strangely that the twins took their own way, and had ventured them out into the wide world thus — they seemed to her still but children —

After this visit of Jammælt's, the unrest in her spirit waxed so great that she could scarce bear to think. If 'twere as the men thought, that 'twould further so much the well-being and safety of the people of the land that this tiny boy in Tunsberg castle should now be called

King of Norway, then this great gain for the folk might
have been won nigh ten years agone had Erlend not —
No! She would not think of *that*, when she thought
of the dead. But she could not help herself, were it but
because she knew that in the sons' eyes their father
stood out glorious and perfect, the foremost of warriors
and chieftains, without spot or blemish. And she herself,
indeed, had thought all these years that Erlend had been
betrayed by his fellows and his rich kinsmen; her husband
had suffered great wrong — but Naakkve overshot the
mark when he said *they* had laid him out to be food for
worms. She, too, 'twas sure, bore her own heavy share of
the blame — but most of all 'twas Erlend's own folly and
his ungoverned self-will that had brought him to his
hapless end.

Nay, but — none the less 'twas bitter to her that Skule
should now be Bjarne Erlingssön's man.

Should she never see the day when she would be set
free from the endless torture of unrest and dread — ?
O Jesus, remembering the care and sorrow Thy blessed
mother suffered for Thy sake, have mercy upon me, a
mother, and comfort me — !

Even for Gaute she had fears. There was the stuff in
the boy for a husbandman of the best, but he was so
headlong in his eagerness to set the fortunes of the house
on their feet again. Naakkve gave him a free hand — and
Gaute had so many irons in the fire. Along with some
other men in the parish he had now taken up the old iron
blast-furnaces in the fells. And he sold away too much;
sold not only of what came in as rent in kind, but of the
stuff from the home farm too. Kristin had all her days
been used to see storehouses and ware-rooms on her
manor full to overflowing, and she was more than a little
wroth when Gaute turned up his nose at rank butter, and
made a mock of the ten-year-old bacon she had hanging.
She had need to feel that on her manor there should never
be lack of food; that no poor folk need be turned away
unholpen from her door, if black dearth should come
again to the countryside. And there should be naught
lacking when days of bride-ales and child-ales and feasting came again to the old manor.

Her high-flown hopes for her sons shrank and dwindled.

She would be content if they would come to rest here in her parish. She could exchange and bring together her estates so that three of them might be settled on their own farms. And Jörundgaard, with the part of Laugarbru that lay this side of the river, would suffice to keep three freeholders. If their lot were not that of great esquires — yet, at the least, poor folk they would not be. And here in the Dale was peace — all this unrest among the chieftains of the land was little heard of and little heeded here. Even if this might be deemed an abatement of the power and worship of the kindred — yet 'twas in God's power to lead those who came after on to greater things if He saw 'twould be for their good. But belike 'twas vain for her to hope she should see them gathered about her in this wise — they would scarce come to rest so easily, these sons of hers who had Erlend Nikulaussön for father.

It was at this time that her soul was wont to find peace and solace if she let her thoughts run on the two little children she had laid to rest up in the graveyard.

Each day in these years she had thought of them — wondered, when she saw children as old as they growing and thriving, what *hers* would have been like now —

When now she went about her daily tasks, deft and diligent as ever, but withdrawn and full of thought, the dead children were ever with her; in her dreams they grew and throve, and their natures were in every wise just as she would have had them: Munan was as faithful to his kinsmen as Naakkve, while in his ways with his mother he was merry and frank as Gaute — but, unlike him, never affrighted her with doubtful plans; he was gentle and thoughtful as Lavrans, but all the strange thoughts that Munan pondered he talked of freely with his mother. In mother-wit he was Björgulf's like, but no mischance darkened his road through life, and thus his wisdom was untouched by bitterness; he was self-assured, strong and bold as the twins, but not so unruly and self-willed —

And all the sweet, joyous memories of her children's lovesomeness when they were little, these she called up again when she thought of little Erlend. He stood upon her lap to be dressed; she held her hands about his fat naked form, and with tiny hands and upturned face and

all his precious body he strained upward towards her face
and her caresses. She taught him to walk — she had laid
a folded cloth across his breast and up below his arm-pits
— in this harness he hung, heavy as a sack, working away
so blunderingly and drolly with his feet, laughing himself
till he twisted him about like a little worm. She bore him
with her on her arm out into the farm-yard to the calves
and lambs; he screamed with joy at the sow with all her
piglets, threw back his head and gaped at the doves up
on the stable loft. He ran beside her in the tall grass by
the stone heaps, cried out for each berry he saw, and ate
them from out her hand so eagerly that her palm was all
wet from his little greedy mouth.

All the joys she had had of her children she called to
mind and lived over again in this dream-life with these
two little ones, and all the sorrows she forgot —

Spring was come for the third time since Erlend was
laid in his grave. Kristin heard no more of Tordis and
Naakkve. But neither did she hear aught of the cloister.
And her hopes grew — she could not help herself: she
was so loath to give up her eldest son to the monkish life.

Just before John's Mass * Ivar Erlendssön came home
to Jörundgaard. The twins had been sixteen-year-old,
growing lads when they set forth from home. Ivar was a
grown man now, near eighteen years old, and his mother
deemed he had grown so fair and manly she could not
look her fill on him.

His mother bore his breakfast up to Ivar the first morning, while he lay abed. Wheaten honey-bread, bannocks,
and ale that she had drawn from the last barrel of the
Yule-tide brew. She sat upon the bed's edge while he ate
and drank, smiled at all he said, stood up and looked at
his clothes, turned and felt each garment, rummaged in
his travelling-bag, weighed his new silver buckle in her
narrow, red-brown hand, drew his dagger from its sheath,
praised it and all his gear. Then she sat her down again
upon the bed, looked on her son, and listened with a smile
in her eyes and about her lips to all the young man's tales.

Then Ivar said:

* 24th June.

" 'Twere best, mother mine, I should tell you what errand has brought me hither — I am come to get me Naakkve's assent to my marriage."

Astounded, Kristin smote her hands together:

"Ivar mine! And you so young — sure you have not been playing any foolish pranks?"

Ivar prayed his mother to hearken. 'Twas a youngish widow, Signe Gamalsdatter of Rognheim in Fauskar. The manor was worth six score silver marks, and the most of it her own; she had it in heritage from her only child. But she had been drawn into a lawsuit with her husband's kin, and Inge Fluga had sought all manner of unlawful gain for himself, if he was to help the widow to her rights. Ivar had grown angry, and had taken the woman's part and gone with her to the bishop himself, for Sir Halvard had shown Ivar fatherly goodwill at all times when he had met with him. Inge Munanssön's doings in his wardenship would ill bear to be looked into sharply — but he had known how to keep friendship with the great people in the parishes, and to frighten the common folk into a mouse-hole — and in throwing dust in the bishop's eyes he had shown great skill; 'twas like too that, for Munan's sake, Sir Halvard was not minded to be over strict. But now things looked none too well for Inge — and so the second-cousins had parted in most unfriendly wise when Ivar took his horse and rode from Inge Fluga's manor. But then it had come to his mind that he might go south and greet the folks at Rognheim ere he left that country-side. That was at Easter-tide, and he had been with Signe since — helped her on her manor in the spring — and now they had agreed together that he should wed her. *She* deemed not that Ivar Erlendssön was too young to be her husband and take her welfare in charge. And he was in favour with the bishop, as he had said — sure enough he was too young and untaught as yet for Sir Halvard to entrust him with any office, but Ivar had good hopes that he would make his way, if he wed at Rognheim.

Kristin sat playing with the bunch of keys in her lap. This, sure enough, was sage and sober talk. And well she deemed that Inge Fluga deserved naught better. But she wondered much what the poor old man, Munan Baardssön, would say to this.

Of the bride she learned that Signe was thirty years old, and of poor and humble stock, but her first husband had prospered, so that now she was in good estate; and she was herself an honourable, kindly, and notable woman.

Nikulaus and Gaute went south with Ivar to see the widow, but Kristin stayed behind to be with Björgulf. When her sons came home, Naakkve brought the tidings to his mother that Ivar was now betrothed to Signe Gamalsdatter. The wedding was to be held at Rognheim in the autumn.

Not long after his home-coming, Naakkve came in to his mother one evening when she sat sewing in the weaving-house. He barred the door within. He said then to his mother that now Gaute was twenty, and Ivar, too, by reason of his marriage, was become his own master, 'twas his and Björgulf's intent to journey north this next autumn and pray to be received as novices into the cloister. Kristin said not much in answer, and what more was said was but of the ordering of the portion that the two eldest sons must now be given from the estate.

But a few days later men came to Jörundgaard to bid them to a feast — Aasmund of Skjenne was to hold his granddaughter Tordis's betrothal-ale with a worthy yeoman's son of Dovre.

Naakkve came in to his mother in the weaving-house that night too, and again he barred the door behind him. He set him down on the edge of the hearth-place, and sat raking with a stick in the embers — Kristin had made a little fire, for the nights were cold that summer.

"Naught but feasting and revelling, mother mine," he said, laughing a little. "Betrothal feast at Rognheim and betrothal feast at Skjenne, and then 'twill be Ivar's wedding — but when Tordis rides to church to her bridal, I shall not be of the company, I trow — I shall have donned the cloister garb by then — "

Kristin answered not for a while. But then she said, without looking up from her seam — 'twas a wedding-coat for Ivar:

"Many had deemed, I trow, that 'twould be a grief to Tordis Gunnarsdatter if you turned monk."

"I had deemed so once myself," said Naakkve.

Kristin let the sewing sink upon her lap. She looked at her son — his face was set and calm. And he was so fair — his dark hair, combed back from his white forehead, clustered so softly behind his ears and over the slender brown pillar of his neck. His features were shapelier than his father's — his face was broader and firmer, the nose not so big and the mouth not so small; his clear blue eyes lay fairly set beneath the straight, black eyebrows — and yet he did not *seem* so comely as Erlend had been. 'Twas his father's animal-like suppleness and grace, the breath of never-fading youth about him, that Naakkve lacked.

The mother took up her work again, but she did not sew. After a little she said, while she looked down and smoothed in an edge of the cloth with her needle:

"Bear in mind, Naakkve, yet have I said no single word against your godly purpose. I dare not be so bold. But you are young — and you, who are much more learned than I, wot well — somewhere in the scriptures 'tis written: Ill beseems it a man to turn and look back over his shoulder when once he has set his hand to the plough."

Not a muscle of her son's face moved.

"I know that for long have you two had this in your thoughts," his mother went on. "Ever since you were children. You understood not then, yourselves, what you would forgo. Now you are come to man's estate — think you not 'twere fit you should prove you a little longer — whether or not you have the call? *You* are born to be the master of this manor and the head of your house — "

"You make bold to counsel me now?" Naakkve drew breath heavily once or twice. He rose — of a sudden he took hold on his bosom, tore apart his coat and shirt, so that the mother looked upon his naked breast, where the birth-mark, the five small blood-red, fiery flecks, shone amidst the black, curling down:

"You thought, maybe, I was too young to understand what you sighed out with tears and moans as you kissed me here when I was a little child — I understood it not then, but the words you spoke I never could forget —

"Mother, mother — have you forgot that father died the most miserable of deaths, unshriven and unhouseled? — And *you* dare to gainsay our purpose?

" — Methinks we brothers know well what we turn us

from — Meseems 'tis none so great a loss if I lose this manor and cut me off from wedlock — and such peace and joy as you and my father had together all the years I can remember — "

Kristin let fall her sewing. All her life with Erlend — the evil and the good — the rich wealth of memories came over her in a flood. *So* little, then, did this child know what he was forgoing. With all his boyish battles, his venturesome deeds, his playing at love and gallantry — naught else was he but an innocent child.

Naakkve saw the tears come into his mother's eyes; he cried aloud:

"*Quid mihi et tibi est, mulier* * — ?" Kristin started in dread, but her son spoke on in a vehement tumult of mind: "God said not these words, I trow, for that He contemned his mother — But He corrected even her, the pure pearl without spot or blemish, when she would have counselled Him how He should use the power He had got from His Father in heaven and not from His mother in the flesh. — Mother, you must not counsel me in this matter — dare not to do it — "

Kristin bent her head upon her breast.

A little after Naakkve said, very low:

"Have you forgot, mother, that you drove me from you — ?" He stopped, as though he could not trust his own voice. But then he went on again: "I would have knelt by you at my father's death-bed — but you bade me begone — Think you not my heart has been wrung in my bosom as often as I thought on it — ?"

Kristin whispered, so low 'twas scarce to be heard:

"Is it therefore you have been so — cold — towards me all these years, since I have been widowed?"

The son was silent.

"I begin to understand — you have never forgiven me this, Naakkve — "

Naakkve looked down, aside.

"Sometimes — I have forgiven you, mother," he said, in a faint voice.

"Often was it not, I trow — Naakkve, Naakkve," she cried in bitter moan, " — think you my love for Björgulf

---

* "Woman, what have I to do with thee?" — John ii. 4.

was less than yours — am I not his mother — am I not
mother to you both? Cruel were you when you ever
barred the door 'twixt him and me — !"

Naakkve's pale face grew yet whiter:

"Ay, mother, I barred the door against you. — Cruel,
say you — ? Jesus comfort you, you know not — " His
voice died away in a whisper, as though the boy's strength
were ebbed away: "Methought you should not — you at
least we must spare — "

He turned sharp about, went to the door, and unbarred
it. But then he stood there unmoving, with his back to
Kristin. At length she called him softly by his name. On
that he came back, and stood before her with bowed
head:

"Mother — I know well this is not — easy — for you — "

She laid her hands upon his shoulders. He hid his face
from her sight, but he bowed down his head and kissed
one of her wrists. Kristin remembered that his father had
done this once — when, she could not recall —

She stroked his sleeve, and on that he lifted his hand
and patted her on the cheek. Afterwards they sat them
down, and sat in silence a little.

"Mother," said Naakkve, in a while, in a steady, even
voice. "Have you still the cross that was my brother
Orm's?"

"Ay," said Kristin: "he told them to pray me never to
part from it."

"I trow that, had Orm known of this, he had given
consent that I should heir it of him. Now shall I, too,
have neither kin nor heritage — "

Kristin drew forth from under her shift the little silver
cross. Naakkve took it from her hand; 'twas warm yet
from his mother's breast. Reverently he kissed the
reliquary in the midst of the cross, clipped the thin
chain about his neck, and thrust the trinket in under his
clothing.

"Have you memory of your brother Orm?" asked his
mother.

"I know not. At times it seems — but mayhap 'tis but
that you spoke so much of him when I was little — "

Naakkve sat on there a little while before his mother.
Then he stood up:

"Good-night, mother!"

"God bless you, Naakkve; good-night!"

He went. Kristin folded up Ivar's bridal coat, laid it with her sewing-gear, and quenched the fire.

"God bless you, God bless you, Naakkve mine — " Then she blew out the candle and left the old house.

It chanced, a little while after, that Kristin met Tordis at a manor in the outskirts of the parish. There was sickness amongst the manor-folk and they had not got in their hay; so the brothers and sisters of Olav's Gild * went thither to lend them a hand with the work. In the evening Kristin bore the girl company part of her way home. She walked slowly, as one well on in years, chatting with the girl; and before long she had led the talk in such wise that Tordis of her own accord had told Naakkve's mother all that had been 'twixt him and her.

Ay, she had been wont to meet him in their home paddock, and last summer, when she lay at the sæter, he had been with her more times than one of nights. But he had never offered to be overbold with her. She knew well what folk said of Naakkve in general — to her he had never done wrong, either in word or in deed. But he had lain by her side upon the bed-covers once or twice, and they had talked together — Once she had asked him if 'twere his purpose to ask for her in marriage; and he had answered that he could not; he had vowed him to the service of Mary Virgin. He said the same this last spring one time they spoke together. And so she would no longer set her against her grandfather's and her father's wills.

"It must needs have brought down evil upon you both, had he broken his vow and you defied your kinsfolk," said Kristin. She stood leaning upon her rake, looking on the young maid — a gentle, round, and comely face this child had, and the fairest bright hair in a heavy plait. "God will surely grant you happiness withal, my Tordis — he seems a gallant, good lad, your betrothed."

"Ay, I like Haavard well," said the girl — and then burst into bitter weeping.

Kristin comforted her with such words as were fitting

---

* See *The Bridal Wreath (The Garland)*, Note 17, Peasant or Farmers' Guilds.

in the mouth of an old and a staid woman. Her own
heart ached with yearning — she had so gladly called this
good, fresh child her daughter.

After Ivar's wedding she stayed a while at Rognheim.
Signe Gamalsdatter was not fair, and she looked worn and
old, but she was gentle and winning. She seemed to
cherish a heart-felt love for her young husband, and she
welcomed his mother and brothers as though she deemed
they stood so far above her 'twas not possible she should
honour and serve them enough. For Kristin 'twas a quite
new thing that any should put themselves about to guess
her wishes and care for her heedfully. Not even while
she was the rich lady of Husaby, with a host of serving-
folk to do her bidding, had any served her as though
they took thought for the mistress's ease and well-being.
She had never spared herself when all work for the good
of the whole household was on her shoulders, and none
else had even bethought them that she should be spared.
So Signe's ready thoughtfulness for her mother-in-law's
well-being all the time she was at Rognheim did Kristin's
heart good; she soon grew to love Signe so well that,
well-nigh as earnestly as she prayed God to bless Ivar's
wedded life, she prayed also that Signe might never have
cause to repent that she had given herself and all she had
to so young a husband.

And so, just after Michael's Mass,* Naakkve and
Björgulf journeyed northward to the Trondheim country.
All that she had heard of them since was that they were
come to Nidaros in good case, and that they had been
received as novices into the brotherhood at Tautra.

Soon now would Kristin have dwelt a year on Jörundgaard with but two of her sons to bear her company. But
she herself wondered — that 'twas but a year. For that
day in autumn of last year when she had been as far as
Dovre with the two, and came riding by the church and
looked down upon the lower slopes, lying sheeted in cold
mist so that she could not make out the houses on her

---

* 29th September.

own manor — she had thought that so must they feel, who ride towards their home knowing that the houses lie there burned to ashes and cold charred wood —

— Now, when she turned homewards by the old path past the smithy garth — this year 'twas all but overgrown, and tufts of yellow bedstraw, bluebells and vetch swept over it from the edges of the rank hay-field — almost it seemed to her that what she saw was a picture of her own life: the weather-beaten, sooty old hearth-place, that never again would have fire kindled upon it. The ground about it was strewn thick with powdered charcoal, but soft, short, glossy grass was springing up over all the plot where the fire had raged. And from the cracks of the old fireplace bloomed the long, pink tassels of the willow-herb, which sows itself in all places.

2

IT would befall at times, when Kristin was gone to rest already, that she would be awaked by folk coming riding into the courtyard. Someone would thunder at the loft door — she would hear Gaute meet his guests with a loud, gay greeting. Serving-folk must up and out. There was a clatter and tramping in the room above — Kristin could make out Ingrid's voice raised in chiding. Ay, she was a good child, that young serving-wench; she would put up with no forwardness from any man. A roar of laughter from young throats greeted her sharp, ready answers. Frida squealed — poor thing, she would never grow wiser; not many years younger than Kristin herself — and yet the mistress had to keep a watchful eye on her —

Then Kristin would turn in her bed and sleep again.

Gaute would be up next morning at cock-crow as was his wont — he slept no longer of a morning for having sat up drinking ale at night. But his guests would not show themselves till the hour of the morning meal. Then they would stay at the manor the day through — sometimes they had a bargain to strike, and sometimes 'twas but a friendly visit. Gaute ever kept open house.

Kristin took heed that everything of the best was set

before Gaute's friends. She knew not herself that she went
about smiling quietly, as she heard once more the sounds
of youth and joyous life on her father's manor. But she
spoke little with the young men and saw but little of them.
Enough for her to see that Gaute was happy and a man
of many friends.

Gaute Erlendssön was as well liked by the small folk as
amongst the rich landowners. Although the doom passed
on Erlend's slayers had borne right hardly upon their
kinsmen, so that there were farms and kindred whose
folk were still most loath to meet with any of the
Erlendssöns, yet Gaute himself had not a foe.

Sir Sigurd of Sundbu had conceived the greatest fondness for his young kinsman. This cousin of hers, whom
Kristin had never met before fate led him to Erlend
Nikulaussön's death-bed, had shown him at that time the
most faithful kinsman to her. He had stayed at Jörundgaard till nigh to Yule-tide, and done all he could to
help the widow and the fatherless young lads. The
Erlendssöns showed their thankfulness fairly and courte-
ously, but only Gaute made close friends with him, and
he had been much at Sundbu since that time.

When this daughter's son of Ivar Gjesling died, the
manor would pass wholly away out of the Gjesling house
— he was childless, and the Haftorssöns were his nearest
heirs. Sir Sigurd was somewhat of an old man already,
and had had a heavy lot to bear — his young wife had
gone from her wits at her first child-bearing. He had
now dwelt with this mad wife nigh on forty years, but
still almost daily he went to visit her and see how things
were with her — she lived in one of the best houses on
Sundbu, and had certain serving-women who did naught
but tend her. "Know you me to-day, Gyrid?" her husband
was wont to ask. Sometimes she made no answer, but at
other times she would say: "I know you well — you are
Ysaias the soothsayer that dwells at Brotveit, northward,
under the Brotveit hill." She sat ever with a spindle in her
hands — when she was at her best she would spin a fine
and even thread, but when 'twas ill with her, she would
pluck her own spinning to pieces and strew the wool
that her handmaidens had carded over the whole room.
After Gaute had told Kristin of this, she ever welcomed
her cousin with heart-felt friendliness, if it chanced that

he came to the manor. But she would not consent to go
herself to his manor — there she had not been since the
day she stood, a bride, in the Sundbu church.

Gaute Erlendssön was much lower of stature than
Kristin's other sons. Beside his tall mother and long-
limbed brothers he looked somewhat short, but he was
of a good middle height. Altogether Gaute seemed to bulk
more largely in every way, now that the two eldest
brothers, and the twins, who came next him in age, were
gone — amongst them he had been quiet in his bearing.
All through the country-side folk deemed him a most
sightly man — and he was comely of face too. With his
flaxen-yellow hair and his big grey eyes, well set beneath
his brows, his oval, somewhat full face, fresh-hued skin
and well-shaped mouth, he was much like his mother's
father. His head was fairly set upon his shoulders, and
his well-formed, large hands were strong beyond the
common. But he was somewhat too short in the lower
body, and his legs were much bowed. For this reason he
went ever in long garments, save when, for his work's
sake, he must needs wear a short coat — though just at
this time 'twas growing more and more the use for men
who would go fine and courtly clad to have their garments of state cut shorter than before. The country
farmers saw this fashion on the great folk who journeyed
through the Dale. But when Gaute Erlendssön came to
church or to banquet in his long, green, broidered holy-
day habit, with silver belt about his slim waist and great
miniver-lined cape thrown back upon his shoulders, the
parish folk would follow the young master of Jörundgaard
with glad and friendly eyes. In his hand Gaute bore ever
a fair silver-mounted axe that Lavrans Björgulfsön had
owned in heritage from his father-in-law, Ivar Gjesling —
and folk deemed it right good to see Gaute Erlendssön
following in his forefathers' footsteps, and, young as he
was, keeping to good old country ways, both in dress, in
manner of life, and in bearing.

And on horseback Gaute was the comeliest man any
could wish to see. He was a most venturous rider, and
folk in the parish boasted there was never a horse in
Norway's land that their Gaute could not tame and ride.
When he was in Björgvin a year agone, 'twas said, he had
mastered a young stallion that no man before him had

been able to back — under Gaute's handling it grew so
gentle that he rode it bare-backed, with a maiden's
hair-riband for bridle. But when Kristin questioned her son
about this matter, he only laughed and would not speak
of it.

That Gaute was light in his dealings with women
Kristin knew, and she misliked it much, but she thought
'twas most because women met the comely young man all
too kindly, and Gaute was open-hearted and forthcoming.
For the most 'twas doubtless sport and jesting — he took
not such things hardly, nor kept them hidden, as Naakkve
had done. He came himself and told his mother when he
had got a child with a young girl over at Sundbu — that
was now two years gone by. With the mother he had
dealt open-handedly, giving her, for her rank, a fitting
maintenance, so Kristin heard from Sir Sigurd; and the
child Gaute would have home with him when 'twas
weaned from the breast. It seemed he was most fond of
his little daughter; he went to see her always when he
was in Vaagaa — she was the fairest of children, said
Gaute proudly, and he had had her christened Magnhild.
Kristin too deemed that, since so it was that the boy had
done amiss, 'twere best he should bring his child home
and be a good father to her. She herself was nowise loath
to have little Magnhild brought thither. But the child
died when a year old. Gaute grieved much when he heard
of it; and Kristin felt 'twas a sore thing that she had never
had a sight of her son's little daughter.

It had ever been most hard for Kristin to chide Gaute.
He had been so sickly when he was little, and after, too,
he had kept by his mother's side more than the other
children. And then he was like her father. And he had
been so steady and trusty as a child — grave and like a
grown-up man, he had gone about with her and done
her many a well-meant hand's turn, such as he deemed in
his childish simplicity must be of the greatest help to his
mother. No, never had she had the heart to be hard with
Gaute — and if he did wrong out of heedlessness or
because at his age he knew no better, he needed naught
but some gentle words of guidance; so sober and clear-
witted was the boy.

When Gaute was two years old, their house priest at
Husaby, who had more than common skill in little chil-

dren's ails, counselled that he should again be given woman's milk, since other means had availed nothing. The twins were then new born, and Frida, who fostered Skule, had much more milk than the little child could drink. But the wench held the poor little being in dread — Gaute was an ill-favoured child, with his great head and his thin and wizen body, and he could neither talk nor stand upon his legs — so she was afeared he might be a changeling, though the child had been sound and comely until the sickness took hold on it at ten months old. Howbeit Frida would nowise put Gaute to her breast; so there was naught to do but for Kristin herself to take him; and he sucked his mother's milk till he was four winters old.

Afterwards Frida could never take to Gaute; she had ever snapped at him, as much as she dared for fear of his mother. Frida sat next to the mistress now on the women's bench, and bore the keys when Kristin was from home. She said to the master and mistress whatever came into her head. Kristin bore with the woman and smiled at her ways, though she was often irked by her too — yet she sought ever to put matters to rights and smooth them over, when Frida had done aught foolish or had let her tongue wag too rudely. Frida took it greatly amiss that Gaute sat in the high-seat now, and was to be the master of the manor. Naught would bring her to account him for aught more than a witless youth; she boasted of his brothers, though most of Björgulf and Skule, whom she had nursed; and she scoffed at Gaute's short stature and crooked legs. Gaute took it in good part:

"Ay, be sure, Frida, had I had you to suck, I had been as good a giant as any brother of them all. But *I* had to be content with my mother's breast — " He smiled at Kristin.

Often mother and son would stroll out together of an evening. In many places the paths across the fields were so narrow that Kristin must follow after Gaute. He walked in front with his long-handled axe, so masterfully — his mother could not but smile behind his back. She felt a mischievous, youthful fancy to run at him from behind, clasp him to her, laugh and toy with Gaute as she had done when he was a child.

Sometimes they went right down to the washing-place

by the river-side, and sat listening to the rushing sound of the stream as it hurried by, bright and swift in the twilight. Most often they spoke but little. But it might happen that Gaute would ask his mother of old times in this country-side and about her own kin. Kristin told of what she had heard and seen in her childhood. Of his father and the years at Husaby no word ever passed between them.

"Nay, mother, you are sitting there shivering, I trow," said Gaute; " — 'tis cold this evening."

"Oh, ay — and I am stiff with sitting on this stone." Kristin got up too. "I am growing to be an old woman, my Gaute!"

On the way up she stayed herself with a hand on his shoulder.

Lavrans was sleeping like a stone in his bed. Kristin lit the little train-oil lamp — she had a mind to sit a little and solace her with the calm in her own soul. And there was ever enough she could busy her fingers with. From overhead came clattering noises — then she heard Gaute climb into his bed up there. The mother straightened her back a moment — smiling a little at the lamp's small flame. Her lips moved; she made the sign of the cross upon her face and breast in the air before her. Then she took up her seam again.

Björn, the old hound, got up and shook himself, stretched him flat upon his fore-paws with a yawn. Then he padded across the floor to his mistress. She patted him, and straightway he put his fore-paws up on her lap — when she spoke to him pettingly, he set to licking her face and hands, thumping the floor with his tail. Then Björn slunk back again — turned his head and looked at the woman; evil conscience looked out from his beady eyes and the whole of his rough, shaggy body, to the uttermost tip of his tail. Kristin smiled quietly and made as though she saw not — then the dog jumped up on her bed and curled himself by the foot-board.

After a while she blew out the lamp, snuffed the wick, and dropped the snuff down into the oil. From without, through the little window-pane, the twilight of the summer night showed dimly. Kristin said over the last prayers for the day, undressed quietly, and crept into bed. She settled the pillows snugly about her breast and shoulders, and the old hound nestled into her back. Soon after she fell asleep.

Bishop Halvard had made Sira Dag his steward in the parish, and from him Gaute had bought the bishop's tithes for the next three years. He bought hides and food stuffs in the parish too, and in winter, when the sleighing was good, he sent the wares to Raumsdal, and on to Björgvin in the spring by ship. Kristin liked not over well these dealings of her son's — she herself had ever sold at Hamar, for so both her father and Simon Andressön had done. But Gaute had joined with his brother-in-law, Gerlak Paus, in a kind of trading fellowship — and Gerlak was a stirring trader, and was near of kin to many of the richest German merchants in Björgvin.

Erlend's daughter Margret and her husband had come to Jörundgaard the summer after her father's death; they made great offerings to the church for his soul's weal. When Margret was a young maid at home at Husaby there had been scant friendship 'twixt her and her stepmother, and she had cared but little then about her small half-brothers. Now she was thirty years old, and had had no children of her marriage; she showed her comely grown-up brothers now much sisterly love, and 'twas she who brought about the understanding 'twixt her husband and Gaute.

Margret was fair still, but she was grown so big and stout that Kristin deemed she had never seen so huge a woman. But all the more room was there for silver plates upon her belt, and a brooch as big as a small hand-shield adorned most fitly the space betwixt her broad breasts. Her mighty body was ever decked out, like an altar, with the most costly stuffs and fairly gilt metal — Gerlak Tiedekenssön seemed to prize his wife exceeding highly.

The year before, Gaute had visited his sister and brother-in-law in Björgvin at the time of the spring meetings, and in the autumn he crossed the fells with a drove of horses which he sold there. That journey brought him so much gain that Gaute swore he would do the like again next autumn. Kristin thought 'twas well to let him have his way in this. Belike he had somewhat of his father's thirst for travel in his blood — he would settle down when he grew older. When his mother saw that he was impatient to get away, she herself hastened his going — the year before he had had to make his way home over the fells after the winter storms had set in.

So he set forth one fair morning of sunshine, just after Bartholomew's Mass.* 'Tis the time for killing goats — and the whole manor smelt of oiled goats' flesh. The folk had eaten their fill and were happy; all summer long they had not tasted fresh meat save on the highest holy-days, but now for many days they had had the savoury meat and rich, fatty broth both at the morning and the evening meal. Kristin was tired, but in good spirits, after the first great slaughtering and sausage-making of the year, as she stood up on the highway and waved the fall of her coif after Gaute and his train. 'Twas brave to look on — fine horses, blithe young men who rode with shining weapons and jingling harness; the high bridge, when they came on to it, resounded with the hoof-beats. Gaute turned in his saddle and waved back with his hat, and Kristin waved again with a dizzy little cry of gladness and pride.

Soon after winter-night,** rain and sleet set in on the lowlands, storm and snow on the fells. Kristin was somewhat uneasy for Gaute, who had not yet come back. But, truth to tell, she was never so fearful for him as she had been for the others — she had faith in this son's fortune.

A week later Kristin was coming from the byre late in the evening, when she was ware of some horsemen up by the manor gate. The mist billowed like white smoke in front of the lanthorn she bore — she went upward in the rain to meet the troop of dark-clad men in furs: was it not Gaute? — 'twas not like that strangers would come so late —

Then she saw that the first rider was Sir Sigurd of Sundbu — he lighted down from his horse with somewhat of an old man's stiffness.

"Ay — I bring you tidings of Gaute, Kristin," said the knight, when they had greeted one another. "He came to Sundbu yesterday —"

---

* 24th August.
** 14th October.

'Twas so dark where they stood that she could not make out his look. But his voice was so strange. And, as he went towards the door of the hall-house, he bade his henchmen follow Kristin's stable-boy to the men's lodging. She grew fearful as he said no more, but she asked calmly enough when they stood alone together in the room:

"What manner of tidings are they, then, kinsman? Is he sick, since he came not home with you?"

"No, Gaute is as well as e'er I saw him. But his company was weary—"

He blew the froth off the bowl of ale that Kristin handed him, drank and praised the ale.

"A good regale for him that bears good tidings," said the mistress, smiling.

"Ay, let us hear what you will say when you have heard my news to an end," he said, most ruefully. "He came not alone this time, your son—"

Kristin stood waiting.

"He has with him—ay, 'tis the daughter of Helge of Hovland—it seems he has taken this—this maid—taken her from her father by the strong hand—"

Kristin still said naught. But she sat her down on the bench in front of him. Her mouth was pinched, with close-pressed lips.

"Gaute begged me to come hither—he feared, I trow, you would be ill pleased at this. He bade me tell you this—and now have I done it," Sir Sigurd ended, weakly.

"You must tell me all that you know of this matter, Sigurd," Kristin prayed, calmly.

Sir Sigurd did so—in a rambling, unclear fashion, with much beating about the bush. 'Twas clear he was himself much dismayed at Gaute's deed. But thus much Kristin made out from his tale: Gaute must have met the maid last year at Björgvin. Jofrid was her name—oh, no, she was not betrothed to any. But Gaute had seen, belike, 'twould be of no avail for him to speak of the maid to her kinsmen—Helge of Hovland was passing rich, of the house that bore the name Duk and had their estates mostly in Voss. So the devil had tempted the two young folk—Sir Sigurd wriggled in his clothes and scratched his head, as though he were lousy all over.

So in summer—when Kristin believed that Gaute was at Sundbu and was out a-hunting with Sir Sigurd after the two big bears among the sæter hills — he had crossed the mountains to Sogn — she was there with a wedded sister; Helge had three daughters and no son. Sigurd groaned miserably — ay, he had promised Gaute then to say naught of it. 'Tis true he had known the boy was after a maid — but how could he dream that 'twas aught so witless Gaute had in mind —

"Ay, 'tis like he will have to pay dear for this, my son," said Kristin. Her face was set and calm.

Sigurd said the winter was setting in now in earnest — the roads would be scarce passable. And when the Hovland men got time to think over the matter, they would maybe deem — 'twere best Gaute were given Jofrid with her kinsmen's consent — since she was his already.

"But if they deem *not* so — if they crave vengeance for the rape of their woman?"

Sir Sigurd twisted and scratched worse than ever:

" 'Tis a felony,* belike," he said, low. "I know not to a nicety — "

Kristin was silent. So Sir Sigurd went on, in a pleading voice:

"He said, did Gaute, that he was well assured you would give them a loving welcome. He said for sure you were not so old that you had forgotten — ay, he meant, you understand, that you got the husband you had set your heart on."

Kristin nodded.

"She is the fairest child I have seen in all my days, Kristin," said Sigurd warmly; his eyes grew wet. " 'Tis an ill thing that the devil's lure has led Gaute astray into this misdoing — but I trow you will welcome these two poor children in friendly wise?"

Kristin nodded again.

The country lay soaking wet, wan and black under drenching rain-showers, when Gaute rode into the courtyard next day about the time of nones.

Kristin felt a cold sweat damp her brow as she leaned forward under the door lintel to look — there stood Gaute

---

* *Ubotamaal*, an offence that cannot be atoned by payment of fine and compensation.

lifting a woman in a dark, hooded cloak from off her horse.
She was small of stature, reaching barely to the man's
shoulder. Gaute would have taken her hand and led her
forward — but she pushed him aside and went alone to
meet Kristin. Gaute set to greeting the house-carls and
giving orders to the men who had been with him. When
he looked again towards the two before the house door,
Kristin stood holding the stranger girl by both hands.
Gaute sprang towards them with a glad greeting on his
lips. In the outer room Sir Sigurd took him by the shoulder, and patted him right fatherly, puffing and panting
now the strain was at an end.

Kristin had been taken unawares when the girl lifted a
face so white and so lovely under the dripping hood of her
cloak — and she was so young, and small as a very child.
When the stranger said:

"I look not that you should welcome me, Gaute's mother
— but now are all doors but this barred against me. If you
will but suffer me here in your manor, mistress, I shall
not forget that I am come hither without goods and without honour, with naught but goodwill to serve you and
Gaute, my master — "

— Then had Kristin taken both the girl's hands ere she
herself knew of it:

"God forgive my son the wrong he has done you, my
fair child — come in, Jofrid — God help you both, as sure
as I will help you all I can!"

Truly she felt, the moment after, that maybe she had
been somewhat over warm in her greeting to this woman
she did not know. But now had Jofrid laid aside her outer
garments. Her heavy winter dress of sea-blue, homespun
wadmal was dripping wet round the bottom, and on the
shoulders, where the rain had soaked clean through her
cloak. And there was a sad, gentle dignity about this childlike girl — she bore her little dusky head graciously, bent
a little forward, and two thick, coal-black plaits hung
down below her waist. Kristin took Jofrid lovingly by
the hand and led her to the warmest place on the bench by
the fireplace wall: "You must be cold?"

Gaute came forward and took his mother vehemently to
his arms:

"Mother — things must go as they are doomed to go —
saw you ever so fair a maid as my Jofrid? I had to have

her, whatever it might cost me — and you will be good to her, my dearest mother — "

Lovely was Jofrid Helgesdatter — Kristin could not take her eyes off her. She was short in stature, broad across the shoulders and the hips, but round and fairly fashioned. And her skin showed so soft and clear that she was fair in despite of her dead-white hue. Short and broad were the features of her face, but the cheeks and the wide, strong arch of the chin made it, too, comely, and she had a wide, thin-lipped and bright red mouth with small, even teeth like a child's milk-teeth. And when she lifted her heavy eyelids, her clear, grey-green eyes were like shining stars under her long black lashes. — Black hair, light eyes — Kristin had deemed these the fairest of all, ever since first she saw Erlend — most of her own fair sons had them —

Kristin set Jofrid in a place on the women's bench by her own side. She sat dainty and bashful amid the strange house-folk, ate little, and blushed brightly each time that Gaute drank to her during the meal.

His face shone with pride and feverish happiness as he sat there in his high-seat. In honour of her son's home-coming Kristin had spread a cloth upon the board and set forth two wax candles in candlesticks of gilded copper. Gaute and Sir Sigurd drank to each other without cease, and the old knight grew more and more wrought up, laid his arm round Gaute's shoulder, and vowed to plead his cause with his rich kinsmen, ay, with King Magnus him-self — 'twould go hard but he would bring Gaute at one with the maid's affronted kinsfolk. Sigurd Eldjarn him-self had not an enemy — 'twas his father's shrewish temper and his own mishap in marriage that had made him so lonely.

At the last Gaute sprang up with the horn in his hand. How proper a man he is, thought Kristin — and how like to father! 'Twas thus her father had been at the beginning of a drinking bout — aglow with joy of life, erect and hearty —

"Now has it so befallen with me and this woman, Jofrid Helgesdatter, that this day we are drinking our home-coming-ale, and have yet to drink our bride-ale hereafter, if God will grant us such good fortune. You, Sigurd, we thank for kinsmanly faithfulness, and you, mother, that you have welcomed us as I looked you would, out of your true, motherly heart — for we brothers oft-times said amongst us, you seemed to us to be the most great-minded of women and the kindest of mothers. Therefore do I beg that you will honour us yet further, and yourself make our bridal bed so fair and stately that I may pray Jofrid without shame to sleep therein with me, and that you will yourself lead Jofrid to the loft, so that she may come to bed in as seemly wise as may be, seeing she has no mother living nor kinswomen here — ".

Sir Sigurd was well on in drink now; he broke into a laugh:

"— But you slept together in the loft at my house — I knew no better, I deemed you two had lain in *one* bed before too — "

Gaute tossed his golden mane loftily:

"Ay, kinsman — but this is the first night Jofrid will sleep in my arms here in her own manor — if God so will.

" — But you good folk I pray to drink and be merry to-night — now you have seen her who shall be my wife, and mistress of Jörundgaard — she and no other woman, I swear it by God our Lord and my Christian faith. I look to you to honour her, all of you, both men and women, and I look that you, my men, will help me to hold her and guard her as befits men of mettle."

Amid the shouting and uproar that followed Gaute's speech, Kristin slipped from the board and whispered to Ingrid to come with her up to the loft.

Lavrans Björgulfsön's stately upper hall had fared ill in the years the Erlendssöns were housed there. Kristin had had no mind to throw away aught else than the most need-ful and the coarsest of bed-gear and loose furnishings on the reckless lads, and she seldom had the hall cleaned out, for 'twas not worth the pains. Gaute and his friends brought in dirt and litter as fast as she had got it swept out. There was a clinging smell as of men-folk who had come in and flung themselves down upon the beds, wet and sweat-drenched and dirty from the forest or the farm; a smell of the stable and of leathern clothes and wet hounds.

Now, hastily, Kristin and the serving-woman swept the room and set it to rights as best they could. And the mistress brought in fine bed-gear, coverlids and pillows; burned juniper to rid the smell, and set the silvern beaker

with the last drop of wine she had in the house, wheaten
cakes, and a wax taper in a metal candle-stick, on a little
board, and moved it close to the bed. 'Twas as fine here
now as she could make it at such short warning.

On the boarded wall by the closet weapons were hanging — Erlend's heavy, two-handded battle-sword and the
smaller sword he was wont to wear, broad-axes, and firewood axes — and Björgulf's and Naakkve's light hand-
axes hung there still. There, too, were two small axes
which the boys seldom used, for that they deemed them
too light — but with them had her father trimmed and
fashioned all kinds of carpentry so featly and surely that
'twas only for finishing he needed to go over the work
with gouge and knife. Kristin bore the axes into the closet
and laid them in Erlend's chest, where were his bloody
shirt and the axe he had in his hand when he got his death-
wound.

When Gaute, laughing, bade Lavrans to light the bride
up to the loft, the boy was both shamefaced and proud.
Kristin saw that Lavrans understood well enough that his
brother's lawless wedding was a perilous game, but he was
dizzied and wrought up by these strange happenings — and
he gazed with sparkling eyes at Gaute and his fair bride.

On the stairs to the loft the candle blew out. Jofrid said
to Kristin:

"Gaute should not have craved this of you, even though
he was drunken — go no farther with me, mistress. Fear
not that I shall forget I am an erring woman, broken away
from my kinsfolk's word."

"Too good to serve you I am not," said Kristin, "until
my son has made amends for his sin against you, and you
can call me mother-in-law with right. Sit you down, that
I may comb out your hair — passing fair it is, child, your
hair — "

But when the household had gone to rest, and Kristin
lay in her bed, she felt again somewhat of disquiet — unwittingly she had been drawn on to say more to this
Jofrid than she was sure she meant — yet. But the girl
was so young — and she showed so clearly she did not
crave to be judged as better than she was — a child who
had fled away from honour and duty.

So *this* was how it looked — when folk had their bridal-
ride and home-faring come before the wedding. Kristin

sighed — once she too had been willing to venture this
for Erlend — but she knew not whether she had dared, if
his mother had been dwelling at Husaby. No, no, she
would not make things worse for the child up there —

Sir Sigurd was still staggering about the hall — he was
to sleep with Lavrans — talking, somewhat mistily but
with the heartiest goodwill, of the two young folk — he
would spare naught that might help them to a good ending of this perilous venture —

The day after, Jofrid showed Gaute's mother what she
had brought with her to the manor — two leathern sacks
of clothes; in a little casket of walrus ivory she had her
trinkets. As if she had read Kristin's thoughts, Jofrid said
that all these things were her own — she had got them
either as gifts or in heritage, for the most from her
mother; she had taken naught that was her father's.

Kristin sat sorrowful, her cheek upon her hand. That
night, long ages ago, when she herself gathered together
her precious things in a casket that she might steal from
home — most of what *she* had laid together were gifts
from the father and mother she had beshamed in secret and
was planning to grieve and dishonour in full light of day —

— But if these were Jofrid's own possessions, and her
heritage, in trinkets alone, from her mother, she must
come from a most wealthy home. Kristin would reckon
the gear she saw here to be worth more than thirty marks
pure silver — the scarlet dress alone, with white fur and
silver clasps and the silk-lined cape that belonged thereto,
had cost ten to twelve marks at the least. If the maid's
father would come to an accord with Gaute 'twould be
good and well — but by no reckoning could he be accounted an even match for this woman. And should Helge
press the matter home against Gaute as hardly as he had
the right and the power to do, then did things look black
indeed.

"This ring," said Jofrid, "my mother wore always — if
you will take it, mistress, at my hands, then shall I know
you judge me not so hardly as a good and high-born lady
well might."

"Nay, then 'twere likest I should strive to stand to you
in a mother's stead," said Kristin smiling, and slipped the
ring upon her finger. It was a little silver ring set with a
fair white agate, and Kristin thought the child must hold

it dear above its worth since it minded her of her mother. "Methinks 'tis but reason I should give you a gift in return." — She fetched her casket, and brought forth the gold ring set with sapphires. "This ring his father laid upon my bed when I had brought Gaute into the world."

Jofrid took the ring and kissed her hand: "But I had thought to beg another gift in return from you — mother — " She smiled so winningly. "Be not afraid that Gaute has brought home a slothful and handless woman. But I have no fitting workaday dress. Give me an old one of yours, and grudge me not the right to help you; mayhap then you will soon like me better than I can look you should now — "

But now 'twas for Kristin to show the young girl what she had in her chests, and Jofrid praised all Kristin's goodly handiwork so understandingly that the elder woman gave her one thing and another — two linen sheets with knotted silk fringes, a blue-hemmed towel, a twilled coverlid, and last of all the long tapestry with the hawking picture on it: "Loth would I be that these things should leave this manor — and by God's and our Lady's help this house will some day be yours." Then 'twas as well they should go across to the storehouses — they spent many hours together there, and the time passed happily.

Kristin would have given Jofrid her green wadmal dress with the inwoven black spots — but Jofrid deemed it all too good for a working dress. Poor soul, doubtless she was striving to please her husband's mother, thought Kristin, hiding a smile. At last they found an old brown kirtle which Jofrid thought would do, if she cut it short below and put patches under the arms and on the elbows. Naught would serve but she must straightway borrow a pair of scissors and sewing-gear, and set her down to sew. Thereon Kristin, too, took up some work, and thus the two women were sitting when Gaute and Sir Sigurd came in for the evening meal.

3

KRISTIN avowed with all her heart that Jofrid was a woman who had good use of her hands. *If* all went well, then Gaute had been fortunate — he would have a wife who was as hard-working and diligent as she was rich and fair. She herself could scarce have found a more notable woman to step into her shoes at Jörundgaard — not if she had searched all Norway through. So she said one day — and afterwards she scarce knew how it was that the words had fallen from her lips — that the day Jofrid Helgesdatter became Gaute's wedded wife, she would make over her keys to the young woman and move into the old hall with Lavrans.

Afterwards, indeed, she thought it had been well if she had weighed the matter more nicely ere she spoke of it. Often already she had been over-hasty when she spoke to Jofrid —

But one thing was that Jofrid was ailing. Kristin had seen it, well-nigh as soon as the young girl came to the manor. And Kristin remembered that first winter when she dwelt at Husaby — *she* was a wedded woman, her husband and her father were bound together in law, howsoever things might go with their friendship when the wrong done came to light. Yet had she suffered sore remorse and shame, had been bitter against Erlend in her heart — and she had been full nineteen winters old; Jofrid was but a bare seventeen. And here was she now, carried off by force and rightless by law, far from her home among strangers, with Gaute's child under her heart. In her heart Kristin denied not that Jofrid seemed much more strong and stout-hearted than she herself had been.

But then Jofrid had not profaned the cloister's holiness, nor broken troth and handfasting, nor lied and deceived and stolen her parents' honour behind their backs. Even though these two young folks in their rashness had sinned against the law of the land, against duty and all seemliness — yet *so* sore a conscience they needed not to have. Kristin prayed instantly for a good issue to Gaute's deed of madness — and she comforted her with the thought that 'twas impossible God's justice could deal out to Gaute and Jofrid a harder lot than had fallen to her and Erlend — and *they* had been wedded; *their* child of sin was borne to be lawful partaker in all his kindred's heritage.

Since neither Gaute nor Jofrid spoke of the matter, Kristin would not bring it forward, albeit she longed to speak to the unlessoned young girl: Jofrid ought to save

her strength now, lie long in the morning and rest instead of being up and about the first of all on the manor —
for Kristin marked that the girl had set her heart on being
up before her mother-in-law, and doing more than she did.
But Jofrid was not one to whom Kristin could proffer help
or pity. She could but quietly take the heaviest work off
her hands, and, for the rest, treat her, both when alone and
before the house-folk, as though she were by lawful right
the young mistress of the manor.

Frida was furious that she must give up her place next
to the mistress to Gaute's — she used an ugly word of
Jofrid, one day she and Kristin were in the kitchen-house
together. For once Kristin struck her serving-woman:

" — Fair words to come from your mouth, old jade
that you are and mad after men!"

Frida wiped away the blood from her nose and mouth:

"Should you be no better, great men's daughters like you
and this Jofrid, than cottar's children — ? You know that
a bride-bed with silken sheets awaits you surely enough —
you must be mad after men and shameless to boot when
you cannot wait, but must make off to the woods with
young blades and get you road-side brats — fie upon such
doings, say I!"

"Be still now — go out and wash you — you are bleeding down into the dough," said the mistress, quietly
enough.

In the doorway Frida and Jofrid met. Kristin saw by the
young girl's face that she must have heard the words that
had passed.

"The poor wretch chatters like the fool she is. I cannot
drive her away — she has nowhere to turn her to." Jofrid
smiled mockingly, and on that Kristin went on: "She fostered two of my sons."

"Gaute she did not foster," answered Jofrid. "Of that
she is never tired of minding both him and me. Can you
not have her wed?" she asked sharply.

Kristin could not but laugh.

"Think you I have not tried? But it never went further,
when once the man had speech with the bride-to-be — "

Should she seize the chance, Kristin thought, and speak
with Jofrid now — let her understand that from her she
need look for naught but motherly goodwill? But Jofrid
looked so cold and angered —

But yet 'twas plainly to be seen now on Jofrid that she bore another life within her. One day, soon after, she was to clean the feathers for new bolsters. Kristin counselled her to bind somewhat over her hair to keep the down from flying into it. Jofrid tied a linen cloth about her head:

"It becomes me better now, too, than a bare head, I trow," she said, laughing a little.

"That may well be," said Kristin, shortly.

She could not understand that, as things stood with her, Jofrid would jest about it.

Some days after, Kristin came out to the kitchen-house, and saw Jofrid standing there cleaning some black game — already blood had spurted up over her arms. In horror, Kristin pulled her aside:

"Child, you must not touch blood *now* — know you not so much as that even — ?"

"Oh, deem you then that 'tis true, all such-like things that women say?" asked Jofrid, doubtingly.

Then Kristin told of the fire-marks that Naakkve had on his breast. Of set purpose she told the tale so that Jofrid might understand she was yet unwed when she watched the church burning.

"You had not thought such things of me, I trow?" she asked, in a low voice.

"Yes, Gaute told me it all — your father had promised you to Simon Andressön, but you ran from home with Erlend Nikulaussön to his mother's sister, and so Lavrans was forced to give consent — "

"Just so 'twas not — we ran not from home. Simon freed me so soon as he knew I loved Erlend better, and on that father gave consent — unwillingly, but he laid my hand in Erlend's — I was his handfasted maid for a year — Deem you that this was worse?" she asked, for Jofrid was grown burning red and looked at the other aghast.

The girl scraped some blood and fibre from her white arm with the knife.

"Ay," she said, low, but right firmly. "Never had I cast away good name and honour needlessly. — Ay, I shall tell Gaute naught of this," she said quickly. "He believes his father carried you off by force because he could not win you by fair suit — "

Most like she was right, thought Kristin.

* * *

As time wore on and Kristin thought and thought upon the matter, it seemed to her 'twere the most honourable way for Gaute to send a word to Helge at Hovland; put his case into his hands and make suit to be given Jofrid to wife on such terms as Helge thought fit to grant them. But when she spoke of this to Gaute, he looked ill pleased and tried to turn the matter aside. At length he asked hotly whether his mother could send a letter over the mountains in winter-time? No, but Sira Dag could doubtless get a letter sent to Nes, and from there along the coast, said his mother; the priests could ever have letters sent forward, even in winter-time. Gaute said 'twould be too costly.

"Then 'twill not be your wife that will bear you a child this spring," said his mother angrily.

"In no case can the matter be set in order so hastily," said Gaute. Kristin marked that he was bitterly wroth.

An ugly, dark fear took hold on the mother as time went on. She could not but see that Gaute's first glowing joy in Jofrid was quite gone; he went about sullen and moody. From the first this matter of Gaute's bride-rape had looked so ill as might be — but his mother deemed 'twould be far worse if the man should now show him affrighted at what he had done. If the two young folk repented their sin, 'twere good and well — but there was an ugly look about it, as though there were here more of unmanly fear of the man he had wronged than of godfearing penitence. Gaute, this one of her sons that she had ever trusted most — it could not be true, as folk had said, that he was untrusty and light with women, that already he was weary of Jofrid, now that his bride was faded and dull, and the time drew near when he must answer to her kinfolk for his lawless deed.

She made excuse for her son — if *she* could let herself be led astray so easily, she who never had aught before her eyes in her girlhood but the virtuous ways of righteous folk — Her sons had known from childhood that their own mother had done amiss, that their father in his youth had children by another man's wife, and had sinned with a married woman when they were already great lads. Ulf Haldorssön, their foster-father, Frida's loose talk — oh, strange it was not if these young men were weak in such things. — Wed Jofrid Gaute must, if he could win her kinsfolk's consent — and be thankful — but 'twere pity of the maid if she could see now that Gaute took her because he needs must, against his will.

One day in the fast-time, Kristin and Jofrid were at work making ready the food-wallets for the wood-cutters. They beat the dried fish thin and flat, pressed butter into boxes, filled wooden bottles with beer and milk. Kristin saw that it irked Jofrid sorely now to stand thus on her feet the whole time, but Jofrid did but grow angry when Kristin prayed her to sit down and rest. To please her a little it came into Kristin's mind to ask of that story of the stallion that folk said Gaute had broken in with a maiden's hair-ribbon for bridle: " 'Twas yours belike?"

"No," said Jofrid angrily, flushing a deep red. But then her mood changed:

" 'Twas Aasa's — my sister's," she said, laughing. " 'Twas her Gaute courted first; but when I came home, he knew not which of us he liked the best. But 'twas Aasa he had looked to find at Dagrun's house last summer when he came down to Sogn. And he grew wroth when I teased him about her — swore before God and all men that he was not such an one as would be overbold with good men's daughters — there had been naught more 'twixt Aasa and him, said he, but that he could sleep in my arms that night without sin. I took him at his word — " She laughed again. When she saw Kristin's face, she nodded defiantly.

"Ay, 'twas my will to have Gaute for my husband, and trust me, mother, I shall get him. Things fall out most often so that I get my will — "

Kristin woke in pitch darkness. The cold bit her cheeks and nose — when she drew the skins more closely about her, she felt they were rimy with her breath. It must be well on towards morning — but she shivered at the thought of rising to look at the stars. She curled herself up under the furs to keep warm a little longer. Of a sudden she remembered her dream.

She thought she lay in bed down in the little hall at Husaby and had even now borne a child. It lay in her arms, wrapped in a lamb's skin which had slipped up and twisted about the little dark-red body — its tiny hands it held clenched over its face; the knees were drawn up

against its body and the feet crossed — now and again it
moved a little. It crossed not her mind to wonder that the
boy was not swaddled, and that there were no women in
the room with them. The warmth of her own body still
enwrapped the child as it lay there close to her; through
her arms she still felt it to the very roots of her heart each
time the child moved. Weariness and pain lay heavy upon
her yet, like a darkness that begins to pass away, while
she lay looking on her son, and feeling joy and love of him
grow unceasingly, as the dawn-rim brightens along a
mountain ridge —

But at the same time as she lay there in the bed, she was
standing without too by the house wall. Beneath her lay
the country-side shining in the morning sun. 'Twas early
morning of a day between winter and spring — she drank
in the sharp, fresh air — the wind was icy cold, but in it
was a smack of the far-off sea and of melting snow; the
ridges right across the dale lay in the morning sun, with
snowless patches around the farms, and the crusted snow
shone silvery white in all the clearings amid the dark-green
woods. The sky seemed freshly swept, clear yellow and
pale blue, with some few dark, wind-driven cloud-wisps
swimming over it — but 'twas cold; where she stood the
snowdrift was stone-hard still from the night's frost, and
between the houses lay cold shadow, for the sun stood
just above the eastern ridge behind the manor. And right
in front of her, where the shadow ended, the morning
wind moved the wan, last-year's grass; it waved and shone,
though steely-bright ice clumps still bound its roots.

Ah! — ah! The moan burst from her breast against her
will. Lavrans she had with her still — she heard the boy's
even breathing from the other bed. And Gaute — he lay
there in the loft, with his paramour. The mother sighed
again, moved restlessly, and Erlend's old dog on the bed-
spread shifted itself closer against her up-drawn legs.

Now she heard that Jofrid was afoot in the loft, walking
about the floor. Kristin crept out swiftly, thrust her feet
into her shaggy fur shoes, and threw on her wadmal dress
and fur coat. In the dark she groped her way to the fire-
place, squatted down, and blew and raked in the ashes; but
there kindled no least spark — the embers had died out
in the night.

She drew out the flint and steel from her belt-pouch,

but the tinder must have got wet — 'twas frozen. At last she gave up the struggle, took the fire-pan and went up to borrow live embers from Jofrid.

A good fire was burning in the little fireplace of the loft, casting its shine out into the room. In the flickering light Jofrid sat sewing the copper buckle more firmly upon Gaute's reindeer coat. Over in the twilight of the bed she could make out the man's naked breast and shoulders — Gaute slept without a shirt even in the bitterest cold. He was sitting up — he had had his morning bait in bed.

Jofrid rose, heavy and matronly — would not mother have a draught of ale? She had warmed up Gaute's morning drink. And mother must take this can to Lavrans — he was to go with Gaute to the timber-felling to-day. 'Twould be cold for the men —

Kristin pursed up her lips in misliking, as she stood in her own room again making up the fire. Jofrid's housewifely busyness, Gaute lying there openly having his woman wait on him — the paramour's thoughtful care for her unrightful brother-in-law — it all seemed to her so immodest and disgustful —

Lavrans stayed behind out in the woods, but Gaute came home to the evening meal, tired and hungry. So the women sat on for a little after the serving-folk had gone out, to keep the master company while he drank.

Kristin saw that 'twas not well with Jofrid this evening. Of a sudden the girl let her sewing sink upon her lap, and twinges of pain passed over her face.

"Are you in pain, Jofrid?" asked Kristin, low.

"Oh, ay, a little — in the feet and legs," answered the girl. She had worked all day long, as was her wont — would hear naught of sparing herself. Now she had got a stitch, and her legs were swollen up.

All at once little tears started out from beneath her lashes. Kristin had never seen a woman weep so strangely — she sat there without a sound, her teeth set hard; and round, bright tears — to Kristin they looked *hard* as pearls — rolled down her marred, brown-flecked face. She seemed angered that she had been forced to give way — unwillingly she let Kristin help her over to the bed.

Gaute came after them:

"Are you in pain, my Jofrid?" he asked, in a chapfallen fashion. He was red as fire in the face from the cold, and

he looked on miserably while his mother made Jofrid easy
on the bed, drew off her shoes and her hose, and began to
tend the swollen feet and legs. "Are you in pain, my
Jofrid?" he went on asking.

"Ay," said Jofrid, in a low voice, with smothered rage.
"Think you, if I were not, I would bemoan me like this?"

"Are you in pain, my Jofrid — ?" he began again.

"Sure you can see it — stand not there gaping like an
oaf, boy!" Kristin turned on her son, her eyes flashing.
The dull coil in her mind — dread for what might come
of it all, impatience at having to suffer the young folks'
lawless life here at her manor, gnawing doubts of her
son's manhood — burst out in furious wrath: "Are you
such a fool, you deem she can be *well*, perchance? — she
sees you are not man enough to dare cross the fells, because, forsooth, 'tis blowing and snowing — You know
well that soon she must down upon her knees, this poor
little thing, and writhe in the worst of torments — and
her child shall be called bastard because you dare not face
her father — you sit warming the bench in the hall, and
dare not so much as lift a finger to safeguard the wife you
have and the child that is coming to you — *Your* father
was not so fearful of my father that he dared not go to
have speech with him, nor so afraid of cold that he durst
not fare on ski over the fells in winter-time. Fie upon you,
Gaute — and woe is me that I must live to call craven
one of the sons Erlend begot with me!"

Gaute took the block-chair in both hands, dashed it on
the floor, ran to the board, and swept off all that stood
upon it. Then he rushed out of the door, with a parting
kick to the block-chair — they heard him run cursing up
the loft stairs.

"Nay, mother — now have you been over hard with
Gaute — " Jofrid raised her on her elbow. "You cannot
look with reason that he should peril his life on the fells
in winter — to find my father and be told whether he must
wed his dishonoured bride with the shift he carried me
off in for portion, or flee the land, an outlaw — "

The waves of anger still ran high in Kristin's heart. She
answered proudly:

"Nevertheless I scarce believe that *my* son can think so!"

"No," said Jofrid, " — had he not had me to think *for*

him — " When she saw Kristin's face, she went on, in a voice that bubbled with laughter:

"Dear mother — hard enough have I had to fight to hold Gaute back — I will not have him do yet more follies for my sake, and part our children from the wealth I can look to have in heritage from my kinsmen, if Gaute can come to such accord with them as will be best and most honourable for us all — "

"What mean you by this?" asked Kristin.

"I mean that if my kinsfolk come in search of Gaute, Sir Sigurd will meet them in such wise that they will see Gaute lacks not kinsmen to back him. He will have to make full amends, but thereafter 'twill be for my father to handfast me to Gaute so that I shall again have right to share with my sisters what he leaves behind — "

"So you yourself must share the blame," asked Kristin, "when your child comes into the world and you still unwed?"

"Since I could flee from home with Gaute, why — None will believe, now, I trow, that he has laid a drawn sword between us in bed of nights — "

"Has he never at all made suit for you to your kinsfolk?" asked Kristin.

"No; we knew 'twould be in vain, even had Gaute been a much richer man than he is." Jofrid broke into laughter again. "See you, mother, father deems himself the shrewdest of all men at a horse-bargain. But 'twould take a man far more wide-awake than my father to get the better of Gaute Erlendssön in an exchange of horses — "

Kristin could not forbear smiling — unglad though she was at heart.

"I know not the law so nicely in such matters," she said gravely, "but I misdoubt me much, Jofrid, 'twill not be easy for Gaute to come to such an accord as you will call good. Should Gaute be doomed outlaw — and your father take you home with him, and let you feel his wrath — or should he require that you go into a cloister and atone your sins — "

"Send me to a cloister he cannot, without giving such rich gifts with me that 'twere a cheaper bargain and more honourable to make accord with Gaute and take amends from him; see you, so could he wed me off and not need to lay out aught in goods and gear. And methinks, for all the love he bears Olav, my sister's husband, he would be loath that I should not share with my sisters in the heritage. Besides, then my kinsfolk would have this child of mine on their hands too. And I trow that father will bethink him twice ere he tries taking me home to Hovland with a bastard child — to make me feel his wrath — he knows *me* —

" — I know not so much of the law either; but I know father and I know Gaute. And now so much time has gone by, that this matter can scarce go forward before I am lightened and grown sound again; and then, mother, you shall not see me weep! Oh, no, sure I am Gaute will win for us such an accord as —

"Nay, mother — Gaute, who is come of nobles and kings — and you who are kin to the best houses in the land — if so be you have had to brook seeing your sons sunk down from the place they were born to stand in, yet shall you see your offspring rise in the world again in Gaute's children and mine — "

Kristin sat silent. 'Twas not unlike, indeed, that things might go as Jofrid wished — she saw that she had had no need to grieve so much for the girl. She had grown thin of face now — her cheeks' soft rounding was quite worn away, and all the more clearly could it be seen how large and strong was her lower jaw.

Jofrid yawned, dragged her up into a sitting posture, and looked round for her foot-gear. Kristin helped her to draw them on. Jofrid thanked her:

"And vex not Gaute any more now, mother. He takes it not lightly himself that we cannot be wed before — but I will not have my child made poor before even 'tis born — "

Fourteen days after, Jofrid bore a son, a great and comely boy. Gaute sent word to Sundbu that same day; and Sir Sigurd came at once to Jörundgaard and held Erlend Gautessön at his christening. But, glad as was Kristin Lavransdatter of her son's son, it vexed her none the less that Erlend's name should be renewed for the first time in a base-born child.

"Your father dared more to win his son his rights," said she to Gaute one evening, as he sat down in the weaving-house watching her make the boy ready for the night. Jofrid was sleeping sweetly already in the bed by the wall. "He loved not old Sir Nikulaus over much, yet would he never have honoured his father so little as give his name to a son not born in wedlock."

"No — Orm — 'twas after his mother's father, was't not?" asked Gaute. " — Aye, ay, mother, maybe this was no seemly speech of a son. But I trow you can understand that all we brothers marked well, what time our father lived, you deemed not then he could be a pattern for us in all things — but now you speak of him late and early as he had been a holy saint — almost. You wot well that we know he was not that. Proud should we all be if any day we should grow to our father's stature — ay, or to his shoulder — we mind ever that he was a chieftain, and a man outdoing all men in all such gifts as adorn a man — but you cannot make us believe he was the meekest and most virtuous of swains in a lady's bower, or the doughtiest of husbandmen —

" — Yet need none wish aught better for you, my Erlend, than that you may grow to be his like!" He took up the child, who was now swathed up for the night, and thrust his chin down on to the little red face in the bright woollen swaddling-cloth: "This well-gifted and hopeful youth, Erlend Gautessön, of Jörundgaard — you must tell your grandmother *you* are not afraid your father will fail you —" He made the sign of the cross over the child and laid it back in Kristin's lap, went over to the bed, and gazed on the slumbering young mother:

" 'Tis as well with my Jofrid as can be, say you? She looks pale — but I trow you understand such things best — God's peace and sound sleep to all in this house!"

A month after the boy's birth Gaute held a great christening-ale, and to it his kinsmen gathered from far and near. Kristin guessed that Gaute had trysted them hither to take counsel with them in this pass — 'twas spring now, and he might soon look to hear news of Jofrid's kin.

Kristin had the joy of seeing Ivar and Skule at home together. And hither came too her cousins: Sigurd Kyrning, who was wed with her father's brother's daughter from Skog, Ivar Gjesling of Ringheim and Haavard Trondssön. She had not seen the Trondssöns since Erlend had drawn the men of Sundbu along with him into mischance. They were of middle age now: they had ever been careless and light-headed, but high-minded and gallant; and they were little changed — they met both the Erlendssöns and their cousin, Sir Sigurd, who stood in their shoes at Sundbu, with the free and open bearing befitting kinsmen. Ale and mead now ran in rivers in honour of little Erlend; Gaute and Jofrid gave their guests as free and unabashed a welcome as had they been lawfully wed and the King himself had made their marriage — all was mirth, and none seemed to call to mind that the two young folks' honour and welfare were still at hazard. But Kristin learned that Jofrid had not forgotten it:

"The more freely and boldly they meet my father, the easier will he yield him," said she. "And Olav Piper could never hide that he loves full well to sit on the same bench with men of the old houses."

The only one that seemed not wholly happy in this gathering of kinsmen was Sir Jammælt Halvardssön. King Magnus had dubbed him knight this last Yule; Ramborg Lavransdatter now bore the name of lady.

This time Sir Jammælt had his eldest step-son, Andres Simonssön, with him. Kristin had begged this of him, when last Jammælt was north, for she had heard a waif word that the boy was strange. A great dread had fallen on her — could it be that he had taken hurt in soul and body from those dealings of hers with him when he was a child? But his step-father said no, the boy was sound and strong, good as gold — and maybe his wits were better than most folks' — 'twas but that he saw visions: he would seem rapt at times, and afterwards would do often the strangest things — even as 'twas last year. He had taken his silver spoon one day — 'twas the very one he had from Kristin as a birth-gift — and a shirt-pin that his father left him — and then he went forth from the manor and down to a bridge that is over the river on the highway near Ælin. There he sat waiting for many hours — at last there came over the bridge three beggars, an old man and a young woman, with a suckling-child. Andres goes up to them, gives them the trinkets, and begs leave to bear the child for the woman. At home they were beside themselves with fear, when Andres came not to the midday meal nor yet to supper — They went out and searched the country-side, and at length Jammælt got word that Andres had been seen far north in the neighboring parish in company with some folk called Krepp and Kraaka; he was carrying their little one. When next day Jammælt got hold of the boy at last, he said, after much asking, that he had heard a voice the last Sunday during Mass, while he stood looking at the picture painted on the panel before the altar. 'Twas God's mother and Saint Joseph journeying with the child to the land of Egypt, and he had wished he had lived in those days, for then would he have prayed that he might have leave to go with them and bear the child for Mary Virgin. Then had he heard a voice, the gentlest and sweetest in all the world, and it promised to show him a sign if he would go to the Bjerkheim bridge on a certain day —

Else was Andres loath to speak of his visions — for their parish priest said they were likely part feigning and part brain-sick wanderings; and he frightened his mother well-nigh from her wits with his strange ways. But he talked much with an old serving-maid, a rarely pious woman, and with a preaching brother who was wont to wander through the parish at Lent and Advent. 'Twas like enough the boy would choose the spiritual life — and so, maybe, 'twould be Simon Simonssön who in time to come would settle down as master at Formo. He was a healthy and a lively child, most like to his father, and Ramborg's darling.

Ramborg and Jammælt had as yet had no children to-gether. Kristin had heard, from folk who had seen her at Raumarike, that Ramborg was grown passing fat and sluggish. She went a-visiting among the richest and mighti-est folk in the south-land, but north to her home country she would never come, and Kristin had not seen her only sister since that day of their parting at Formo. But Kristin deemed she could see that Ramborg still nursed the old grudge against her. She lived happily with Jammælt, and he cared for his step-children's welfare with love and fore-thought. He had taken order that the eldest son of the man who would be his chief heir if he died childless should wed Ulvhild Simonsdatter; thus, at the worst, Simon Darre's daughter would have the good of his estates after him. Arngjerd had been wedded with Grunde of Eiken the year after her father's death; Gyrd Darre and Jam-mælt had made her as rich a portion as they knew Simon meant to give this child of his, and she was happy,

Jammælt said — Grunde let himself be guided in all things by his wife, and they had three fair children already.

Kristin was strangely moved when she saw Simon and Ramborg's eldest son once more. *He* was Lavrans Björgulfsön's living likeness — much more even than Gaute. And in these last years Kristin had had to give up her belief that Gaute was so like her father in his frame of mind.

Andres Darre was now in his twelfth year, tall and slender, fair-haired and comely, and somewhat quiet in bearing; though he seemed healthy and happy of mood, had good strength of body, and a good stomach to his food, save that he would eat no flesh. Somewhat there was that marked him out from other boys, but Kristin could not say *what* it was, though she watched him narrowly. Andres was soon good friends with his mother's sister, but he never let fall aught of his visions, and fell not into any raptures while he was in Sil.

The four Erlendssöns seemed to take pleasure in being together in their mother's manor, but Kristin got but little speech with her sons. When they talked among themselves, she felt that their lives and their concerns were slipping now beyond her range of sight — the two who had come from without had parted them from their home already, and the two who dwelt on the manor would soon, for sure, be taking its governance out of her hands. The meeting fell in the middle of the spring dearth, and she saw now that Gaute must have made ready for it by saving fodder in winter more than was common, and he had borrowed fodder from Sir Sigurd too — but all this he had ordered without taking counsel with her. And all the parleyings about Gaute's affair went on, as 'twere, over her head, even though she sat in the room with the men.

So 'twas little marvel to her when one day Ivar came and said that Lavrans would keep him company when he went back to Rognheim.

Howbeit one day Ivar Erlendssön said to his mother that he deemed 'twere well she should come to him at Rognheim when once Gaute was wedded:

"Signe were a more towardly daughter-in-law to bide in a house with, I trow — and easy for you sure it cannot be to give up the reins here, where you have been wont to rule." For the rest, 'twas plain he liked Jofrid, he and all the other men. Only Sir Jammælt seemed to look upon her somewhat coolly.

Kristin sat with her little grandson in her lap, and thought, easy 'twould scarce be for her either at the one or the other place. 'Twas a hard matter, growing old. So lately, it seemed, 'twas she herself who was the young woman — then it was about her fate that the men's strife and counsels tossed. Now she had drifted into a backwater. And not long ago her own sons had been even as this one here. She bethought her of her dream of the new-born babe — At this time the thought of her own mother rose often in her mind — her mother that she could not remember as other than an ageing, heavy-hearted woman. Yet she had been young, she too, when she lay and warmed her baby girl with her body's warmth; her mother too had been marked in youth, body and soul, by the bearing and nourishing of children; and she had thought perchance no more than Kristin herself, when she sat with that sweet young life at her breast, that so long as they two lived each single day would lead the child farther and farther from her arms.

"When you yourself had borne a child, Kristin, me-thought you would understand," her mother had said once. Now she understood that her mother's heart had been scored deep with memories of her daughter, memories of thoughts for her child from the time it was unborn and from all the years a child remembers nothing of, memories of fear and hope and dreams that children never know have been dreamed for them, until their own time comes to fear and hope and dream in secret —

At length the gathering of kinsmen broke up, so far as that some took up their abode with Jammælt at Formo, and some went with Sigurd over to Vaagaa. But at last one day two of Gaute's tenants from south in the Dale came galloping into the manor with tidings: the Warden was on his way north to seek out Gaute at his home, and the maid's father and kinsmen were in his train. Young Lavrans ran straightway to the stable — Next evening it looked as though an army was gathered at Jörundgaard: all Gaute's kinsmen were there with their armed followers, and his friends in the parish had come to tryst too.

Then came Helge of Hovland with a great following to crave his right against the ravisher. Kristin caught a glimpse of Helge Duk, as he rode into the courtyard alongside of Sir Paal Sörkvessön, the Warden himself. Jofrid's father was an oldish, tall and bent-backed man of a sickly look — when he lighted from his horse 'twas seen one leg was shorter than the other. The sister's husband, Olav Piper, was short, broad, and thick-set, red of skin and hair.

Gaute went forward to meet them; he bore him gallantly, with head held high — and behind him he had the whole array of kinsmen and friends; they stood in a half-circle before the upper-hall steps, in the midst the two elder men of knightly rank, Sir Sigurd and Sir Jammælt. Kristin and Jofrid watched the meeting from the shed of the weaving-house, but they could not hear the words that fell.

The men went up into the loft, and the two women turned in to the weaving-house. They could not speak. Kristin sat by the hearth-place; Jofrid walked the floor, bearing her child in her arms. Some time went by thus — then Jofrid wrapped a coverlid about the boy and went out with him. An hour after, Jammælt Halvardssön came in to his sister-in-law as she sat there alone, and told her the outcome.

Gaute had proffered to Helge Duk sixteen marks in gold in amends for Jofrid's honour and for carrying her off by the strong hand — 'twas the same as Helge's brother had got for his son's life. And he stood ready to espouse Jofrid at her father's hands, making her a fitting morning-gift and extra-gift; but on his part Helge should accord him and his daughter his full forgiveness, so that she should have a like portion with her sisters, and share with them in the heritage. Sir Sigurd, on behalf of Gaute's kin, stood surety that he would keep his bond. Helge Duk seemed willing to fall in with the proffer straightway; but his son-in-law, Olav Piper, and Nerid Kaaressön, who was Aasa's betrothed, spoke against it, and said that Gaute must be the most brazen of all men, to presume to fix terms himself for his wedding with a maid he had dishonoured while she was in her brother-in-law's manor, and thereafter borne away by force — or to crave that she should share in her sisters' heritage.

'Twas easy to see, said Jammælt, that Gaute himself liked but little this haggling over the price he should pay for wedding a well-born maid, whom he had led astray and who had now borne him a son. But 'twas easy to see, too, he had been made to learn both the lessons and the sermon by heart, so that he needed not to read them from a book.

While yet they were in the midst of the parleyings, and friends on both sides were seeking to bring them to accord, Jofrid came in with the child in her arms. At that her father broke down, and could not keep back his tears. So 'twas settled as she had wished.

That Gaute could never have paid such amends was clear; but Jofrid's portion was so fixed that the one quit the other. Thus, in very deed, the outcome of the bargain was that Gaute took Jofrid, and got little more with her than what she had in her wallets when she came to the manor, while for her extra-gift and morning-gift he gave her by deed the most of what he owned, his brothers consenting thereto. But some day great riches would come to him through Jofrid — if, indeed, the marriage were not childless, said Ivar Gjesling laughing — all the men joined in the laugh; but Kristin flushed red, for Jammælt sat listening to all the gross jests that now flew about.

The next day Gaute Erlendssön handfasted Jofrid Helgesdatter, and forthwith she held her churching, with as much honour as she had been a wife — Sira Dag said she had a right to this now. Then she journeyed with the child to Sundbu and abode in Sir Sigurd's ward until the wedding.

That day month, just after John's Mass,* the bridal was held; 'twas a brave and a stately one. The morning after, with great solemnity, Kristin Lavransdatter made over her keys to her son, and Gaute fastened the bunch to his wife's girdle.

Thereafter Sir Sigurd Eldjarn gave a great banquet at Sundbu, and thereat he and his cousins, the former owners of Sundbu, solemnly swore friendship and confirmed the oath with their hands and seals. With a bounteous hand, Sir Sigurd made gifts from the treasures that were at his

---

* 24th June.

manor, both to the Gjeslings and to all the guests according
to the nearness of their kinship and friendship — drinking-
horns, table-plate, trinkets, weapons, fur robes, and horses.
And thus all folk deemed that Gaute Erlendssön had
brought this matter of his bride-theft to a most honourable issue.

4

ONE summer morning the year after, Kristin was in the
penthouse in front of the old hearth-room house, setting
in order some gear in the chests that stood there. A noise
came to her ears of horses being led out, and she went and
looked forth between the small pillars of the penthouse. One
of the house-carls was leading out two horses, and Gaute
came forth from the stable doorway; the child Erlend was
sitting astride his father's shoulder. The bright little face
looked out about the man's yellow hair, and Gaute held
the boy's little hands in his great brown one up under his
chin. He handed the child to a maid who came across the
yard, and mounted his horse. But when Erlend screamed
and reached up after his father, Gaute took him again and
set him on the saddle-bow before him. At that moment
Jofrid came from the hall.

"Would you take Erlend with you — whither you are
riding?"

Gaute made answer. he was bound for the mill — the
river was like to carry it away, " — and Erlend has a mind
to go along with father, he says."

"Are you out of your wits — ?" She caught the boy
quickly to her arms, and Gaute laughed loud:

"I believe verily you deemed I meant to take him with
me!"

"Ay — " His wife laughed too: "You drag the poor
thing about with you everywhere — I well believe you
would do as the lynx does — eat the little one up ere you
let any other get him — "

She waved with one of the child's hands to Gaute as he
rode from the manor. Then she set the boy down on the
sward, crouched over him a moment, and talked to him

a little, and then ran across to the new storehouse and up
to the loft.

Kristin stood still, watching her grandson — the morning sun shone so fair on the little red-clad child. Young
Erlend toddled round in rings, gazing down into the grass.
Now he grew ware of a heap of chips, and straightway
set to work, painfully heaving them about. Kristin laughed.

He was fifteen months old, but forward for his age, his
parents thought, for he both walked and ran, and could
say two or three words to boot. Now he steered his way
straight for the little water-gutter that ran across the bottom of the courtyard and swelled to a purling beck when
rain had fallen in the fells. Kristin ran out and took him
up in her arms:

"Mustn't — mother will be angry if you wet you — "

The boy pouted — pondering belike if he should cry
because he was kept from paddling in the beck, or if he
should give in — to get wet was the deadly sin for him —
Jofrid was all too strict with him in such-like things. But
he looked so sage — laughingly Kristin kissed the boy,
set him down, and got her back to the penthouse. But her
work went but slowly — for the most part she stood looking out on the courtyard.

The morning sun shone so soft and fair on the three
storehouses over against her — 'twas as though Kristin
had not seen them rightly for a long time past — how
brave the houses were, with their loft-balconies adorned
with pillars and rich carving. The gilded vane on the gable
cross of the new storehouse glittered against the blue
haze that hung over the fell behind. This year, after the
wet early summer, the grass on the roofs was so fresh and
green.

Kristin sighed a little, looked once more on little Erlend, and turned to her chests again.

All at once there came from without a child's wailing
cry — she flung down all she had in her hands and rushed
out. Erlend stood shrieking, looking from his finger to a
half-dead wasp lying on the grass, and back again. When
his grandmother lifted him up with pitying words, he
shrieked still louder, and when, with yet more sounds of
pity and compassion, she bound wet earth in a cold green
leaf upon the sting, his wailing grew fearful to hear.

Lulling and caressing him, she bore him into her room, and he shrieked as though his last hour were come — and stopped short in the midst of a yell: he knew the box and the horn-spoon which his grandmother took from the door lintel. Kristin dipped bits of soft bannock in honey and fed him with them, while she went on petting him, rubbing her cheek against his neck, where the fair hair was still short and crinkled from the days when he had lain still in his cradle and worn it away on the pillow. And Erlend had forgotten his woes now — he turned his face up to the woman and offered to pat and kiss her with sticky hands and mouth.

In the midst of these doings, Jofrid stood in the door:

"Have you brought him in? — surely 'twas not needful, mother — I was but up in the loft."

Kristin told of the mischance that had befallen Erlend: "Heard you not how he shrieked?"

Jofrid thanked her mother-in-law, " — but now we will not trouble you longer — " She took the child, that now reached out to its mother and was fain to go to her, and went her way.

Kristin put away the honey-box. Then she sat on, her hands in her lap: the chests in the penthouse might wait till Ingrid came in.

It had been meant that she should have Frida Styrkaars-datter to wait on her when she moved over into the old hall. But then Frida was wedded off to one of the jackmen who had come over with Helge Duk — a lad that might have been her son.

" 'Tis the use in our quarter of the land that our underlings hearken to their masters when they counsel them for their good," said Jofrid, when Kristin marvelled that this match was come about.

"And in this country-side," said Kristin, "the common folk are unused to obey us further than 'tis reason they should, or to hearken to our counsel except 'tis for their good as fully as for ours. 'Tis good counsel I give you, Jofrid, when I pray you to bear this in mind."

" 'Tis as mother says, Jofrid," said Gaute — but passing meekly.

— Even before he was wed with her, Kristin had seen

that Gaute was most loath to cross Jofrid. And he was grown to be a most compliant husband.

The mother-in-law denied not that in many things Gaute might do well to give ear to his wife — she was shrewd, notable, and hard-working far beyond the common. And *she* was so more wanton than Kristin herself had been. She too had trodden underfoot her duty as a daughter and sold her honour, because she could not win the man she had set her heart on at a cheaper rate; but once she had won her will, she was the most faithful and modest of wives. Kristin knew that Jofrid loved her husband passing well — that she was proud of his good looks and of his noble birth; her sisters were richly wed, but their husbands were best seen at night when no moon was shining, and of their forefathers the less said the better, Jofrid let fall scornfully. She was jealous of her husband's welfare and his honour, as she understood them, and at home she spoiled him all she could — but if Gaute ventured to be of another mind than his wife in the least of trifles, Jofrid would first agree in such a fashion that Gaute faltered straightway — and then she would set to work and talk him round.

But Gaute throve and was content. None could doubt that the two young folks lived well together. Gaute was happy with his wife, and both were marvellous proud of their son, and loved him beyond all measure.

So now everything might have been for the best. If only Jofrid Helgesdatter had not been — ay, she was niggardly; Kristin could not call it aught else. Had she not been so, 'twould have vexed Kristin less that her son's wife was so set on her own will.

The very first autumn, when she was but newly wedded and come to be the mistress, Kristin had seen at the harvest-time that the work-folk were ill content — though they scarce said a word. But the old mistress marked it none the less.

It might have happed in Kristin's time, too, that the folk had to eat herring that had gone musty, bacon as yellow and high-smelling as fir-root splints, and tainted meat. But then all had known that the mistress would surely make up for it with some extra good titbit at another time, milk-porridge or fresh cheese, and good ale out of season. And when food came round that had got a bad taste and must be eaten up, all knew 'twas but the over-flow, as it were, of Kristin's bursting storehouses — and when folk were in sore need, then the abundance of the Jörundgaard store-houses was a blessing to the whole parish. Already folk felt less sure that Jofrid would prove open-handed in deal-ing out help in food, when the common folk felt the pinch of dearth.

This it was that vexed the mother-in-law — for it seemed to minish the honour of the manor, and of its master.

That even in this one year she herself had been made to feel that her daughter-in-law favoured her own part un-duly was a thing that touched her less nearly. It had shown already at Bartholomew's Mass,* when she had been given two of the slaughtered goats instead of the four she should have had. True, the glutton had made havoc among the small stock in the fells that summer — still Kristin deemed it shameful to take count of two goats on so great a manor; but she held her peace. And 'twas the same with all her dues from the manor — autumn slaughtering, corn and flour, fodder for her four cows and two saddle-horses — she was ever given short measure or poor wares. She marked that Gaute misliked this and was ashamed — but he dared not do aught for fear of his wife, and so he made as if he saw it not.

Gaute was as open-handed as were all Erlend Nikulaus-sön's sons. In his brothers the mother had called it waste-fulness. But Gaute was a worker, and content with little for himself — had he but the best of horses and hounds and some good hawks, he cared not, for the rest, to live in other wise than the small farmers of the Dale. But, if folk came to the manor, he was a free-handed host to guests of every kind, and bountiful to beggars — and therein he was a house-master after his mother's heart; 'twas thus she deemed great folk should live who dwelt upon their udal lands in their own country-side, making their goods yield increase, wasting naught uselessly, but neither sparing aught when love of God and of His poor, or care for the honour of the house, required that they should give from their store.

_____

* 24th August.

She saw now that Jofrid set most of Gaute's rich friends and kinsmen of worship. Howbeit in this matter Gaute seemed least willing to be guided by his wife — he tried to hold fast to the old comrades of his youth — brother tipplers, Jofrid called them; and indeed Kristin learnt now that Gaute had been somewhat wilder than she knew of. But those friends came not unbidden to his manor after he was become a wedded man. And so far 'twas sure no poor man had been sent away empty by Gaute. But he gave much smaller gifts when Jofrid was looking on. Behind her back he would give more, as 'twere by stealth. But 'twas not much that could happen behind Jofrid's back.

And Kristin saw that Jofrid was jealous of her. His mother had had Gaute's friendship and trust so wholly and fully all these years, since he was her poor sick child that was able neither to live nor die. Now she marked that Jofrid liked it not if Gaute sat him down by his mother, asked her counsel, or got her to tell stories as in the old days. If the man forgot the time, and lingered a little by her down in the old hall, 'twould not be long ere Jofrid found an errand thither —

And she would grow jealous if her mother-in-law made too much of little Erlend.

— Out in the yard there grew in the short, trodden grass certain herbs with coarse, dark, leathery leaves. But now, in the sunny days of midsummer, there sprang a little stalk, with clear, pale-blue flowerets, up from the middle of each flattened whorl. To Kristin it seemed that the old outer leaves, scarred as they were by every foot of man or beast that had trampled them, must love the sweet bright flowering heart-shoot even as she loved her son's son.

He seemed to her to be life of her life and flesh of her flesh, as surely as her own children, but yet more sweetly. When she had a chance to hold him in her lap, and saw that the boy's mother watched the two jealously the while, took him away as soon as for shame's sake she might, laid him, secure in her ownership, to her breast, and pressed him to her greedily — then it dawned on Kristin Lavransdatter as never before that the preachers of God's word were right. The life of the body was tainted with unrest beyond all cure; in the world where men mixed, begot new generations, were driven together by fleshly love, and loved their own flesh, there came heart-ache and broken hopes, as surely as rime comes in autumn; both life and death sundered friends at last, as surely as winter parts the tree from its leaves.

Now it befell one evening, fourteen days before Olav's Mass,* that a band of mumpers came to Jörundgaard, and prayed the loan of a house for the night. Kristin was standing on the balcony of the old storehouse — it was to be at her disposal now — she heard Jofrid come out and answer the beggars: food they should have, but she could not give them shelter: "We ourselves are many, and we have our mother-in-law living on the manor — she has the half of the houses — "

Wrath flamed up in the one-time lady of the manor — never had it happed before that wayfarers had been denied a night's shelter at Jörundgaard — and the sun was already touching the western ridges. She ran down and went across to Jofrid and the beggars:

"They can have lodging in my house, Jofrid, and, being there, 'twill be well I should give them their meat too. Never before on this manor have we denied a fellow-Christian shelter, when he asked it in God's name."

"Do as you think fit, mother," answered Jofrid, fiery red in the face.

When Kristin had looked more nearly at the beggars, she well-nigh repented her proffer — 'twas not quite without reason that the young wife was loath to have these folk on the manor overnight. Gaute and the house-folk were away on the far meadows up by the Sil water, and would not be home at even; Jofrid was alone at home, with the parish bedes-folk, an old couple and two children, and Kristin and her servant in the old hall. And many and strange as were the kinds of folk Kristin was used to see in wandering bands of beggars, she liked the looks of these but ill. Four were big and strong young men — three of them red-haired, with small wild eyes. These seemed to be brothers; but the fourth, who had had both his nostrils slit and wanted his ears, spoke a broken tongue, as though he were an outlander. Besides these there were two old folks — a little crooked fellow, yellowish-green in face, hair, and beard from dirt and age, with

---

* 29th July.

belly swollen as from some ailment — he went on crutches — and an old woman, her neck and hands covered with sores, and her head-cloth reeking with blood and matter. Kristin shuddered at the thought that this creature might have come near to Erlend. But, none the less, 'twas well for these wretched old folk that the band should not need to wander about the Hammer-fells that night.

But the beggars behaved them peaceably enough. Once the earless one tried to catch a hold of Ingrid as she was setting food on the board; but Björn straightway bristled up and growled. For the rest they seemed out of heart and weary — they had suffered much ill and got but little gain, they answered to the mistress's questioning — 'twould be better at Nidaros maybe. The woman was pleased when Kristin gave her a goat's horn full of good grease made of purest lamb's fat and little children's water — but she would not have it when Kristin offered to steep her head-clout in warm water and to give her a clean linen cloth — the cloth, indeed, she took.

All the same, Kristin had Ingrid, the young serving-maid, sleep innermost in her bed. Once or twice during the night Björn growled, but else all was still. A little after midnight the dog ran to the door and gave a couple of short barks — Kristin heard hoofbeats in the courtyard, and knew that 'twas Gaute coming home. She guessed that Jofrid had sent word to him.

Kristin filled the beggars' wallets well the next morning; and they were gone but a little way beyond the manor gate when she saw Jofrid and Gaute making for her house.

Kristin sat her down and took up her spindle. She greeted her children fairly when they came in, and asked Gaute about the hay. Jofrid sniffed — the guests had left a fusty smell behind them. But her mother-in-law made as if she marked naught. Gaute shifted about uneasily and seemed to find it hard to bring out his errand. On that Jofrid took the word from him:

"There is one matter, mother, that I deem 'twere best we spoke of now. I see well you think that I am more saving that you deem befits the mistress of Jörundgaard. I know that you think this, and you deem that I minish Gaute's honour thereby. Now I will not say aught of how I was afraid last night to take in this band, seeing that I was alone on the manor with my baby child and a few old parish folk, for I saw you understood it, so soon as you had come to sight of your guests. But I have marked before, too, that you deem I am a niggard with food and ungentle to the poor.

"I am not so, mother; but Jörundgaard is no longer the seat of a king's man and a rich man, as it was in your father's and mother's time. A rich man's child were you; you went about amongst rich and mighty kinsfolk; you were wedded richly, and your husband lifted you up to yet greater power and station than you were brought up to. None can look that you should fully understand in your old age how far otherwise it is with Gaute, who has lost his father's heritage, and who must share the half of your father's riches with many brothers. But *I* dare nowise forget that I brought little more to his estate than the child I bore beneath my heart, and a heavy burden of amends for my love to pay — seeing that I was party to the wrong he wrought my kin. Time may make that good — but 'tis my duty to pray God to grant my father long life. We are young folk, Gaute and I, we know not how many children 'twill be our lot to have — You *must* believe, mother-in-law, I have no other thought in all I do but for the good of my husband and our children — "

"I believe it, Jofrid." Kristin looked gravely into her daughter-in-law's flushed face. "And never have I meddled with your house-holding, nor denied that you are a notable woman and a good and faithful wife to my son. But you must let me deal with my own as I am used to do. As you say, I am an old woman, and no longer apt to learn new ways."

The young folk understood that the mother had naught more to say to them, and soon after took their leave.

As ever, Kristin felt she must own that Jofrid was right — at first. But when she bethought her, it seemed to her — no, right she was not, after all; 'twas against reason to liken Gaute's alms with her father's. Gifts for the soul's peace of the poor and strangers dying in the parish; dowry gifts to fatherless maids; ale-feasts on the holy-days of her father's best-loved saints; doles to sick folk and sinners journeying to seek Saint Olav — even had Gaute been much richer than he was, none had looked that he should put himself to such costs; Gaute thought no more of his

Maker than he needs must. He was free-handed and good-hearted; but Kristin had seen that her father held the poor he helped in reverence, because Jesus had chosen a poor man's lot when He came in the flesh. And her father had loved hard work and deemed that all handicraft was honoured, since that God's mother, Mary, chose to be a working-woman who spun to win bread for herself and hers, though she was a daughter of rich folk and came of the kindred of the kings and high-priests of the Jewish land.

Two days after, early in the morning, while Jofrid was still going about half clad and Gaute lay abed, Kristin came in to them. She had on a kirtle and cloak of grey wadmal, wore a wide-brimmed, black felt hat above her coif, and strong shoes upon her feet. Gaute flushed deeply when he saw his mother in this garb. Kristin said she was minded to go afoot to Nidaros to Saint Olav's feast, and she prayed her son to see to her affairs the while.

Gaute strove eagerly to shake her purpose — he would have had her at least borrow horses and groom from him and take her serving-maid with her — but, as was most like, coming from a man lying in his naked bed before his mother's eyes, his words carried little weight. So abashed was he, that in pity Kristin bethought her to say she had had a dream.

"I think long, too, till I see your brothers again — " but at that she had to turn her away; she had not yet dared to confess to her own heart how she yearned and feared to meet her two eldest sons again.

Gaute was set on bearing his mother company the first part of her way. While he dressed himself and had a bite of food, Kristin sat laughing and playing with little Erlend — he crowed, and chirped, new wakened and in a twitter with morning life. She kissed Jofrid at parting, and this she had never done before. In the courtyard all the household was gathered — Ingrid had spread the tidings that mistress Kristin was going on pilgrimage to Nidaros.

Kristin took the heavy, iron-shod staff in her hand, and, as she would not ride, Gaute laid her double wallets across his horse and drove it on before him.

Up on the church-green Kristin turned about and looked down upon her manor — so fair it lay in the dewy, sun-bright morning. The river shone white. The house-folk stood there yet — she could make out Jofrid's light dress and coif, and the child, a patch of red, upon her arm. Gaute saw his mother's face grow pale with the fullness of her heart.

The road bore upwards through the woods under the shadow of Hammer-fell. Kristin walked as lightly as a young maid. She and her son spoke not much together. And when they had walked for two hours, they came where the way bears off over Rostkampen, and the whole Dovre country-side lies spread before one northward. Then Kristin said Gaute must go no farther with her; but she would sit a while and rest before going on.

Down beneath them lay the Dale, with the river's greenish-white riband wandering through it, and the farms like small green patches on the forest-covered slopes. But higher up the upland mosses arched, brownish or yellow with lichen, inward towards the grey screes and the bare heights flecked with snow-drifts. Cloud shadows drifted over the Dale and the uplands, but northward all was clear among the fells; the heaped-up hills had flung off their cloaks of mist, and shone blue, one behind the other. And Kristin's yearning moved with the cloud-flocks northward on the long road that lay before her, hurried over the Dale, in among the great mountains that blocked the way, and along the steep tracks across the uplands. A few days more, and she would be wending her way downward through Trondheim's rich, green dales, following the river's windings towards the great fjord. She shuddered at the memory of the well-known places by the sea, where she and youth had gone about together. Erlend's fair form moved before her sight, with changing looks and bearing, swift, unclear, as though she saw him mirrored in running water. Last of all she would come forth on Feginsbrekka, by the marble cross — and there would lie the town by the river mouth, between the blue fjord and the green ridge of Strind, and on the river bank the mighty, shining church with dizzy towers and golden vanes, the evening sunlight burning on the rose midway on its breast. And far up the fjord, under Frosta's blue hills, lay Tautra, low and black like a whale's back, the church tower standing up like the steering-fin. Oh, my Björgulf; oh, Naakkve —

But when she looked back over her shoulder, she could still see a little of the home fell below Hövringen. It lay in shadow, but her well-used eye could see where the sæter path went through the woods. She knew the grey mountain-tops that rose above the cloak of forest — they ringed about the Sil dwellers' old sæter fields.

From the hills above came stray notes of a cow horn — a few clear high tones, that died away and came again — it sounded like children practising them in blowing. Far off tinkling of bells — and the muffled roar of the river, and the deep sighs of the forest in the still, warm day. Kristin's heart trembled with unrest in the stillness. She was drawn as with home-sickness onward, as with home-sickness back-ward to the parish and the manor. Visions swarmed be-fore her sight — pictures of daily life: she saw herself running with the goats on the path through the sparse woods south of their sæter — a cow had got mired in the bog — the sun shone brightly; when she stood a moment and listened, she felt her own sweat bite into her skin. She saw the courtyard at home in a flurry of snow — a grey day of storm, darkening into a wild winter night — She was all but blown back into the outer room when she opened the door, the storm took her breath away; but there they loomed up, two shapeless bundles of men in snow-smothered fur coats: Ivar and Skule had come home. Their ski sank deep into the big drift that ever heaped itself together right across the yard when 'twas blowing from the north-west. On such days there were always deep drifts in two places in the courtyard — and all at once 'twas as though she must think with love and longing of these two snowdrifts that she and all folk on the manor had cursed each winter — 'twas as if she were doomed never to see them more.

It seemed as if these yearnings burst her heart in sunder —they ran hither and thither like streams of blood, seeking out ways to all places in the wide-stretched land where she had lived, to all the sons she had wandering in the world, to all her dead beneath the moulds — She wondered — could it be that she was fey? She had never felt the like of this before —

Then she saw that Gaute was sitting staring at her. And she smiled quickly, as if in excuse — 'twas time they should say farewell, and she go on her way.

Gaute called to his horse, that had wandered forward grazing along the green track. He ran after it and brought it back, and they said farewell. Kristin had her wallets over her shoulder already, and her son had set his foot in the stirrup — then he turned and took a step forward:

"Mother!" For a moment she looked deep into his be-shamed, helpless eyes. "You have not — you have not been over well content this last year, I trow — mother, Jofrid means well, she holds you in great reverence — but mayhap even so I should have said more to her, of what manner of woman you are and ever were — "

"How come you to have such thoughts, my Gaute?" His mother spoke gently and wonderingly. "I know well myself that I am no longer young, and old folk, they say, are hard to please, but so old I am not yet that I have not wit to know your worth, yours and your wife's. An ill thing would I count it were Jofrid to deem it had been all vain and thankless toil, all she has done to spare me from work and care. Think not so of me, I pray you, my son, as to deem I set not all due store by your wife's worth and your faithful, duteous love — if so be I have not shown it as much as you could with reason look for, you must even bear with me, remembering that 'tis the way of old folk — "

Gaute stared at his mother, open-mouthed — "Mother — " Then he burst into tears, and leaned against his horse, shaking with sobs.

But Kristin kept a firm hold on herself; her voice be-wrayed naught but wonder and motherly kindness.

"My Gaute, you are young in years, and true it is that you were my pet lamb, as your father was wont to say. But none the less you must not take this parting thus, son, now you are a man grown and the master of a house. If I were bound for Rome or Jerusalem, then indeed — but on this journey I shall scarce meet with such great perils — I shall find folk to bear me company, you know, for sure when I come to Toftar, if not before. For each morning at this season pilgrim troops set out from thence — "

"Mother, mother — forgive it us! so as we took all power and all rule out of your hands, thrusting you aside — "

Kristin shook her head with a little smile: "I fear me you children must deem me a woman over fond to rule — "

Gaute turned him to her: she took his hand in one of

hers and laid her other hand on his shoulder, while she begged him once more to believe she was not unthankful to him or Jofrid, and prayed that God be with him. Then she turned him round towards his horse, and laughingly smote him between the shoulders for good luck.

She stood looking after him, till he sank from sight below the brow of the hill. So comely as he was on the big, dark-grey horse.

She felt her mood a strange one — all things without her came so sharply to her sense: the sun-steeped air, the warm breath of the pine wood, the twitter of tiny birds in the grass. Yet at the same time, looking within herself, she saw pictures like the visions that high fever brings — within her was an empty house, wholly soundless, dark, and breathing desolation. The vision changed — a strand at ebb, the tide far withdrawn from it; pale, worn stones; heaps of dark, lifeless tangle; all kinds of driftage —

Then she settled her bag more easily on her shoulder, grasped her staff, and set forth on her way down into the Dale. — If 'twere not fated that she should come hither any more, then 'twas God's will — useless to be afraid. And most like 'twas but that she was growing old — She crossed herself and went her way with firmer step — willing all the same to get down to the hill-slopes where the road ran among the farms.

Only from one short stretch on the highway could one see the houses at Haugen, high on the topmost mountain ridge. Her heart set to throbbing at the thought.

As she had thought, she met with pilgrims not a few when she came to Toftar late in the day. Next morning they made a little troop as they set off up the fells in company.

A priest, with his servant, and two women, his mother and sister, were on horseback and soon were far ahead of those on foot. Kristin felt a pang in her heart as she looked after the second woman, who rode between her two children.

In Kristin's company there were two oldish yeomen from a little farm here on Dovre. Then there were two younger men from Oslo, craftsmen of the city, and a farmer with his daughter and her husband; quite young people, these two; they were journeying with the young folks' child, a little maid, a year and a half old maybe, and had a horse they rode by turns. These three were from a parish far south in the land, Andabu by name — Kristin knew not where it was. That first evening Kristin begged to look at the child, for it cried and whimpered without cease — it looked wretchedly, with a great, hairless head and small, slack-jointed body; it could neither speak nor sit upright yet. The mother seemed ashamed of it — and when next morning Kristin proffered to bear her daughter a while for her, she was left with it on her hands — the mother pushed on far in front; she seemed to be a cuckoo mother. But they were over young, both she and her husband, scarce eighteen years old, and she might well be weary of bearing a heavy child that was ever puling and weeping. The grandfather was an ugly, sulky, cross-grained man; but 'twas he who had been set on journeying to Nidaros with his daughter's daughter, so he seemed to have some kindness for her. Kristin walked beside him and the two Franciscan monks at the tail of the troop — and it vexed her soul that the man from Andabu never thought to lend the monks his horse a while — all could see that the younger monk was grievously sick.

The elder, Brother Arngrim, was a round little man, with a round, red, freckled face, lively brown eyes, and a foxy-red ring of hair about his pate. He talked endlessly, most of the poverty they lived in, the barefoot monks of Skidan — the order had but newly got a house in that town, but they were so parlous poor they were scarce able to keep going the services, and the church they had been minded to build would never come to aught for sure. He laid the blame on the rich nuns of Gimsöy, who pursued the poor begging friars with envy and spite, and now had a suit at law against them; with glib-tongued relish he told all kinds of evil tales about them. Kristin misliked to hear the monk talk in this fashion, and his tales of how 'twas said their abbess had been chosen uncanonically, and how the nuns missed the offices in slothful slumber and were given to tattling and to unchaste talk over the board in the refectory, seemed to her little to be trusted — ay, of one sister he said right out that folk deemed she had not kept her vows of chastity. But she saw that Brother Arngrim was otherwise a good-hearted and kindly man. He bore the sick child long stretches when he saw that Kris-

tin's arms were weary, and, when it screamed too grievously, he would set off at a run over the upland, with his
gown kilted high, so that the juniper flogged his black,
hairy legs and the mire splashed up from the bog holes,
while he shouted and bawled to the mother that now she
must bide for them, for the child was thirsty. Then he
trotted back to the sick man, Brother Torgils; to him he
was the tenderest and most loving of fathers.

With the sick monk 'twas impossible to come to Hjerdkinn that night; but the two Dovre men knew of a stone
hut by a tarn a little southward in the waste, and the
pilgrims made towards it. The evening was grown cold
by now. The ground by the edge of the water was
swampy, and white mist rose from the marsh, so that the
birch trees dripped with wet. A thin sliver of moon hung
over the mountain-tops in the west, its pale yellow scarce
showing in the yellow evening sky. More and more often
Brother Torgils was forced to stand still; he coughed so
sorely 'twas pitiful to hear. Brother Arngrim held him up
in these bouts, and after wiped his face and mouth, then
with a shake of the head showed Kristin his hand — 'twas
bloody with the sick man's spittle.

They found the hut, but it had fallen into ruin. So they
sought out a sheltered spot and made them a bonfire. But
the poor folk from the south had not thought that night
on the fells would be so icy cold. Kristin took from her
sack the cloak that Gaute had forced upon her because
'twas so passing light and warm — of fine boughten cloth,
lined with beaver fur. When she wrapped Brother Torgils
in it, he whispered — he was so hoarse he could scarce
speak — that he would be fain to have the child lie in it
with him. So they put the child in with him; it whimpered
and wailed, and the monk coughed; but between-whiles
both of them got some sleep.

Part of the night Kristin kept watch with one of the
Dovre men and Brother Arngrim, looking to the fire. The
pale yellow light drew round to the northern sky — the
tarn lay at their side white and still; fish rose and made
rings upon the water — but under the hill on the farther
side of the water mirrored black darkness. Once an uncanny barking screech came to their ears from over there
— the monk started and gripped the other two hard by
the arms. Kristin and the farmer deemed 'twas some beast

—then they heard a stone roll, as if someone was walking on the hill-side screes, and another cry like a gruff voice of a man. The monk began to pray aloud — she caught the words: *"Jesus Christus, Soter,"* and *"vicit leo de tribu Juda"* * — then they heard a door shut to, away under the mountain.

The faint grey dawn began to show, the scree across the lake and the clumps of birch came into sight — then the other Dovre man and the man from Oslo took their place. The last thing Kristin thought, ere she fell asleep, close in to the fire, was that, should they make such short marches — and give an alms to the beggar monks she must when they parted — 'twas like she would have to beg her meat at the farms when they came down into Gauldal.

The sun was well up already, and the morning wind was darkening the lake in little squalls, when the frozen pilgrims gathered about Brother Arngrim while he said the morning prayers. Brother Torgils sat crouched together, with chattering teeth, striving to keep back his cough as he mumbled the words over after him. When she looked at the monks' ashen-grey gowns with the sun shining on them, Kristin called to mind that she had dreamed of Brother Edvin — she could not remember her dream, but she kneeled and kissed the monks' hands and prayed for their blessing on the company.

The sight of the beaver-skin cloak had shown the other pilgrims that Kristin was not come of small folk. And when she chanced to say that she had journeyed twice before by the king's highway over the Dovre-fjeld, she became a sort of guide and leader to the band. The Dovre men had never been farther north than to Hjerdkinn, and the folk from Viken were, of course, quite strange here.

They came to Hjerdkinn before the hour of vespers, and, after the service in the chapel, Kristin went out into the hills alone. She would fain have found again the path she had followed with her father, and the spot by the beck where she had sat with him. These she could not find, but she deemed she had found the hillock she had clambered up that she might gaze after him as he rode away from

---

* Jesus Christ, the Saviour. — The lion of the tribe of Judah has conquered.

her. So she thought — but the little stony ridges along the pathway here were much alike.

She knelt amid the bearberry vines at the top of the knoll. The summer evening was growing dusk — the birch-tree slopes on the hill-sides, the grey screes, and the brown stretches of marshland melted together, but, above the wide-stretched mountain waste, the evening sky arched its clear, fathomless bowl. All the pools shone whitely, and the heavenly brightness was given back, broken and more faint, from the little mountain beck that hurried, chafing restlessly over stones, to flow out between pale gravel banks into a little moorland tarn.

Again there came upon her that strange, feverish inner vision — the stream seemed to show her a picture of her own being; thus had she hurried restlessly through the waste of these earthly years, foamed up in turbulent chafing at every stone in her path — 'twas but weakly and fitfully and palely that the everlasting light could mirror itself in her life. — But it dawned upon the mother dimly, that in anguish, and care, and love — each time the fruit of sin ripened into sorrow — it had been granted to her earth-bound, wilful soul to catch a reflection of the heavenly light.

Hail, all hail, Mary, rich in mercy! Blessed art thou among women, and blessed the fruit of thy womb, Jesus, who gave His sweat and blood for our sake —

While she said over the five Aves in memory of the redemption's mysteries of pain, she felt 'twas through her sorrows only that she dared seek shelter under the cloak of God's mother. Her sorrow for the children she had lost, her heavier sorrows for each stroke of fate that fell upon her sons and that she could not ward from them. Mary, the perfect in purity, in meekness, in obedience to the Father's will, had sorrowed the most of all mothers, and her mercy would see and understand the pale and weak reflection from a sinful woman's heart, that had burned with hot and ravaging fleshly love and with all the sins that fleshly love brings with it — untowardness and defiance, a stony, unforgiving spirit, stubbornness, and pride — yet was a mother's heart in despite of all.

Kristin hid her face in her hands. For a moment it seemed to her more than she could bear, that she was parted now from them all — from all her sons.

Then she said over the last Paternoster. She thought of
her parting from her father on this spot all these long years
agone, of her parting from Gaute but two days back. In
childlike thoughtlessness her sons had offended against her
— yet she knew that, even had they offended against her
as she against her father — wilfully and in sin — it could
never have changed her heart toward them. 'Twas easy to
forgive one's children —

Gloria Patri et Filio et Spiritu Sancto — she said the
words, and kissed the cross her father had given her,
humbly thankful to feel that, despite of all, despite of her
ungoverned spirit, yet had it been granted to her restless
heart to catch a faint gleam of the love she had seen mirrored in her father's soul, clear and still, even as the brightness of the sky was thrown back now by the great still
moorland tarn.

Next day the weather was so grey and windy and cold,
with mist and rain-storms, that Kristin deemed she scarce
dared go on with the sick child and Brother Torgils. But
the monk himself was the most eager — she saw he was
fearful he might die ere he came to Nidaros. So they took
their way across the upland; but the fog was so thick at
times that Kristin dared not venture down over the headlong tracks, with cliffs both above and below, that she
remembered led down to the pilgrims' shelter in Drivdal.
So they built a fire when they were come to the top of the
glen and rested there for the night. After evening prayer
Brother Arngrim told them a goodly saga of a ship in peril
of the sea that was saved by an abbess's prayers to Mary
Virgin; the morning star came out over the sea at her
command.

The monk seemed to have taken a liking to Kristin.
While she sat by the blaze, lulling and hushing the child
that the others might get to sleep, he edged close to her
and began to tell about himself in a whisper. He was a
poor fisher's son, and when he was fourteen years old, he
lost his father and brother at sea one winter night, but was
saved himself by another boat. He had deemed this a sign
and token, and besides he had grown afeared of the sea;
and thus the thought came to him that he should turn
monk. But for three years more he had had to tarry at
home with his mother, and they toiled and starved, and he

was ever afeared when in a boat — but then his sister was wed, and her husband took over the house and the share in the boat, and he could betake him to the Minorites of Tunsberg. There they had mocked at him at first for his low birth — but the guardian was kind and stood his friend. And, since Brother Torgils Olavssön was come into the brotherhood, all the monks had grown much more pious and peaceable, for he was passing pious and meek, though he was the best born of them all, of a rich yeoman kindred away in Slagn — and his mother and sisters were most bounteous to the cloister. But since they were come to Skidan, and since Brother Torgils was fallen sick, all things were grown much harder again. Brother Arngrim gave Kristin to understand that he marvelled Christ and Mary would make the path so stony for their poor brethren's feet.

"They chose poverty themselves, while they lived on earth," said Kristin.

" 'Tis easy for you to say such things, rich woman as you doubtless are," said the monk angrily. "I warrant you have never proved what it is to go fasting — " and Kristin must even avow that so it was —

When they were come down among the tilled lands, and fared through Updal and Soknadal, Brother Torgils got now a ride and now a drive for stretches of the way; but he grew weaker and weaker, and Kristin's company was ever changing, for folk parted from them and went forward, and new pilgrims came up with them. When they came to Staurin, none of them who had crossed the mountains with her were left in her company, saving the two monks. And in the morning Brother Arngrim came to her weeping, and said that Brother Torgils had had a sore blood-spitting in the night; he could go no farther — now, belike, they would come to Nidaros too late, and would miss the festival.

Kristin thanked the brothers for their company, and for ghostly guidance and help on the journey. Brother Arngrim seemed to be astonished at the richness of her farewell gifts, for his face lighted up — ay, she must have a gift in return from him, he said; he drew forth from his wallet a case with some letters in it. On them was written a goodly prayer with all God's names at the end thereof; an open place was left in the scroll wherein to print the name of the supplicant.

Kristin told herself that 'twas not like the monk should know aught of her, with whom she had been wed, or her husband's fate, even if she gave her father's name. Yet did she pray him to write only: "Kristin, widow."

Down through Gauldal she took the paths on the out-skirts of the parishes, for she thought that if she met folk from the great manors it might well befall that one or other would know the sometime mistress of Husaby again, and she was loath to be known, though she scarce knew why. The next day she climbed by the forest tracks up over the ridge to the little church on Vatsfjeld, that was sacred to John the Baptist — but the folk thereabout called it Saint Edvin's.

The chapel stood in an opening in the thick woods; it and the knoll behind were mirrored in a pond that fed the healing spring. A wooden cross stood by the beck, and round about lay crutches and staves, and on the bushes near by hung tatters from old bandages.

About the church was a little fenced-in plot, but the gate was fast shut. Kristin kneeled down without, and thought of the time she had sat within there with Gaute on her lap. Then she was clad in silks, one of the company of bravely clad great folks, men and women, from the country-side all around. Sira Eiliv stood close by, hold-ing Naakkve and Björgulf firmly; in the throng without were her serving-maids and henchmen. Then had it been the burden of her burning prayer, that might this poor, unhappy child but be made whole in body and in wits, she would crave for naught more — not even to be freed herself of the sore hurt in her back that had plagued her since ever the twins were born.

She thought of Gaute, sitting his great iron-grey, a brave and goodly horseman. And she herself — not many women of her age, nigh to half a hundred years, were blessed with such health; she had marked it well on her journey across the mountains. Lord, give me but this and this and this — then will I thank Thee and crave no more than this and this and this —

Never, it seemed to her, had she prayed to God for aught else than that He might grant her her own will.

And she had got always what she wished — most. And now she sat here with a bruised spirit — not because she had sinned against God, but because she was miscontent that it had been granted her to follow the devices of her own heart to the journey's end.

She had not come to God with her garland, nor with her sins and her sorrows — not so long as the world still held a drop of sweetness to mix in her cup. But she came now, now she had learned that the world is like a tavern — where he who has naught more to spend from is cast out at the door.

She felt no joy in her resolve — but it seemed to Kristin that 'twas not she herself who had resolved. The poor beggars who came in to her house had come to bid her go forth. Another will than her own had set her in the company of the poor and sick, and bidden her go with them, away from the home where she had been the mistress and had ruled as the mother of men. And if now she obeyed the call without too ill a grace, she knew 'twas because she saw that Gaute would thrive the better when she was gone from the manor. She had bent fate to her will, she had had the lot of her own choice — but her sons she could not fashion after her will; they were as God had fashioned them, and their natures drove them on; striving with them she must be worsted. Gaute was a good farmer, a good husband and faithful father, a doughty man, and as honourable as most folk — but the stuff for a chieftain he was not, nor was he of a mood to long for what she had coveted for him. But he loved her enough to be troubled, when he knew she looked for more from him than he could give. Therefore was she now minded to beg for harbour and sanctuary; though 'twas bitter to her pride to come in such utter poverty that she could bring no offerings in her hands.

But she knew that she was called to come. The fir woods on the knoll stood drinking in the sunlight that sifted through them, and sighing so gently; the little church lay there shut and silent, breathing forth a smell of tar. Yearningly Kristin thought of the dead monk who had taken her hand and led her into the radiance of God's enfolding love when she was an innocent child; had put forth a hand time after time to lead her home from the paths of transgression, both while he lived on earth and since — And of a

sudden she remembered as clear as day what she had
dreamed of him that night upon the fell:

She had dreamed that she stood in the sunshine in the
courtyard of some great manor, and Brother Edvin came
towards her from the hall-house door. His hands were full
of bread, and, when he came to her, he broke off a great
piece and gave it her — she understood that she had had
to do as she had thought, beg for alms when she came
down into the parishes; but in some way or other she had
joined company with Brother Edvin, and they two were
faring on together, begging — But at the same time she
knew that the dream had a two-fold meaning: the manor
was not only a great manor, but it seemed to her to betoken a holy place, and Brother Edvin was one of the
household there; and the bread which he brought and gave
to her was not the simple bannock it looked like — it betokened the host, *panis angelorum*, and she took the bread
of the angels at his hands. And now she gave her promise
to Brother Edvin's keeping.

5

So at last she was at her journey's end. Kristin Lavransdatter sat resting on a haycock by the wayside below Sions-
borg. There was sunshine and a blowing wind; the part of
the meadow that was not yet mown waved red and silky
bright with seeding grass. Nowhere but in the Trondheim
country were the meadows red like this. Below the slope
she could see a glimpse of the fjord, dark blue and flecked
with foam; fresh white sea spray dashed up against the
bluffs, as far as she could see along the strand below the
forest-clad Byness.

Kristin drew a deep breath. After all, 'twas good to be
here again; good, though 'twas strange as well to know
that she should never go from here any more. The grey-
clad sisters out at Rein followed the same rule, Saint Bernard's rule, as the brothers at Tautra. When she rose at
cock-crow and went to the church, she would know that
now Naakkve and Björgulf too were going to their places
in the monks' choir. Thus, after all, she would come to live

out her old age with certain of her sons — although not in the fashion she had thought.

She drew off her shoes and stockings and washed her feet in the beck. Into Nidaros she would walk barefoot.

Behind her on the path up the castle hill some boys were playing noisily — they were hard at work below the barbican, trying to find a way into the tumble-down work. When they grew ware of her, they fell to calling down foul words at her, laughing and hooting the while. She made as if she did not hear, till a little imp — eight years old the boy might have been — came rolling down the steep sward and almost bumped into her, shrieking out some ugly words he had picked up in wantonness from the older boys. Kristin turned towards him and said smiling:

"No need to shriek so to let me know you for a troll imp, for I see you have the rolling-breeches * on you — "

When the boys marked that the woman answered, they came bounding down, the whole pack. But they fell silent and abashed when they saw 'twas an ageing woman in pilgrim's garb, and that she chid them not for their bad words, but sat looking at them with great, clear, calm eyes and a stealthy little smile on her lips. She had a lean, round face with broad forehead and small rounded chin; she was sunburnt and much wrinkled under the eyes, but after all she looked not so exceeding old.

So the boldest of the boys took to talking and asking questions to hide the sheepishness of the troop. Kristin felt she could have laughed — these boys seemed so like her own rascals, the twins, when they were small, though she prayed to God that *hers* had never been so foul-mouthed. These seemed to be children of common folk in the town.

And when the moment came that she had longed for all through her journey, when she stood below the cross on Feginsbrekka and looked down on Nidaros, it came not so that she could collect her thoughts for prayer or meditation. All the bells of the town burst forth at that moment to ring to Vespers, and the boys all talked together, wanting to point out all that was before her —

Tautra she could not see, for a squall of wind, with mist

---
* See Note 6.

and scudding showers, was sweeping over the fjord beneath Frosta.

In the midst of the flock of boys she took the steep path that led down the Steinberg heights — and now cow-bells clinked and herdsmen whooped around them — the cows were bound homewards from the town pastures. At the gate in the town wall across the Nidareid, Kristin and her young attendants had to wait while the cattle were driven through — herdsmen hallooed, shouted, and cursed, oxen butted, cows were crowded and crushed together, and the boys named the owners of this bull or that as they passed. And when they were through the port and were passing towards the town lanes, Kristin had more than enough ado to pick her way with her naked feet amid the cow-dung on the poached-up track.

Some of the boys followed her unbidden even into Christ's Church. And as she stood in the dim forest of pillars and gazed towards the lights and the gilding of the choir, the boys plucked ever at the stranger-woman's gown, and would fain have shown her all such things as most draw children's eyes — from the patches of coloured sunlight falling through the rose-window among the arches, and the tombstones on the floor, to the canopies of costly stuffs above the altars. Kristin was given no peace to collect her thoughts — but each word the boys said wakened the dull yearning in her heart — for her sons first and foremost, but for the manor too, the houses, the outhouses, the cattle — for the toil and the sway of motherhood.

She had still that loathness to be known again of any who had been her friends or Erlend's in days gone by. They were wont ever to be in their town houses at festival tide and to have guests living with them — she shrank at the thought of meeting a company of them. Ulf Haldorssön she must seek out, for, as her bailiff, he had charge of the shares she still had in some farms north of the fells and meant now to give in payment for her commons in the Rein cloister. But 'twas like he would have with him now his kinsfolk from the farm at Skaun; so she must wait. But she had heard that a man who had served among Erlend's men-at-arms in the days he was Warden had his dwelling in a small yard out on Bratören; he

worked with the dolphin- and porpoise-fishers on the
fjord, and kept a lodging for seafarers.

When she came thither she was told that all the houses
were overfull already; but then came the man himself,
Aamunde, and knew her straightway. 'Twas strange to
hear him cry out her old name:

"Now I ween — is't not Erlend Nikulaussön's lady of
Husaby — all hail, Kristin — how can it be that you are
come hither to my house?"

He was full glad that she would be content with such
shelter as he could give her for the night, and he promised
he would sail her out to Tautra himself, the day after the
festival.

Till far on in the night she sat out in the courtyard
talking with their one-time house-carl, and it moved her
deeply when she marked that they that had been Erlend's
men still loved their young chieftain's memory and held
it in high honour — again and again Aamunde spoke of
him as "young." From Ulf Haldorssön they knew of his
hapless death, and Aamunde said, never did he meet any
of his old fellows of Husaby days but they drank to the
memory of their gallant master — and twice some of them
had put their money together and had masses said for him
on his death-day. Aamunde asked much after Erlend's
sons, and Kristin too asked of old acquaintance. 'Twas
midnight ere she got to bed by the side of Aamunde's
wife — naught would serve him at first but that they both
should give up their bed to her, and at last she was fain
to accept with thanks of his proffer that at least she should
take his place.

Next day was Olav's Wake. From early morning Kristin walked about the shore by the river mouth, looking at
the bustle on the wharves. Her heart beat faster when she
saw the Lord Abbot of Tautra step ashore — but the
monks who were with him were all elder men.

Long ere nones folk were streaming towards Christ's
Church, bearing or holding up their sick and cripples, so
that they might come near the shrine when it was borne
out in procession next day after High Mass.

As Kristin came up through the booths set up by the
fence round the churchyard — they sold, for the most,

meat and drink, wax-candles, and mats woven of rush or birch twigs to lay beneath one on the church floor — she stumbled upon the folk from Andabu, and Kristin took the child while the young wife got herself a draught of ale. At that moment came the procession of English pilgrims with songs and banners and lighted tapers; in the press and crush, as they made their way through the throng of folk by the booths, she lost the Andabu folk and could not find them again.

For long she wandered hither and thither on the out-skirts of the crowd, lulling the shrieking child. When she laid its face against her neck and would have comforted it with caresses, it mouthed about and sucked at her skin; she saw that it was athirst, and she knew not what to do. It seemed vain to seek for the mother; she must go down into the streets and ask where she could get it milk. But when she came out on to Upper Langstræte and would have gone northward, there was again a great press of folk — from the south came a train of knights, and at the same time the men-at-arms from the palace marched into the space betwixt the church and the Crossed-friars' House. Kristin was thrust aside into the nearest lane; but here, too, folk were hurrying to the church ahorse and afoot, and the press grew so great that at length she had to take refuge up on a stone dyke.

The air above her was full of the noise of bells — the cathedral chimes ringing out *nona hora*. The child stopped shrieking at the sound — it looked up at the sky, and a gleam of understanding showed in its dull eyes — it smiled a little. Touched with pity, the mother of other children bent and kissed the poor little creature. Then she saw that she was sitting on the stone wall around the gar-den of the Nikulaus house, their old town mansion.

— Well should she know the stone-built chimney rising through the turf roof — the back of their hall-house. Close by her stood the houses of the spital whose right to share the garden with them had roused Erlend's wrath.

She pressed the stranger-woman's child to her breast, kissed it and kissed it. Then someone touched her knee —

— A monk in the white gown and black cowl of the preaching brothers. She looked down into a pale yellow, furrowed, old man's face — a long, narrow, in-fallen mouth, two deeply sunken, amber eyes.

"Can it be — is it you yourself, Kristin Lavransdatter?" The monk laid his crossed arms upon the dyke and buried his face in them. "Are you here?"

"Gunnulf!" At that he moved his head so that it touched her knee where she sat: "Deem you 'tis so strange that I am here — ?" Then she called to mind that she was sitting on the garden wall of this house that had been his first and her own afterwards, and thought, 'twas strange indeed.

"But what child is this you have on your knee — sure, this cannot be Gaute's son?"

"No — " At the thought of little Erlend's healthy, sweet face, and strong, well-made body, she pressed the poor little stranger-child to her, overcome with pity: " 'Tis the child of a woman that crossed the fells along with me."

— But then there dawned upon her what Andres Simonssön had seen in his childish wisdom. Filled with reverence, she gazed on the pitiful creature that lay upon her lap.

But now it wept again, and before aught else she had to ask the monk if he could tell her where she could get milk for the child. Gunnulf led her eastward round the church to the House of the Preaching Friars, and got her a bowl of milk. While Kristin was feeding her foster-child, they talked together, but their talk went but haltingly.

"So long a time has gone by, and so much has befallen since last we met," she said sorrowfully. "And heavy to bear for you, too, the tidings must have been — the tidings of your brother?"

"God be merciful to his poor soul," whispered Brother Gunnulf in a shaken voice.

Only when she asked about her sons at Tautra did Gunnulf speak something more freely. With great gladness had the convent welcomed these two novices, come of the best kindreds in the land. Nikulaus seemed to have such excellent gifts of mind and made such strides in learning and godliness that the abbot must needs call to mind his noble forefather, the Church's well-gifted champion, Bishop Nikulaus Arnessön. That was in the first days. But a while after the brothers had taken the cowl, Nikulaus had misbehaved him grievously, and had wrought much trouble in the cloister. Gunnulf knew not the causes of the trouble fully — *one* was that Abbot Johannes would not suffer that young brothers should be ordained priests before they were full thirty years old, and he would not depart from this rule for Nikulaus' behoof. And as the reverend father deemed that Nikulaus read and pondered more than sorted with his measure of spiritual ripeness, and that he was breaking down his health with pious exercises, he thought fit to send him to one of the cloister's cattle-farms on Inderö, to work there, under some of the elder monks, at the planting of an apple orchard. Then, 'twas said, Nikulaus had broken out into flat disobedience to the abbot's behests, had charged his brethren with having wasted the cloister's goods in high living, with sluggishness in the worship of God, and with looseness in their talk. The matter, said Gunnulf, was kept, for the most part, within the convent walls, as was but reason; but 'twas said, too, that he had defied the brother whom the abbot appointed to chasten him. For some time he had lain in the penitentiary cell, Gunnulf knew, but since then he had humbled him, when the abbot threatened to part him from Brother Björgulf, and to send one of them to Munkabu — 'twas like it had been the blind brother that egged him on. But on this threat Nikulaus had grown meek and contrite.

" 'Tis their father's nature that is in them," said Gunnulf bitterly. "None could look that my brother's sons should find it easy to learn obedience, or that they should show steadfastness in the godly life — "

" 'Tis as like to be their heritage from their mother," answered Kristin, sorrowfully. "Disobedience was the chief of my sins, Gunnulf — and I too was unsteadfast. All the days of my life have I longed both to go the right way and to follow my own wildered paths as well — "

"Erlend's wildered paths, mean you?" said the monk, darkly. " 'Twas not once only that my brother lured you astray, Kristin; I trow he lured you astray each day you lived with him. Such forgetfulness he wrought in you that you remembered not, when you thought thoughts you yourself blushed at, that you could not hide the thoughts of your heart from an all-knowing God — "

Kristin gazed before her.

"Now I know not, Gunnulf, if you are right in this — I wot not that I have forgotten at any time that God saw into my heart — all the greater, belike, is my sin. And, moreover, 'tis not so, as you deem perchance, that I had most need to blush for my immodest wantonness and for my weakness — rather must I feel shame that my thoughts of my husband were many a time more bitter than the poison of serpents. But like enough it must needs have come to this — 'twas you who once said to me, that they who have loved one another with the fieriest desire come in the end to be as two vipers biting each other's tails.

"But it has been my comfort in these years, Gunnulf, as often as I thought how 'twas Erlend's lot to go before God's judgment-seat unhouseled and unholpen, struck down with wrath in his heart and blood upon his hands — that *he* did not grow to be — what you said, and what I became. He bore in mind anger, and wrong done him, as little as he bore aught else in mind — Gunnulf, he was so fair and he looked so peaceful when I had laid his body out — I wot that the all-knowing God knows that Erlend never bore a grudge to any man, for any cause — "

The brother gazed at her with wide-opened eyes. Then he nodded.

After a while the monk asked:

"Know you that Eiliv Serkssön is priest and counsellor to the nuns out at Rein?"

"No?" said Kristin, beaming with gladness.

"I deemed 'twas therefore you had chosen to enter there," said Gunnulf. Soon after, he said that he must go back to his cloister.

The first nocturn was begun already when Kristin came into the church. In the nave and about all the altars there was a throng of folk, but one of the vergers, who saw that she bore a most sickly child in her arms, pushed her forward through the press till she came right in front among the many cripples and sick folk in sorest need, who were gathered in the middle of the church under the great dome and in full view of the choir.

Many hundred lights burned in the church — the church servants took the pilgrims' tapers and fixed them upon the little hillock-shaped towers studded with spikes, that were set up all down the nave and aisles. As the light of day died out behind the many-coloured panes of glass, the church grew warm with the smell of the burning wax, and ere long it was filled, too, with the sour stench from the rags of the sick folk and the poor.

When the song of the choir soared under the vaulting, and the organ pealed, and the noise of flutes, drums, and stringed instruments resounded, Kristin understood why it might be that the church was called a ship — in the mighty house of stone all these folk seemed to be on board a vessel, and the singing was like the noise of the sea whereon it was upborne. Ever and anon it came to rest, as when the billows are stilled, and a single man's voice bore the lesson out over the listening throng.

The close-packed faces grew paler and more weary as the wake-night wore on. Scarce one went out between the services, not at least of those who had places midway of the church. Between the nocturns they dozed or prayed. The child slept well-nigh the whole night — once or twice Kristin had to lull it a little, or give it milk from a wooden flask that Gunnulf had gotten for her from the cloister.

The meeting with Erlend's brother had stirred her strangely — the more so that every step of the road hither had brought her nearer and nearer home to the memory of the dead man. She had *thought* little on him in these last years, while her work for her growing sons gave her little time for memory of her own fate — none the less the thought of him had been ever, as it were, close behind her, only that she had not had the time to turn her towards it. Now she seemed to see her soul as it had been in these years; it had lived as folk live on a manor through the busy summer half-year, when they move out of the great hall and bide in the storehouse loft. All day long they go to and fro past the winter hall, never thinking of going in thither, though they have but to lay their hand on a latch and push open a door. And when at last some day they have an errand thither, the house has grown strange and almost solemn, because of the air of loneliness and quiet that has come to it —

But while she was speaking with him who was the last living witness of the interplay 'twixt seed-time and harvest in her life with the dead man, it seemed to her that she had come to look out over her life in a new way: as when a man comes up on a height above his native place where he has never climbed before, and looks down from it into his own dale. He knows each farm and fence, each thicket, the gully of each beck; but he seems to see for the first time how these things all lie on the face of the land. And seeing things in this new way, she had found all at once words that swept away both her bitterness against Erlend and her terrors for his soul, borne off by sudden death. Ill-will he had never borne to any; she saw it now, and God had seen it always.

So at last she was come so far that she deemed she could look on her own life as from the uppermost step of a glen. Now did her road lead down into the darkling valley, but ere she took that road she had been given grace to understand that, in the loneliness of the cloister and at the gates of death, there waited for her one who had ever beheld the life of mankind as men's parishes look, seen from the mountain brow. He had seen the sin and sorrow, the love and hate, in the hearts of men, as one sees the rich manors and the humble cots, the teeming cornfields and the abandoned wastes, all borne on the bosom of the same countryside. And he had descended; his feet had trodden the peopled lands, and stood in palaces and in huts; he had gathered up the sorrows and the sins of rich and poor, and lifted them aloft with him upon a cross. Not my happiness and my pride, but my sin and my sorrow, O my sweet Lord — She looked up where the crucifix stood, uplifted high over the triumphal arch.

— While the morning sun lit up the high-set coloured panes deep among the pillars of the choir, and a glory, as of red and brown and green and blue gems, dimmed the light from the tapers on the altar and from the golden shrine behind, Kristin listened to the last vigil — the matins. She knew that the lessons in this service told of God's healing miracles through the power vouchsafed to his faithful knight King Olav Haraldssön. She lifted the sick stranger-child up towards the choir, and prayed for it.

But she was so icy chill from her long vigil in the cold of the church that her teeth chattered; and she felt faint from fasting. The smell of the many folk, and the sickening fumes of the sick and the beggars, mingled with the smoke of the wax-candles and sank down in a heavy, strangely greasy and clammy cloud upon the people kneeling on the stone floor, cold in the cold morning. But a fat, kind, cheerful countrywoman who had sat dozing a little against the foot of the pillar just behind them, with a bear-skin below her and another over her lame legs, awoke now and drew Kristin's weary head down

upon her wide lap: "Rest a little now, sister — you have
need of it, I trow — "

Kristin slept in the strange woman's lap, and dreamed:

She stepped over the threshold of the old hearth-room
house at home. She was young and unwed, for she saw her
own uncovered thick brown plaits hanging forward over
her shoulders. She was in company with Erlend, for he
was even now drawing him upright, after going through
the doorway before her.

By the hearth her father was sitting, binding arrow-heads
on the shafts — he had his lap full of bunches of sinew
string, and on either side of him on the bench lay piles of
arrow-heads and sharpened shafts. Just as they stepped in,
he bent him forward over the heap of embers and made
to take up the little three-legged metal cup that he ever
used to melt resin in. But swiftly he caught back his hand,
shook it in the air, and then he stuck his burnt finger-tips
into his mouth and sucked them, while he turned his head
towards her and Erlend, and looked up at them with a
wrinkled brow and a smile about his lips —

Then she awoke, her face wet with tears.

She kneeled through the High Mass, when the Archbishop himself served the holy rite before the high altar.
The clouds of incense rolled through the echoing church,
where many-coloured sunlight was mingled now with the
wax tapers' shining; the fresh, spicy scent of the frank-
incense spread abroad and overcame the smell of poverty
and sickness. With a heart that seemed bursting with ruth
for the flock of the infirm and the needy in whose midst
God had set her, she prayed in a rush of sisterly tenderness
for all who were poor as she, and who suffered as she herself had suffered —

— "I will arise and go to my father — "

6

THE CONVENT stood on a rising ground near the fjord, so
that, with most winds, the roll of the surf on the beach
drowned the soughing of the pine woods that covered
great part of the ridge's slopes, north and west, and hid
the sea from sight.

Kristin had seen the church tower above the trees when she sailed by with Erlend, but the pilgrimage out to the nunnery that his forefather had founded, which Erlend had sometimes said they must make, had never come about. She had never landed at Rein Cloister before she came to make it her abiding-place.

She had thought that the life here would be like that she knew at the nunneries in Oslo or at Bakke, but here much was otherwise than there, and 'twas far more quiet. Here the sisters were truly dead to the world. Lady Ragnhild, the abbess, made it her boast that 'twas five years since she had been in to the market town, and as long since some of her nuns had set foot outside the bounds of the cloister.

There were no children here to be nurtured, and, at the time Kristin came to Rein, there were no novices either; so long was it since any young maid had sought to be taken into the sisterhood, that 'twas six winters already since the last, Sister Borghild Marcellina, had taken the veil. Youngest in age was Sister Turid, but she had been sent hither in her seventh year by her father's father, who was priest of Clement's Church, an exceeding strict and earnest man, and the child had had a shrivelled hand from birth and was besides something of a cripple, so she had donned the habit as soon as she reached the age for it. Now she was thirty years old, and sadly frail, but she had a lovesome face, and from the first day she came to the cloister Kristin took great joy in serving her, for she deemed that Sister Turid minded her of her own little sister Ulvhild, who died so young.

Sira Eiliv said that low birth should assuredly not stand in the way of any maids who were minded to come hither to serve God. Nevertheless, so it had been that, ever since the convent had been set up, few but the daughters or widows of mighty and high-born men of the Trondheim country entered there. But during the evil and restless days that had been in the realm since King Haakon Haalegg, of blessed memory, died, piety seemed to have fallen away greatly amongst the great nobles — now 'twas the daughters of townsmen and well-to-do farmers for the most part who turned their thoughts to a convent life. And they betook them rather to Bakke, where many of them had been nurtured in godliness and womanly handicrafts, and where the sisters for the most were come of homely people — there, too, the rule was not so strict, and the cloister lay not so far removed from the highway.

Howbeit, 'twas not often that Kristin had the chance to speak with Sira Eiliv, and she soon saw that the priest's duties and his footing in the cloister were both toilsome and ticklish. Though Rein was a rich cloister and the sisterhood scarce numbered half as many nuns as the foundation might well have fed, yet its money affairs were in great disorder, and it was hard put to it to meet its outgoings. The last three abbesses had been more pious than worldly-wise; none the less they and their convent had fought, with tooth and claw, to make good their freedom from the Archbishop's obedience — so far did they go in this that they would not even take counsel proffered in fatherly goodwill. And the brethren of their order from Tautra and Munkabu, chosen to be priests of the convent church, had ever been old men, that no colour might be given to evil speaking, and their guidance of the cloister's worldly weal had been none too skilful. When King Skule built the fair stone church and gave his udal manor to the cloister, the houses were first built of wood; and they had burnt down thirty winters agone. Lady Audhild, who was abbess then, began the building of them up again in stone; much was done in her time for the betterment of the church, and the goodly convent hall was built. She had journeyed also to the general chapter at the mother house of the order, Tart * in Burgundy, and from that journey she had brought back the noble ivory tower that stood in the choir near the high altar — a fitting tabernacle for God's body, the church's greatest adornment and the nuns' pride and darling treasure. Lady Audhild left behind her the fairest renown for piety and worth, but her unskilful conduct of the building works, and her unwise dealings with the convent lands, had wrought mischief to the cloister's welfare and the later abbesses had not had the skill to repair the ill.

How it had come about that Sira Eiliv was sent thither as priest and counsellor, Kristin never learned; but so much she understood, that from the first the abbess and the

---

* See Note 7.

sisters had met him, as a secular, with misliking and mistrust; and so 'twas Sira Eiliv's task at Rein to be the nuns' priest and spiritual guide, to set the husbandry of the estates on its feet again, and bring order into the convent's money affairs, while deferring to the abbess's overheadship, the sisters' right of self-governance, and the right of the abbot of Tautra to oversee all, and keeping friends with the other priest at the church, a monk from Tautra. His age and his name for unstained purity of walk and conversation, humble fear of God, and skill both of the canon law and of the law of the land, stood him in good stead, but he had to walk most warily in all his goings. Together with the other priest and the church servants, he dwelt in a little house lying north-east from the cloister. 'Twas there, too, that the monks lodged who came out from Tautra on divers occasions. Kristin knew that, if she lived so long, some time, when Nikulaus had come to be ordained priest, she should hear her eldest son say Mass in the convent church.

Kristin Lavransdatter had been received at first as a commoner.* But after she had taken a vow of chastity and obedience to the abbess and the sisterhood, before Lady Ragnhild and the sisters, in presence of Sira Eiliv and two monks from Tautra, and, in token that she forwent all rights over worldly goods, had put her seal into Sira Eiliv's hands to be broken in pieces, she was given leave to wear a garb like to the sisters', but without the scapular; a grey-white woollen robe, white head-linen and black veil. The intent was that, after some time had gone by, she should seek to be received into the sisterhood as a professed nun.

But 'twas still a hard matter for her not to think overmuch on what had been. To read aloud during meal-times in the refectory, Sira Eiliv had written out in the Norse tongue a book of the life of Christ, made by the general of the Minorites, the most learned and godly doctor Bonaventura. And while Kristin listened to it, and her eyes filled with tears as she thought how blessed they must be who could love Christ and His mother, pains and afflictions, poverty and humility, in such wise as was there written — yet all the time she could not but remember the

---

* See *The Bridal Wreath (The Garland)*, Note 13.

day at Husaby when Gunnulf and Sira Eiliv had shown her the Latin book from which this was taken. 'Twas a thick little book, written upon parchment so thin and shining white that she had never believed calfskin could be wrought so fine; and there were the fairest pictures and capital letters in it, the colours glowing like jewels against the gold. And while she looked, Gunnulf spoke laughingly, and Sira Eiliv gave assent with his quiet smile — of how the buying of this book left them so penniless, they had to sell their clothes and get them meat along with the alms-folk in a cloister, till they came to know that some Norse churchmen were come to Paris, and made shift to raise a loan from them.

When, after matins, the sisters went back to the dormi-tory, Kristin would tarry behind in the church. On summer mornings 'twas sweet and delightsome to her there — but in winter it was bitterly cold, and she was fearful in the dark among all the tombstones, even though she kept her eyes bent fixedly on the little lamp that burned always before the ivory tower with the host in it. But, winter or summer, while she tarried in her corner of the nuns' choir, she thought of how Naakkve and Björgulf were now watching and praying for their father's soul; and that 'twas Nikulaus who had begged her to join with them in these prayers and penitential psalms each morning after matins.

Ever, ever she saw before her those two, as she had seen them that grey day of rain she went out to the monks' cloister: when Nikulaus stood before her in the parlour of a sudden, marvellous tall and strange in the grey-white monk's habit, with his hands thrust under the scapular, her son, and yet so changed. 'Twas most of all his likeness to his father that moved her so deeply — 'twas as though she saw Erlend in monk's garb.

Whilst they sat talking together, and he had her tell him of all that had befallen at the manor since he took his way from home, she was waiting, waiting. At length she asked fearfully if Björgulf would not come soon.

"I know not, mother," answered her son. A little after he said: "For Björgulf it has been a hard struggle to bow beneath his cross and serve God — And it seemed to af-fright him when he heard that you were here — lest too many thoughts should be called up again — "

Thereafter she sat on, deathly sad, gazing at Nikulaus while he talked. He was much sunburned in the face, and his hands were worn with toil — he said, with a little smile, now had he had to learn after all how to guide a plough and work with scythe and sickle. In the hostel that night she could not sleep, and she hasted to the church when the bell rang to matins. But the monks stood so that there were but few whose faces she could see, and her sons were not amongst these.

But next day she walked in the garden with a lay brother who worked there, and he showed her the many rare plants and trees it was renowned for. While they so walked, the clouds broke, the sun came forth, and with it the scent of celery and onion and thyme, and the clumps of yellow lilies and blue columbines that decked the corners of the beds glittered with great raindrops. And then came her sons; they came forth, both of them, from the little arched door of the stone house. And Kristin deemed that she had a foretaste of the joy of Paradise when she saw the two tall brothers in light-hued raiment come down towards her on the path beneath the apple trees.

Yet they spoke not much together; Björgulf was silent well-nigh all the time. He had become a giant in frame, now he was full-grown. And it seemed as though in the long time they had been sundered her sight had grown keener — now, for the first time, she understood to the full what the battle was that this son of hers had fought, that doubtless he was still fighting, while he grew so great and strong of limb, while his inward sight waxed keen, and he felt his eyesight grow dim —

Once he asked after his foster-mother, Frida Styrkaars-datter. Kristin told him that she was wed.

"God bless her," said the monk. "She was a good woman — to me she was a good and faithful foster-mother."

"Ay, methinks almost she was more a mother to you than was I," said Kristin, sadly. "Little must you have marked of the mother's heart in me, when you were tried so sorely in your youth."

Björgulf answered low:

"I thank God, none the less, that the enemy was never suffered to bow me to such unmanliness as to try the mother's heart in you — though I felt it, of a truth — but

I saw that you bore too heavy a burden already — and after God 'twas Nikulaus here who saved me, those times I was like to fall into the Tempter's power —"

No more was said of this, nor of whether they were happy in the cloister, nor of how 'twas said they had done amiss and brought disgrace upon themselves. But it seemed to give them great joy when they heard 'twas their mother's purpose to take the veil in Rein convent.

When, after this hour of prayer, Kristin went back through the dormitory and saw the sisters sleeping two and two on sacks of straw in the beds, clad in the habits which they never put off, she thought how much unlike she must be to these women, who from their youth up had done naught but serve their Maker. The world was a master whom 'twas not easy to fly, when once one had yielded to its dominion. Ay, and in sooth she had not fled the world — she had been cast out, as a hard master drives a worn-out servant from his door — and now she had been taken in here, as a merciful lord takes in an old serving-maid and of his mercy gives her a little work, while he shelters and feeds the worn-out, friendless old creature —

From the nuns' sleeping-house a covered way led to the weaving-house. There Kristin now sat alone, and spun. The nuns of Rein were famed for their linen, and those days in summer and autumn, when all the sisters and lay sisters went to work in the flax-fields, were like feast days in the cloister; but most of all the day the plants were pulled. The nuns were busied in most of their working-hours with making ready the flax, spinning the thread, weaving the linen, and making vestments from it. Here were none who copied or adorned books, as the sisters in Oslo under Lady Groa Guttormsdatter had done with such great skill, nor did they practise much the craft of broidering with silk and gold thread.

In a while she would hear with joy the sounds of the wakening farm-yard. The lay sisters went to the kitchen-house to make ready the food for the serving-folk; the nuns touched not meat nor drink till after the Mass of the day, saving when they were sick. When the bell rang for primes, Kristin went to the sick-ward, if any lay there, to take the place of Sister Agata or of whichever other nun was there. Sister Turid, poor soul, lay there often.

Soon, now, she might begin to look forward to the morning meal, which followed after the third hour of prayer and the Mass for the cloister's serving-folk. Each day alike Kristin took joy in this comely and solemn repast. The refectory was timber-built, but a fair hall notwithstanding, and there all the women in the cloister ate together — the nuns at the upper board, where the abbess sat in the high-seat, and where the three old dames who were commoners like herself had also seats — and the lay sisters further down. When the prayer was ended, the meat and drink borne in, and all sat eating and drinking in silence, with still, seemly behaviour, while often one of the sisters read aloud from a book, Kristin would think that, could folk in the world without but take their meals in such goodly wise, they might well come to see more clearly that food and drink are gifts from God, and they would begrudge them less to their fellow-Christians, and think less on scraping together for their own and their children's behoof. But she herself had felt quite otherwise, when she spread her board for a flock of wild, riotous men, amid laughter and uproar, while the dogs snuffed about beneath the board, or thrust up their noses and got a meat bone or a thwack, as the mood of the boys might chance to be.

Travellers seldom came hither. At times a vessel with folk from the nobles' seats around would put in when sailing down or up the fjord, and men and their wives, with children and young folk, would go up to Rein to greet a kinswoman among the sisters. Then there were the bailiffs from the cloister's farms and fisheries, and a messenger from Tautra now and then. At the feast-tides that were kept with greatest state — Mary Virgin's Mass days, Corpus Christi, and the day of Saint Andrew the Apostle — folk sought the nuns' church from the parishes on both sides the fjord, but otherwise 'twas but those of the cloister's tenants and work-folk who dwelt nearest that came thither to the Masses. They took up but little room in the great church.

Then there were the poor — the alms-folk who had their doles of ale and meat at fixed times under rich folk's testaments, in requital of yearly masses for the donors' souls — and who, besides, drifted up to Rein well-nigh

daily, sat by the kitchen-house wall and ate, and when the
nuns came out into the courtyard made up to them to
talk of their sorrows and troubles. Sick folks, cripples,
and lepers wandered out and in — there were many here
who suffered from leprosy, but 'twas ever so in the sea
parishes, said Lady Ragnhild. Tenants came to crave abate-
ments in their rents or grace time for their payments, and
these had ever much to tell of hardships and adversity.
The more wretched and hapless these folk were, the more
open and unashamed they were in telling the sisters of
their condition, though most often they blamed others for
their ill-fortune, and had pious words ever on their lips.
'Twas not strange that the nuns' talk at recreation and in
the weaving-house ran much on these folks' lives — nay,
Sister Turid avowed to Kristin that when the nuns met in
convent to take counsel together concerning bargains and
the like, the talk would often wander, and turn to gossip
about the folk who were mixed in the matters in hand.
Kristin marked, by what the sisters said, that they knew
little of what they talked of, save what they had heard
from the folks themselves or from the lay servants who
had been out into the parish. They were passing easy of
belief, whether their underlings praised themselves or
spoke ill of their neighbours — and she thought with anger
of all the times she had heard godless lay folk, ay, even a
beggar monk like Brother Arngrim, cry down the nunneries for dens of scandal, and tax the sisters with greedy
swallowing of waif rumours and immodest gossip. The
very folk who came hither and dinned Lady Ragnhild's
ears, or any of the sisters' they could get speech of, full
of idle talk, would be the first to blame the nuns for talking
among themselves of the tidings that reached them from
the world they had renounced. It seemed to her 'twas the
same with the talk of the convent ladies' luxurious living
— it came from folk's mouths who had many a time had
both morning bite and breakfast at the sisters' hands, while
these servants of God watched, prayed and laboured fasting, ere they all met for their first solemn meal in the
refectory.

So Kristin served the nuns with loving reverence in the
time that must go by before she might make profession.
A good nun she could never be, she thought; she had scattered abroad all too much what gift she might have had

for meditation and piety — but she would be as meek and
as steadfast as God would give her grace to be. 'Twas now
well on in the summer of the year 1349; she had dwelt in
the Rein convent two years, and ere Yule-tide came she
was to take the veil. And the glad tidings came to her that,
for her dedication, both her sons would come out thither
in Abbot Johannes' train. Brother Björgulf had said, when
he heard of his mother's purpose:

"Now is my dream like to come true — I have dreamed
twice this year that before Yule we should both see her —
though *wholly* as it appeared in my dream it cannot be, for
in my dream I *saw* her."

Brother Nikulaus, too, had been overjoyed. But at the
same time she heard other tidings of him that were not so
good. He had sorely mishandled certain farmers up the
fjord near Steinker — they were at odds with the cloister
over some fishing-rights, and when the monks came upon
them one night while they were busy breaking up the
cloister's salmon weir, brother Nikulaus had hurt one man
grievously and flung another into the river and there-
withal had sinned heinously in the matter of cursing and
swearing.

7

A FEW days after, Kristin went to the pine woods with
some of the nuns and lay sisters, to gather moss for green
dye. This moss is somewhat hard to come by, growing
most on wind-fallen trees and dry branches. So the women
soon scattered through the woods, and lost one another
from sight in the fog.

For some days now this unwonted weather had held —
windless, with a thick mist, that showed a strange leaden
blue out over the sea and away against the hill-sides, when
now and again it thinned so much that the eye caught
glimpses of the country round. Between-whiles it thickened
to a drizzling rain; then again it lightened so much that a
whitish patch showed where the sun hung amid the towering mists. But there brooded ever a strange, heavy warmth,
as of a bath-house, that was unwonted down here by the
fjord, in especial at this time of the year — 'twas two

days before Nativitas Mariæ * — so that all folk talked of
the weather and marvelled what it might betoken.

Kristin sweated in the lifeless, damp heat, and the
thought of this tidings that she had heard of Naakkve
weighed upon her breast. She was come down to the skirts
of the wood, to the log fence by the path up from the sea,
and, as she stood there scraping moss from the fence, Sira
Eiliv came riding homewards through the fog. He stopped
his horse and said some words of the weather, and so they
fell in talk. Then she asked the priest if he knew aught
of this matter of Naakkve — though she knew 'twas in
vain, for Sira Eiliv ever made as though he had no knowledge of the inside affairs of the Tautra cloister.

"I trow, Kristin, you need have no fear that 'twill hinder
his coming hither in the winter, this mischance," said the
priest. " 'Tis that you feared, belike?"

" 'Tis more than that, Sira Eiliv. I fear me Naakkve never
was meant to be a monk."

"Think you that you dare judge of such things?" asked
the priest, bending his brows. He lighted down from his
horse, bound it to a fence log, and leaned over the fence,
gazing fixedly and searchingly at the woman. Kristin said:

"I fear 'tis hard for Naakkve to bow beneath the rule
of the order — and he was so young when he withdrew
him from the world, he knew not what he forwent, and
knew not his own mind. All that befell in his young days
— the loss of his father's heritage, the sight of the discord
'twixt his father and mother, that ended in Erlend's death
— so wrought in him that he lost all heart to live in the
world. But I could never mark that it made him godly — "

"You could not? — It may well have been as hard for
Nikulaus as for many another good monk to bow him
beneath the order's rule; hot of mood is he, and a young
man — too young, maybe, to have understood, ere he
turned his back on the world, that the world is as hard a
taskmaster as any other lord, and in the end a tyrant without mercy. Of that, I ween, you yourself can judge,
sister —

"And if so it be that Naakkve entered into the cloister
more for his brother's sake than from love for his Maker
— none the less I believe not that God will let it go un-

---

* 8th September.

requited that he took up the cross for his brother's sake. God's mother Mary, whom I know that Naakkve honoured and loved from his boyhood up, will surely show him clearly one day, that her son came hither to this earthly home to be his brother and bear the cross for him —

" — Nay — " The horse whinnied, with its nose against the priest's breast; he caressed it, while he said, half to himself: "From his childhood up my Nikulaus had a wondrous gift of loving and of suffering — I deem that he should be right well fitted for a monk.

"But you, Kristin," he said, turning to the woman, "you should have seen so much now, methinks, that you might trust in God Almighty with a surer trust. Have you not yet understood that He bears up every soul so long as the soul lets not go its hold on Him? Think you, woman, child that you still are in your old age, that 'tis God punishing the sin, when you must reap sorrow and humiliation because you followed your lusts and your overweening pride over paths that God has forbidden His children to tread? Would you say that *you* had punished your children if they scalded their hands when they took up the boiling kettle you had forbidden them to touch, or if the slippery ice broke under them that you had warned them not to go upon? Have you not understood, when the brittle ice broke beneath you — that you were drawn under each time you let go God's hand, and you were saved from out the deep each time you called on Him? Was not the love that bound you and your father in the flesh together, even when you defied him and set your wilfulness against his will, was it not a comfort and a solace none the less when you had to reap the fruits of your disobedience to him?

"Have you not understood yet, sister, that God has helped you each time you prayed, though you prayed half-heartedly and with feigning, and helped you much beyond what you prayed for? You loved God as you loved your father, not so hotly as you loved your own will, yet none the less so that you ever sorrowed much when you forsook Him — and therefore His mercy towards you suffered good to grow, amidst the evil harvest you must needs reap from the seed of your stubborn will —

"Your sons — two of them He took to Himself while

they were innocent little children; for them you need
never fear. And the others have turned out well — even
if they have not turned out as *you* would have had them.
Doubtless Lavrans deemed the like of you —

"And your husband, Kristin — God be merciful to his
soul — I wot you have blamed him in your heart early and
late for his reckless unwisdom. Yet meseems it had been
much harder for a proud woman to remember that Erlend
Nikulaussön led you with him through shame and deceit
and blood-guiltiness, if you had seen but *once* that the man
could do aught with cold contrivance. And almost I believe, too, 'twas because you were steadfast in anger and
hardness as in love, that you were able to hold Erlend
fast so long as you both lived — with him 'twas out of
sight, out of mind, with all things else but you. God help
Erlend; I fear me he never had the wit to know true
repentance for his sins — yet did your husband repent
and sorrow truly for his deeds wherein he sinned against
you. That lesson, we may dare to trust, has profited Erlend now that he is dead."

Kristin stood still and silent; neither did Sira Eiliv say
any more. He loosed the reins, gave her a "Peace be with
you," mounted his horse, and rode away.

When, a little after, she came back to the cloister, Sister
Ingrid met her at the door with word that one of her sons
was come to greet her — Skule he called himself; he was
at the parlour gateway.

He was sitting talking with his boat-folk — he sprang
up when his mother came to the door. Ah, she knew her
own by the quick nimbleness — the small head, borne high
above broad shoulders, the long-limbed, slender form.
Beaming with joy she went towards him — but she stopped
suddenly and caught her breath at the sight of his face —
oh, who had done this to her fair son — ?

His upper-lip showed as though kneaded out thin — a
blow must have crushed it, and afterwards it had grown
together flat and long and misshapen, barred with a net-
work of white scars; it had left his mouth twisted awry,
fixed in what seemed a sneering grimace — and the bone
of his nose had been broken and had set again crooked.
He lisped a little when he spoke — he wanted one front
tooth, and another was blue-black and dead.

Skule reddened under his mother's gaze: "I trow you know me not, mother?" He laughed a little, and passed a finger over his lip — 'twas not sure whether he pointed to his blemish, or whether 'twas but a chance movement.

"So long parted, I trow, we have not been, my son, that your mother should not know you again," Kristin answered calmly, with an untroubled smile.

Skule Erlendssön was come two days before with a light sloop from Björgvin, with letters from Bjarne Erlingssön for the Archbishop and the Treasurer of Nidaros. Later in the day, mother and son walked in the garden beneath the ash trees, and, now that they were alone, he gave his mother the news of his brothers:

Lavrans was in Iceland still. — His mother knew not even that he had gone thither! Ay, said Skule, he had met his youngest brother in Oslo the winter before at the gathering of the nobles; he was with Jammælt Halvardssön. But, as she knew, the boy had ever had a longing to come abroad and look about him in the world, and so he took service with the Bishop of Skaalholt and sailed away —

Ay, he himself had gone in Sir Bjarne's train to Sweden, and thereafter to the war in Russia. His mother shook her head gently — she had known naught of *that* either! Skule had liked the life, he said, laughing — it had given him his chance to greet the old friends his father spoke so much of — Karelians, Ingrians, Russians. No, that brave scar of honour was not won in war — he laughed a little — ay, 'twas in a fight; the fellow that gave it him would never have need now to beg his bread. More of it, or of the war, Skule seemed to have little mind to tell. Now he was captain of Sir Bjarne's horsemen at Björgvin, and the knight had promised to get back for him some of the manors his father had owned in Orkladal, that were now under the Crown — but Kristin saw that Skule's great, steel-grey eyes took on a strange, dark look as he said this.

"You deem you cannot put much faith in such a promise?" asked his mother.

"No, no." Skule shook his head. "The deeds are even now being drawn. Sir Bjarne has kept all he promised when I took service with him — calls me kinsman and friend. Almost I have the like place in his household that

Ulf had at home with us" — he laughed; and the laugh became his marred face ill.

But he was the comeliest of men in bodily form, now that he was full-grown — he wore garments of a new-fashioned cut, tight hose and a small close-fitting *kothardi* that barely reached to the middle of his thigh and was buttoned with small brass buttons all down the front — it showed up in well-nigh unseemly wise his body's supple strength. He looked as though he went about in his under-garments, thought the mother. But his forehead and his comely eyes were not changed.

"You look as though something were weighing on you, Skule," the mother ventured.

"No, no, no." 'Twas but the weather, he said, shaking himself. There was a strange red-brown glow in the fog as the hidden sun went down. The church stood out above the garden tree-tops, strange and dark, melting into the dull red mist. They had had to row the whole fjord, from the very mouth, 'twas so calm, said Skule. Then again he shifted a little in his clothes, and began to speak once more of his brothers.

He had been an errand south in the land for Sir Bjarne this spring, so he could give her fresh tidings of Ivar and Gaute, for he had ridden up overland and made his way across the fells from Vaagaa home to the west country. All was well with Ivar; they had two little sons at Rogn-heim, Erlend and Gamal, comely children. "But at Jörund-gaard I chanced upon a christening-ale — and Jofrid and Gaute deemed, as you were dead to the world now, they might name the little maid after you; Jofrid is so proud that you are her mother-in-law — ay, you laugh, but, now that you are not to dwell under one roof, be sure Jofrid knows well it has a brave sound when she talks of 'my mother-in-law, Kristin Lavransdatter.' But I gave Kristin Gautesdatter my best finger-ring, for she has such winsome eyes; almost I deem she will be like you — "

Kristin smiled sadly:

"Soon will you bring me to think, my Skule, that my sons deem me as great and good as old folk are wont to be, once they are beneath the sod."

"Speak not so, mother," said the man, with a strange vehemence. Then he laughed a little: "You wot well that all we brothers, ever since we were breeched, deemed you

were the bravest and most high-minded of women —
though you clinched us full tightly under your wings
many a time, and we flapped back, maybe, somewhat hard
again ere we scaped from the nest —

" — But it has proved, sure enough, that you were right
in deeming Gaute the one of us brothers that was born to
be a chieftain," said he, laughing loud.

"No need to mock me for that now, Skule," said Kristin — and Skule saw that his mother flushed with a young,
tender red. At that he laughed all the more:

" 'Tis true, my mother — Gaute Erlendssön of Jörundgaard is grown a mighty man in the northern dales. This
theft of his bride brought him such renown" — Skule
laughed loudly, with the laughter that so ill became his
ravaged mouth. "They sing a ballad of it; ay, they sing
now that he took the maid with iron and with steel, and
he fought her kinsmen three livelong days on the mountain — and the feast that Sir Sigurd held at Sundbu, and
whereat he made peace betwixt the kinsmen with silver
and with gold, for that too Gaute gets all the honour in
the ballad — and it seems to make no matter that 'tis all
a lie; Gaute rules the whole parish and somewhat beyond
— and Jofrid rules Gaute — "

Kristin shook her head, with her little sad smile. But she
grew young of face as she gazed on Skule. Now seemed it
to her that *he* was most like his father — after all, the
young warrior with the ravaged face had the most of
Erlend's gallant mettle — and that he had so early had to
take his fate into his own hands had given him a cool
firmness of spirit that filled his mother's heart with a
strange security. With Sira Eiliv's words of the day before in mind, she saw all at once — fearful as she had been
for her headstrong sons, and hard as she had often laid
hand upon them by reason of her dread — yet had she
been much less content with her children had they been
meek and unmanly.

Then she asked again and again of her grandson, little
Erlend — but him had Skule given small heed to, it
seemed — ay, he was strong and comely, and was wont to
have his way at all times.

The uncanny glow in the fog, as of clotted blood, faded
away; the dark was falling. The church's bells began to
ring; Kristin and her son rose. Then Skule took her hand:

"Mother," he said in a low voice. "Mind you that I once lifted my hand against you? I threw a bat at you in anger, and it struck you on the brow — mind you of it? Mother, while we two are all alone, tell me that you have forgiven me!"

Kristin drew a long breath — ay, she remembered. She had bidden the twins go on an errand up to the sæter — but when she came out into the courtyard the horse was there, grazing, with the pack-saddle on its back, and her sons running about and playing at ball. When she chid them angrily for this, Skule flung the bat from him in a towering rage — But she remembered best what came after — How, as she went about after, one eye quite closed by the swelling of the lid — the brothers looked at her and at Skule, and shrank from him as though he were a leper — though Naakkve had beaten him mercilessly first. And Skule wandered away, and sat boiling with defiance and shame under a hard, scornful mien. But when in the evening she was standing putting off her clothes in the dark, he stole up to her — said nothing, but took her hand and kissed it. And, when she touched his shoulder, he cast his arms about her neck and pressed his cheek to hers — his was cool and soft and still a little rounded; she felt 'twas a child's cheek still — he was but a child, after all, this headstrong, fiery youth—

"That have I, Skule — so fully, that God alone knows, for I cannot tell you, how fully I have forgiven it you, my son!"

A moment she stood with her hand on his shoulder. Then he grasped her wrists, gripped them so tight that she winced with pain — and the next moment he flung his arms about her with the same passionate, fearful, bashful tenderness as that other time.

"My son — what ails you?" whispered the mother, in fear.

She felt in the dark that the man shook his head. Then he let her go, and together they went upward to the church.

During the Mass Kristin called to mind that she had forgotten to bring in blind Lady Aasa's cloak, from where they had sat together on the bench outside the priest's door that morning. After the service she went round to fetch it.

Under the archway stood Sira Eiliv, lanthorn in hand, and Skule. "He died as we came alongside the wharf," she heard Skule say, in a strangely wild, despairing voice.

"Who?"

Both men started violently when they saw her.

"One of my ship-folk," said Skule, low.

Kristin looked from one to the other. At the sight of their blank, strained faces in the lanthorn's glimmer she broke unwittingly into a little cry of fear. The priest set his teeth in his under-lip — she saw that his chin quivered a little.

" 'Twere best, my son, you should tell your mother. Better that we all make us ready to bear it, if 'tis God's will this folk too shall be awaked by so hard a — " But Skule uttered a kind of groan and said no word; and on that the priest spoke: "Pestilence has come to Björgvin, Kristin — The great and deathly sickness that we have heard say is laying waste the lands in the world around — "

"The black death — ?" whispered Kristin.

"It boots not to try to tell you how things were in Björgvin when I sailed from there," said Skule. "None can think it that has not seen it. At first Sir Bjarne took the hardest measures to quench the fire where it broke out, away in the houses around Jons cloister; he would have cut off the whole Nordnes from the town with a chain of his men-at-arms, though the monks of the Michael cloister threatened him with the Church's ban — There came an English ship that had the pest aboard, and he would not suffer them to unload the lading or to leave the ship; every man on the sloop died, and then he had her scuttled. But some of the wares had already been brought to land, and some of the burghers smuggled more ashore one night — and the friars of the Jons church stood to it that the dying must have ghostly comfort — Then folk began to die throughout all the town, so 'twas bootless, we saw — Now is there not a living soul in the city save the bearers of the dead — all flee the town that can, but the pest goes with them — "

"O Jesus Christus!"

"Mother — mind you the last time 'twas lemming-year

at home in Sil? The throngs that rolled along all the roads
and paths — mind you how they lay and died in every
bush, and rotted, and poisoned every runnel with stench
and festering foulness — ?" He clenched his fists; his
mother shuddered:

"Lord, have mercy on us all — Praise be to God and
Mary Virgin that you were sent hither even now, my
Skule — "

The man ground his teeth together in the dark:

"So said we too, my men and I, the morning we hoisted
sail and stood down Vägen out to sea. When we were
come north to Moldö Sound, the first fell sick. We bound
stones to his feet and a cross upon his breast when he was
dead, vowed a mass for his soul when we came to Nidaros,
and cast his body into the sea — God forgive us. We put
in to shore with the next two and got them help for their
souls, and Christian burial — for 'tis bootless to flee from
fate. The fourth died as we pulled into the river, and the
fifth last night — "

"Is it needful that you go back to the town?" asked his
mother a little later. "Can you not bide here?"

Skule shook his head, with a joyless laugh:

" — Oh, soon, methinks, 'twill matter naught where one
is. Useless to be afeared — a man in dread is half dead. But
would that I were as old as you are, mother!"

"None knows what they are spared who die young,"
said his mother, low.

"Be still, mother! Think on the time when you yourself
were three-and-twenty winters old — would you have
missed the years you have lived since then — ?"

Fourteen days later Kristin saw for the first time one
sick of the plague. Rumour that the pest was raging in
Nidaros and spreading through the country-side had come
to Rissa — how, 'twas not easy to understand, for folk
kept their houses, and every man fled to the woods or
thickets if he saw an unknown wayfarer on the road; none
would open his door to stranger-folk.

But one morning two fishers came up to the cloister
bearing a man between them in a sail; when at daybreak
they came down to their boat, they had found a strange
bark at the wharf, and in its bottom lay this man, senseless
— he had found strength to make his boat fast, but not to

get out of it to land. The man had been born in a house owned by the cloister, but his kindred had all left the country-side.

The dying man lay on the wet sail in the midst of the grass-grown courtyard; the fishermen stood afar off talking with Sira Eiliv. The lay sisters and serving-women had fled into the houses, but the nuns stood in a cluster at the door of the convent hall — a throng of startled, trembling, despairing old women.

Then Lady Ragnhild stepped forth. She was a little, thin old woman, with a broad, flat face and a little round, red nose like a button; her great, light-brown eyes were red-rimmed, and always watered a little.

"*In nomine patris et filii et spiritus sancti,*" she said in a clear voice, then gulped once. "Bear him into the guest-house — "

And Sister Agata, the eldest of the nuns, elbowed her way through the throng and, unbidden, went with the abbess and the men who bore the sick man.

Kristin went in thither late at night with a remedy she had made ready in the pantry, and Sister Agata asked if she durst bide there and tend the fire.

She deemed herself she should have been hardened — well used as she was to births and deaths, she had seen worse sights than this — she strove to think of all the worst that she had seen — The plague-stricken man sat upright, for he was like to choke with the bloody spittle that he brought up at each coughing-fit — Sister Agata had slung him up in a band passed across his lean, yellow, red-haired chest, and his head hung forward; his face was leaden grey-blue, and fit on fit of shivering shook him. But Sister Agata sat calmly saying over her prayers, and, when the cough took him, she rose, put one arm about his head, and held a cup below his mouth. The sick man roared loud in his agony, rolled his eyes fearfully, and at length thrust a black tongue far out of his gullet, while his lamentable cries died away in pitiful groaning. The nun emptied out the cup into the fire — and while Kristin threw on more juniper, and the wet branches first filled the room with a stinging, yellow smoke, and then burst hissing into flame, she saw Sister Agata settle the cushions and pillows under the sick man's back and arm-pits, wipe his face and cracked brown lips with vinegar-water, and draw the fouled cover-

lid up about his body. 'Twould soon be over and done, she
said to Kristin — he was cold already; at first he had been
hot as fire — but Sira Eiliv had prepared him already for
his going. Then she sat her down beside him, thrust the
calamus root into its place in her cheek with her tongue,
and fell again to prayer.

Kristin strove to overcome the fearful horror that she
felt. She had seen folk die a harder death — But 'twas in
vain — this was the plague, a chastisement from the Lord
for all mankind's secret hardness of heart, of which He
alone had knowledge. She felt as if she were rocked giddily
on a sea, where all the bitter and angry thoughts she had
ever thought towered up like one huge wave amid a thousand, and broke in helpless woe and lamentation. Lord,
help us, for we perish —

Sira Eiliv came in late in the night. He chid Sister Agata
sharply that she had not followed his counsel to bind a
linen cloth dipped in vinegar over her mouth and nose.
She mumbled testily that 'twas of no avail — but both
she and Kristin had now to do as he bade them.

The priest's quietude and steadfastness put some measure
of courage into Kristin — or awoke a feeling of shame —
she ventured out of the juniper smoke and began to help
Sister Agata. A choking stench came from the sick man,
that the smoke availed not to deaden — filth, blood, sour
sweat, and a noisome smell from his throat. She thought
of Skule's words about the lemming swarm; once more
there came upon her the awful longing to fly, though she
knew there was no place whither one could flee from this.
But when once she had taken heart of grace and touched
the dying man, the worst was over; and she helped as well
as she might until he had breathed his last. He was black
in the face already when he died.

The nuns walked in procession, with the holy relics,
crosses, and burning tapers, round the church and the
cloister hill, and all in the parish who could walk or
crawl went with them. But, not many days after, a woman
died near by at Strömmen — and then the deadly sickness broke out at a stroke on every hand throughout the
country-side.

Death and horror and direst need seemed to bear away
the land and its folk into a timeless world — 'twas not more

than a few weeks that were gone by, if one were to reckon the days, and already it seemed as if the world that had been, ere pestilence and death stalked naked through the land, was fading from folks' memories, as a sea-coast sinks when one stands out to sea before a rushing wind. 'Twas as though no human soul could keep in memory that once life and the daily round of work had seemed sure and near, death far away — or had the power to conceive that so it would be again — if so be all men did not die. But "Belike, we shall all die," said the men who came to the cloister with their motherless little ones; some said it with dull, hard faces, some with weeping and lamentations; they said it when they fetched a priest to the dying, they said it when they bore the corpses to the parish church down the hill and to the graveyard by the cloister chapel. Often the bearers themselves must dig the grave — Sira Eiliv had set the lay serving-men — such as were left — to work at saving and garnering the corn from the cloister's fields; and wheresoever he went in the parish he admonished the folk to get their crops housed, and to help one another to care for the cattle, that so they might not perish in the dearth the plague was like to leave behind when it had spent its rage.

The nuns in the cloister met the visitation at first with a kind of bewildered calm. They settled them down for good in the convent hall, kept a fire blazing night and day in the great masoned fireplace, slept there, and there took their food. Sira Eiliv counselled that great fires should be kept up in the courts and in all the houses where there were fireplaces; but the sisters were afraid of fire — they had heard so many tales from the oldest sisters of the burning of the convent thirty years before. Meal-times and working-hours were kept no longer, and the divers offices of the sisters could not be kept apart, by reason of the many children who came from without, praying for food and help. Sick folk were brought in — these for the most were well-to-do folk who could pay for a gravestead in the cloister and for masses for their souls, or the poorest and loneliest of the poor who could get no help at home. Those of a middle station lay and died in their own houses. On some manors every human being died. But amid all this the nuns had as yet made shift to keep up the hours of prayer.

The first of the nuns who fell sick was Sister Inga, a
woman of Kristin's age, near fifty years; but none the less
was she so afeared of death that 'twas horrible to see and
hear her. The shivering fit came upon her in the church
during Mass, and she crept on hands and knees, shaking
and with chattering teeth, praying and beseeching God
and Mary Virgin for her life — Before long she lay in a
burning fever, groaning, and sweating blood from all her
body. Kristin's heart shuddered within her — doubtless
she, too, would be as wretchedly afraid as this when her
time came. 'Twas not alone that death was sure — 'twas the
awful horror that clung about death from pestilence.

Then Lady Ragnhild herself fell sick. Kristin had wondered a little that this woman had been chosen to an abbess's high office — she was a quiet, somewhat peevish old
woman, unlearned, and, it seemed, lacking any great gifts
of the spirit — but, when death laid his hand upon her,
she showed she was in truth a bride of Christ. Her the sickness smote with boils — she would not suffer even her
spiritual daughters to bare her old body, but under one of
her arms the swelling grew at last as big as an apple, and
under her chin too boils broke out and waxed huge and
blood-red, and at last turned black; she suffered unbearable
pains from them, and burned with fever; but as oft as her
mind was clear, she lay there a pattern of holy patience,
sighing to God for forgiveness of her sins, and praying in
fair and heartfelt words for her cloister and her daughters,
for all sick and sorrowful, and for the salvation of all
souls who now must part from hence. Even Sira Eiliv
wept, when he had given her the viaticum — and *his* steadfastness as well as his unwearied zeal in the midst of all
this misery had been a thing to wonder at. Lady Ragnhild
had many times already given her soul into God's keeping
and prayed Him to take the nuns into His ward — and
then at last the boils on her body began to burst. But this
proved a turning towards life, not death — and after, too,
folk deemed they saw that those whom the sickness smote
with boils were sometimes healed, but those to whom it
came with a bloody vomit, died every one.

It seemed as though the nuns took new courage from
the abbess's steadfastness, and from the having seen one
stricken with the pest who yet did not die. They had now
to milk and tend the byres themselves, to make ready their

own food, and themselves fetch home juniper and fresh
pine branches to burn for cleansing smoke — each one had
to do what came to her hand. They cared for the sick as
best they could, and doled out remedies — theriac and
calamus root had given out; they dealt round ginger, pep-
per, saffron and vinegar to ward off the poison; and milk
and meat — the bread gave out and they baked at night —
the spices gave out, and folk must needs chew juniper-
berries and pine-needles against the infection. One by one
the sisters dropped and died; passing-bells rang from the
cloister church and the parish church early and late in
the heavy air; for the strange, uncanny mist still lay upon
the land; there seemed to be a secret privity 'twixt the fog
and the deadly sickness. Sometimes it turned to a frosty
fog and sifted down in small ice-needles and a half-frozen
drizzle, and the land grew white with rime — then came
mild weather and mist again. Folk deemed it a sign of evil
omen that the sea-fowl, that else were wont to flock in
thousands along the creek that runs inland from the fjord
and lies like a river between the low stretches of meadow,
but widens to a salt-water lake north of Rein cloister —
that they suddenly vanished, and in their stead came ravens
in countless numbers — on every stone by the water-side
the black birds sat amidst the fog, making their hideous
croaking; while flocks of crows, so huge that none before
had seen the like, settled on all the woods and groves, and
flew with ugly screechings over the stricken land.

Now and again Kristin thought of her own — the sons
who were scattered so far and wide, the grandchildren
she should never see — little Erlend's golden head wavered
before her sight. But they were grown to seem far off and
pale to her. Almost it seemed as though all mankind in this
time of need were alike near to each other and alike far
apart. And then she had her hands full all day long — it
stood her in good stead now that she was used to all kinds
of work. While she sat milking, she would find beside her
suddenly little starving children she had never before set
her eyes on, and she would scarce remember to ask
whence they were or how things were with them at home;
she would give them food and lead them to the shelter of
the chapter-hall, or some other place where a fire was
burning, then stow them away in a bed in the dormitory.

She marked, with a kind of wonder, that in this time of

calamity, when more than ever there was need that all should be vigilant in prayer, she scarce ever found time to meditate or to pray. She would fling her down in the church before the tabernacle when she found a vacant moment, but naught came of it but wordless sighs, and Paternosters and Aves uttered by rote. She herself knew not that the nun-like ways and bearing she had fallen into in these two years were dropping from her more and more, and that she was growing ever liker to the housewife of the old days — as the flock of nuns dwindled, the round of cloister duties fell into disarray, and the abbess still lay abed, weak and with half-palsied tongue — and the work grew more and more for the few that were left to do it.

One day she learned by chance that Skule was still in Nidaros — his ship-folk were dead or fled away, and he had not been able to get new folk. He was whole yet, but he had plunged into wild living, as had many young men in this desperate pass. For him who was afraid, death was sure, they said, and so they deadened thought with drink and riot, gambled and danced and wantoned with women. Even honourable burghers' wives and young maids of the best kindreds ran from their homes in this evil time; in company with the women of the bordels they caroused in the inns and taverns amongst the wildered men. God forgive them, thought the mother — but 'twas as though her heart were too weary to sorrow much for these things.

But in the country-side too, for sure, there was enough of sin and distraction. They heard little of it at the cloister, for there they had no time for much talk. But Sira Eiliv, who went about everywhere, without rest or respite, to the sick and dying, said one day to Kristin that the folk's souls stood in yet direr need than their bodies.

There came an evening when they were sitting round the chimney-place in the convent hall — the little flock of folk that were left alive in Rein cloister. Four nuns and two lay sisters, an old stableman and a half-grown boy, two bedeswomen and some children, huddled together round the fire. On the high-seat bench, where a great crucifix gleamed in the dusk on the light-hued wall, lay the abbess, and Sister Kristin and Sister Turid sat at her hands and feet.

It was nine days since the last death among the sisters, and five days since any had died in the cloister or the nearer houses. The pestilence seemed to be lessening throughout the parish, too, said Sira Eiliv. And for the first time for near three months something like a gleam of peace and hope and comfort fell upon the silent and weary folk that sat together there. Old Sister Torunn Marta let her rosary sink upon her lap, and took the hand of the little girl who stood at her knee:

"What can it be she means? Ay, child, now seems it as we should see that never for long does God's mother, Mary, turn away her loving-kindness from her children."*

"Nay, 'tis not Mary Virgin, Sister Torunn, 'tis Hel.* She will go from out this parish, with both rake and broom, when they offer up a man without blemish at the graveyard gate — to-morrow she'll be far away — "

"What means she?" asked the nun again, uneasily. "Fie upon you, Magnhild; what ugly heathenish talk is this? 'Twere fit you should taste the birch — "

"Tell us what it is, Magnhild — have no fear" — Sister Kristin was standing behind them; she asked the question breathlessly. She had remembered — she had heard in her youth from Lady Aashild — of dreadful, unnamably sinful devices that the devil tempts desperate men to practise —

The children had been down in the grove by the parish church in the falling dusk, and some of the boys had strayed through the wood to a turf hut that stood there, and had eavesdropped and heard some men in it laying plans. It seemed from what they heard that these men had laid hold on a little boy, Tore, the son of Steinunn, that lived by the strand, and to-night they were to offer him up to the pest-ogress, Hel. The children talked eagerly, proud that the grown-up folk were paying heed to what they said. They seemed not to think of pitying the hapless Tore — maybe because he was somewhat of an outcast. He wandered about the parish begging, but never came to the cloister, and if Sira Eiliv or any sent by the abbess sought out his mother, she ran away, or she kept a stubborn silence, whether they spoke lovingly or harshly to her. She had lived in the stews of Nidaros for ten years,

---

* See Note 8.

but then a sickness took hold on her, and left her of so ill
a favour that at last she could not win her livelihood so as
she had used her to do; so she had forsaken the town for
the Rein parish, and now dwelt in a hut down by the
strand. It still befell at times that a chance beggar or some
such stroller would take lodging with her for a while. Who
was father to her boy she herself knew not.

"We must go thither," said Kristin. "Here we cannot sit,
I trow, while christened souls sell themselves to the devil
at our very doors."

The nuns whimpered in fear. These were the worst men
in the parish; rough, ungodly fellows; and uttermost need
and despair must have turned them now into very devils.
Had Sira Eiliv only been at home, they moaned. In this
time of trial the priest had so won their trust, that they
deemed he could do all things —

Kristin wrung her hands:

"Even if I must go alone — my mother, have I your
leave to go thither?"

The abbess gripped her by the arm so hard that she
cried out. The old, tongue-tied woman got upon her feet;
by signs she made them understand that they should dress
her to go out, and called for her golden cross, the badge
of her office, and her staff. Then she took Kristin by the
arm — for she was the youngest and strongest of the
women. All the nuns stood up and followed.

Through the door of the little room 'twixt the chapter-
hall and the choir of the church they went forth into the
raw, cold winter night. Lady Ragnhild's teeth began to
chatter and her whole frame to shiver — she still sweated
without cease by reason of her sickness, and the pest-boil
sores were not fully healed, so that it must have wrought
her great agony to walk. But she muttered angrily and
shook her head when the sisters prayed her to turn, clung
the harder to Kristin's arm, and plodded, shaking with
cold, on before them through the garden. As their eyes
grew used to the darkness, the women made out the dim
sheen of the withered leaves strewn on the path beneath
their feet, and the faint light from the clouded sky above
the naked tree-tops. Cold waterdrops dripped from the
branches, and puffs of wind went by with a faint soughing sound. The roll of the waves on the strand behind the
high ground came to them in dull, heavy sighs.

At the bottom of the garden was a little wicket — the sisters shuddered when the bolt, fast rusted in its socket, shrieked as Kristin withdrew it by main force. Then they crept onward through the grove down towards the parish church. Now they could see dimly the black-tarred mass, darker against the darkness; and against the opening in the clouds above the low hills beyond the lake they saw the roof-top, and the ridge turret with its beasts' heads and cross over all.

Ay — there were folk in the graveyard — they felt rather than saw or heard it. And now a faint gleam of light was to be seen low down, as of a lanthorn set upon the ground. Close by it the darkness seemed moving.

The nuns pressed together, moaning almost soundlessly amid whispered prayers, went a few steps, halted and listened, and went on again. They were well-nigh come to the graveyard gate. Then they heard from out of the dark a thin child-voice crying:

"Oh, oh, my bannock; you've thrown dirt on it!"

Kristin let go the abbess's arm, and ran forward through the churchyard gate. She pushed aside some dark shapes of men's backs, stumbled over heaps of upturned earth, and then was at the edge of the open grave. She went down on her knees, bent over, and lifted up the little boy who stood at the bottom, still whimpering because the dirt had spoiled the good bannock he had been given for staying quietly down there.

The men stood there frighted from their wits — ready to fly — some stamped about on the same spot — Kristin saw their feet in the light from the lanthorn on the ground. Then one, she made sure, would have sprung at her — at the same moment the grey-white nuns' dresses came into sight — and the knot of men hung wavering —

Kristin had the boy in her arms still; he was crying for his bannock; so she set him down, took the bread, and brushed it clean:

"There, eat it — your bannock is as good as ever now — And now go home, you men" — the shaking of her voice forced her to stop a little. "Go home and thank God you were saved from the doing of a deed 'twere hard to atone." She was speaking now as a mistress speaks to her serving-folk, mildly, but as if it could not cross her mind that they would not obey. Unwittingly some of the men turned towards the gate.

Then one of them shrieked:

"Stay a little — see you not our lives at the least are forfeit — mayhap all we own — now that these full-fed monks' whores have stuck their noses into this! Never must they come away from here to spread the tidings of it — "

Not a man moved — but Sister Agnes broke into a shrill shriek, and cried in a wailing voice:

"O sweet Jesus, my bridegroom — I thank Thee that Thou sufferest Thy handmaidens to die for the glory of Thy name — !"

Lady Ragnhild pushed her roughly behind her, tottered forward, and took up the lanthorn from the ground — no one moved a hand to hinder her. When she lifted it up, the gold cross on her breast shone out. She stood propped on her staff, and slowly turned the light upon the ring about her, nodding a little at each man she looked on. Then she made a sign to Kristin to speak. Kristin said:

"Go home peaceably and quietly, dear brothers — be sure that the reverend mother and these good sisters will be as merciful as their duty to God and the honour of His Church will suffer. But stand aside now, that we may come forth with this child — and thereafter let each man go his way."

The men stood wavering. Then one shrieked out as though in direst need:

"Is't not better that *one* be offered up than that we should all perish — ? This child here who is owned by none — "

"Christ owns him. 'Twere better we should perish one and all than to hurt one of His little ones — "

· But the man who had spoken first shouted again:

"Hold your tongue — no more such-like words, or I cram them back down your throat with this" — he shook his knife in the air. "Go you home, go to your beds and pray your priest to comfort you, and say naught of this — or I tell you, in Satan's name, you shall learn 'twas the worst thing you ever did to put your fingers into our affairs — "

"You need not to cry so loud for him you named to hear you, Arntor — be sure he is not far from here," said

Kristin calmly, and some of the men seemed affrighted, and pressed unwittingly nearer to the abbess, who stood holding the lanthorn. "The worst had been, both for us and for you, had we sat quiet at home while you went about to make you a dwelling-place in hottest hell."

But the man Arntor swore and raved. Kristin knew that he hated the nuns; for his father had been forced to pledge his farm to them when he had to pay amends for man-slaying and incest with his wife's cousin. Now he went on casting up at the sisters all the Enemy's most hateful lies, charging them with sins so black and unnatural that only the devil himself could prompt a man to think such thoughts.

The poor nuns bowed them terrified and weeping under the hail of his taunts, but they stood fast around their old mother, and she held the lanthorn high, throwing the light upon the man, and looking him calmly in the face while he raved.

But anger flamed up in Kristin like new-kindled fire:

"Silence! Have you lost your wits, or has God smitten you with blindness? Should we dare to murmur under His chastisement — we who have seen His consecrated brides go forth to meet the sword that has been drawn by reason of the world's sins? They watched and prayed while we sinned and each day forgot our Maker — shut them from the world within the citadel of prayer while we scoured the world around, driven by greed of great and small possessions, of our own lusts and our own wrath. But they came forth to us when the angel of death was sent out amongst us — gathered in the sick and the defenceless and the hungry — twelve of our sisters have died in this plague — that you all know — not one turned aside, and not one gave over praying for us all in sisterly love, till the tongue dried in their mouths and their life's blood ebbed away — "

"Bravely speak you of yourself and your like — "

"*I* am *your* like," she cried, beside herself with anger; "I am not one of these holy sisters — I am one of you — "

"You have grown full humble, woman," said Arntor, scornfully; "you are frighted, I mark well. A little more and you will be fain to call her — the mother to this boy — your like."

"That must God judge — He died both for her and for me, and He knows us both. — Where is she — Steinunn?"

"Go down to her hut; you will find her there sure enough," answered Arntor.

"Ay, truly someone must send word to the poor woman that we have her boy," said Kristin to the nuns. "We must go out to her to-morrow."

Arntor gave a jeering laugh, but another man cried, uneasily:

"No, no — She is dead," he said to Kristin. " 'Tis fourteen days since Bjarne left her and barred the door. She lay in the death-throes then — "

"She lay in — " Kristin gazed at the men, horror-struck. "Was there none to fetch a priest to her — ? Is the — body — lying there — and no one has had so much compassion on her as to bring her to hallowed ground — and her child you would have — ?"

At the sight of the woman's horror, 'twas as though the men went clean beside themselves with fear and shame; all were shouting at once; a voice louder than all the rest rang out:

"Fetch her yourself, sister!"

"Ay! Which of you will go with me?"

None answered. Arntor cried:

"You will have to go alone, I trow."

"To-morrow — as soon as 'tis light — we will fetch her, Arntor — I myself will buy her a resting-place and masses for her soul — "

"Go thither now, go to-night — then will I believe you nuns are choke-full of holiness and pureness — "

Arntor had stuck his head forward close to hers. Kristin drove her clenched fist into his face, with a single loud sob of rage and horror —

Lady Ragnhild went forward and placed herself at Kristin's side; she strove to bring forth some words. The nuns cried out that to-morrow the dead woman should be brought to her grave. But the devil seemed to have turned Arntor's brain; he went on shrieking:

"Go now — then will we believe on God's mercy — "

Kristin drew herself up, white and stiff:

"I will go."

She lifted the child and gave it into Sister Torunn's arms, pushed the men aside, and ran quickly, stumbling

over grass tussocks and heaps of earth, towards the gate,
while the nuns followed wailing, and Sister Agnes cried
out that she would go with her. The abbess shook her
clenched hands towards Kristin, beckoning her to stop;
but she seemed quite beside herself and gave no heed —

Suddenly there was a great commotion in the dark over
by the graveyard gate — next moment Sira Eiliv's voice
asked: who was holding Thing here. He came forward
into the glimmer of the lanthorn — they saw that he bore
an axe in his hand. The nuns flocked around him; the men
made shift to steal away in the dark, but in the gateway
they were met by a man bearing a drawn sword in his
hand. There was some turmoil and the clash of arms, and
Sira Eiliv shouted towards the gate: woe to any who broke
the churchyard peace. Kristin heard one say 'twas the
strong smith from Credo Lane — the moment after, a tall,
broad-shouldered, white-haired man appeared at her side
— 'twas Ulf Haldorssön.

The priest handed him the axe — he had borrowed it
from Ulf — and took the boy Tore from the nun, while
he said:

" 'Tis past midnight already — none the less 'twere best
you all came with me to the church; I must get to the
bottom of these doings this very night."

None had any thought but to obey. But, when they were
come out on to the road, one of the light-grey women's
forms stepped aside from the throng and turned off by the
path through the wood. The priest called out, bidding her
come on with the others. Kristin's voice answered from
the darkness — she was some way along the track already:

"I cannot come, Sira Eiliv, till I have kept my promise — "

The priest and some others sprang after her. She was
standing leaning against the fence when Sira Eiliv came
up with her. He held up the lanthorn — she was fearfully
white of face, but, when he looked into her eyes, he saw
that she was not gone mad, as at first he had feared.

"Come home, Kristin," he said. "To-morrow we will go
thither with you, some men — I myself will go with
you — "

"I have given my word. I cannot go home, Sira Eiliv, till
I have done that which I vowed to do."

The priest stood silent a little. Then he said in a low voice:

"Mayhap you are right. Go then, sister, in God's name."

Like a shadow, Kristin melted away into the darkness, which swallowed up her grey form.

When Ulf Haldorssön came up by her side, she said — she spoke by snatches, vehemently: "Go back — I asked not you to come with me — "

Ulf laughed low:

"Kristin, my lady — you have not learnt yet, I see, that some things can be done without your asking or bidding — nor, though you have seen it many a time, I ween — that you cannot alway carry through alone all that you take upon you. But this burden of yours *I* will help you to carry."

The pine woods sighed above them, and the boom of the rollers away on the strand came stronger or more faint as the gusts of wind rose or died away. They walked in pitch darkness. After a while Ulf said:

" — I have borne you company before, Kristin, when you went out at night — methought 'twere but fitting I should go with you this time too — "

She breathed hard and heavily in the dark. Once she stumbled over somewhat, and Ulf caught her. After that he took her hand and led her. In a while the man heard that she was weeping as she went, and he asked her why she wept.

"I weep to think how good and faithful you have been to us, Ulf, all our days. What can I say — ? I know well enough 'twas most for Erlend's sake, but almost I believe, kinsman — all our days you have judged of me more kindly than you had a right to, after what you first saw of my doings."

"I loved you, Kristin — no less than him." He was silent. Kristin felt that he was strongly stirred. Then he said:

"Therefore meseemed 'twas a hard errand when I sailed out hither to-day — I came to bring you such tidings as I myself deemed it hard to utter. God strengthen you, Kristin!"

"Is it Skule?" asked Kristin softly in a little. "Skule is dead?"

"No; Skule was well when I spoke with him yesterday

— and now not many are dying in the town. But I had news from Tautra this morning — " He heard her sigh heavily once, but she said naught. A little after he said:

" 'Tis ten days now since they died. There are but four brothers left alive in the cloister, and the island is all but swept clean of folk."

They were come now where the wood ended. Over the flat stretch of land in front the roaring of the sea and the wind came to meet them. One spot out in the dark shone white — the surf in a little bay, by a steep, light-hued sand-hill.

"She dwells there," said Kristin. Ulf felt that long, convulsive shudders went through her frame. He gripped her hand hard:

"You took this on yourself. Remember that, and lose not your wits now."

Kristin said, in a strangely thin, clear voice, that the blast caught and bore away:

"Now will Björgulf's dream come true — I trust in God's and Mary's grace."

Ulf tried to see her face — but 'twas too dark. They were walking on the strand — in some places 'twas so narrow under the bluffs that now and then a wave washed right up to their feet. They tramped forward over tangled heaps of seaweed and great stones. After a while they were ware of a dark hump in against the sandy bank.

"Stay here," said Ulf, shortly. He went forward and thrust against the door — then she heard him hew at the withy bands and thrust at the door again. Then she was ware that the door had fallen inwards, and he had gone in through the black hole.

'Twas not a night of heavy storm. But it was so dark that Kristin could see naught save the little flashes of foam that came and vanished the same instant on the lifting sea, and the shining of the waves breaking along the shores of the bay — and against the sand-dune she could make out that black hump. And it seemed to her that she was standing in a cavern of night, and that 'twas the forecourt of death. The roll of breaking waves and the hiss of their waters ebbing among the stones of the beach kept time with the blood-waves surging through her, though all the time 'twas as though her body must shiver in pieces, as a vessel of wood falls apart in staves — her breast ached as if something would burst it in sunder from within; her head felt hollow and empty and as 'twere rifted, and the unceasing wind wrapped her round and swept clean through her. She felt, with a strange listlessness, that she herself had surely caught the sickness now — but 'twas as though she looked that the darkness should be riven by a great light that would drown the roar of the sea with its thunder, and that in the horror of this she should perish. She drew up her hood, blown back from her head by the wind, wrapped the black nun's cloak close about her, and stood with her hands crossed beneath it — but it came not into her thought to pray; 'twas as though her soul had more than enough to do to work a way forth from its mansion trembling to its fall, and as though it tore at her breast with every breath.

She saw a light flare up within the hut. A little after, Ulf Haldorssön called out to her: "You must come hither and hold the light for me, Kristin" — he was standing in the doorway — as she came, he reached her a torch of some tarred wood.

A choking stench from the corpse met her, though the hut was so draughty and the door was gone. With staring eyes and mouth half open — and she felt her jaws and lips grow stiff the while and wooden — she looked round for the dead. But there was naught to see but a long bundle lying in the corner on the earthen floor, wrapped in Ulf's cloak.

He had torn loose some long planks from somewhere and laid the door upon them. Cursing his unhandy tools, he made notches and holes with his light axe and dagger, and strove to lash the door fast to the boards. Once or twice he looked up at her swiftly, and each time his dark, grey-bearded face grew more hard set.

"I marvel much how you had thought to get through this piece of work alone," he said as he wrought — then glanced up at her — but the stiff, death-like face in the red gleam of the tar brand was set and unmoved as ever — 'twas the face of a dead woman or of one distraught. "Can you tell me that, Kristin?" he laughed harshly — but still 'twas of no avail. "Methinks now were the time for you to say a prayer."

Stiff and lifeless as ever, she began to speak:

"*Pater noster que es in cælis. Adveniat regnum tuum. Fiat voluntas tua sicut in cælo et in terra* — " Then she came to a stop.

Ulf looked at her. Then he took up the prayer:

"*Panem nostrum quotidianum da nobis hodie* — " Swiftly and firmly he said the Lord's prayer to the end, went over and made the sign of the cross over the bundle — swiftly and firmly he took it up and bore it to the bier that he had fashioned.

"Go you in front," he said. "Maybe 'tis somewhat heavier, but you will smell the stench less there. Throw away the torch — we can see more surely without it — and see you miss not your footing, Kristin — for I had liefer not have to take a hold of this poor body any more."

The struggling pain in her breast seemed to rise in revolt when she got the bier poles set upon her shoulders; her chest *would* not bear up the weight. But she set her teeth hard. So long as they went along the strand, where the wind blew strong, but little of the corpse smell came to her.

"Here I must draw it up first, I trow, and the bier after," said Ulf, when they were come to the steep slope they had climbed down.

"We can go a little farther on," said Kristin; " 'tis there they come down with the seaweed sleighs — there 'tis not steep."

She spoke calmly, the man heard, and as in her right mind. And a fit of sweating and trembling took him, now it was over — he had deemed she must lose her wits that night.

They struggled forward along the sandy track that led across the flat towards the pine wood. The wind swept in freely here, but yet 'twas not as it had been down on the strand, and, as they drew farther and farther away from the roar of the beach, she felt it as a homefaring from the horror of utter darkness. Beside their path the ground showed lighter — 'twas a cornfield that there had been none to reap. The scent of it, and the sight of the beaten-down straw, welcomed her home again — and her eyes filled with tears of sisterly pity — out of her own desolate terror and woe she was coming home to fellowship with the living and the dead.

At times, when the wind was right behind, the fearful

carrion stench enwrapped her wholly, but yet 'twas not so awful as when she stood in the hut — for the night was full of fresh, wet, cold, cleansing streams of air.

And much stronger than the feeling that she bore a thing of dread upon the bier behind her, was the thought that Ulf Haldorssön was there, guarding her back against the black and living horror they were leaving behind — and whose roar sounded fainter and more faint.

When they were come to the edge of the pine woods they were ware of lights: "They are coming to meet us," said Ulf.

Soon after, they were met by a whole throng of men bearing pine-root torches, a couple of lanthorns and a bier covered with a pall — Sira Eiliv was with them, and Kristin saw with wonder that in the troop were many of the men who had been that same night in the churchyard, and that many of them were weeping. When they lifted the burthen from her shoulders she was like to fall. Sira Eiliv would have caught a hold of her, but she said quickly:

"Touch me not — come not near me — I have the pest myself; I feel it — "

But none the less Sira Eiliv stayed her up with a hand below her arm:

"Then be of good cheer, woman, remembering that our Lord has said: 'Inasmuch as ye have done it unto one of the least of these My brethren or sisters, ye have done it unto Me.'"

Kristin gazed at the priest. Then she looked across to where the men were shifting the body from the stretcher that Ulf had fashioned to the bier they had brought. Ulf's cloak slipped aside a little — the point of a worn-out shoe stuck out, dark wet in the light of the torches.

Kristin went across, kneeled between the poles of the bier, and kissed the shoe:

"God be gracious to you, sister — God give your soul joy in His light — God look in His mercy on us here in our darkness — "

Then it seemed to her as 'twere life itself that tore its way from out of her — a grinding, inconceivable pain, as though something within her, rooted fast in every outermost fibre of her limbs, were riven loose. All that was within her breast was torn out — she felt her throat full of it, her mouth filled with blood that tasted of salt and foul copper — next moment her whole dress in front was a glistening wet blackness — Jesus! is there so much blood in an old woman? she thought.

Ulf Haldorssön lifted her in his arms and bore her away.

At the gate of the cloister the nuns, bearing lighted candles, came to meet the train of men. Already Kristin scarce had her full senses, but she felt that she was half borne, half helped, through the door, and she was ware of the whitewashed, vaulted room, filled with the flickering light of yellow candle flames and red pine torches, and of the tramp of feet rolling like a sea — but to the dying woman the light was like the shimmer of her own dying life-flame, and the footfalls on the flags as the rushing of the rivers of death rising up to meet her.

Then the candlelight spread out into a wider space — she was once again under the open, murky sky — in the courtyard — the flickering light played upon a grey stone wall with heavy buttresses and high, tall windows — the church. She was borne in someone's arms — 'twas Ulf again — but now he seemed to take on for her the semblance of all who had ever borne her up. When she laid her arms about his neck and pressed her cheek against his stubbly throat, 'twas as though she were a child again with her father, but also as though she were clasping a child to her own bosom — And behind his dark head there were red lights, and they seemed like the glow of the fire that nourishes all love.

— A little later she opened her eyes, and her mind was clear and calm. She was sitting, propped up, in a bed in the dormitory; a nun with a linen band over her lower face stood bending over her; she marked the smell of vinegar. 'Twas Sister Agnes, she knew by her eyes and the little red wart she had on her forehead. And now 'twas day — clear, grey light was sifting into the room from the little glass window.

She had no great pain now — she was but wet through with sweat, woefully worn and weary, and her breast stung and smarted when she breathed. Greedily she drank down a soothing drink that Sister Agnes held to her mouth. But she was cold —

Kristin lay back on the pillows, and now she remembered all that had befallen the night before. The wild dream fantasies were wholly gone — her wits must have wandered a little, she understood — but 'twas good that she had got this thing done, had saved the little boy, and hindered these poor folk from burdening their souls with such a hideous deed. She knew she had need to be over-joyed — that *she* had been given grace to do this thing just before she was to die — and yet she could not rejoice as 'twas meet she should; 'twas more a quiet content she felt, as when she lay in her bed at home at Jörundgaard, tired out after a day's work well done. And she must thank Ulf too —

— She had spoken his name, and he must have been sit-ting hidden away by the door, and have heard her, for here he came across the room and stood before her bed. She reached out her hand to him, and he took and pressed it in a firm clasp.

Suddenly the dying woman grew restless; her hands fumbled under the folds of linen about her throat.

"What is it, Kristin?" asked Ulf.

"The cross," she whispered, and painfully drew forth her father's gilded cross. It had come to her mind that yesterday she had promised to make a gift for the soul's weal of that poor Steinunn. She had not remembered then that she had no possessions on earth any more. She owned naught that she could give, saving the cross she had had of her father — and then her bridal ring. She wore that on her finger still.

She drew it off and gazed at it. It lay heavy in her hand; 'twas pure gold, set with great red stones. Erlend — she thought — and it came upon her now 'twere liker she should give this away — she knew not wherefore, but it seemed that she ought. She shut her eyes in pain and held it out to Ulf:

"To whom would you give this?" he asked, low, and as she did not answer: "Mean you I should give it to Skule — ?"

Kristin shook her head, her eyes tight closed.

"Steinunn — I promised — masses for her — "

She opened her eyes, and sought with them the ring where it lay in the smith's dusky palm. And her tears burst forth in a swift stream, for it seemed to her that never be-fore had she understood to the full what it betokened. The life that ring had wed her to, that she had complained

against, had murmured at, had raged at and defied — none
the less she had loved it so, joyed in it so, both in good
days and evil, that not one day had there been when
'twould not have seemed hard to give it back to God, nor
one grief that she could have forgone without regret —

Ulf and the nun changed some words that she could not
hear, and he went from the room. Kristin would have
lifted her hand to dry her eyes, but she could not — the
hand lay moveless on her breast. And now the pain within
was sore; her hand felt so heavy, and it seemed as though
the ring were on her finger still. Her head began to grow
unclear again — she *must* see if 'twere true that the ring
was gone, that she had not only dreamed she had given it
away — And now too she began to grow uncertain — all
that had befallen last night: the child in the grave; the
black sea with its swift little flashing waves; the corpse
she had borne — she knew not whether she had dreamed
it all or had been awake. And she had no strength to open
her eyes.

"Sister," said the nun, "you must not sleep now — Ulf
is gone to fetch a priest for you."

Kristin woke up fully again with a start, and fixed her
eyes upon her hand. The gold ring was gone, that was sure
enough — but there was a white, worn mark where it had
been on her middle finger. It showed forth quite clearly
on the rough brown flesh — like a scar of thin, white
skin — she deemed she could make out two round spots
on either side where the rubies had been, and somewhat
like a little mark, an M, where the middle plate of gold
had been pierced with the first letter of Mary Virgin's holy
name.

And the last clear thought that formed in her brain was
that she should die ere this mark had time to vanish — and
she was glad. It seemed to her to be a mystery that she
could not fathom, but which she knew most surely none
the less, that God had held her fast in a covenant made
for her without her knowledge by a love poured out upon
her richly — and in despite of her self-will, in despite of
her heavy, earthbound spirit, somewhat of this love had
become *part* of her, had wrought in her like sunlight in the
earth, had brought forth increase which not even the hottest flames of fleshly love nor its wildest bursts of wrath
could lay waste wholly. A handmaiden of God had she

been — a wayward, unruly servant, oftenest an eye-servant in her prayers and faithless in her heart, slothful and neglectful, impatient under correction, but little constant in her deeds — yet had he held her fast in his service, and under the glittering golden ring a mark had been set secretly upon her, showing that she was His handmaid, owned by the Lord and King who was now coming, borne by the priest's anointed hands, to give her freedom and salvation —

Soon after Sira Eiliv had given her the last oil and viaticum, Kristin Lavransdatter again lost the knowledge of all around. She lay in the sway of sore fits of blood-vomiting and burning fever, and the priest, who stayed by her, told the nuns that 'twas like to go quickly with her.

— Once or twice the dying woman came so far to herself that she knew this or the other face — Sira Eiliv's, the sister's — Lady Ragnhild herself was there once, and Ulf too she saw. She strove to show she knew them, and that she felt 'twas good they should be by her and wished her well. But to those who stood around it seemed as she were but fighting with her hands in the throes of death.

Once she saw Munan's face — her little son peeped in at her through a half-open door. Then he drew back his head, and the mother lay gazing at the door — if perchance the boy might peep out again. But instead came Lady Ragnhild and wiped her face with a wet cloth; and that too was good — Then all things were lost in a dark red mist, and a roar, that first grew fearsomely; but then it died away little by little, and the red mist grew thinner and lighter, and at last 'twas like a fair morning mist ere the sun breaks through, and all sound ceased, and she knew that now she was dying —

Sira Eiliv and Ulf Haldorssön went out together from the room of death. In the doorway out to the cloister yard they stopped short —

Snow had fallen. None had marked it, of them who had sat by the woman while she fought with death. The white gleam from the steep church roof over against the two men was strangely dazzling; the tower shone white against the ash-grey sky. The snow lay so fine and white on all the window-mouldings, and all buttresses and jutting points, against the church's walls of grey hewn stone. And 'twas as though the two men lingered because they were loath to break with their footprints the thin coverlid of new-fallen snow.

They drank in the air. After the noisome smell that ever fills the sick-room of one pest-stricken, it tasted sweet — cool, and as it were a little thin and empty; but it seemed as though this snowfall must have washed the air clean of all poison and pestilence — 'twas as good as fresh spring water.

The bell in the tower began to ring again — the two looked up to where it swung behind the belfry bars. Small grains of snow loosened from the tower roof as it shook, rolled down, and grew to little balls — leaving spots where the black of the shingles showed through.

"This snow will scarce lie," said Ulf.

"No, 'twill melt, belike, before evening," answered the priest. There were pale golden rifts in the clouds, and a faint gleam of sunshine fell, as it were provingly, across the snow.

The men stood still. Then Ulf Haldorssön said low:

"I am thinking, Sira Eiliv — I will give some land to the church here — and a beaker of Lavrans Björgulfssön's that she gave me — to found a mass for her — and my fostersons — and for him, Erlend, my kinsman — "

The priest answered as low, without looking at the man:

" — Meseems, too, you might think you had need to show your thankfulness to Him who led you hither yester-even — you may be well content, I trow, that 'twas granted you to help her through this night."

"Ay, 'twas that I thought of," said Ulf Haldorssön. Then he laughed a little: "And now could I well-nigh repent me, priest, that I have been so meek a man — towards her!"

"Bootless to waste time in such vain regrets," answered the priest.

"What mean you — ?"

"I mean, 'tis but a man's sins that it boots him to repent," said the priest.

"Why so?"

"For that none is good saving God only. And we can do no good save of Him. So it boots not to repent a good

deed, Ulf, for the good you have done cannot be undone;
though all the hills should crash in ruin, yet would it
stand — "

"Ay, ay. These be things I understand not, my Sira. I
am weary — "

"Ay — and hungry too you may well be — you must
come with me to the kitchen-house, Ulf," said the priest.

"Thanks, but I have no stomach to meat," said Ulf Haldorssön.

"None the less must you go with me and eat," said Sira
Eiliv — he laid his hand on Ulf's sleeve and led him along
with him. They went out into the courtyard and down
towards the kitchen-house. Unwittingly, both men trod
as lightly and charily as they could upon the new-fallen
snow.

NOTES

THE CROSS

P. 83.   1. *Grace-deed*

SIMON, having committed an offence punishable with out-lawry, has to obtain a grace-deed permitting him to remain at home unmolested until his case is judged. See *The Mistress of Husaby*, Note 14.

P. 118.   2. *Debtors*

The word (*skyldnere* in the original) is, of course, used in the sense which it bears in the Lord's Prayer. In the text it has sometimes been necessary to render it by the equivalent phrase: "they that trespass against us."

P. 156.   3. *The Comb-maker's Seed*

King Sverre's putative father — the husband of his mother — was a comb-maker. He claimed to be an illegitimate son of King Sigurd Mund; but his opponents strenuously denied this.

P. 220.   4. *Friggja-grass*

Grass of Parnassus — *Parnassia palustris*. Popularly supposed to be an aphrodisiac, and hence named after the goddess of love.

P. 251.   5. *Oath with Compurgators*

The original has "*sættared eller tylvtared.*" In certain cases the accused might clear himself of a charge by taking oath to his innocence, along with five, or eleven, compurgators (*mededsmænd*). The oath with five compurgators was termed "*sættared,*" that with eleven, "*tylvtared.*" The compurgators swore, not to the facts of the case, but to their knowledge of the accused and their persuasion that he was telling the truth. According to Norse law, the compurgators in the case of a woman accused of an offence must be women.

P. 371.   6. *Rolling-breeches*

In the popular tales trolls are sometimes equipped with

423

"rolling-breeches" (*trille-brok*) —breeches which enable them
to lie down and roll rapidly after prey, or from their pursuers.

P. 382.   7. *Tart in Burgundy*

Now Tart l'Abbaye, in the Côte d'Or department, near
Citeaux, the cradle of the Cistercian order. Tart was the mother
house of all the Scandinavian Cistercian nunneries.

P. 405.   8. *Hel*

In Norse folk-lore the plague was personified as a hideous old
woman carrying a rake and a broom. Where she used the rake,
some part of the population survived; where she used the
broom, she swept the country-side of every living soul. It
would be natural, in the fourteenth century, for the popular
imagination to identify her with Hel, the death goddess of the
old mythology.

ABOUT THE AUTHOR

SIGRID UNDSET (born 1882) grew up in Oslo, Norway, the daughter of a Norwegian archaeologist, whose early death left his family in difficult circumstances. From 1899 to 1909, she supported her family as an office clerk, writing at night, and won her first success in 1912 with her third novel, *Jenny*, the story of an urban working girl. Other modern novels followed during her thirteen-year marriage to a painter, during which she also raised six children. But her interest in the Middle Ages gave rise to her masterpieces: the three-volume *Kristin Lavransdatter* (1920–22), and the four-volume *The Master of Hestviken* (1925–27). She was awarded the Nobel Prize for Literature in 1928. Undset was divorced in 1925, and turning her back on the liberal, feminist circles of her youth, converted to Roman Catholicism the same year. Her later novels (she published fourteen during her lifetime) returned to modern settings and were overtly religious in tone. During World War II, she escaped to the United States, having been a vocal and bitter opponent of Nazism. She returned to Norway to die in 1949.

KRISTIN LAVRANSDATTER

by
Sigrid Undset

A sweeping epic of medieval life in Norway, **KRISTIN LAVRANSDATTER** takes its golden-haired heroine from her wondrous childhood in the misty valley of Jorundgaard to maturity and the wisdom of age in a convent far from home. This richly textured trilogy abounds in color and high drama: feasts in the great hall, ancient bridal customs, witchcraft, rape and adultery among nobles, a plot against the crown, childbed agonies and penitential journeys in sackcloth and bare feet. Yet it is most powerful in its portrait of one woman moving through the ordinary events of her life, changing through first love, loss of innocence, marriage, motherhood and age. Ancient in setting, but unerringly modern in its psychological treatment of character, it is as vital today as when it won the Nobel Prize for Literature in 1928.

THE BRIDAL WREATH (Volume I) A novel of passion. Her father's favorite child, Kristin is ready to accept his choice of bridegroom—until she meets the rakish Erlend Nikulausson, a renegade nobleman exiled for living in sin with another man's wife. For Erlend she sacrifices her honor, her father's favor, her own peace, and persists against all obstacles to marry him.

THE MISTRESS OF HUSABY (Volume II) A novel of marriage. A pregnant Kristin weds Erlend and becomes mistress of his neglected estate, Husaby. She bears him seven children, living in years'-long cycles of resentment, rage, reconciliation and renewed passion. Not until Erlend is arrested and sentenced to death for treachery does Kristin fully realize the absolutely fated quality of their love.

THE CROSS (Volume III) A novel of leave-taking and reconciliation. Husband, sons, wealth—all slip away, leaving Kristin alone, but still indomitable. Journeying through a land ravaged by the Black Death, she is chastened by the suffering around her. She ends her days in a cloister, nursing victims of the plague, until she herself contracts the disease, having glimpsed only at the end the spiritual fulfillment she has sought all her life.

Be sure to read all three volumes of **KRISTIN LAVRANSDATTER,** to be available at Bantam Books, wherever paperbacks are sold. **THE MISTRESS OF HUSABY** will be on sale October 1st, **THE CROSS** will be available November 1st.

THE NAMES THAT SPELL
GREAT LITERATURE

Choose from today's most renowned world authors—every one an important addition to your personal library.

Hermann Hesse

☐	2906	KNULP	$1.95
☐	11916	MAGISTER LUDI	$2.25
☐	12024	DEMIAN	$1.95
☐	10060	GERTRUDE	$1.95
☐	11978	THE JOURNEY TO THE EAST	$1.95
☐	12529	SIDDHARTHA	$2.25
☐	10352	BENEATH THE WHEEL	$1.95
☐	12509	NARCISSUS AND GOLDMUND	$2.50
☐	11289	STEPPENWOLF	$1.95
☐	11510	ROSSHALDE	$1.95

Alexander Solzhenitsyn

☐	10111	THE FIRST CIRCLE	$2.50
☐	12677	ONE DAY IN THE LIFE OF IVAN DENISOVICH	$2.25
☐	2997	AUGUST 1914	$2.50
☐	11300	CANCER WARD	$2.50
☐	12079	LENIN IN ZURICH	$2.95

Jerzy Kosinski

☐	12465	STEPS	$2.25
☐	12460	THE PAINTED BIRD	$2.25
☐	2613	COCKPIT	$2.25

Doris Lessing

☐	11870	THE SUMMER BEFORE THE DARK	$2.25
☐	10425	THE GOLDEN NOTEBOOK	$2.25
☐	12461	THE FOUR-GATED CITY	$2.95
☐	11717	BRIEFING FOR A DESCENT INTO HELL	$2.25

André Schwarz-Bart

☐	12510	THE LAST OF THE JUST	$2.95

Buy them at your local bookstore or use this handy coupon for ordering: